DOVETAIL

Bernard Pearson

Cover design Ian Mitchell. Typesetting Amanda Cummings.

ISBN 978-1-5272-2331-8

Other publications

The Discworld Almanak (2004)
Terry Pratchett with Bernard Pearson

The World of Poo (2012)
Terry Pratchett and Bernard and Isobel Pearson

The Compleat Ankh-Morpork City Guide (2012)
Terry Pratchett and the Discworld Emporium

Mrs Bradshaw's Handbook (2014)
Terry Pratchett and the Discworld Emporium

The Compleat Discworld Atlas (2015)
Terry Pratchett and the Discworld Emporium

A Glastonbury Tale (2021)

This is a novel about good and evil and the darker side of the antiques business. It is also a story about the power of friendship that spans generations.

Like the antiques he restores, master craftsman Bill Sawyer knows that his interesting past could lead to a fragile future. In the autumn of his life, as his body begins to betray his skill, his dwindling days are about to become very interesting. The value of Bill's experience has not gone unnoticed, because things of value often attract dangerous attention.

But it's no use growing old if you don't get artful.

There is an old adage in the antiques trade that says 'not all that glistens is gold'. So you better believe that not all that's said to be Elizabethan is old. It might well be have been made yesterday.

Note from me:

This book is all about friendship, it is woven into the plot.

This book could not have happened without the help of my friends:

Jean Tillson whose Herculean task was to mentor me as she edited the damn thing. Elin Woodger Murphy who eagle-eyed proof read and my mate Ian Mitchell who created the cover design.

There was also Terry Wright who was bullied into printing it and Amanda Cummings who said yes and typeset it. Friends, all of them and I hope after all my mithering they still are.

So to them who made it happen and to you who are reading this – thank you.

To Isobel – of course.

Dovetail, dovetail joint: *n.* A mortise joint formed by interlocking tenons and mortises. Difficult to make, requiring skilful and practised craftsmanship. An impossible joint to break without destroying the construction.

THE FIRE

The match flared, and its phosphorus smell overcame for an instant the pungent odour of petrol. The man stepped back and dropped the burning match onto the ground. Everything seemed to happen in slow motion: the match falling to earth like a comet, the silent explosion as the petrol vapour ignited, then a dull *whoomph* as the line of petrol made a fiery trail through the open door of the huge house. The man walked away quickly, the night sky now illuminated by flames.

'Any moment now,' he thought, as he drove his van quickly down the gravelled drive and into the lane beyond. Almost at once he heard a violent blast from behind him and sighed with satisfaction. The Calor gas cylinders he had left gently hissing into the room had definitely made a difference. The fact that everything on the ground floor of the house – including the bodies – had been doused in petrol had made quite a difference, too.

The house was a long way from its nearest neighbours and set back from the road along an extensive drive, so no one saw the flames until they lit the area like a beacon. On any other night this would have caused calls to the emergency services from miles around, but not tonight. Not November the fifth. And if the burning mansion was the brightest light that shone out in the darkness, many others only slightly less brilliant were to be seen on the soft round hills of the Somerset landscape.

About a mile from the burning mansion the man stopped his vehicle in a field entrance and got out. The smell of petrol was making him gag; some of it must have splashed onto his clothes. He opened all the doors to let the fumes disperse, then leaned over and vomited, the revolver in his jacket pocket making dull thunking sounds against the van as he wretched.

Resting against the side of the vehicle, he admired the glow in the distance. Breathing cool, fresh air at last, his adrenalin levels began to return to normal. This left him leaving him feeling weak and exhausted, but the thought of what he had done was seared into his brain as bright as the flames that now engulfed the house.

Eventually he gathered enough strength to drive home, the events of that evening playing over and over like a movie behind his eyes.

Chapter 1

THREE MONTHS EARLIER

Bill Sawyer lived a very simple life and, in some ways, was a very simple man. Not simple as in stupid, but simple in the single-minded way of a fine craftsman. At sixty-seven, with decades of experience, he could take a piece of indifferent furniture of any era from Medieval to Regency and turn it into something collectors would clamour to own. He did this by 'simply' selecting the right woods, using the right glues (even if that meant rendering rabbit skins down to an evil-smelling broth), hand-making screws and pins to fit the age of the piece, and, finally, anointing the work with stains and polishes made to his own very secret recipes.

Stocky, broad-shouldered, balding, and with the ruddy face of the countryman, Bill had an easy grin and soft Somerset burr that lulled those who didn't know him well into believing he was indeed simple. People who did know him well, however – and these were very few – sometimes noticed a sparkle in his eyes like the gleam on the honed edge of a chisel.

Bill's expertise with old furniture was second to none. To call him an antiques restorer didn't do justice to his almost mystical ability to commune with the pieces he touched, to listen to the songs of time the wood sang to him as he held it. Furniture was brought to him to establish its age and identity or, occasionally, for a very specialised kind of restoration. A restoration that could defy time, define a maker, and fool even the best museum curator, let alone a buyer in an antiques shop. He was never short of work if he wanted it, but now only took on projects that really interested him.

If a stranger had happened by his place today, however, all they would have seen was an old man sitting at a bench in an enormous workshop that had once been a large barn. The stones that made up the walls were of a size that would not have disgraced a castle, nor indeed the abbey they had originally come from. A massive arch that once held a great oaken door was now made up of tar-washed timbers set with grimy glazed windows. Instead of one massive door, however, there were now two that created an opening about ten feet wide. It was a beautiful piece of craftsmanship sadly hammered by time and gentle neglect, but it did the job, which was all Bill wanted of anything.

Once upon a time the barn had been the heart of the farm, where wagons were brought in and grain was stored and threshed. Huge timbers held up a roof that would have done justice to a medieval hall and probably once had. The roof itself was lost in gloom, but the lower beams were festooned with cobwebs still holding wisps of ancient straw along with the more recent wood dust that coated almost everything else.

A bench ran the entire length of the long wall, its various surfaces of marble, slate, and timber stained and disfigured by chemicals. At one end was a melamine kitchen worktop in which was set a butler sink with a tap above it. Dominating that corner of the room was a vast cast-iron stove, its black shape liberally sprinkled with wood dust like dandruff on an undertaker's collar.

Great piles of cut timber were stacked against one wall: oak, beech, ash, and mahogany in planks. Piled everywhere was furniture of all ages resembling the carcases of dead animals with their skeletal structures on display. Innumerable shelves held myriad jars, tins, and boxes.

Under various low-hanging lights stood machines of all sorts and ages. Planes, finishers, routers, saws, and drills, each one in its own unique bed of sawdust or chippings like strange metal birds in nests of wood.

Bill no longer traded in antiques himself as getting stuff to and from the auctions was quite literally a pain these days. The ache in his chest was getting worse, he seemed always to be short of breath, and just of late he had noticed spots of blood on his handkerchief after he had had one of his increasingly frequent coughing fits. He occasionally thought of going to see his doctor, but each time he managed to convince himself his problem was just the ever-present dust.

Normally, Bill didn't stop for lunch, but today his chest was playing him up something rotten, so he set his current project aside and started to do what he always did at the end of a working day: put away his tools. This routine activity did more to quieten his mind than anything else could have done. Some of the small tools went into a box he had made for them at least forty years before. The box itself was a work of art, with his initials carved on the top and the smallest dovetail joints it was possible to make holding the panels together. Each tool had been known to his hands for decades, and they were more a part of him in some ways than people ever had been.

He picked up the claw spike that had been given to him by his first boss, the man he had been apprenticed to. Shaped like some medieval instrument of torture, it was designed to take pins out of upholstery, or at least that was what he used it for. It had been hand-forged and was old, but still worked despite being worn.

'Just like me,' Bill thought. 'For now, at any rate.'

He sat back in his chair. The familiar sensation of the piece of steel in his hand brought to mind his first big break and the man who had unwittingly provided it so long ago.

~~~

Harry Pexton was a short, squat, grizzled man to whom Bill had been apprenticed as a school leaver at age 16. An upholsterer, Harry had a workshop in one of the back streets of Bath that he had started up with the gratuity he had received from the army when he was demobbed in 1946. Harry's business was all about taking in furniture and repairing or re-stuffing it with whatever he could get his hands on, then covering it with a material based on what the client could afford. Sometimes this turned out to be curtains that had been 'liberated' from some empty house in the county. Harry had a cavalier regard to private ownership and was a great one for liberating stuff.

It was the late 1950s, Britain was still buttoned up tight, even the television stopped at 11 pm, and none of the local girls seemed to be interested in a spotty youth who smelt of leather and glue. Bill spent his days stripping rotting upholstery off furniture that exuded nose-clogging dust and the odour of dogs long dead (he sometimes even found fossilised turds, turned by time into small black pellets that broke apart as his fingers encountered them). But he enjoyed the process of making something new from sagging wrecks with broken springs poking out of rents in their coverings. He felt he was helping them come alive again.

Bill knew that once his apprenticeship was over, Harry would fire him and get some other poor sod to do all the shit jobs rather than pay Bill a man's wage. There was no formal agreement, nor any bit of paper at the end of it, but three years in that workshop had taught him a lot. Most importantly, it taught him that he had a way with wood and a feel for antique furniture. When not working, he haunted the many antiques shops in Bath and got to know the trade from the inside out.

Sure enough, when Bill turned nineteen Harry told him he would have to go. To salve his conscience, Harry gave him a last job reupholstering a large, winged club chair that had come in from a lady who had bought it from an auction in London. Harry pompously informed Bill that he could keep the lion's share of the profits as a parting gift, but when Bill saw the estimate he thought, 'If there's anything left over from this I'll be bloody lucky!' Still, money was money, and he knew he would need all he could get.

Bill set to work on the gigantic chair, its leather worn smooth on the arms and its deep, rich, red stained to a dull maroon by having countless drinks slopped over it. There were burns from cigarettes, cigars, and dropped matches. The back was not buttoned, which was a blessing as redoing all of that would have taken hours. It was a typical club chair, probably 1890s, mahogany frame, horsehair stuffing under leather worn thin and shiny by the fat backsides of the gentry. It would be a pleasure to turn this back into something lovely. The leather would have to be stripped off – he might be able to reuse that on the back – but the seat was cracked and torn and the inside padding in need of replacement. Also, by the feel of it, the springs under the seat were shot.

Bill used his new claw spike to prize the studs away from the frame. He would keep as many of those as he could and use them again. Slowly the frame of the chair came into view as the horsehair and hessian were pulled carefully away from the strings that bound them down. He would do the removable seat last; that was always the smelly job and by the look of this one it had seen a lot of action. 'Oh, the tales it could tell,' he thought, 'and all from the bottom up!' He reached the hessian shroud that covered the layer of horsehair now showing through in dirty clumps, and there, in the join between the seat and the back, right down almost out of sight, something shone.

Bill had often found coins when stripping the upholstery from old furniture. Harry regarded these as treasure trove and occasionally shared the spoils, but not very often. He had told tales of finding diamond rings and wallets, but Bill had never come across anything like that before. He reached in now and with strong, nimble fingers brought out a pocket watch of such intricacy and beauty it almost took his breath away. There were the remains of a gold chain attached to the bow. It was a full hunter watch with a spring-hinged front cover to protect the crystal and dial.

He took the watch over to the light. The front cover clicked open, probably for the first time in many years. There was no name on the elegant white dial. It had simple Roman numerals, dark-blue steel hands, and a small subdial marked off into seconds. There was a hallmark on the stem, and going to a dusty chart that hung on the wall, he looked up the symbols. These told him the watch had been made in Birmingham in 1876 and was eighteen carat gold.

He sat down and carefully, very carefully, opened the back cover. One thing about hanging around with antique dealers, you picked up all the tricks of the trade, so he knew just how to prise it open without leaving a scratch. Inside, still as bright and as crisp as the day it was engraved, was the name 'Woodley, London, St Swithin's Lane' in beautiful cursive letters. He closed the back with a gentle pressure and was rewarded with a very crisp click.

He turned it over, extended the stem, and put the time right by a cracked alarm clock that was the only timepiece in the room. The hands moved in silky precision. He pushed in the stem and, as gently as he could, wound the movement a few turns. Putting it to his ear he heard a clear tick evenly marking the passage of time. He took out his handkerchief, put the watch on it, and just stared as the small hand on the second dial went around and around in an even sweep.

He could see no damage on the watch case from its long interment in the bowels of the chair. A slight rubbing perhaps, but apart from that the watch looked as good as it must have done when it was lost. How long had it been there? Whose had it been? And, most importantly, whose was it now?

He wrapped the watch in his handkerchief, then in a piece of clean rag, and put it in the pocket of his jacket that hung on a nail by the door. Then Bill got on with the job in hand.

He went to the rolls of leather that Harry kept as dust-free as anything could be in that place and, instead of using the skin that had been left out for the job, chose the best there was. Rich, dark green, full-grain leather; the cost of this alone would leave a hole in Harry's pocket.

Bill left Harry's employ a bit earlier than he had originally been planned, and with curses rather than a reference, but to the *people who knew Harry and his winning little ways, that was a reference in itself.*

Bill went to work for the father of a school friend, a joiner and cabinet maker in a nearby village. He learned even more from this kindly and clever man, who recognised in young Bill the makings of a good craftsman. But Bill simply wasn't interested in new doors and window frames, no matter how well they were made. He missed the feel of old wood under his fingers, of antiques and the treasures of the past.

Bill decided the time was right, and he sold the watch for quite a lot of money. Enough to equip his own workshop and set out on the road he had travelled ever since.

Chapter 2

TUESDAY, 14 AUGUST

When the tools were back in their box, Bill put it on a shelf behind him and turned off the radio. Then he put on his old tweed jacket and started the ritual Packing of the Pockets. Pipe, tobacco pouch, and lighter all went into the same pockets they had done ever since the jacket was new. Bill didn't give a damn how he looked so long as he was comfortable. He had been a sartorial wreck since the day his wife, Beryl, had left him.

He didn't blame her, really. When their boy, Philip, was just thirteen she had told Bill she was off to 'find herself', and, to be honest, it had been a relief. That was over thirty years ago, and he didn't know if she had ever found herself, but she *had* found financial security with an estate agent named Stanley. There were no hard feelings, though, and he had sent them a rather nice Victorian money box as a wedding present.

The Packing of the Pockets always acted as a signal for his dog and sole companion, Bess, who rose from her basket next to the stove and gazed up at him with pure love in her liquid brown eyes. She was a small lurcher Bill had acquired from a gypsy as part payment for a Welsh dresser he had fitted into the traveller's caravan. The dresser had been nothing special, at least not until he had incorporated into it a very secret compartment lined with steel and made fireproof with asbestos. Bill had done a lot of work for the travelling community, one way and another. He liked them. He didn't entirely trust them, of course, but he liked them. They put two grubby fingers up to society and got on with their lives, just like he did.

Bess had been a puppy then, the last of a litter of whippet and bearded collie crosses, with long hair like grey and black clouds breaking into white over her chest, a long snout, and big eyes under a tuft of soft fur. He fell in love with her at first sight, and she with him. It was the only relationship in Bill's life that was totally without an edge.

'The only time you buy love is when you buy a dog,' the gypsy had said to him. 'But to you, Bill, I give her out of friendship and, say, £20 off the price, eh?'

Bill didn't even haggle. The two men shook hands on the deal, and Bill reckoned it was the best one he had ever made. Bess took to training like a professional athlete and after a while could catch rabbits on the run, break their necks, and bring them back unmarked to Bill's feet without ever making a sound. A true gypsy dog.

He turned off the power, locked up, and headed to the house. Previously part of a large farm, it had been bought it as an investment. Bill had told his wife they could make a packet when it was done up and resold, persuading her that moving from the small bungalow she had inherited from her mother to this rambling heap would be the opportunity of a lifetime. It wasn't, of course. It could have been, but there was so much to do that when they had the time they didn't have the money, and whenever they did have any money, Bill put it back into his business.

No wonder his son had become an accountant. He'd seen the arse hanging out of his father's trousers all his life and knew that wasn't for him. Philip was better with his brains than his hands, anyway, which disappointed Bill in one respect but comforted him in another. On the whole, he was glad his son had an indoor job with no heavy lifting.

Crossing the yard and passing through a small porch, he entered a large kitchen that had once been part of the buttery when the house was young. This room was really all he used now. A vast, black, iron kitchen range took up the whole of the wide fireplace. On the mantle above was an ornate 18th-century French clock he had restored as a wedding present for his wife. She never liked it and he never wound it; that said it all, really. Time was actually kept by a large, round, wall-mounted railway clock whose ticking was sometimes the only sound Bill heard. A pine Welsh dresser bore a few fine china plates like medals on a war hero. The huge farmhouse table in the middle of the room he had dragged out of a barn in rural Wales; it had taken him weeks to clean off the engine oil and chicken shit, but the wooden top was now beautiful. Around the table were six fine Windsor chairs, all different, their fruitwood frames mellowed by time and his craftsmanship. It was a room full of memories, and not just his. Each piece of furniture, each painting: they all had stories of their own, all had lived in other lives, been useful and loved.

From a large, white, incongruously modern refrigerator (a leftover from the Beryl days), he took out a large piece of cheese and the remnants of a pork pie of indeterminate age.

These were his regular rations: cheese, a bit of pie or pasty, and an apple or two to follow. All washed down with the cloudy delights of a straw-coloured cider he got by the barrel from a mate of his who owned a farm nearby. He had helped old Jimmer to repair his cider press and even, in a dark part of the man's cowshed, build a contraption of copper piping and vessels that distilled the rough cider into a lethal and entirely illegal spirit Bill found invaluable in concocting his own wood stains.

His home, a manor in centuries past, sat behind a bulwark of hedges and old stone walls hard against the road itself. This minor road joined up the hamlet of Ayleham via tiny lanes and narrow ways to the village of Brewton. Slap bang in the middle of the county of Somerset amidst gentle hills, fields, and meadows, and occasional woodland, it was as remote as you could get in this part of England.

The front of the house was simple and geometric, with a Georgian façade behind which it rambled away to itself in a muttering of stone walls and lathe and plaster. It was old, very old – parts of it medieval, probably – but with 17th–19th century additions, subtractions, and general mucking about. There was a front door, but it was never used. The path to it from the road was completely overgrown, which was fine because the wrought-iron gate was so rusted it wouldn't open in any case. And even if it had, Bill would probably have padlocked it, but as it was, Mother Nature had done the job for him.

Privacy was important to him, and it showed in the way he allowed his hedges to grow high and his trees to flourish however they wanted to grow. There was even a small garden on the south side of the house that most people didn't know existed. It was tucked away in a corner created by one side of the barn and the gable end of the house, its entrance guarded by an old yew and nearly hidden by the ivy-clad walls. Bill was no gardener, but he liked the roses that climbed over the old stones, and the honeysuckle that ran riot in summer. He had planted a couple of fruit trees here, but the only one that had thrived was a cherry. Sometimes he picked the fruit, but mostly he just enjoyed the shade and seclusion it provided.

On the north side of the house was a leafy lane with a 'No Through Road' sign almost hidden by undergrowth and saplings. Near the house, the lane was wide due to vehicles and carts turning in and out of the entrance to the farmyard. Once past the farm buildings, however, the lane narrowed until it became a small green drain with hedges either side that led up a gentle hill, the top of which was crowned with a ring of trees. In the middle of the ring, with only the roof showing when the trees were in leaf, was the cottage of Bill's nearest neighbour, Miss Templeton.

Miss Templeton was her name and 'Miss Templeton' Bill always called her, with sincere reverence for her advanced years and character. She was stick thin, with grey hair shot with silver that reminded Bill of polished pewter. Always dressed in a mishmash of homemade garments that hung on her in colourful layers, she was a one-off and Bill liked her a lot. On occasions when his business took him away from home, he would leave Bess in her care. In return he kept her sheds and chicken house in good repair.

Taking up the entire back of Bill's house was a large, square farmyard. Forming almost one whole side was the barn he used as his workshop. The other buildings – cart shed, stables, grain store, milking parlour – made up the rest of the square.

They all faced inwards to the farmyard and most didn't even have windows. The majority of the buildings were two-storey, but Bill doubted if the upper floors would take so much as the weight of a man now. Wood rot and rain coming in through roofs from which the slates had fallen out ages ago made them more stone shells than buildings. The farm had been almost derelict in parts when he bought it over thirty years before, and the only repairs Bill had made were to those buildings he used regularly; others were just used to store junk.

Around dusk, Bill took Bess outside for a walk. Just as they were returning to the house, the lights of a car turned up the green drain that led to the house, and a shiny, new, white Range Rover turned into the gate and parked. Two men got out and walked to where he and his dog were standing. Oozing the false bonhomie that politicians and used-car salesmen wear like aftershave, one of them held out a hand for Bill to shake.

'I'm Darryl Skates,' he said, and Bill got the impression the man thought he was somehow conferring a great honour on him by saying it.

Mr Skates looked to be in his early forties, very tan and extremely well dressed, with dark hair and a widow's peak that made him look like a character out of a vampire film. This effect was enhanced by small, piercing eyes under highly defined eyebrows that arched across his forehead as if they had been painted on. As Bill moved forward to shake the man's hand, Bess went to his heel and let out a low growl. Odd, thought Bill, she hardly ever does that.

'I know you by sight, Mr Skates, but I don't think we've ever met before,' said Bill.

'My associate, Richard Warren,' said Skates, indicating the

man at his side.

Warren said nothing. Though not large, he was the most intimidating man Bill had ever seen, and he had seen a few in his long life. This bloke, though, was in a league of his own, with a face like a scar under a head completely devoid of hair. His thin lips were a bloodless cut line under his nose. Muscular in a very compact way, he held himself like a man ready for a fight anytime with anyone.

Bill did not know Skates, but he had heard of him. He was one of those people who dabbled in antiques, and his mansion was reportedly stuffed with all sorts of treasures. He wasn't a dealer, though; more of a fixer who was none too worried about provenance or recent ownership issues. He was reputed to have contacts in all the dark corners of the antiques trade, in which lurked some very nasty villains, as Bill was well aware – people he avoided like the plague.

Skates had money and liked to show it off, but quite where the money came from no one seemed to know. His voice was cultured, with a veneer of public school under which Bill thought he heard just a hint of South London. Bill had seen him at a couple of big auctions around the area, and once in London at Christies. He never seemed to be bidding, yet was treated with oily deference by the auction house staff, which indicated he was worth money to them. Quite a lot of money, judging by the level of grovelling.

The only insight Bill had to the man himself was a scene he had witnessed about three years back in a car park at an auction in Taunton, one of the last he had attended. Bill had gone outside for a smoke, and from the shelter of the doorway in which he was standing, he saw Skates on the other side of the car park talking to a tall, well-dressed young woman with red hair. They were a few dozen yards away, and he could hear Skates raving at the girl, but not what he was saying. Warren was there, too, leaning over the poor woman, who had her back against a parked car. He couldn't hear what she was saying, if anything, but the way she was standing looked as if she was certainly on the defensive. Then they had all got into the car and driven away at breakneck speed, scattering gravel and pedestrians as they left.

Now the two men stood silently in his yard, just looking at him. Not examining the surroundings, the weather, or anything else, just looking at him.

Wishing to end this strange vigil, Bill said, 'Come into the workshop and I'll make us a cup of tea. Or I have some cider if you prefer it.'

'No, thank you, to the drinks, but I would be happy to see your workshop,' said Skates with great condescension. 'I've heard a lot about you, Bill. I'm told you're a very clever man.'

Bill led them the short distance to the barn. There was a small deal table and two chairs in front of the cast-iron stove, and Bill directed them to these. Pulling out the two chairs and getting another from nearby, he invited them to sit down. Skates sat in the chair opposite Bill's, but Warren stood just behind Skates, hands in pockets, no discernible expression on his face.

Bill filled his pipe, and Bess, instead of going to her basket as usual, laid down at his side as if on guard.

Skates sat back in his chair looking relaxed and self-assured. His mouth was formed into a smile, but his eyes were cold and his manner patronising.

'I'm told you can work wonders, Bill. That you're a real

miracle worker with wood.'

Bill made no reply, just smoked his pipe.

'Do you know anything about Elizabethan furniture?' asked Skates.

'I've worked on a few pieces in my time,' said Bill. 'I've worked on a lot more Jacobean, though. It's much more common.'

'But you can turn your hand to some Elizabethan if you have to, am I right?' asked Skates.

'Yes,' said Bill, 'but I have all the work I want right now.'

Skates ignored this. 'My sources tell me you did a nice little job for the V&A a while back. A Tudor chest that had taken a battering during a move? No one else would touch it, but you had the thing right as rain in the end.'

'I can't comment on that,' said Bill, smiling. 'Those kinds of jobs come with a vow of silence.'

It was true. 'Trappist jobs' they were called in the trade, and no matter how good you were, you wouldn't get any more work from a really big museum if they heard you'd bandied their name about.

'Have you ever heard of the Blakeney Chairs?' asked Skates. He took a cigarette from a gold case and lit it with a gold lighter the size of a small brick.

'I've heard of them, of course,' said Bill, 'but they've not been seen in years, decades even. They're a bit like the holy grail to the right collector, and just as elusive.'

'Yes, just like the holy grail,' smiled Skates, 'but no longer quite so elusive. I've got them. Three of them, anyway.'

Bill sat back, surprised. These things happened in the antiques trade, of course, but not often.

'How?'

'That's not something with which you need concern yourself,' answered Skates loftily.

Bill had heard enough. Such high-profile pieces came with all sorts of trouble. He thought it was time to bring this conversation to a close and began to rise from his chair to see this man out of his workshop and his life.

At nearly seventy years of age it's an affront to be manhandled, especially in your own workshop. But it wasn't so much the act itself that took Bill's breath away; it was the speed with which it was done. Skates must have made some sign because in the blink of an eye Bill went from almost standing to being pinned in his chair, his shoulders gripped by hands of steel. It was as if two huge vices had him in their grasp. He could no more have struggled out of that grip than fly. Warren had him pinned like he was nothing. That was the frightening thing; like he was nothing. Just an old man too slow and frail to defend himself.

Warren let go, and Bill resisted the urge to rub some life back into his shoulders. Skates had not moved. He now made a motion with one carefully manicured hand, and Warren walked back to where he had been standing prior to assaulting Bill.

Skates smiled and said, 'Let's not get off on the wrong foot, Bill. I have a very special commission for a very special craftsman, and you are that craftsman. There is no one else capable that I know of. And you will be well paid, I assure you.'

Bill left his face in neutral, but his mind was racing. 'What is it you want me to do?'

'I have a set of chairs so famous and so valuable they would form the pinnacle of anyone's collection. They are also of great historical importance. You, Bill, will use your talents to create for me a set of four museum-quality chairs.'

'Four chairs,' said Bill. 'I thought you only had three?'

'Well, to be absolutely truthful, I have two in good condition and one that is, oh, let's say, past its prime. What I want is to have four Elizabethan chairs, all genuine, but with 'some restoration'.'

'So you want me to do a shuffle, then. A mix and match.'

'Exactly,' said Skates, 'but one that only you and I will know about. And Mr Warren here, of course, but he can be as silent as the grave when he needs to be.'

The thought went through Bill's mind that if Mr Warren stayed silent it was probably only so he could more easily appreciate the screams of his victims.

Bill leaned back in his seat. 'Without seeing the chairs I have no idea if what you're asking is even possible. The older the piece, the more difficult it is to make the components good enough to match.'

'And why is that?' asked Skates, without any real interest in the answer.

'Making good and making more is fine for anything 18th century and beyond. All the components were much the same. There are slight differences, of course, because they're handmade, but nothing like with really early stuff that is all to pot, no two legs being the same, let alone any carvings or decoration.'

Skates remained silent.

'Mr Skates, I have been in this game all my working life and I do know what I'm talking about. If you want four museum-quality chairs made from two-and-a-bit old wainscots, then you need a fucking magician, not a furniture restorer.'

'Let's not be hasty,' purred Skates, uncurling himself from his chair. 'I shall bring you the chairs and then we can decide how to proceed. I'll give you a call in the next day or two and fix a time to come over.'

It wasn't a question, so there was no answer for Bill to make. He supposed he could at least look at the job before deciding it couldn't be done.

Skates walked to the door followed by Warren. He turned just before he left and said, 'Not a word about this to anyone, Bill, is that clear?'

Bill said nothing, but nodded his head.

The door closed behind them. As he heard the car drive away, Bill collapsed into his chair and started to cough – long, hacking coughs that racked his whole body. At last, taking a wad of tissue from his pocket, he slowly wiped his mouth, drained by this and by them.

Eventually, Bill rose and locked up, then he and Bess went back into the house. He ate some supper, not because he was hungry but because he felt he must. He also drank far more than he should have done. When he eventually reached his bed, his sleep was patterned with dreams, none of them very nice.

Chapter 3

WEDNESDAY, 15 AUGUST

The next morning Bill woke with a hangover, which was only made worse by remembering the previous night's visit. He fed Bess, the smell of the dog food making him even queasier. Then he went to his bookshelves. He knew what he was looking for, but as he searched through his vast collection, the pile beside him grew and grew. There were books he hadn't looked through in years. Books, though, are like old friends; they never let you down. He selected the most relevant ones, then sat at the kitchen table drinking strong coffee and refreshing his memory.

The Blakeney Chairs had a unique provenance. Made of oak in 1560 by an unknown master craftsman, they were a set of four wainscots owned by Sir Edmund Blakeney of Darrington Hall in Somerset. Oak chairs of this quality were not so rare as to be of enormous value, but what made these so special was who had used them and when.

During the summer of 1560, Queen Elizabeth I and her huge entourage of courtiers, favourites, hangers-on, and servants were making their way from Bristol to the hall of Sir John Thynne at Longleat. It was an extensive journey on bad, almost nonexistent roads during particularly foul weather. There came a point when the going got so bad that the Queen sent a courtier off to find a place of shelter with words to the effect that 'be it hovel or castle, I heed not, just find it!'

From the old Roman road where the mud had been churned into a foul soup by the horses and carts that made up the convoy, a track had been found that led to a former abbey set in a small valley half a mile away. This ancient building had been turned into a comfortable home after the Dissolution of the Monasteries and was owned by a man of some substance but no standing at court. In fact, his neighbours barely counted him a gentleman.

The records do not tell of the confusion that must have reigned when a soaked, worried nobleman rode into the courtyard of this house. All that is recorded is that one Edmund Blakeney did provide such victuals and refreshments as could be wished for by a drenched and exhausted monarch. She stayed the night, with only her close companions sharing the accommodation, the rest making what shift they could in the farm buildings.

Before leaving the next day, with the sun shining after a dry and comfortable night's rest, the Queen knighted Edmund and gave him the title Lord of the Manor. From then on Sir Edmund Blakeney's fortunes were assured, and to commemorate the event he had the 'four great chairs that seated the Queen of our realm and her noble lords carved anew with the rose of her father she so proudly bears'. So reads an entry in the accounts book kept by the new knight.

The same chairs figured in Sir Edmund's will in 1602 and were part of the estate of his heirs who lived in Darrington Hall in an unbroken line until the 1920s. The chairs were included in photographs of the hall and, because of their quality, history, and unique decoration, featured in various books and journals about Tudor and Elizabethan furniture.

Unfortunately, the set was broken up when the last of the family died in 1925. His only son had been killed on the Somme in 1916, and his wife had died in the flu epidemic of 1918, after which Sir Fredrick Blakeney became a recluse and lived in genteel but grinding poverty. With the mansion falling down around his ears, the lonely old man was forced to sell off part of his estate and such possessions as would fetch any money. Upon his death, a local house-clearance firm was called in, and in due course a few items found their way to a small auction house. The lots included a pair of Elizabethan chairs that were purchased by Simon Morse, a well-known collector and dealer in antique oak furniture. He identified the chairs as being part of the original Blakeney set, and they were catalogued as being in his possession in 1935. No trace was ever found of the other two chairs, however, and it was assumed they had been sold during Sir Frederick's lifetime, or possibly even burned as firewood, things having become that desperate.

When Simon Morse died in 1960, his records showed that the two Blakeneys he owned had been sold to a private collector in 1953. Neither the name of the purchaser nor the price paid was recorded, suggesting it was likely to have been a cash sale.

Bill closed his books, sighed, and took Bess outside. While she trotted about on her own business, he looked around at the stone walls of the sheds and barns that were grey and pitted by time and lichen. It had started to rain, and the damp, colourless surroundings matched his mood. After a bit he called Bess and, walking across the yard to the barn, opened up his workshop.

Lighting first the huge stove and then his pipe, Bill pulled up a chair near the growing warmth. Bess lay looking up at him from her basket beside the stove. It was at times like this that Bess really proved her worth. Talking through a problem with yourself may help sort things out in your head, but the dialogue is all one-way. Talk to your dog, however, and you get sage advice with no interruptions, deviations, or repetitions.

'No doubt about it, Bess, darling, that bastard Skates is not going to leave us alone unless we can come up with a bloody good reason for him to.'

Bess said nothing, but wagged her tale a fraction to let him he was not alone in this.

Bill sat back and enjoyed Bess's company and his pipe of tobacco. Eventually he found his hands needed something to do, so he got up and fetched his current project, a Windsor chair he was doing up for an old mate of his, Jerry Sparks.

Bill had first met Jerry years ago when he still worked the auctions himself. Going into the big Illminster antique auction held in the town hall, he'd spotted the usual suspects of dealers and traders weaving their wicked ways through the punters like sharks through shoals of minnows. The thing about antique auctions in those far-off days was that they were invariably bent. Those in the know, such as dealers, had the objects of their interest marked well before the auction started, even if they hadn't attended the preview. They knew what was on offer from their contacts in the auction house itself. Never mind the man with the gavel, who often was not only the boss but usually did a bit of collecting on the side, too. The porters were always good for a tip if you looked after them regularly.

Dealers in the same locality tried not to step on each other's toes too much. If you were after a nice bit of Spode that had surfaced and it didn't cut across anyone else's plans, then on a nod and a wink the other members of this magic circle would not bid against you when it came under the hammer. If, on the other hand, there was something two or three of the circle were after, then only one of them would bid at the auction, thus keeping the price as low as possible. After the main auction had finished, there would be a subsequent private auction held around a table of the favoured pub where the object in question would be sold to the one most determined to possess same.

The fly in the auction ointment was, of course, the general public. These people had a nasty habit of bidding through the roof on something that took their fancy, with absolutely no consideration for the real value of the piece and the fact that there were poor sods out there who were scratching a living buying and selling these little bits of yesterday. No consideration, some people.

Jerry Sparks had stood out from the crowd because, for one thing, he dressed in the loudest check suiting Bill had ever seen outside a circus. He also had a booming voice so rich in aristocratic tone that he was almost unintelligible. His tall, slim frame was invariably topped by a battered Fedora, and his sartorial elegance was marred only by a constant fall of ash from the Turkish cigarettes he smoked. Bill had bumped into him, literally, in the gents at the Bull Inn in Watchett. A small auction was taking place in the old reading rooms next door. Jerry was drunk, as he often was, and his aim wandered as he stood at the urinal, loudly declaiming in his Etonian drawl, 'For this relief, Horatio, we thank you!'

His aim was so bad that a stream of urine went all over Bill's shoes. Bill was not amused, but seeing no malice aforethought in the action, and softened by the anguished apologies of the perpetrator, he allowed himself to be taken into the bar to dry off one end and wet the other. When Jerry found out Bill's trade he was beside himself with glee and bought another round—doubles and chasers. They both missed the auction but struck up a firm friendship. Jerry, it turned out, was a dealer in fine antique furniture with good connections in America. He took container loads from his warehouse in Bath to the USA where he sold it on to top-end antique furniture shops. Always on the lookout for some tasty item that might have owed some part of its past to that nice Mr Chippindale or his ilk, Bill was able to conjure up some very fine mostly antique items to their mutual advantage.

These days, the whole American bubble had all but burst, and Jerry kept a shop in Bath whilst getting old disgracefully. His trade was still upper-end but now catered for the home decorator rather than the serious collector. Windsor chairs for big new kitchens and chaise longue for loft apartments. He never quibbled over Bill's charges, and when they went out for a drink after Bill had delivered a piece, they drank little and smoked less amidst the gaggle of tourists that now infected every pub in Bath. How times had changed.

Bill finished the work around five, phoned Jerry, and told him he wouldn't be able to deliver the chair himself, which Jerry said was not a problem. He gave Jerry the price and received a raspberry down the line.

'It's far too much, you old fraud, but I'll beggar myself and pay it anyway.'

He laughed as he said it, though, because they both knew Bill was charging yesterday's prices for today's work.

As Bill covered the lovely chair in a blanket for the journey, he thought to himself that this might be one of the last he did. He was comforted in the knowledge that this old Windsor, made by some forgotten craftsman two hundred years or more ago, would live again in someone's life. He hoped they would cherish it and enjoy the skill that had gone into making it back then, and making it better now. He had not signed the work; the man who had bent the yew back rail centuries before had not, so what right had he?

Chapter 4

THURSDAY, 16 AUGUST

It was not long into the next morning when the phone rang. Skates imperiously informed Bill he would be dropping in sometime late afternoon to deliver the chairs. Time dragged after this, and Bill found it hard to concentrate. He did things about the workshop in a half-hearted way, and then, of course, the unexpected happened, because it always does at times like this.

Bill was sitting at his bench, smoking and moodily staring into time and space when he heard a car drive up. His heart sank; it was only eleven. They were hours early, the bastards! But it turned out to be his daughter-in-law, Gloria, and his one and only grandchild, Jack, who was nine years old and the light of his grandfather's life.

Gloria was a lovely woman who always reminded Bill of summer days and gymkhanas. From an old, local farming family, she had gently defied her parents and married Bill's son, Philip, a chartered accountant ten years her senior with no interest in hunting, shooting, or fishing, and who regarded horses as something to be avoided at all costs and never, ever climbed on as a means of transport, let alone recreation.

'What on earth are you doing here?' he asked Gloria. Philip and Gloria lived in Dorchester, about an hour's drive away.

'Daddy's not well again,' she explained, 'so I brought Jack over to see him, and I stopped by to share some news with you.'

A small, tousle-haired boy threw himself into Bill's arms. Bill held the squirming child close to his chest and gave him a huge whiskery raspberry on his exposed neck, just as he always did, and as always the boy gave a laugh that was more of a tonic to Bill than any medicine on earth. Jack got down and ran off to explore the workshop, kicking up clouds of wood shavings as he went.

'Stop that!' scolded his mother. 'Poor granddad will have to clear that up after you, you horror.'

Bill caught his grandson under his arms and carried him out of the workshop into the yard.

'Let's all have a cup of tea and then you can tell me your news. Would you like some lunch? We could go down the road.'

That meant the pub, of course, but Gloria said a cup of tea would be fine and she had brought lunch with them. The fact was she hadn't wanted to embarrass her father-in-law, who, she guessed rightly, did not have enough food in the house for three.

'Oh, a picnic!' said Bill, relieved not to have to do anything other than enjoy time with his family. 'What a great idea, eh, Jack?'

'Can I take Bess for a walk, Granddad?'

'If you like,' said Bill, 'but come in first and have some lunch and, if you can find it, a little treat because you're such a jolly rotter.'

This was another ritual. Bill had an old ginger jar in which he kept sweets for his grandson. The game was for Jack to close his eyes while Bill moved the jar from its regular place on the dresser to somewhere else in the room. Then there would be a game of 'Am I warmer or colder?' as the child got nearer or further away from the jar. For many years Bill had been an absent father to his only son, and not a terribly good one at that. You can't turn back the clock, but you can do things better next time, given the chance. And this precious child was Bill's chance of doing things better.

The game began. Starting in one corner, Jack moved away, asking if he was warmer or colder. He knew he would eventually get the treat, but enjoyed both the anticipation and the fun with his grandfather, so he entered into the spirit of the thing with laughs and giggles.

Bill started to laugh along with Jack, but the laugh turned into a bout of coughing that got worse and worse until he was completely bent over and shaking with the effort. Jack stopped what he was doing and looked horrified. Gloria just stared.

'How long has this been going on?' she asked as she walked over and gently rubbed his back. Her warm touch gave Bill real comfort; the hacking subsided, but once again he felt completely drained by the experience.

'Not long,' he lied. 'It's just the dust. Just a bit of dust I must have breathed in. Find the jar, Jack, you're very warm now.'

Gloria was not to be fobbed off, however, and as she busied herself unpacking the sandwiches and making the tea she asked Bill if he had seen the doctor.

'Going to,' said Bill. 'But it's just the dust. That's all it is, dust.'

Jack had found the jar and Bill lifted it out of its hiding place and got out a tube of chocolate buttons for the boy.

Jack was delighted and sat at the table with a glass of milk and the sweets.

'How's my wicked son?' Bill asked Gloria.

When Beryl had left him, she had taken Philip with her. It was only when the lad was in his late teens that Bill really got to know his son, and it came as a surprise to them both that they got on so well. Since then all his hopes of what the future might hold revolved around Philip and his family.

'Oh, he's fine,' Gloria said, sitting down next to him and pouring the tea. 'Working as hard as ever. Must be in his genes; he never stops.'

'But otherwise things are fine?'

'Yes,' she said, a brief shadow crossing her face. 'He would really like to have his own practice, of course. They keep promising him a partnership but nothing ever comes of it. He could go out on his own, he has enough clients who would follow him, but that takes money.'

She shrugged, then, with a look of concern, asked Bill, 'What's wrong?'

Bill played down the coughing episode and blamed the dust again, saying nothing of Skates and his damned chairs. Instead he turned the conversation back to his son's problems.

'How much money does he need to go out on his own?' he asked.

'Oh, lots,' replied Gloria with a rueful laugh. Then her face lit up. 'And we have an added extra on the way.'

'Wonderful news!' Bill cried. 'Wonderful! When?'

'February.'

Bill was overjoyed. This news quite eclipsed any thoughts of his dealings with Skates.

Lunch over – and it really had been a picnic, so Bill had no washing up to do – they followed Jack and Bess into the yard. Of course Jack wanted to explore his grandfather's workshop, which was for him a place of magic and dusty mystery.

'You will phone the doctor,' Gloria told Bill, the tone of her voice brooking no argument.

'I'll do it from the workshop phone right now. There's a calendar in there so I can fix a date and everything.'

They went into the workshop, and even before Bill had put on all the lights, young Jack scooted inside.

Bill called out to his grandson, 'No climbing! Remember what happened last time, right?'

Turning to Gloria, he said, 'Same as his dad, never could resist a pile of chairs', and started to laugh.

This time the coughing fit brought on by the laughter was not as bad, but it was enough to send him over to a dusty, wall-mounted phone next to which hung a battered address book on a string. He looked up his doctor's number and was soon talking to someone in the surgery. During the conversation another coughing fit came on, and he was put in as an emergency with an appointment for the following Monday. With the call made, it seemed to Bill he had made a start at sorting out at least one of his problems.

He sat down. Gloria sat opposite him on a wheelback chair and rubbed her hands over the beautiful polished wood of the arms.

'Is this very old?' she asked.

'Older than me by a couple of centuries,' said Bill, somewhat absently. He looked everywhere but at Gloria.

'Bill, is there anything bothering you apart from the cough?'

He looked at her. There was, of course, and he suddenly found he wanted to talk to her about it. Gloria was clever, and he really needed someone else's opinion, a fresh pair of eyes on the problem.

'The fact is,' he said, 'I've been asked to do a job for a right villain. I don't trust the . . .' He was going to say 'bastard' but measured his language in case small ears were flapping. '. . . swine, and it's a real moody job he wants done.'

He got up, put a piece of soft wood in a vice on his bench, took out a small hammer and a tin of wire nails, called Jack over, and showed him what awaited. With a huge smile the boy picked up the hammer and started to bang in the nails in a line along the wood.

'Be careful,' said Bill, 'and remember to keep the hammer head straight and leave a gap between each nail like I taught you.'

The sound of hammering filled the workshop, which gave Bill and Gloria a chance to talk without being overheard.

'I've been a bloody fool most of my life and I've done some slightly dodgy deals as you have to now and again to make a shilling, but not for years now. Don't need to anymore.'

He paused, looking around his workshop as if the place itself would confirm the truth of what he said.

'I know that sounds daft, but I love what I do, I'm still good at it, and I really don't want to embark on something shady at this time of life. I don't need the money and I don't need the stress.'

Gloria nodded sympathetically, but said nothing, not wanting to interrupt his flow of thought.

'What it boils down to is that I'm being asked to fake up

a set of chairs that will then be worth big money – really big money – and that's when things always start to get interesting. By which I mean difficult and possibly dangerous.'

'Why is that?' asked Gloria.

'Well, lass, when a lot is at stake, including reputations, then what's being sold is looked at very carefully indeed. The history of the piece—its provenance—well, that has to match with what the furniture looks like, feels like, tells you about itself. There can't be any gaps or mistakes. The right joint, the right age of the wood, those are the easy things to replicate. It's the subtle traces that experts will really be looking for, and those are the hardest to reproduce.'

Gloria was fascinated. Philip had told her that his father was a master of some of the dark arts in the antiques trade, and she knew by the furniture he had given them that Bill was a superb craftsman, but this was a side of the business she knew nothing about.

'How would you go about doing it? If you were going to do it, I mean.'

Bill walked over to a pile of chairs that stood against the wall, selected the top one, and brought it back to sit between them like a third at bridge.

'Consider,' he said. 'This is a nice little Hepplewhite-inspired, shield-shaped dining chair, 19th century, and in quite good condition, considering. But it's only one chair and therefore not worth very much.' As he spoke, his hands stroked the carved wood, his fingers following the arabesques, curves, and elegant shapes in the mahogany chair back.

'Lovely, isn't it?'

'Not my taste,' said Gloria, 'but mummy has a set just

like them.'

'Well, let's say your mum's chairs are the real thing. Hepplewhite, Sheraton, or even Chippendale dating from the 1760s and a set of four without carvers. Let's also say that two of them are a bit worn and rocky and in need of some care and attention. And let's also say your mum wanted to trade them in for a few bob and get something else with the cash. Not that she would of course,' he added hurriedly, 'but just as an example.'

Gloria smiled. 'Go on, then.'

'Dealers always like to sell chairs in sets of four, six, or eight. And they charge a premium for supplying the whole set; a big premium if they can get away with it. So it would be worth your mum's while to have her two distressed chairs tidied up a bit before trying to sell them. Now, it is not wrong or illegal to restore a piece of furniture. It's not even wrong or illegal to copy a piece of furniture outright. Plenty of people make an honest living from doing so. What *is* a crime, however, is passing off the result as an original, known in the trade as a 'naughty'.'

'But could you actually make a chair good enough to fool an expert?' asked Gloria.

Bill couldn't help smiling at the question. 'Well, yes, a very good craftsman could. You see, a chair has four legs, sometimes two arms, a stretcher – that's the bit that keeps the legs apart and strengthens them – a seat, and a back. Lots of clever bits of wood shaped to do what they need to do so the chair will support a bum as heavy as mine or as pretty as yours.'

Gloria laughed. Bill really was an old charmer. He continued the lesson, warming to his theme in spite of himself.

'You take the two damaged chairs, strip them down, and you mix original parts with new as far as you can. When it comes to backs and seats, you usually have to make up new ones, but always using the originals as a guide. Use the same sort of wood, use the same method of jointing, and use the right glues, such as rabbit skin or hoof. Make everything just the same, but don't make exact copies. All antique furniture was handmade, so there are always slight differences in the carving or shapes. You use old tools, or new tools forged or made in the same ways the old ones were. That way if some suspicious bugger uses a magnifying glass to examine a piece, the work marks are the same. But the real skill, of course, lies in the finishing.'

'Do you mean the polish?'

'That's part of it,' said Bill, 'but what I really mean is 'making age'. Carefully, ever so carefully, recreating the wear and tear of the centuries.'

He got up and went over to a dining chair that stood nearby. 'Furniture gets lived with and lived on for years and years; wear happens in all sorts of ways. Hands and clothes rub on the arms and back, chair legs get scuffed from being dragged across floors, and everything just generally gets knocked about in a busy household.'

As he explained this, he showed Gloria the way time and use had made marks on the piece. He went on to tell her of the methods that could be used to replicate age; the careful rubbing down of certain surface areas, and the use of wire wool, scrapers, and subtle blades to pair away the new to reveal the old.

'What about woodworm and the like?' asked Gloria.

Bill lit his pipe, filling the space with fragrant smoke. The regular sound of hammering told them that Jack was still engaged in bashing nails into wood.

'Yes,' he said, 'woodworm holes are very difficult to fake.

The little buggers leave holes that have bends just fractions of an inch in from the surface, so a small drill hole or hot nail won't do. No bend, see, and that's suspicious.'

'What happens if you get found out?'

'You're in a world of pain, my love,' said Bill. 'A world of pain, and possibly prison.'

'And someone is trying to pressure you into doing this?'

'I'm afraid so.'

'Well, just tell them no!' said Gloria. 'They can't make you do it, for heaven's sake. What can they do apart from get angry?'

'Lots,' said Bill. 'And none of it nice.'

'Can't you go to the police?'

'My darling,' said Bill, 'the police are the last ones to go to. Bloody useless, they are. All these people have to say is that they asked me to make a reproduction. Nothing illegal in that, and I'm left looking like an idiot and still on the hook.'

The banging stopped. Jack came over to where they were sitting and proudly showed his grandfather the piece of wood he had decorated with small nails.

'What do you think, Granddad?' he asked, his eyes alight with enthusiasm and his clothes covered with dust.

'Wonderful job!' said Bill. 'All in line and neatly done. You'll be my apprentice in a year or three if you want.'

Jack looked pleased at that. He really wanted to be a Star Wars fighter pilot, but he thought he might be able to do both, if his mother let him.

Gloria was still looking worriedly at Bill.

'I'll sort it out, don't you fret,' he said, patting her hand and smiling with a confidence he didn't feel.

They stood up and Gloria kissed him, after which he bent

down and picked up his grandson for a goodbye hug.

As their car started off, he looked at his watch. It was half past three. Before Gloria's car could even reach the gate, Skates's Range Rover drove in, blocking her exit. She backed up, giving him room to pass, then continued on her way. Jack turned to wave from the back seat, and Bill could see him smiling at him as they drove away.

'Family?' asked Skates, walking over from where he'd parked.

'Just a customer,' said Bill. 'Looking for a table.'

'Oh, I thought it was your daughter-in-law,' smirked Skates. 'She drives a remarkably similar car, and that boy in the back looked just like your grandson.'

Skates's eyes were hard and stared meaningfully into Bill's. 'I don't have a family myself,' he said. 'No "hostages to fortune" for me. So many nasty things can happen; I'd be a nervous wreck.'

He turned to Warren, who was getting the chairs out of the back of the vehicle. 'You haven't got family either, have you, Mr Warren? No little Warrens to impede your "great enterprises of virtue or *mischief*". As he stressed the last word, he winked at Bill, obviously very pleased with himself for being able to continue the quotation.

Warren said nothing, as usual. He carried the chairs, wrapped in blankets, into the workshop. Bill could just make out their shapes. Polished wood showed through a gap in the cloth.

Skates turned to Bill and said, 'I'm off to attend some auctions in New York, which should give you plenty of time to look over the chairs and decide how you're going to deal with them. But don't worry; Mr Warren here will be close by in case you get lonely.'

As Bill stood there helplessly fuming under another of Skates's significant leers, the two men got back in the Range Rover and drove away.

Going back into his workshop, Bill uncovered the chairs and carried them to a section of bench that could be illuminated by a whole battery of lights that left no shadows. Kept clean of dust, mostly, it was where he could photograph furniture or examine it in forensic detail. Each of the three chairs was looked at more closely than it had probably ever been before. He utilised all his skills as a maker and restorer, as well as that expert eye that comes only after years of study and experience. He wanted a reason, any reason, to duck out of having to do this job. If a chair had been faked or there was even any doubt as to its credentials, that might be enough, though Bill was starting to worry if even that would convince Skates to back off.

Two of the chairs were good, with slight damage commensurate with their age in places where he would expect such damage to occur. Their patina was lovely, and one that only age (or a very, *very*, skilful hand) could give. The highlights in their polished surfaces were golden with hints of light raw umber merging into a brown madder by way of a van Dyke brown. Beautiful. His hands traced the centuries written upon the silk surface of the wood. If there was artifice here, it was beyond his ability to see, and therefore there probably wasn't any.

The back panels of the chairs were carved in a vigorous rustic style, the central motif being the Tudor Rose. This alone would not date the chairs, though, as it had been used from King Hal's time onward, being one of the first pieces of royal branding.

Henry had them stuck all over the place, and many a piece of furniture was given a patriotic makeover by carving these roses on them.

Underneath, in large, simple letters, the initials 'ER' were carved, again in relief. Bill looked closely at the carving. It was well done, but not abbey quality. That indicated a local craftsman rather than one of the elite who travelled from job to job on the ecclesiastical payroll.

The panels themselves were definitely from the original chairs and, looking at the slight variation in the angles of some of the petals in the rose, were probably carved in situ rather than on new wood. Sure enough, when Bill took a rough measurement of the thickness of the chair back, it told him a lot of wood had been taken away; the rose and the initials were a sort of bass relief. All the undercuts that gave depth to the design left the wood thin in places where the carver had gone in deep with his gouge. All this made sense because wood had to be cut, planed, and shaped by hand in those days, which took a long time and was very expensive.

The rose was set in a simple border with no foliage to the flower head; that was definitely an Elizabethan rather than a Jacobean addition. The Queens's initials would probably have been added later, but with old furniture you never really knew for sure. The problem with pieces of this age was that they were always being mucked about with. Extra carvings were done to make something look new or to tart up a plain piece. Even the Victorians did this, and later on, fashionable homeowners who were bitten by the 'Gothic Revival' bug became downright vandals and chipped bits off to sex up perfectly good late medieval furniture. But as hard as Bill looked, both these chairs seemed 'right'.

The third chair could have been from the same set, but it was difficult to be sure. Age had certainly wearied and the years condemned this poor bugger. Only three legs were complete and all the stretchers were damaged. Thankfully, the frieze rail was still good, as was the seat. One arm was missing, and the carved back panel was split but repairable. One seat rail was split and the other water-damaged. It was not good, not good at all. It could be restored, but it would not be easy. However, when finished, one would be able to get away with describing it as 'original with some restoration'.

There was, of course, no fourth chair. That would have to be made from mixing and matching with bits of the other chairs and making the missing parts from scratch. That would be a hugely difficult job, especially now that Bill was not firing on all cylinders. He had a vast stock of old timber, both in antique furniture parts and in rough-cut planks and baulks lurking in the dark, dust-encrusted corners of his workshop, so finding English oak would not be a problem, but working old oak was a right bastard. Nothing blunted even the best steel as quickly as old oak.

But the real problem, Bill decided, would be the back panel carving. He had done a bit of carving once upon a time, but never to the quality this job would require.

He decided that was his get-out and felt a bit better for it. He covered up the chairs, but left them where they were so he could talk through the problems with Skates and slip out from under this bloody job. The bugger of it was, he thought, that a few years ago, and with a different client, he would have leapt at the project. It would be fascinating, a real challenge, and a damn good earner. But not for Skates, and not now.

Chapter 5

FRIDAY, 17 AUGUST

The next day Bill went hunting. He wanted to find out more about Skates. He was sure in his own mind that the man was dangerous, and that his nasty sidekick, Warren, was a psychopath (if he wasn't, he made a damned good job of appearing as one). But so far all they had really done was bully him. How serious were Skates's badly veiled threats? Was Skates the sort of person who would actually use violence against Bill or his family to gain his ends?

Bill racked his brains to think of someone canny enough to know what Skates's game was. Jerry Sparks? No, he was too far removed from the scene of action now, but thinking of Jerry reminded him of someone who might be in a position to know (or find out) and, more importantly, one he could trust to keep his mouth shut.

That meant a trip to London, to Bermondsey market, where for a few years Bill had enjoyed the company and devious wiles of one of the shrewdest antiques dealers he had ever had the pleasure to know. Manny Traviss was a dealer of the old school (i.e., you needed to count your fingers after he'd shaken your hand), but if he took a liking to you, he was as good as gold.

He even had a set of highly illegal assay stamps (as used by HM assay offices to mark precious metals) to prove that it really was gold he was as good as. Bill had not been to London for a few years and hadn't been in contact with Manny during that time, so it was a long shot, but it was the only shot he could think of.

Bill took Bess to Miss Templeton's and explained that he had to go to London on business and was unsure when he would be back, but he didn't think it would be more than a day or two. She said it was not a problem and wished him luck.

Bill drove to Castle Cary railway station and boarded the train to Paddington. From there, he made his way to the Elephant and Castle underground station, from which it was just a short walk to the Bermondsey Road. It was an area he knew well. For years it had been one of the hubs of the antiques trade, not least because this market had been one of the few places where dodgy gear could be sold legitimately.

Thanks to a law going back centuries, if something was stolen and then sold in an 'open market' – which Bermondsey was right up until 1995 – then it was fair game, and no matter the provenance, whoever brought it could legally keep it. This meant, of course, that amidst the hundreds of stalls, barrows, and piles of junk, rare gems of antiques could be picked up for a good price, especially if one was in the know.

As Bill walked through the market thronged with stalls and crowded with punters, he checked out the wares. It was rubbish mostly, but occasionally something would take his eye and he'd have to restrain himself from going to take a closer look. Old habits die hard. He didn't recognise any stall holders; these people were obviously here just to flog tat to the unwary tourist. What he was looking for was a 'face': someone who knew the trade and was a part of it. It seemed it had all changed, but then so had he.

Disappointed, Bill went into a café he used to frequent and ordered a mug of tea and a bacon sandwich. He was told he could have something called a 'panini', but that the café was vegetarian. They did, however, offer a broad range of organic teas, both herbal and estate grown, and which one would he like?

He got up to leave, but as he reached the door he was stopped by a tall woman with straw-blonde hair piled up in an old-fashioned beehive. She was festooned with costume jewellery and wore a moth-eaten fake-fur coat. Her thick makeup cracked as she grinned hugely, took him by the shoulders, and shrieked, 'Bill Sawyer, as I live and breathe and fuck on Sundays, what the hell are you doing in these parts? We all thought you were dead!'

'Hello, Dolly,' he said, trying to extricate himself from her bejewelled talons.

After a brief but painful coughing fit brought on by her dreadful perfume, Bill found himself returned to the seat he had just vacated and in the company of a dubious contact of years gone by. One with whom he had done some very shady business at one time. As he ate the strange concoction placed in front of him and drank a mug of hot, flavourless liquid, Dolly caught him up on the doings of the market: who had given up the trade, who was still clinging to the wreckage, and who had gone on to that great saleroom in the sky,

As Dolly kept saying (far too loudly), 'We're old partners in grime, darling!'

Indeed they had been. During hard times, Bill would take a

rather indifferent stick of furniture apart and, with great skill, guile, and very special stains and polishes, produce a piece that would pass, to even a moderately educated eye, as something rare and desirable. Then Dolly would put the word around that she was about to receive some gem of an antique that had fallen from the French windows of a nice house in one of the home counties. Not coming right out and saying it was stolen, of course, but dropping enough hints that those mugs who thought they were part of the 'special end of the trade' would mosey round and have a look. If enough people were interested, Dolly would hold an impromptu 'Dutch' auction – sealed bids opened at lunch time, winner to collect and pay before the market closed – to add to the illusion that the piece was dodgy.

Dolly had always wanted more than Bill thought prudent to provide, and he eased himself out of the relationship as soon as he could. Dolly, however, got greedy and took on another partner, one who was nothing like as skilled as Bill, and the inevitable happened. She was rumbled, and one of her former customers was angry enough about the refunds he had to give as a result of her activities (or rather their discovery) that he gave her a severe beating. When Bill heard about that he came up to London to visit her in hospital, bearing a huge bunch of flowers that concealed a bottle of gin. That's when he found out that 'Dolly' was really Dennis and had once been a drag act at Danny La Rue's nightclub in Soho.

As they talked of bygone days, Bill carefully slipped in an offhand enquiry as to whether old Manny was still alive. It seemed he was, but he had retired from the trade.

'Well, dear, he must be 80 if he's a day, and all that drink and sex in the House of Lords has got to take it out of you!'

bellowed Dolly.

Apparently Manny had a nice little council flat nearby; she knew the street but not the number. Bill quickly moved the conversation on, and after another hour of weak tea and detailed descriptions of Dolly's current medical problems, Bill was able to get away.

He had no trouble finding the street Manny lived in. It contained a row of two-storey council flats with their doors all painted the same colour blue. Not a long street, it must have been bombed during the war and these dwellings put up in the 1950s. Not at all the sort of place he imagined Manny would have ended up. A mews cottage in Kensington perhaps, or maybe some little thatched number in Surrey that would make for an easy journey to the Oval, but not one of these humble workers' dwellings.

Walking up the street as near to the houses as he dared, Bill looked into all the front windows. The last thing he wanted was some busybody calling the police and accusing him of being a peeping Tom, but he couldn't think of anything else to do.

Luckily, the street was deserted, and before very long Bill found a front window containing a vase so large it must have blocked out all the available light to the room. It was garishly ornate and had a picture of a very bored-looking Queen Elizabeth II on one side. Bill knew this vase well, and the story behind the monstrosity.

On the succession to the throne of our gracious Queen, Royal Doulton in Stoke-on-Trent created 100 of these huge urns to commemorate the happy event. No expense was spared, and distribution was limited to heads of state and fellow royals attending the coronation. However, the Doulton potters, glazers, kiln packers, and all the other workers were firm monarchists, and extra urns had to be made for glazing tests and in case of accident. Of course there were 'rejects'.

Not too long after all the celebrations were over, the new Queen was on a tour of her realm and eventually rocked up in Stoke for a look around the Doulton factory and other places of civic interest before a knife-and-fork tea at the town hall. Her open-topped car was driven down a small, typical street in which many of the Doulton pottery employees lived. So, having been told by the great and the good of Royal Doulton that only 100 coronation urns bearing her likeness were ever made, what does the lovely young Queen see but urn after urn proudly displayed in the front-parlour windows of these workers' homes!

Doulton management were furious and threatened to fire and prosecute for theft any worker found to possess one of the illicit urns. Fortunately, saner heads prevailed; an amnesty was declared and a small reward given to those who handed the things in for destruction. Most were destroyed, but the few that weren't became even more highly sought after than the official run of production. Bill had seen this self-same vase before and heard the story of its making from dear old Manny, antiques expert, staunch monarchist, and well-connected fence, as he reverently dusted the revolting object.

Bill rang the bell on the council-blue door and eventually heard a slow, shuffling sound that gradually grew nearer. Bolts were withdrawn with great difficulty and the door was finally opened as far as the security chain would allow. A face appeared in the gap between door and frame; a face that was folded in as if made from wet flannels, but with a pair of sharp eyes peering out from the layers.

Suddenly the door swung open and a reedy voice twittered, 'Bill, darling, well I never! I never did, indeed, how splendid, do come in!'

Bill entered a short hallway, every wall of which was covered with paintings in shabby gilt frames. He was pushed along by Manny, who was trailing a cloud of Chanel Number Five and wintergreen ointment, to a door at the end. This opened into a small room made even smaller by a mountainous chaise longue and two enormous overstuffed club chairs covered with myriad shawls and throws. Small, brass-topped occasional tables were loaded with bric-a-brac and photographs in silver frames. As in the hallway, every wall was covered with oil paintings, watercolours, and huge gilded mirrors that went from floor to ceiling. There were more pictures here, Bill thought, than in most provincial galleries.

Bill was waved to one of the chairs and sank into a morass of silk shawls. Manny sat on the chaise and adopted as coquettish a pose as his arthritis would allow.

His first words were 'You look a mess, Bill, darling.'

Bill looked at him and said simply, 'Manny, I think I'm really in the shit this time.'

Manny got painfully to his feet again and said, 'Well, we're both going to need a cup of tea, then. I'll make it, and you feel free to wander around and smoke that foul pipe of yours.'

Bill had known and liked Manny from his earliest days in Bath working for Harry Pexton. He would sometimes ask Bill up to his hotel room when he was staying over, but never took it personally when Bill refused. Manny admired Bill's enthusiasm for his craft and love of old and interesting things and would answer all of Bill's many questions at length. He even loaned him books on restoration and, when Bill finally left the clutches of Harry Pexton, gave him an original 1803 copy of *The Cabinet Dictionary* by Thomas Sheraton. It was worth a fortune; Bill still treasured it.

Manny's special area of expertise was Russian icons, and he had made many visits to Soviet Russia during the Cold War when visas were almost impossible to obtain. But obtain them he did, thanks to his specialized knowledge and the universal freemasonry of 'the exuberantly joyful'. Manny knew them all, from cabinet ministers to East End gangsters and, as he liked to say with a twinkle in his eye, 'all stations in between'.

Bill was still walking down memory lane when Manny returned with a tray bearing two large mugs, a teapot, and a bottle of Navy rum.

'Just like old times,' said Manny as he set the tray down beside him on the chaise and passed a mug to Bill. 'A bit of Navy for you?' he asked with smile.

'No, thanks, I might have to do some walking later and I'll need my wits about me in this wicked city.'

Bill took a sip of tea, choked on it, and started to cough; one of his bad episodes that went on and on. Finally, wiping his mouth on his handkerchief, he looked up. Manny sat on the chaise looking at him with eyes that were as full of cunning as ever, but also something else: friendship and concern.

'You're ill,' he said.

'No, not really. It's just all that bloody dust I've sucked up over the years.'

'Well, tell me about this shit you're in, then,' said Manny with a wry smile that creased his old face further.

Bill put his handkerchief in his pocket, sat back, and told

Manny the story of Skates and the chairs. Manny was a good listener and let Bill tell the story without interruption. He didn't ask any questions, and when Bill stopped halfway through to have another coughing fit, he simply waited, his eyes never leaving Bill's face. When he finished his story, Bill felt spent, as though he had been running, but also slightly more relaxed. He hadn't realized how tightly his nerves had been stretched until they loosened a bit.

'Right,' said Manny, 'I'll go make some discreet phone calls, and then we'll have a bit of lunch.'

Manny went into his bedroom to use the phone as Bill finished his tea. When he came back, Bill followed him into a small but surprisingly modern galley kitchen filled with every conceivable appliance, but not a single antique. They chatted as Manny fussed around making eggs and toast.

Bill said, 'Last I knew, you were living in Kensington. When you weren't in Russia, anyway.'

'Yes, well, there was plenty of money to be made in those days, my dear, but after the dissolution of the Soviet Union, the quality of the clientele went steadily downhill, I can tell you. 'Rough trade' wasn't in it! Dreadful people, and there came a point when I simply couldn't stick it any longer.'

'And what then?'

'I decided to take a holiday away from smoky old London. Picked up a lovely boy in Nice, reminded me of David Hockney, though he couldn't paint to save his life, bless him. He did try though.' Manny paused and sighed. 'Alas, he was very trying in the end.'

'What happened?'

'Well, once the money ran out, the little tart buggered off

with the few valuables I had left and I was broke. Stony broke. The mews flat gone, my business gone, and no capital with which to start again.'

Manny served up the scrambled eggs and a huge pile of toast, made another pot of tea, and they carried everything into an elegant if overcrowded dining room. The plates were valuable Ceres, but the cutlery was strictly Woolworths.

'So, what about this lot?' asked Bill, waving a piece of toast at all the pictures and objets d'art around them.

'Oh, friends,' said Manny, coyly. 'I still have friends, *some* of whom even come to see me when they're not in trouble.'

Manny laughed, but Bill still felt slightly guilty.

'No, but life's easier now,' Manny continued. 'I have a bit of a pension, a dear friend got me this place as I was technically homeless and just a wee bit disabled. To earn a crust, I act as a consultant to those whose pockets are deeper than their knowledge and who want a bit of advice as to what is good and what—like sex with a guardsman in Hyde Park—should be treated with caution. I also make discreet arrangements when some old darling wishes to dispose of a few family treasures without the heirs finding out and getting their greedy young paws on the proceeds.'

Same old Manny, thought Bill with a smile. Still fixing and mixing, and not a stone's throw from the market. He always was a cunning bugger.

The phone rang and Manny went into his bedroom to take the call. Bill helped himself to another slice of toast and tried to keep his nerves from contracting again. After what seemed like ages, Manny came back,

'Right, listen up, Bill darling. Skates is known. Back in the

80s and 90s he was a property developer in and around the East End, the type who is frequently troubled by suspicious fires in buildings that can't be developed because they are either listed or contain little old ladies with long tenancy agreements. My informant is a porter for Spink now, but he used to be a restorer for one of the big auction houses. He lived in Islington in a flat taken over by your friend Skates, and sure enough, his building caught fire one dark night. He and a lot of other people barely escaped with their lives. He can't use one hand properly now because it got burned while he was helping another tenant leave the building. He told the police he saw Skates and Warren on the stairs and Warren attacked him. There was enough evidence to charge them both, but at the trial Skates paraded a wife who swore blind he was at home with her all the evening and had driven her to church for an early service the next morning. Skates even had a priest to swear it was him driving the car that dropped his wife off. Warren, on the other hand, pled guilty, swore he acted alone, and went down for five years.'

'Jesus, what a pal!' said Bill. 'Why on earth would he do that?'

'Who knows? But eventually Skates sold off some of his flats and gentrified the rest just as places like Islington were going upmarket. Made a fortune and apparently decided to educate a few shillings by putting them into antiques. Speaking of which, I think I may have found a connection with those chairs. After he made his pile, Skates did a little social climbing and bought his way into the late Lord Deverill's set.'

Bill had heard of Lord Deverill. At one time he had owned a vast collection of Elizabethan furniture and artefacts, but it was never fully catalogued because some of the items were of dubious provenance. What he was mostly known for, however, was his passion for gambling and his rotten luck.

'Rumour has it that Deverill was deeply in debt to Skates at one time and, after receiving various threats to life and limb, gave him some of the dodgier items from his collection in lieu of payment.'

Bill thought for a moment, then said, 'Very interesting. But getting back to the trial, you mentioned a wife. The last time I saw Skates he said he had no family. So, what happened to the wife?'

'He must have dumped her,' said Manny. 'Is it important?'

Bill thought it was. If he could talk to Skates's wife, she might give him some sliver of information that could be useful in the days ahead. And he thought he knew where to start looking for her.

Bill spent the night on Manny's sofa. They talked into the early hours, remembering past times and the ghosts that now peopled them. They also agreed that Bill needed to find a way to get out of this damned chair job. After another of Bill's coughing fits, Manny said perhaps that was the key.

'Cover the bastard's boots with that horrible green stuff and he might just leave you alone.'

Bill laughed and said yes, but thought no, it would take more than that to put Skates off.

He woke early the next day with a rotten headache, which he attributed to an overdose of violet room freshener. When he went to say goodbye, Manny was propped up in bed, the pain from his arthritis and whatever else was slowly destroying him clearly showing in his creased and tired face. But he beckoned Bill over and opened his arms wide. Poor old Manny, thought

Bill, but at least he has a safe haven here amongst his treasures and memories. Bill held his old friend for a moment, smiled his thanks, and then left.

Chapter 6

SATURDAY, 18 AUGUST

W onderful places, libraries. As a boy, Bill loved going to his local one and bringing back his three books, which if his dad was not too tired he would read to him at bedtime. He hadn't been to a library for years now, however, and the few books he read these days came from car boot sales or junk shops. He didn't have much use for adventure stories or spy fiction anymore; for him a good book was one about antiques, woodworking, or, surprisingly, chickens. For some reason he liked chickens.

Luckily, Ilford had a library, and thanks to the fact that he had come up to London by train, he could wander the capital using public transport. Ilford was just outside the East End, which he knew quite well because of its links to the furniture trade.

From Manny's informant, he knew Skates's trial had been held in early 1990 and he had stated at the time that he lived in Ilford. After acquiring the relevant microfiche, Bill trawled the local papers starting from the first of January. He fought his way through the coverage of a seemingly infinite number of dog shows, jolly sports days, and local government meetings, and eventually found what he was looking for in the *Ilford Record* for 15 March 1990. 'Local Man Found Not Guilty of Fire Crime. Mr Darren Skates, of 48 Peal Road, Ilford was found not guilty . . .'

Now Bill had an address to start from; one concrete link with Skates he hoped he could build on. Of course, this article was from seventeen years ago. He doubted Skates would still keep a house in such a place, but it was the only chance he had at the moment, and it might at least provide another lead.

Leaving the library, he found a small café, one of a sort that was fast disappearing from the world. In the fuggy, steamy embrace of its rundown interior, he enjoyed a huge breakfast. A bit of good ballast before becoming a gumshoe, he thought to himself. He liked the anonymity of the place. The man in the creased white apron who stood behind a marble-topped counter on which a giant urn steamed away had hardly glanced up at him as he took Bill's order. Shelves behind the man held mugs and cups and sauce bottles as well as a dispenser for selling cigarettes, though this last item was empty. Now that the law was being changed to ban smoking in any place that might offend the sensibilities of the general population, it would undoubtedly remain so.

He selected a table at the back of the room where he could see the door and the other customers, and lit his pipe. The damp air laced with cooking smells gave him an appetite. Bill ploughed his way through an artery-clogging meal washed down with mahogany-brown tea. The meal contained more fat and calories than he normally consumed in a week from his own frying pan (the weapon of choice for a man who lives on his own).

After breakfast he was able to get an A–Z of London at a newsagent's and soon found Peal Road. Luckily, it was only a short walk away. Bill had spruced himself up at Manny's and even wore a clean shirt (one left behind by a 'friend' of Manny's) under his old tweed jacket. His shoes were clean, his corduroy trousers unpatched. He looked at his reflection in the shop window. With his stocky physique, close-cropped grey hair, and ruddy complexion he might not pass as a city gent, but perhaps he could pass for a civil servant. Not a high-born Brahmin of the species, of course, but maybe a hewer of civic wood or a carrier of local authority water.

He turned, went back into the newsagent's, and bought himself a clipboard, a pen, and a pad of paper. You could go anywhere with a clipboard and ask all sorts of questions. Whether you got any answers was another thing entirely, but it made a start.

Peal Road was one of many containing an unbroken row of Edwardian houses, each the same as its neighbour, with a bay window next to the front door and a tiny front garden between it and the pavement. He found number forty-eight. It looked a bit more dilapidated than its neighbours. The paintwork on the door was flaking off, and all the curtains were drawn.

He rang the bell. Nothing happened. He waited, rang again, and finally heard steps coming toward the door. It was opened by a tall, thin woman in her late thirties or early forties wearing a faded silk kimono. Her face had probably once been pretty but now seemed drained of all vitality. It was framed by unkempt blond hair that came down to her shoulders.

In a tired voice she asked Bill, 'Is that woman complaining about the dog again?'

'Who?' asked Bill.

'The cow two doors up. She hates dogs. Look, come in, he's under control, you'll see for yourself. She hates dogs, that woman.'

Bill said no more but followed her into the house, clutching his clipboard in front of him like a shield. Despite the rundown exterior, the inside of the house was quite clean, and the few pieces of furniture were worn, but not worn out. The living room had French windows opening onto a small garden.

He was invited to sit down on an easy chair opposite a threadbare sofa covered in a plaid blanket. On the blanket lay a huge, mostly grey dog of very mixed parentage who, seeing Bill, got up on long legs and padded over to greet him, tail wagging happily. Bill loved dogs, but was usually wary when he didn't know the beast in question. This one just oozed friendliness, however, and was soon practically in Bill's lap being patted, petted, and told what a good boy he was. The dog looked to be in better condition than his mistress and was obviously well cared for.

Seeing Bill being so kind to her dog, the woman relaxed somewhat. 'Would you like a cup of tea?' she asked.

Bill said yes, please, and she went into the small kitchen next door and, through an open hatch that joined the two rooms, asked him how he took it. Bill thought her voice had a slight county accent.

Looking about him, Bill decided the place actually had a homely, comfortable air about it, but one that showed there wasn't much money to go around. There were no photographs on the mantelpiece or on the shelf unit that took up one wall. Few pictures (and those cheap reproductions) adorned the walls, and there was only a small television. The big dog continued to demand attention; Bill scratched the animal behind its ears and did all the things he knew would please his new friend.

The tea was brought in, and Bill noticed that during the brewing the lady had brushed her hair. She didn't look quite as old as she had in the doorway, but there was still a wariness about her that he thought was caused by something more than just having a stranger in her home; the wariness of the hunted rather than the hunter.

'I'm sorry,' Bill said, 'I didn't get your name. Mine's Bill Sawyer.'

'It's Marshall. Lucy Marshall.'

'Have you lived here long?' asked Bill.

'A few years,' she replied with a frown, 'but you must know that already if you're from the council.'

'The thing is,' Bill said, deciding to trust his instinct and simply tell her the truth, 'I'm not from the council. I'm here because I need your help.'

'My what?' She stood up quickly and Bill could see that she was shaking. 'Get out! Get out now or I'll call the police!'

Bill lifted up both hands in a gesture of entreaty. 'No, please,' he said, keeping his voice low. 'Please hear me out. Let me explain, please.'

The last couple of days had all but drained Bill of the slight reserves of energy he had. Illness and worry had combined to etch lines of fatigue on his face. Lucy, despite her panic, must have noticed these because she sat back down.

'Go on, then,' she said. 'But this better be good.' Her voice and eyes were still cold and untrusting.

'There's a man called Skates who has threatened me and my family. I believe it's a real threat and I need to know more about him before I can even begin to think of how to protect myself and, more importantly, them.'

'Go to the police,' said the woman, but her voice was less sharp than before.

'From the little I know already, I don't think that would make any difference. And besides, I don't think the police or even a bloody brigade of Guards could stop a mad bastard called Warren who works for Skates.'

Bill's voice trailed off; he started to cough, and this time the spasm shook him to the core. It took Lucy by surprise and she found herself hoping the poor old thing wasn't going to collapse in front of her. That was all she needed!

With a great effort, Bill straightened up and muttered an apology, trying to smile as he did so, but his face was grey and drawn. Though he had tricked his way into her house, Lucy detected none of the guile in him she would have expected in a con artist. She had reason to know she was not the best judge of character in the world, but he just seemed to be an old man who was in some form of trouble. Trouble that came from someone she loathed, feared, and hated. She sighed.

'You'd better tell me all about it,' she said. 'I was married to him once. But the last thing I want right now, or ever, is more trouble coming from that direction.'

Bill sank back into his chair and smiled. Something in Lucy's voice and the way she had relaxed gave him a glimmer of hope.

'Hang on,' she said. She rose to her feet and headed back to the kitchen. As she passed him, her hand rested lightly on his shoulder for a moment, sending a glow of warmth into him. Returning, she set down two glasses and a bottle of whisky on a coffee table within easy reach of them both. After pouring two healthy measures, she picked up her glass and nodded at Bill to proceed.

He told Lucy his story from start to finish. He spoke of where he lived, the work he did, and how her ex-husband had come into his life. He told her about Warren pinning him to his chair and how helpless and furious it had made him feel, and about his family and the threats Skates had made concerning them. He told her he had found out about Skates's past, looked up the trial, and found the address that had led him to her.

By the time he had finished, he was wiped out. Seeing this, Lucy told him to stay where he was, have another drink, and she would see to a bit of lunch for them both. She opened the French windows and the dog went out and did what dogs do with a gusto that Bill envied. He felt exhausted, but also as if a huge weight had been lifted from him.

Lucy came back into the room dressed in jeans and a large sweater, with her hair in a ponytail.

'Come on,' she said. 'You look like you could do with some food.'

Lucy had set the small dining table with two places and put out a pile of sandwiches and two rather nice Spode cups without saucers and, he was pleased to see, without any cracks. She saw him pick up his cup and carefully examine the bottom.

In answer to her look, Bill said, 'It's old habits, I'm afraid. People in my trade always look for the right marks. These are nice pieces; must have had a few gallons of tea through them in the last hundred or so years.'

'Well, they're all I've got left of that set now, what with one thing and another. Anyway, lunch is just cheese, I'm afraid,' she said with an embarrassed smile. 'Times are a little hard at the moment.'

'Why?' asked Bill.

'It's a long story. But you told me yours, so I'll tell you mine. I had a breakdown a few years ago. Fact is, I was in a nuthouse for a while. Eventually they decided they'd done all they could do for me and I ended up here. I have a very small income from some money my grandmother left me, but that's it.'

She smiled ruefully at Bill. 'I keep thinking I'm going to start my life over again just as soon as I pull myself together, but I've been working at it for a few years now and I still feel pretty scattered.'

'Don't you have any friends or family?' asked Bill. 'No one who could help you?'

'No, not really. I haven't seen my mother in years; after father died she remarried, but I never visited.'

As they ate the meagre lunch, Lucy continued her story.

'My father was a brute. No, that's not fair; he felt he was washed up and useless, and it made him bitter. He was sort of retired and much older than mummy. He had been a half colonel and was dumped by the MOD in one of their defence department cuts. Anyway, he required instant obedience in all things at all times. He never got another real job, but he would try to help out at charities and things until someone upset him, and then he'd storm off back home and take it out on us. Mummy, bless her, had a little problem with the bottle, and provided there was enough booze in the house, would while away her time making happy hour last all day and, if possible, most of the evening as well. The truly bizarre part is that her second husband is a man exactly like my father.'

She looked down into her cup, sad and silent for a while,

shoulders hunched, closed in on herself like a book that has been slammed shut. Then, with slight shrug, she looked at Bill and continued.

'I met up with Darren after I left home. Ditched A-levels and never went back.'

'How old were you?' asked Bill.

'Old enough to know better, young enough not to care,' laughed Lucy wryly. 'I thought I knew it all. It was 1985, I think; summertime, anyway.'

She sat back, her mind in the past when, for just a little while, her world was a simpler and much kinder place.

'Some friends from school and I joined a load of hippies and became part of the Peace Convoy. We were making our way to Stonehenge for a free festival. Old coaches, families in trucks and caravans; it was really cool, something special.'

Bill said, 'I remember that. It was in all the papers, wasn't it? Pictures of police brutality and all sorts of horrors.'

'They didn't show the half of it. It was terrible, really terrible.'

Lucy sat silent for a while, sadness wrapped around her like a cloak. The past she was seeing now was no summer of love, just men in uniforms beating women and children and smashing their homes and dreams. Bill said nothing; he wished he could light his pipe but didn't want to disturb her.

After a moment or two, she carried on. 'Anyway, the upshot of all that was I found myself headed to London. I certainly wasn't going back home. I had no idea what I could do, but one of the travellers had given me the address of a commune in a squat and I was making for that.'

'How the hell were you going to get there?' asked Bill.

'Hitch. I was a bit dazed, I suppose, but I really didn't give it much thought. I just reckoned if I could get to London and find this place I would be safe. Stupid, I know.'

'Not stupid,' said Bill. 'You had been in a war zone; you were just beating a hasty retreat from all sorts of shit.'

'I suppose you're right. When the uniforms were smashing into all those lovely people and shouting and swearing at them, all I could think of was my father and how he used to shout and swear at mummy and me. So I ran away. Again.'

Bill didn't want to cause her more pain, but he had to find out how Skates fitted in; where and when that bastard had begun his part in wrecking her life. It was as though Lucy had read his thoughts and she carried on with her story.

'I got a lift with a bloke in a van. He thought any hippy girl was up for a screw, of course. 'How about a bit of free love, then,' he said, and he pulled over into a lay-by. I tried to get out, but he was too quick for me. It was horrible. He stank and his hands were everywhere at once.'

Bill felt ashamed as he sat listening to this, as though he represented his entire gender. Lucy noticed his look and smiled at him to show she knew the sin was not his.

'I was ridiculously naive. I really believed all that peace and love stuff. I wanted nothing but happiness for others and I thought that would somehow protect me. You know, karma and all that shit.'

'So what happened?' asked Bill.

'Well, would you believe it, another car was parked in the same lay-by and the driver was having a piss in the hedge, so Mr Hands didn't see him. I was half out the passenger door screaming blue murder when this man came back, saw me, went over to the driver's door of the van, wrenched it open, and gave the swine a damned good hiding.'

'It was Darren Skates, wasn't it?' said Bill.

'The very man,' said Lucy. 'And that's when things really started to go downhill, though of course I didn't know it at the time. He put me in his car and drove away. Unfortunately, I left my bag behind with what few clothes I had and, more importantly, that damned bit of paper that had the address of the commune in London on it.'

She got up and went to make more tea; Bill munched his way through another sandwich. The cheese was dry, not like the stuff he was used to back in Somerset, and the bread was slightly stale. Lucy came back in and sat down. She had not eaten much.

Bill passed her the plate of sandwiches and said, 'Come on, eat something. You can't cut down brambles in memory lane without something in your stomach.'

Lucy laughed and took a sandwich. 'I like you,' she said. 'Have you ever been married?'

Bill told her about his very ex-wife, Beryl. Like so many young couples in the early 1960s, after she discovered she was pregnant there was a traumatic interview with her parents, followed by Handel's *Largo* played on shotgun bolts by her furious father, who thought she could have done a lot better for herself. This was a view that Beryl increasingly shared until she finally left Bill some thirteen years later.

But all that was a long time ago now, and he had taken the advice of his favourite philosopher and drinking companion, Sid, whose answer to any metaphysical conundrum was, 'Don't fuck about, just get on with it.' So Bill had.

Bill was pleased to see Lucy was actually eating something

at last; not a lot, but something.

'Right about now I would normally light up my umpteenth fag of the day,' she said.

'Why don't you? I'd light my pipe, but it makes me cough. You go ahead.'

'No,' she said, 'I've given them up. I can't really afford them and it's a crutch I'm trying to do without. I'm done with crutches, or at least I'm trying to be.'

'Brave you,' said Bill. 'It's not easy breaking with the past. Or the habits of the past, I should say.'

Looking out of the window, he saw the sun had come out.

'Come on,' he said. 'Let's take that dog of yours for a walk. Do us both good to get outside for a bit.'

Lucy, startled, sat back in her chair. 'I don't go out much. I don't really like leaving the house.'

Bill smiled at her and said, 'Come on, let's give those nosy neighbours something to twitch their curtains at.'

Lucy laughed, suddenly relaxing. 'You're right,' she said. 'Let's take Clive for a walk in the park. There's a small one not far up the road. He'll love it.'

The park turned out to be a few trees dotted around a set of swings and other rusting metal constructions for children to play on. The place had an air of municipal desolation. It was clearly uncared for and used mostly by rebellious youths as a hangout when all else failed. The one small shelter had no roof and showed the usual signs of unimaginative vandalism.

'What they don't smash they write 'fuck' on,' said Lucy. 'Sad, really. This could be a nice place if it was planted up and looked after.'

'You sound like someone who likes the countryside.'

'We had a big garden and our house was on the edge of the countryside, so there was horse riding and the like. I didn't appreciate it at the time, but I do miss it a bit now, I suppose. I certainly didn't expect to end up here, that's for sure.'

They walked side by side like prisoners in an exercise yard, with slow, even strides that made talking easy. They walked and talked while Clive had a mad half hour chasing nothing at all as fast as he could go.

'One thing I would like to ask,' said Bill. 'No need to answer if you don't want to.'

Lucy looked at him warily and said, 'Go on.'

'Why 'Clive'?'

Lucy laughed. 'My father's name. I grew up hearing 'Stop that, Lucy!', 'Come here, Lucy!', and 'Be quiet, Lucy!' So when my therapist suggested I get a dog, I thought it would do me good to be able to say things like 'Get down, Clive!', 'Stop barking, Clive!', and 'Don't shit there, Clive!'

Bill's turn to laugh now. They continued to walk slowly beside each other, their shoulders occasionally touching, like conspirators in a film. Eventually, one happy dog and two slightly less-troubled people walked back to the small house together.

Like every antiques dealer or trader, Bill kept a small stash separate from his spending money just in case he saw a bargain. With this in mind, he said to Lucy, 'Let me take you out to dinner. Where would you like to go?'

Suddenly she looked troubled again. 'I really can't. I hate going out when it gets dark. Please, let me cook something.'

Thinking of the dry cheese and stale bread they'd had for lunch, Bill asked, 'How about a takeaway? Something foreign.

We don't get foreign in Somerset. Well, not London foreign, anyway.'

Lucy thought for a bit. 'Do you like curry? There's a place just on the High Street. I've had them deliver stuff before and it's really nice. Not too hot if you don't like that sort of thing.' She looked at him and smiled. 'They do chips.'

It was a really good curry, one of the best Bill had ever tasted. They had called in at a small corner shop first and bought a few tins of lager and a bottle of white wine.

After the meal, they sat in the back room, he on an easy chair, she on the sofa with Clive next to her and the bottle of wine on the table beside her. After a few glasses she shared the rest of her story with Bill. It was no fairy tale, nor did it have a happy ending.

Skates had rescued her from her attacker. She had nothing but the clothes on her back and some very bad experiences from the Peace Convoy onwards. Truth to tell, she was probably in shock. Skates acted the gentleman all the way to London. He stopped off at a service station to put some food into her and then offered her a place to stay for the night. He took her to his flat in Notting Hill and showed her to a bedroom.

'It's all yours, darling,' he said, 'and it even has a key in the lock so you can feel safe.'

Lucy was exhausted and took the bait. She had no option, really, and Skates had said he knew all of the commune squats so they could look them out the next day. As she told Bill, she didn't even lock the door, she was that naive.

The following day her Galahad took her shopping in the King's Road and fitted her out, no expense spared. And, of course, when they went looking for the commune, she was wholly unprepared for the filthy condition of the squats. She didn't have a name to ask for, anyway, let alone anyone she recognised from the Peace Convoy.

So it was back to the flat, a meal out in a good restaurant, and all the while Skates telling her not to worry, she could stay with him as long as she liked, and bolstering her ego with constant flattery. He told her he was 'in property', and he certainly seemed to have a lot of money. There were more fancy restaurants, soon followed by the trendiest nightclubs, which meant more expensive clothes.

It also meant limitless amounts of cocaine. Lucy had smoked plenty of pot with her hippie friends, but cocaine was a rich person's drug, so her experience with it was limited. Skates was never without a supply, nor without a personal assistant, nearly always one Richard Warren.

He worked her like a fish on a hook, thought Bill, or more like a butterfly in a spider's web. It wasn't long before Skates convinced her he was in love with her, and she moved into his bedroom. He was gentle at first – she was still not much more than a schoolgirl, after all – but that honeymoon didn't last long.

'I'm your bit of rough,' he told her and was, sometimes, very rough, but she didn't want to seem unsophisticated, so she put up with it. She also increased the amount and number of drugs she took. The clubs were full of them, and she knew all the right people now.

Things got worse, however, when Ricky Warren became involved.

One night Skates and Warren had both gone out, leaving Lucy behind in the flat. They came back drunk and, with as little ceremony as if he was offering him a cup of coffee, Skates gave Lucy to Warren to play with.

Bill gasped, but Lucy didn't appear to hear him.

Unfortunately, that night was only the first of many, and she soon found that the only thing Skates liked better than hurting her himself was watching Warren do it.

Skates and Warren had quite a history, she told Bill. They grew up together in some sort of children's home on the Isle of Man.

'Ricky's a little younger than Darren, so by the time he got there Darren was already practically running the place. Apparently one night Darren came across a gang of older boys taking turns raping Ricky and he intervened. Not because of any finer feelings, mind you, but because they hadn't gotten Darren's permission first. Anyway, after that Ricky pretty much became Darren's slave.'

Lucy look up at Bill. 'I suppose it just goes to show there are always reasons for why people are the way they are. I mean, there may even be a reason why Darren is such an evil bastard.'

'Yes, lass, there are always reasons, but reasons are not excuses. Nothing could ever excuse what those two did to you.'

Lucy looked thoughtful at that. 'Anyway, my life became a blur of drugs and pain after that. Skates stopped even pretending to be my lover and started bragging about being my owner. 'And what I own I never let go of', he'd say. And I'd been raised to be obedient, so I was used to discipline. I didn't *enjoy* it; in fact I hated it. But it was *familiar*. I had learned to cope with it as a child and now, of course, I had all these wonderful drugs to help me escape into my head.'

'How on earth did you end up married to the swine?' Bill

asked her.

These glimpses into the hell Lucy must have suffered during her years with Skates turned his stomach. You don't get to 67 without running into heartless pricks now and again, but he had never come across anything like this before. It horrified him.

Lucy told him how, after he and Warren had been charged with arson, Skates had needed a good, cast-iron alibi. He thought that if Lucy married him, she could never act as a witness against him, and her testimony on his behalf would carry more weight. (Bill knew that was all cock, but if it was in Skates's head, then no amount of learned council would shift it.) So it was a rushed registry office marriage with the detestable Warren as the only witness.

'What about the other witness at the trial, the vicar?'

'Someone they had their hooks into, I expect,' said Lucy. 'I never met the man, but he had to be bent to tell the police what he did. Bent or terrified. Probably both. Besides, Ricky pleaded guilty and swore Darren wasn't with him, so what could they do? Ricky got five years, but was out in two.'

'And how did you finally manage to get away from them?'

'I became ill. Between the drugs and the abuse, I had a complete mental and physical breakdown.' Lucy looked down at her hands. 'There were . . . miscarriages. After the last one I tried to top myself, so I got sectioned.'

'Oh, Christ,' said Bill. 'I'm so sorry.'

She smiled at him. 'That was a few years ago now, but thanks. Anyway, after all that, I wasn't any 'fun' anymore. This house was still on Darren's books and it wasn't worth much. One of his creeps had been living in it; it was Darren's letterbox to keep the Notting Hill place private. So he divorced me and put half of this place in my name so I would have somewhere to live that he still controlled. He never lets go, remember? I can't sell the place and he knows I don't have enough money to leave. Thinking he has me trapped here probably makes him feel all warm and powerful.'

Lucy had talked herself almost hoarse and looked utterly drained. Bill suddenly noticed the time and knew he had no chance of getting home that night; the last train from Paddington would have left already. He didn't want to impose on Lucy or appear to be taking advantage in any way. He liked her. He saw her weaknesses, but he also saw a strength she probably didn't realise she had, or had forgotten how to use. The woman was a bit of a mess, but he didn't mind messes; he was one himself. He just didn't want to add to her problems.

Lucy solved the conundrum for him. Preparing to take the empty food cartons out to the dustbin, she turned to Bill and said, 'There's a spare room. I haven't aired the sheets or blankets on the bed in ages, but will that do you?'

'It will, and nicely. I really wasn't relishing a long journey. I'm so tired I could sleep in a bath.'

When Lucy came back, Bill got up slowly, his legs stiff with sitting for so long, and reached out and gently took her hand.

'Thank you, lass. Sleep well.'

She walked up the stairs, Clive at her heels, and went into her bedroom. Bill turned off the lights and found his way to the spare room. As he passed Lucy's door on the landing, he saw that it had two Yale locks. It was not an ordinary domestic door but one of the heavy-duty sort used as a fireproof barrier in offices. It was there to keep things out, but Bill was afraid it also served to keep some things in.

Chapter 7

SUNDAY, 19 AUGUST

B ill awoke the next morning in that half-conscious state that comes with the new day for nearly everybody except small children. Eyes blurred, mind dulled, and with gritty bits lurking in moist corners. Not to mention that the start of each day was now heralded by a body-racking coughing bout. He felt like shit. He sat on the edge of the small bed and ran through what he now knew, then made his way downstairs.

Lucy and Clive were in the living room, some toast and a pot of coffee on the small table. Lucy looked tired, but relaxed.

'You look dreadful,' she said. 'I could hear you coughing from here. You really should do something about that. Soon.'

Bill smiled at her but said nothing. It was eight o'clock. They ate the toast, drank the coffee, and talked about nothing very much, the way friends do. And they were friends now. They both knew it, though neither of them could have explained it.

Finally, Bill said, 'I've got to get back to Somerset today. I'll try for the afternoon train, but first I've got some errands to run. Will you and Clive come with me?'

After only a slight hesitation, Lucy said yes, which pleased him. They walked to the High Street and Bill found a bank that had just opened. Lucy and Clive waited outside while he went in and drew out some money, then they went into a couple of shops and bought bread, cakes, and a whole box of dog biscuits for Clive. Little, ordinary, domestic things that somehow seemed special and pleasantly different from their usual solitary lives.

Their walk back to her house took in the small park they had visited the day before. Clive dashed madly about, sniffing at and piddling on every tree, lamp post, and railing.

'My Bess is far too much of a lady to do that,' said Bill, and he told Lucy about his beloved gypsy dog. She held his arm as they walked back to the house. Bill liked the feel of that very much.

As they neared the house, Lucy let go of his arm and Bill saw tension return to her features. He thought she looked like someone in a spy film checking for watchers. The past was never very far away from Lucy, and it never would be while she lived here.

Once in the house, she seemed to relax again. She headed to the kitchen to make more coffee. Bill got out the cakes and put them on the paper bag they had come in, then opened the box of dog biscuits and fed a couple to Clive. Much tail thumping and drool resulted.

Lucy came back in with the coffee and, seeing the cakes piled up on the split paper bag, started laughing. 'You've been living alone for too long. You've lost what few social graces you might once have had. I'll get the plates.'

As she turned and went back into the kitchen, Bill heard a snatch of a song, quietly sung, that lightened his heart. They sat down opposite each other and shared the coffee and cakes.

Time to get back to the real world, thought Bill. It saddened him, but he couldn't stay much longer and things had to be done. He had a lot of thinking and planning to do. Thankfully, the train ride home would give him time to sort out in his head all that Lucy had told him yesterday.

'Right, my girl,' he said. 'I have an idea to put to you.'

Lucy looked at him, anxiety reappearing in her eyes.

Bill took his wallet out of his pocket and extracted most of the cash he had withdrawn from the bank earlier.

'Here is £500 for you to be getting on with,' he said, and held out the wad of cash to her.

Lucy looked at him, astounded. 'I can't take that! We ... we hardly know each other.'

'Look, you need it, I've got it, and it will help you move forward and get out of that man's clutches forever.'

'But I'll never be able to pay you back. This is daft of you. It's really, really generous, but I can't take it. I can't.'

Bill shook his head. 'Money is just a tool, lass, use it like one. Please. I can afford it, really.'

Lucy just sat there, not saying anything, and not touching the money Bill had now placed on the table.

'Lucy,' said Bill, 'you have to get out of here and find a place where you can't ever be tracked down by those bastards. Buy a car, some old banger that still goes, and when you have, get in touch with me, okay?'

'But I hate going out the front door, let alone driving around. I haven't driven for years, I'm not even sure I still can.' She seemed near to tears. 'It's all too much, Bill. Too much too soon. I just can't, I'm sorry.'

Bill smiled at her. 'Either too soon or too late. No, you're probably right. I didn't mean to upset you.'

He bent down to pet Clive for a moment, then said, 'Keep the cash, but use it as you see fit. It's a gift. Just a gift, that's all, really. Here's my address and phone number,' he added, handing her a slip of paper. 'I'll have kicked Skates into touch within a week or two, and then you can come and stay for a bit, if that appeals.'

They stood up and hugged briefly, then Bill left and walked away to the station and the journey home. He looked back at Lucy's closed door and suddenly felt completely alone again.

~~~

Bill's journey back to Somerset was not a good one. As the concrete gave way to fields and countryside, his mind was still back in that terraced house in its suburban street. He tore himself up for interfering in Lucy's life. And he had gone to London looking for answers, not to get himself enmeshed in someone else's problems. Not to mention it would probably be stupid for Lucy to come to him in Somerset – the same county those bastards were currently living in – but where else could she go? At least from his place she could look for somewhere safe in which to start her life over again.

The countryside rolled by as if it, rather than the carriage, was moving. Bill thought over all that Lucy had told him about Skates and Warren. It was clear that Skates himself was little more than a bully, though a seriously twisted one. Still, if he only had Skates to deal with, he would have sent him and his damned chairs packing. But Warren . . . Warren actually enjoyed causing people harm. Skates only had to point out his chosen victim.

Lucy's story played over and over again in Bill's mind. He kept coming back to the phrase she used so often about Skates: 'He never lets go.' Never lets go, eh?, thought Bill. Never lets go. Just like the monkey and the nuts . . . never lets go.

The sound of the train as it passed over the tracks, rhythmically clacking out the miles, turned into a chant: never-lets-go, never-lets-go, never-lets-go. The monkey and the nuts. It was an old parable. To catch a monkey, place a pile of nuts in a small wooden box. Make sure the lid is well secured. Put a hole in the lid just large enough for a monkey's hand to reach inside, but not large enough for it to be drawn back out with a handful of nuts. And a monkey never lets go. Trapped by its own greed and stupidity. Trapped until it's either released or killed.

Bill's train arrived in the late evening, and he decided to go straight to Miss Templeton's to get Bess. His van had not picked up a parking fine, which pleased him, and the joyous greeting he received from Bess took his mind off the journey he had made in more ways than one.

He reached his house, parked, and wandered around just to see if everything was as he had left it. He was tired and not minded to open the workshop that night, so just headed to the kitchen. In the small porch outside the door was an enamel bread tin he used as a mail box. It contained a couple of letters and some of the usual circulars.

When he pushed the door open, he saw an envelope with his name written on it lying on his kitchen table. He opened it and read:

Look forward to seeing you soon. Hope London was

worthwhile.
    Keep healthy, D.S.

The contents of the letter didn't bother Bill – he was not at all surprised that Skates knew he had been to London – but the fact that it had been left on his kitchen table with the back door locked, now that was scary. Bill checked all over the house, every window and even the front door, which hadn't been opened in years. Nothing, nothing at all to show how an entry had been made, and it had to have been a break-in because he was the only one with a key.

He went out, followed by Bess, and this time opened up the workshop. The chairs were where he had left them, still covered in blankets. Nothing here had been touched as far as he could tell. The workshop had an ancient, formidable padlock on a hasp securing the doors. The windows had never been opened and were covered in dust, so any marks of entry there would have shown.

He went back to the house and, with the aid of a torch, looked closely at the lock on the back door. It was as old as the door itself and not exactly state of the art for burglar proofing. It never crossed his mind it would need to be, but tomorrow he would visit an ironmongers for a whole new bit of kit. Bill didn't think he would have any more visits that night, but even so he didn't go to bed until after he got a huge, rusty bolt on the kitchen door working again.

Chapter 8

MONDAY–TUESDAY, 20–21 AUGUST

Monday morning Bill went into town and bought a good, modern lock. Though not happy about having to disfigure the old door to fit it, he felt better when it was on. And the other security stuff he had purchased as well: door chains, window locks, and the like. It all cost a pretty penny, but he didn't begrudge the money as he would have done a week ago.

He made his home, if not a fortress, then at least a more secure place than it had been. He really resented having to do this. In all the years he had lived there, he had never once felt insecure or even in need of strong gates. When he went to the pub he often left the kitchen door unlocked. The gate to his yard had not been closed in years.

To top it all off, that afternoon he had an appointment with Chris Hall, his local GP. Bill's cough was worse now than it had been even a few weeks ago, and that trip to London had really taken it out of him, so cancelling the appointment was not an option. He helped Bess up into the passenger seat of his van and off they went. It was almost like old times when they used to go to auctions or deliver pieces he had worked on.

Almost, but not really.

It seemed unfair somehow to be ill in summertime. You could understand having a cold or the flu in winter, but when you felt like shit on a bright, warm summer day, you felt betrayed by your own body. But at least Bill knew and liked Dr Hall, and had been able to do him a few favours when he tried to dabble in antiques. They enjoyed each other's company when they met in the pub, too, but going to see him professionally was not something Bill relished.

The good doctor saw him on time and examined him in his small consulting room, as Bill had expected. What he hadn't expected was to then be immediately hauled off to Chris's study in his house next door and asked to look at a small bureau the doc had recently bought and wanted an opinion on. This 'professional examination' was accompanied by a cup of coffee and a bright 'hello' from Chris's wife, who then left them to their discussions. These eventually included Bill's symptoms.

He was told in no uncertain terms that his smoking and the dust he inhaled all day long was doing him no good at all. He might have a very bad infection or it might be something more serious – very serious, in fact.

Bill looked at Dr Hall. 'Right,' he said. 'Are we talking about the 'Big C' here?'

'We can't discount that, but we won't know for certain until we've done some tests. Anyway, let's not go down that road until we have to, eh? It could well be just a severe infection of the lungs.'

Bill was given a prescription for painkillers and antibiotics and told to get as much rest as possible and throw that bloody pipe away! He was also given a referral to the local hospital for x-rays and tests.

'Sooner rather than later. Phone the hospital and get an appointment as soon as possible, right?'

Right it was, and a very thoughtful journey home from the surgery into the bargain. Even Bess caught his mood and drooped in her seat rather than watching out the window for rabbits as she usually did.

Bill sat in his kitchen that night, radio on, unopened book beside him, and looked around as he pondered on the day. All the new locks on the windows and door shone against the old paintwork. They were an intrusion; he hadn't needed them before Skates. His life had been comfortable, gentle, even well-ordered. Now his routine had been shattered, his health was in question, his loved ones were threatened, and for the first time since he was a child, he felt utterly helpless. He kept remembering Warren's hands on his shoulders, pinning him to his chair . . .

When he finally went to bed, the windows he would normally have left open to catch the fragrant breeze on the warm night air were closed and locked. The room was hot and humid, and sleep was elusive. When he did slip off, his dreams were troubled. Waking from them, he found he was worrying about Lucy in addition to all his other problems.

Suddenly, with the sheets clinging to him like a shroud, he hauled himself out of bed, put on the light, and yelled, 'Bugger this for a game of soldiers!' He opened the windows in his bedroom, then stomped downstairs and, with many a ripe curse word, opened every window on the ground floor. Bess padded sleepily after him, taking her master's expletives and strange behaviour in her stride. He just did these things sometimes.

~~~

The next morning was bright and warm. The sweaty anxieties of the previous night were dispelled by the strong sunshine that cast dark shadows under the open-sided cart shed and would have bleached the woodwork even more if that had been possible. Bill decided to spend the day pottering. His ostensible reason for doing so was in order to put a few considered trifles into some local sales to recoup some of the money spent on all those locks and chains, but the fact was something in the back of his mind told him time was no longer on his side. He was ill, and he wasn't getting better. Putting it all down to dust was, he knew, just a cop-out.

But he put that aside as he sat in his workshop, both doors propped open, the sun shining in and the radio tuned to its usual station. He heard a scrunching sound in the yard and, looking up, saw the thin shape of Miss Templeton astride a bike silhouetted in the doorway.

Bess wandered over and got a genteel greeting from the old lady. Bill invited her into the house and brewed tea. He sat opposite her, his arms on the table holding his big mug of tea, listening in polite silence whenever she spoke. After a short but apparently necessary exchange of small talk, the real reason for Miss Templeton's visit rose to the surface like a pike in a garden pond.

'Two nights ago it was a full moon and a mild night and, being restless, I took a walk,' she said.

Bill nodded; he sometimes saw her strolling in the moonlight when he came back late from the pub.

'I was on the field edge just up the path from here when I

saw a large, white vehicle drive slowly up the lane and turn into your yard.' She went on to describe how a man had gotten out of the car and seemed to fiddle with Bill's back door. She indicated the one behind her, and the wise old eyes noticed the new lock and the cleaned bolt, then swept over the new hardware on the kitchen windows.

'I see you have taken precautions,' she said. 'That is just as well. I didn't like the look of that man, or rather the way he moved. He was obviously up to no good. I had Bess with me, so I knew you were not expecting visitors.'

'Visitors?' asked Bill. 'There was more than one man?'

'Yes. The one in the passenger seat stayed in the car while the driver went into your house.'

'You . . . you didn't speak to them, did you?' asked Bill.

'Certainly not.'

'I'm glad,' said Bill with relief. 'They are not very nice people. But you mustn't worry, I don't think they'll pull a stunt like that again. I'm sorry if you were frightened.'

Miss Templeton looked at him hard and drew herself up. 'Mr Sawyer,' she said, 'I have not been frightened of any man since my training in 1942. And, although old, I am not without resources. I could see them; they could not see me.'

'No, no, of course not, Miss Templeton,' Bill replied quickly, but inside he was thinking, *1942*! That may as well have been a hundred years ago!

Bill was sitting upright in his chair now and felt as if he were being judged in some way and probably found wanting.

Miss Templeton held his gaze with china-blue eyes that were as hard as diamonds, but in her usual refined manner said,

'Not all young women stayed at home knitting or working the land in those dreadful days. Some of us took a more active part in the proceedings.'

Then, having shared her news, she departed, telling Bill she would keep an eye on his home and he was to let her know if he was going away again. She also said that, as he drove up to his house, there was a gap in the trees through which he could see her attic window. She told him she would have a lamp lit in that window if there was any danger, and if he saw it he was to drive straight up to her cottage with his lights off.

Bill thanked her appropriately, though as she cycled off he thought, 'That's all I need, an eccentric old lady watching over me.' But, strangely, it did give him some comfort to know there was another pair of eyes looking out for him. He certainly slept better that night than he had the night before.

Chapter 9

WEDNESDAY, 22 AUGUST

The next day the good August weather continued, and Bill thought it was about time he caught up with his family. It was coming to the end of the school holidays, and he felt it would be a criminal shame not to have a day in their company. Bill telephoned and it was agreed that a trip to the seaside was in order. They chose Seaton because it was less than a two-hour drive for them both.

The small seaside town of Seaton was just on the Devon/Somerset border. No longer a big crowd puller, it was run-down in a gentrified sort of way that had always suited Bill. It was one of those towns that had grown up from a fishing port and become, with the benefit of the railway, an Edwardian resort of genteel pretensions. The beach was nothing special, but it had a plethora of charity shops, a few pubs and cafés, and a nice prom to walk on.

Climbing into the van, rolling down the windows, and tuning the radio to something mindless, he and Bess set off. Bess, as always, sat on the front passenger seat with her tongue lolling out, scanning the fields and hedges for rabbits. Bill looked at her lovingly. She was probably the most sensible friend he had. She was certainly the most loyal and, except for insisting on eating what Bill considered to be a particularly posh (and expensive) dog food, undemanding.

The van purred along country roads that wove their way across an ancient landscape. Bill was as happy as he could be that morning, all things considered, and was the first to arrive at the agreed-upon car park. He let Bess out, filled her water bowl, and sat in the open back of the van, admiring a very colourful caravan park that was clinging to a hill above the town. Before long his family arrived. With Bess at his heels, he walked over and hugged his son, his daughter-in-law, and, with a great laugh full of joy, his grandson.

In the back of Bill's van were three antique deckchairs and all the other old beach equipment he had been able to find. Passing some of this to his son to carry – and, of course, the 'most important' piece to young Jack – Bill and his family made their way onto the sand.

Once the venerable constructs much amended by Bill with the help of bailing twine and scrap timber had been erected, they had a camp: deckchairs, a small and very rocky picnic table, and a windbreak. Jack and Gloria were despatched with a £10 note to buy ice creams and a ball plus any other essential that had not been essential until Jack spotted it.

The sun shone, Bess lolled in the shade, and Bill wore his holiday hat. This was a strange, straw device that might once have been an elegant Panama but was now discoloured and tatty as only a much-loved hat can be. He even took off his habitual tweed jacket and showed the world that a true Englishman wore both braces and a belt.

Gloria had brought a wonderful picnic, and as they ate it

Bill thought what a lucky man his son was. As they sat amidst the ruins of the feast, Bill took from the jacket at his side a small, thin, elegantly turned cylinder of wood, glowing a mellow yellow in the warm sunlight. He put it to his lips and blew a long, pure note like that of a bird or perhaps an angel.

Jack looked up, then literally sprang to his feet. Bess lifted her head and thought about springing up, too, but decided it was too soon after lunch for so much activity. Philip laughed out loud, and Gloria turned to look at Bill.

'What is it?' she asked.

'It's a recorder,' said Bill, 'but a small one. They used to be called flutes years ago.'

He blew a few more notes, then paid for his efforts with a spasm of coughing. His family looked at him with concern. Bill raised both his hands to silence them before they could speak.

'It's all right,' he said, a bit breathlessly. 'I've got it in hand.'

Gloria gave him such an old-fashioned look it might have come from the last century, but simply asked 'Did you make it?'

'Yes, years ago,' replied Bill. 'I found it during a clear-out and gave it a bit of a polish.'

He turned to Jack and asked him if he would like to try it. Jack took the flute and, putting it to his lips, blew. No clear, bright sound this time; just a shrill noise. Poor Jack looked desolate.

'Not as easy as it looks, eh? Go on, give it to yer dad and see what he can make of it.'

Jack did so and Philip put the instrument to his lips and blew three clear notes that danced in the seaside air like gulls in the clear blue sky. Jack looked up at his father, wonder on his face. This was a skill he had no idea his dad possessed. This was a bit of magic and, love him as he did, he had never thought of his father as being magical before. A man in his mid-forties, not very tall, balding, and with glasses over which he sometimes looked at you like a quizzical owl. That was his dad, not this amazing being sitting back in his deckchair, shirt open at the neck, playing a sea shanty that had his mother laughing and his grandfather clapping along.

Finishing the tune, Philip gave a bow to them all and handed the flute back to Jack. 'I'll teach you how to play it if you like,' he said. 'Your granddad taught me when I was about your age.'

Gloria put her arm around her husband and kissed him on his forehead. Sitting back, she looked at him and said, 'Philip Sawyer, I never knew you had it in you. Sod the accountancy; become a busker and we'll travel around in a gypsy caravan!'

Jack thought about that. He hoped that if they did, he would still be able to have his computer.

Gloria then turned back to Bill. 'So how did all this come about, and why didn't Philip take up music rather than boring sums?'

Bill looked at Philip but said nothing.

'My mum would never have allowed that,' Philip said. 'Besides, though I liked music, it was never a burning ambition with me. And I knew I would never have my father's skilled hands, so I opted for working in an accountant's firm as soon as I finished my A-levels.'

'How about you, Bill?' asked Gloria. 'Would you have liked to be a musician?'

Bill thought a bit then said, 'All I ever wanted to do is what I did. Make things in wood. When Philip needed a flute for school, I bought a couple from a house sale and repaired them as best I could so he'd have his own instrument and not one knocked about by other kids. To do the job properly, of course, I had to know how they worked.' He grinned at Philip. 'And that meant many an excruciating hour for anyone within earshot as I taught myself to make sounds that didn't frighten the barn cats.'

Philip grinned back at his father. 'Tell her about the year we did the Glastonbury Festival.'

Jack had wandered off a little way to make sandcastles by this time, so Bill was able to tell Gloria the story with no interruptions.

It was 1981, Philip was 17 and visiting his father on holiday. He had tried to get a ticket for the festival but with no luck; they were all sold out. He was extremely upset because his favourite group, Hawkwind, were playing, and he moped until Bill finally got him to say what the misery was all about. Of course, Bill knew someone who knew someone and they got in as traders. They had to be there early to set up, and they had to agree that a portion of their take would go to help fund CND as that was the aim of this festival.

'Well, that was all right, but we were buggered as to what we could sell. I had a load of old tat from auctions and the like, but that was all wrong for Glastonbury, and besides, we wanted something that would be cheap. Then up came the idea of flutes and whistles.'

Both Bill and Philip burst out laughing as the memories came flooding back.

'Dad set up the big lathe,' said Philip, 'and hollowed out some hardwood dowels he had got for a job but never used. They were great lumps of wood and he turned them down into ten-inch lengths and bored a hole right through!'

'Then I just cut a simple notch, shaped the mouth end, and glued in a smaller dowel to make the part called a 'fipple'. This gave us a simple whistle, and when we had worked out roughly where to drill the finger holes, job done.'

'Did they work?' asked Gloria.

'Well, after a fashion,' said Bill with a chuckle.

They had made about fifty and took them in on the Friday, selling out almost immediately. While Philip stayed behind, Bill sloped off to make as many more as he could from whatever suitable wood he could find.

'Even used some old chair legs,' said Bill, smiling at the memory.

'We had a blast,' said Philip. 'It was the coolest thing ever, and we made a mint.'

'How much did you sell them for?' asked Gloria.

'Well, we started at a pound each, then kept upping the price all weekend till those that had a bit of colour on them and looked suitably ethnic we banged out at a fiver each,' said Bill.

'Mind you,' he added, 'after that husband of yours stuffed some 'herbal tobacco' in my pipe, I really didn't know what was going on. Good time, though, eh, son?'

'It was, Dad,' said Philip. 'The best. Really the best.'

'Ever since then,' Bill said, 'when I have a bit of cash from a silly job, or one that's just off the corner as it were, I call that 'flute money'.'

Gloria looked with admiration at Bill and Philip. Both were good men, had big hearts, and were not afraid of life. Well, Bill wasn't. There were things Philip wanted to do that he was still too insecure to pursue yet, but that might change, she thought, as she cleared away the detritus from the picnic.

A few hours later, Bill, Philip, and Jack, with much laughter, dismantled the encampment and loaded it back into the van. The family parted with hugs all round and a big kiss from Jack to his granddad.

Still warmed by their love and the bit of sun he had caught in spite of his hat, Bill drove home. It had been a wonderful day, and he felt lucky to have such a family.

All was quiet under a gentle moon as Bill drove into his yard. In the magic of this summer's night, the farm looked as if the centuries had done little to change their appearance. But Bill was a cautious man and had placed discrete markers around his property that would tell him if anyone had been into the yard or near the front of the house. Luckily, all was as it should be, but even so, the need to have checked took some of the sunshine out of the day.

He went into his kitchen, put on the radio, made a pot of tea, and sat in his comfy armchair by the stove. Bess curled up in her basket, exhausted by the sea air and unaccustomed activity. As he sat there, relaxed and tired, smoking his pipe, a large mug of tea at his side, Bill savoured the memories of the day as only the old can. When you have more time behind you than you do in front, he thought, such memories are very precious indeed.

Chapter 10

LATE AUGUST

August was dwindling towards September, and the light changed subtly, intensifying the colours of the countryside. Sometimes when he and Bess were out walking the fields that girded the house and yard or in the small lanes round about, Bill would stop and take note of the timber the landscape might yield. Sit him down, put a pint of cider in his hand, give him time to stoke and light his pipe, and he would wax lyrical about trees: their wood, their particular uses, and even the folklore that surrounded them. He could also tell you where the best unharvested trees were to be found and how many years it would be before they would be at their most useful.

He hadn't heard from Skates and assumed he must still be in New York, so was able to put off worrying about the chairs for a bit longer and continue clearing out some of the tumble-down sheds that were once a vital part of the farm. An urge as old as mankind itself was telling him it was time to take stock – to discard what was of no use, and to make a tally of that which still had virtue. It was his autumn as well as that of the land around him, so he delved into forgotten sheds and buildings he hadn't looked in for years.

The farm had never been a very successful one. The land around it was decent pasture but the fields under the plough had given a reasonable harvest only when the weather was kind. Along with many other family farms in this part of the world, it had slowly decayed as the men who might have worked it moved away to earn livings elsewhere or died in various wars.

Having purchased only a tiny bit of land with the buildings, Bill had moved in and got working just as soon as he could. The big barn had become his workshop, some of the larger buildings were used for storage or lumber, and there was even an outhouse with its bucket still under the now worm-eaten seat. Sheds that had been stuck like limpets onto other buildings were now covered in ivy so dense their doors were no longer visible. The corrugated iron roof of one of these was rusted into a mere tracery above his head. Light trickled through ivy and through the branches of an ancient yew tree that had woven themselves around and through the building. There amongst the dry leaves and fallen shelves he found a large, rusted device that, when he uncovered it, chilled him to the bone.

It was a man trap. Taking it out into the yard, he set it down. It was rusty, but the steel was still good, with pointed teeth that would grab and tear the leg of any poor sod who stepped in it. With its metal jaws grinning, it certainly looked like a thing of evil intent. He had seen its like before, and knew that old ones such as this were sought after by collectors. People had them cleaned and blackened to adorn their walls, neither knowing nor caring how many unwary men (ostensibly poachers and other trespassers) they had maimed. Bill put the thing in the back of one of the stables, up high where Jack wouldn't stumble across it during one of his excursions.

As the shadows lengthened, he realized he was thirsty and felt he had earned a trip to the pub. After washing some of the rust and dirt from his hands and face, he called Bess to him and they headed out. They walked along a small lane that was crowded on both sides by vegetation that towered above sunken sections of the track. From the lane, a gate opened onto a footpath that led to the village and the dubious pleasures of The George, his local watering hole. He called it a watering hole because the beer was watered and it was indeed a hole, but it suited him.

Run-down and dirty, with an interior redolent of tobacco smoke and sweat, the pub had a back bar that contained chairs that 'belonged' to certain regulars. George Hapkins, for instance – a great big fat man who took a fiendish snuff that caused massive expectorations on anyone in his immediate vicinity – adorned an old Windsor that had been in the pub for years; one that Bill knew was an original and probably worth more than the entire stock of the bar. On its ancient seat was a cushion covered in what had once been a floral pattern. This was now just a shapeless lump that lurked on the seat like a dead badger and smelled about the same. Any careless traveller who wandered into the back bar and sat in this chair would certainly go away with memories, most of them olfactory, as the vile juices from the dreadful cushion soaked into his trouser seat.

Same with the long bench that ran down one wall: 'Death Row' it was called, because all the old boys who sat along it slowly died off like flowers in winter. Their flowering had been as young men in khaki, but now they were no longer fit enough to work in their gardens, and being at home with their wives was not a habit they had ever acquired. So they nursed their pints and slowly smoked pipes or rollups, making both last for as long as they could.

Bill went into the almost deserted public bar. It was too early for some, and the others had already headed home. Betty, the landlady, pulled him a pint of cider without his even having to ask. She was a gaunt lady with a shock of white hair and a smattering of makeup, and she hated the customers almost as much as she hated her husband, whom no one ever saw because he was always pissed by midday. The sympathy of the regulars was squarely with this man; they reckoned you couldn't live with a malevolent old witch like Betty and stay sober. Still, provided you never asked for credit and were not ill on or over the premises, she would serve you. But you needed to watch your change if you'd had a few; she was as artful as a bag of monkeys.

Bill took his cider over to a small, round table that was placed as close to a meagre, smoky fire as possible, and sat down opposite a thick-set man who looked as if he had been there since the place was built. This was Sid. Bill had known him for decades now, ever since Bill had first moved to the farm. Sid knew his way around any sort of vehicle or machinery, and hired himself out by the job whenever he needed to earn a little money. As well as being a jack of all mechanical trades, Sid was a certified rat catcher, which always secretly impressed Bill. They had got on well from the start, especially after it had been established that Bill always paid in cash and never tried to knock Sid down on his prices.

Sid had a beer belly that entered a room just a second or two before he did, and people tended to think of him as jolly, even harmless. His round face was more moulded than chiselled, but if you looked closely there was scar tissue under his ruddy complexion. Huge, bushy eyebrows hung over sharp eyes that missed nothing. For all his girth, he was very strong, having been in the Royal Marines in his younger days, and was the anchor for the pub's tug-of-war team.

In addition to admiring his mechanical skills and rat-catching abilities, Bill appreciated Sid's wicked sense of humour. No one had ever proved it, but Bill knew it was Sid who had hidden a kipper under the seat of the chairman of the magistrates in the small court next to the police station in Castle Cary. How he had got into the place without being caught Bill never found out, but the fact that Sid had been up before the selfsame magistrate earlier that week for various minor motoring offences was probably no coincidence. It was a local legend how the smell of the rotting fish defied all attempts to remove it. These included digging up the floors looking for dead rats, cleaning the drains, and even investigating the plumbing in the magistrate's very own personal convenience.

Bill lit up, and clouds of tobacco smoke curled around them. Bess sat at his feet, patiently waiting for the biscuit she knew he had in his pocket.

'There now, lass,' Bill said, as he gave it to her. 'Now we've both got a little treat, eh?'

Bess gently took the biscuit from his hand and lay down to eat it. After that she would stretch out and go to sleep, knowing the two men would be there for a good long while.

Both men supped their cider, in no hurry to talk, just enjoying each other's silent presence. Finally, Sid asked the

question that had been on his mind since he had seen .
friend walk in.

'You look bushed, mate. You been working too hard or what?'

Bill smiled and shook his head, took another swallow, then replied, 'I wish that was all it was. I could cope with that.'

Then he told Sid how Skates was putting the screws on him to take a commission that was likely to be a right bastard from start to finish.

'I could do it all right enough,' he said, 'and years ago I might have jumped at the chance, but I'm older and wiser now. No, too dodgy by half, Skates and his damned chairs.'

When Bill described how his house had been broken into and a note left on his kitchen table, Sid looked serious. This was more than just an intrusion, it was a downright threat.

'A man's home is his castle, all right, but only until some fucking rat crawls up the drain pipe,' Sid said. 'Want me to weld up a few bars? Firm up that old door of yours?'

Bill said no, he had all that in hand. 'Still,' he added grimly, 'that's Londoners for you. Never had this sort of goings-on in the past.'

Sid had no intention of being fobbed off, however. 'So what can I do to help, you stubborn old bugger?'

'Sid, I really don't want you involved. It's just a bit of a bastard job, that's all. Well, that and this bloody cough that won't shift.'

'You ill?' asked Sid.

'Not as such,' said Bill. 'Just feel like shit some of the time, but working with wood dust all your life, you're bound to get your tubes bunged up a bit. Anyway, I'm having tests.'

Then he remembered he still hadn't phoned the hospital.

To change the subject, he asked Sid, 'And what have you been up to? Any new work for the Frigging Brigadier?'

Brigadier Archie Stanhope-Smythe, Royal Army (retired), known to all and sundry as the Frigging Brigadier, lived a mile or so up the road in what had been a farmhouse of grand proportions. He rode and kept good horses, the right sort of dogs, and the wrong sort of wife. She was much younger than him and pretty in a plumpish kind of way that made some of the older men think of Singapore and its ladies of negotiable affection. She was also kind and generous, and had no airs or graces.

Her husband was the exact opposite. Mean, arrogant, and deeply suspicious of the lower classes, he was a tall, gaunt man with a toothbrush moustache that looked like an angry ginger caterpillar under his long, bony nose. He had a large military pension, and his wife had the fortitude to put up with a man many years her senior who had been institutionalised from boarding school onwards. However, having had enough of being sneered at by the other officer's wives and ignored entirely by the regimental servants, she had prevailed upon her husband to take the offer of retirement and head back to Blighty. He chose the place and she chose the gardener. It was rumoured (well, not so much rumoured as stated as fact by their cleaner, Mabel) that Mrs Brigadier Stanhope-Smythe, Royal Army (retired) was a bit of a lass when it came to strong young men who were good with their hands.

Now, it was not true that time stood still in that part of Somerset, but things did tend to move forward at their own pace. When things needed to be done, they were done, eventually. If you were a local, then by default you were part of a tribal network that covered most trades and skills. This resulted in a largely cash economy that relied on tradition and, in many cases, a useful cousin. Strangers or 'blow-ins' could tap into this network if they were not 'up 'emselves' and, more importantly, if they had the right contacts.

If you needed a car fixed and you knew and were known, then there were several good blokes in garages or sheds who could fix you up cheaper and better than a main dealer in any of the big towns nearby. The same with building work: if you were part of the tribal network, you'd know who to ask and you'd be told who would be good for what and when. The downside, of course, was always that 'when'. A job would be looked at and pondered on, and a date of starting agreed upon, both parties understanding that this date was not just flexible but downright elastic. But if you knew how the game was played and were content to trust in fate and strong cider, then all would be well.

But that was not good enough for the Frigging Brigadier. Therefore, shortly after he moved to the area, he had hired a reputable builder in Salisbury to widen, flatten, and generally improve the long drive up to his house, carry out some hard landscaping, and eventually dig out an old cesspit and fill it in. The reputable builder immediately employed a local subcontractor. Two men with one mechanical digger were soon being welcomed each morning by a lady who liked to watch them as they worked. She took them tea, cooling lemonade, and, as they got to know each other better, her husband's whisky.

Of course, the brigadier had views on how things should be done, and so each day he would stalk down to see what progress had been made and to tell the workers what they were doing wrong. It was no surprise, therefore, that the work took a lot longer than had originally been anticipated. It all came to a head one day when the brigadier found one of the men helping his wife to 'move some straw' in the stable loft. Strong words were used, including the phrase *horse whipping*, which resulted in a fast exit by the subcontractor's only digger driver.

So Sid, who had frequently worked for this subcontractor before, was asked to step in and operate the digger. He had not been on the site for five minutes when up sprang the Frigging Brigadier to look over his new man. Striding up, red-faced and full of his own piss and importance, he saw Sid atop the digger. Sid was no fool and the money was good, so he stopped the machine, got down, and, to the amazement of his co-worker, stood to attention and threw a very smart salute to the brigadier. The old boy was as pleased as punch and, although they were both in civvies, returned the salute with that elegant wave that only the true Sandhurst-trained officer can pull off. Honour was not just satisfied, it marched up and down in ranks.

Thus it came to pass that whenever the difficult old bugger needed a job done, he demanded that Sid be in the workforce. He only ever spoke to Sid and always addressed him as 'Sergeant', which suited Sid's mate who owned the equipment.

Now Sid answered Bill's question with a smile. 'The driveway is pretty much done, so we're starting on the landscaping soon. I asked him, 'You expecting an attack, sir? Shall I dig a few foxholes, tank traps, or what?' The silly old sod says 'No, and if I was, I wouldn't ask a ruddy marine to do it!'

Sid laughed and continued. 'What he's actually after is for that bottom field he used to exercise his horses on to have a bit of a scrape to level it out and for new top soil to be put on. I don't know what my mate's charging him to keep that digger hanging about, but it suits me.'

The two old friends (three if you counted Bess fast asleep at their feet) smoked and gossiped till almost closing time. Sid knew Bill had not told him everything that was troubling him, but was sure he eventually would, so respected his silence for now.

Chapter 11

LATER THAT AUGUST

The next few days passed uneventfully. Bill made himself call the hospital to set a date for the tests Dr Hall had ordered. Skates was on his horizon but not in his life at the moment, and he was happy to consign any thought of that bastard (and the dreaded hospital visit) to the future.

Right now it was a bright Sunday, and he was meeting up with his family to celebrate Gloria's birthday. Bill was determined to pay, even though it was going to be at a posh pub that had recently changed hands and become all gourmet and upmarket. He just hoped they served good-sized helpings, none of this new-age rubbish and bits of what looked like snot dribbled over square plates full of not very much at all.

The pub was the Old Harrow. He pulled up in his van and parked alongside big, four-wheel-drive vehicles that had never seen a clump of mud in their entire mechanical lives. The place had been tarted up something rotten. He remembered it as it used to be when it was the den of the infamous South Somerset Free Trade Association. Membership was by invitation only, and you were carefully vetted for any contacts you might have with the police or any other tiresome barriers to a liberal and free-thinking attitude to commerce. Having a criminal record was not necessarily a bar providing it was for the receiving or handling of liberated goods or some other offence not involving violence or household robbery. There was a standard to be maintained, after all, and nobody wanted to share a table with the sort of scum who turned over some poor sod's home and made off with a few keepsakes and granddad's watch.

Now the former inn had been renovated, and its new, trendy paintwork was like make-up on an aging hooker. It hid the cracks and brightened up a few bits, but underneath were old bones steeped in cider and larceny.

Inside, Bill hardly recognised where he was. The snug in which gamblers had played poker for days on end was gone. The saloon bar had been knocked into the public bar and an extension built on to accommodate a large dining area. It was all clean and bright, with tools and farm implements on the walls and a carpet underfoot. Anything vaguely wood was made to look like stripped pine: new 'old' furniture, not his taste at all. Not only that, but no one was smoking. A big sign hung over the long bar that took up one entire wall and proclaimed, in elegant lettering, 'Thank You For Not Smoking'. Stuff this, thought Bill.

As he stood resenting this insult and all the other changes that had been made, his arm was suddenly grabbed by his grandson. All thoughts of the old place and the old days were driven out of his mind as he was pulled lovingly to where his family were sitting. A chair was pulled out for him between his son and Jack. Gloria sat opposite and looked a million dollars as she leaned across and kissed him in welcome.

Bill turned to Jack and asked him if he had washed behind

his ears that morning. This was one of Jack's favourite games; he knew just how it would turn out and loved every minute of it.

'Yes, Granddad, but you better check just in case.'

He squirmed in his seat as Bill looked in one of his ears, then turned his head dutifully and allowed the other ear to be pulled gently, and – well, would you believe it, a pound coin had appeared in his grandfather's hand!

'You didn't make much of a job of it! Look what I found lurking behind your lug 'ole, boy.'

This not-so-sleight of hand brought a smile to Philip's face and a gasp of theatrical astonishment from Gloria. Tradition had been maintained.

'In my day it was only a penny,' said Philip.

'Ah, well, that's inflation for you,' said Bill, and he hugged his grandson.

They ordered from a lengthy menu proffered by a waitress whose smile was purely professional. Bill's chest had been bad that morning, but the clean atmosphere in the restaurant was actually therapeutic. The conversation drifted round the table, taking in Philip's job, Gloria's parents (who were still hanging in there and moaning about the neighbours), and of course the goings-on in the life of his grandson.

The meal arrived, and Bill had to admit it was good. Not the largest helpings he had ever been subject to in his time, but large enough. It was the size of the Yorkshire puddings that started a conversation centring around Bill's mother, May, kicking off with 'they don't make Yorkshire puddings like they used to'.

Anecdotes about his mother were demanded by Gloria, who was fascinated by Bill's rich past and the vanished clan he belonged to. Philip sat back and listened to the familiar stories of his grandmother. He remembered his paternal grandmother well; she really had been the stuff of legends and a very wise old bird. His mother's side of the family were all as dull as ditchwater and he had seen little of them growing up.

As they waited for the puddings to arrive, Bill turned to Gloria and said, 'She would have liked you, lass, she really would. Not one for airs and graces, but she knew people and could sniff out a wrong 'un. She had been in service, see, before the war and saw all the goings-on and goings-wrong of the county set in the twenties and thirties. She was born in a workhouse in 1908 and died owning her own home in 1978.'

'What about your dad?'

'Dad was a plumber, he died when I was eleven. That's when mum went back to her sister in Illminster, but they didn't get on, so we rented a dreadful little cottage on a farm for a while. She had a tough life, she did, but so did most of that generation what with the wars and all that.'

Gloria said nothing, but thought of her own buttoned-up, middle-class parents who had spent more effort on planning their annual holiday than they had on raising their children. She had never really got on with them. The she smiled to herself, suddenly remembering the time she had turned up to her father's masonic lodge's Ladies' Night wearing a punk outfit with extra safety pins in various interesting places.

Philip was explaining to his father the plans he had for the future and how he was almost ready to branch out on his own. Bill listened and wished he could lay his hand on a few grand to help his son out. He couldn't, of course, but his house would be worth a bit; there was no mortgage and prices were always on the up for property in his neck of the woods.

Bill said to his son, 'Look, lad, if I sold the house and workshop, that would make a bit, especially if there was planning permission to build where the barns and sheds are ...'

But before Bill had time to say more, he saw Skates walk into the restaurant. He was wearing a cream linen jacket and a smug expression as he led the way with two Sloane Rangers in tow. Talking loudly and showing off like spoiled children, they made their way to a table on the other side of the room. The place was crowded with diners and staff, so Bill kept his head down and hoped the meal would finish quickly and he could bugger off without being seen.

No such luck. Skates was walking towards the lavatories now, which were on Bill's side of the room. Seeing Bill and taking in the situation at a glance, Skates made a quick detour and fetched up behind Jack's chair. He stood a moment not saying anything, his hands resting on the top of the chair back, close, so very close, to Jack's head. Philip and Gloria looked up at him, friendly but puzzled.

'Please don't let me disturb your meal. I'm a friend of Bill's,' said Skates. 'You must be his son,' he said, extending his hand to Philip, who rose and shook it.

'Yes,' said Philip, 'and this is my wife, Gloria, and our son, Jack.'

Skates nodded at them. 'Yes, I saw you when I visited Bill recently. You were driving away as I drove in. I'm Darren Skates.'

Skates always said his name as though he expected it to be greeted with gasps of recognition and gratification, but there was only silence around the table. Bill kept his face neutral, but inside he was boiling and would have given much to be able to take up his spoon and gouge the smug bastard's eyes out.

Gloria, sensing that something was wrong, filled the awkward gap by asking Skates how he knew her father-in-law and was he in the same line of business?

He gave a short laugh with absolutely no humour in it. 'Well, no, not really, I'm more of a collector. A collector of considerable trifles, eh, Bill?'

Bill grunted and then, because of the tension that had built up within him, launched into a dreadful coughing fit. Philip patted him on the back; Gloria passed him a glass of water. Skates just stood there, hands on the back of Jack's chair, his lips stretched in a smile as false as a politician's promise, as Bill struggled to get his breath back.

Finally, he said, 'Enjoy your family, Bill. I'll be in touch soon and we can get that little job we discussed under way, okay?'

Bill grunted, neither a yes or a no, just a 'piss off' without words. Skates continued on his journey to the loos. When he was gone, Jack said, 'I didn't like him. He smelled like perfume.'

'That's not nice,' Gloria told Jack. 'I'm sure he's a very ... nice ... man.' She looked at Bill, her eyes saying something else entirely.

Philip put his hand on his father's arm. 'You in trouble, Dad?'

'No,' said Bill. 'He's just some joker who wants a job done in a hurry. I shan't take the job. Not my bag any more.'

The puddings arrived, and the conversation around the table returned to all the inconsequential things that make gatherings amongst family such a pleasure. For Bill, however, the meal had been spoiled; sullied somehow by that bastard turning up and making more veiled threats.

They did not hang about after the meal as they ordinarily would have done. Bill made some excuse about getting back to let Bess out, and as they parted there were more things unsaid than said. His son would not let him pay for the meal, and for once Bill was too preoccupied to make any fuss, just thanked him, gave him a hug, kissed Gloria, and held his grandson close before getting into his van and driving home.

Once there, he called Bess from her bed by the stove and received a sincere, if slightly subdued, greeting. She was too old now to leap up, grasp her lead off the back of Bill's chair, and drop it at his feet as she used to do. Instead, she just nuzzled him as he gently stroked the soft fur of her head and looked up at him adoringly.

'Come on, girl,' he said. 'Let's walk this problem off.'

They set off from the yard at a gentle pace on their normal route round the fields that lay at the back of the house. Bill had his pipe clenched in his jaws out of habit, but it wasn't lit. Bess wandered a little this way and that, smelling the world about her, but never very far from Bill. They walked slowly and companionably as dusk fell around them, turning the landscape into a watercolour painting, the colours so transparent that the trees and the hedges seemed to be ghosts of themselves. If Bill had been a whimsical man he might have imagined he and Bess were walking through the twilight lands between the living and the dead. As it was, he only knew that something bad was brewing and hoped to all the gods he would have the strength and the wit to weather it.

Chapter 12

SATURDAY–SUNDAY, 1–2 SEPTEMBER

The next morning Bill was in his workshop with the big doors open, letting in the sun, dust motes dancing in the bright light. There were always jobs to be done, especially if you were someone who earned a living making things that other people would pay good money to possess. Bill had no need to tout for work now; dealers and collectors came to him, and although he declared to all who would listen that he was 'winding down', if some old friend dropped a piece off and it was a job he liked to do, then Bill would take it on. Always under the condition that it would be done when it was done, and that would be when he got round to doing it.

But now, in the dark recesses of his workshop, sat three chairs. Three chairs that, despite their beauty, brought the threat of an Elizabethan tragedy into this mild, 21st-century Somerset summer.

At about one o'clock Bill took Bess out for a pee and a wander, then made himself a cup of tea. Not a dunk of a teabag into a stained mug, but tea immersed in freshly boiled water in his mother's 'just for best and snotty visitors' bit of old Spode.

Her pride and joy and the one thing he himself cherished. It always cheered him up, this tea ceremony. The visit to the doctor and the pile of medications he now took every day brought home to Bill the whole bloody getting old game. Mortality was a right bugger, and you could only opt out, never in.

He sat in his kitchen surrounded with 'things' and 'stuff'. He drank his tea, relishing the taste that only a properly brewed pot can give, and then stood up. Slowly, he turned around and around, like a radar antenna, taking in every object his eyes lit upon, seeing as a stranger might the room he stood in and all its contents.

All the cooking paraphernalia, copper pots and pans, innumerable books on shelves that, whether they had ornate cast iron brackets or simple wooden ones, were all coated in generations of paint. Chinese tea jars, kettles, crockery, and all the old furniture he had acquired over the years filled every surface and corner. The antiques trade was the worst profession any hoarder could have. That which didn't sell – or needed repairing before it could be sold – followed you home and never left.

And this was just one room. One room! Christ, he thought, who is going to want this and all the other rubbish I have accumulated over the years? Some of it was good and worth a bit; other objects, like this teapot, only had value to someone who could remember where they came from and who had loved them in their time.

He decided to start getting rid of the real rubbish. He knew a bloke who did house clearances and would get him over to do a deal. This was a man he had done some valuations for and, in one case, a bit of addition and subtraction on a nice antique wardrobe. Thus, in the loose freemasonry that was the antiques game, Bill was owed a favour.

His hands held the old teapot. There was a sugar bowl and milk jug somewhere, too. For some reason he thought of Lucy and smiled. Perhaps he would wrap it up carefully and send it to her. No note, no letter, just a tea set. He liked that thought. Well, that was one bit of 'stuff' he could find a new home for. It was a start.

He wasn't hungry, so he just fed Bess her usual portion of overpriced dog food and for the umpteenth time said to her, 'What's wrong with tripe then, eh? You used to like it well enough. Too much the grand old lady, now, are you?'

Later, as they walked towards the workshop, he said to her, 'All said and done, it's only stuff, eh, girl? What's real is what's warm in your heart and warm to your hand.'

That thought stayed with him as he opened the door, put on the lights, and, in defiance of doctor's orders and his own sore chest, lit his pipe. It was wonderful.

~~~

That evening he and Bess went for their traditional ramble round the fields and enjoyed the soft air and silence of the countryside. Harvest would be beginning soon, and that meant a bit of rabbit shooting. The land was farmed by two brothers, Hugh and Alan Dawlish. They had inherited the farm from their father, who had inherited it from his, and so on back as far as anyone could remember. Hugh was the real farmer, though; Alan was more of a businessman who only wore tweeds at the weekend, but they both enjoyed a bit of 'rough shooting' and even raised a few game birds for more formal shoots. One of the bonuses of living in a home that had been occupied by the same family for countless generations was a gunroom full of old shotguns. Bill himself had never owned one, but Hugh would always loan him some ancient piece of artillery with which he would blast away more in hope than expectation.

Bill liked the times he spent with men like that. Honest and hardworking, but with just a dash of villainy that made their company great fun. Whenever he happened to hear *The Archers* on the radio, the posturing of its so-called 'country folk' was so far removed from the real sons of the soil he knew personally as to be a joke.

That thought stayed with him after he and Bess got back home, and by way of proving it to the universe, he put on his radio just as *The Archers* theme tune fired up. At the same time, he heard a car drive into the yard. His heart sank. It had to be Skates; no one else would call on him so late. Oh, well, he thought, let's get it over and done with. As *The Archers* began their usual inanities, he walked out into the yard to meet them. Later, much later, whenever he heard that theme music, he would rush to turn off the radio, or throw it across the room, depending which way the mood took him.

The Range Rover parked up near Bill's back door and Skates and Warren walked towards him. Skates looked as dapper and sleek as ever; sleek like a shark with a wide grin and stone cold eyes. Warren was just half a pace behind him, his movements somehow predatory, as if anticipating opportunities for mayhem.

Skates spoke, making a lazy effort to sound friendly. 'Bill, old chap, we were just driving by and thought we would pop in and see what you thought about those chairs of mine.'

Bill effected a harmless look, the sort you give to policemen or dogs you think might bite.

'I'm glad you came. I've been giving them the once-over and I was going to ring you tomorrow to discuss them with you. Come into the workshop and I can show you the problems.'

He headed towards the barn. Bess, who had followed him outside, stayed close to him all the way. Opening the shop, Bill led Skates to the chairs and put one of them under a spotlight.

'Now, there is no doubt in my mind that this and the other complete chair are 'right', he said. 'I've examined them closely and there seems to be no sign of repair or renewal. They're kosher, all right, and in remarkably good nick for their age.'

Talking about his subject with these lovely examples in front of him, Bill almost forgot his listeners were two such shits.

'The carving on the back panels was done after the chairs were made, maybe a year or two after, but that's impossible to know for certain. What is for certain is that it would be criminal to break them up for a mix-and-match job.'

Skates said nothing. Taking the damaged chair and putting it under the light so the full state of the piece could be clearly seen, Bill carried on.

'The third chair is a wreck. It could be repaired, but it would need a lot of work and you might even have to make an entirely new back because this one has split, as you can see. You can also see that this chair has had a good dose of the worm. My guess is that it was kept in a barn or shed for a good few years. Perhaps someone was going to get round to mending it or just couldn't bear to chuck it out, but in any case it's in very bad shape.'

'But it is repairable,' said Skates.

'Yes, it's repairable, but it's a big job and wouldn't be cheap.'

'Well,' said Skates, 'I agree it would be a shame to break up these good chairs.' He bent forward and examined one of the chairs, his hand stroking the top rail. 'And it would probably be less work to restore the broken chair and make a completely new fourth one.'

'Make a new one!' said Bill in astonishment. 'Christ, that's a whole new ball game, that is.'

'But if anyone can do it, Bill, you can,' said Skates, smiling greasily.

'But it's a huge job. It would take months and really soak up the money.'

'Don't worry your pretty head about money,' said Skates. 'That's my problem, not yours.'

Skates walked over to the seats in front of the stove where Bill had 'entertained' him the first time he had come here. He sat down and stretched out his legs. His polished handmade shoes were speckled with wood dust. After fastidiously wiping them with his handkerchief, he indicated to Bill that he should sit down opposite him. Warren moved to stand behind his master's chair.

'What you don't seem to understand, Bill,' said Skates as if he were explaining something to a child, 'is that this is probably the most important job you will ever do.'

'Why's that, then?' asked Bill, resigned to hearing the man out before turning him down.

'Because it's for me.'

Bill started to say something, but Skates put his hand up to signal he was not finished.

'I don't know what you found out about me in London and

question that had been on his mind since he had seen his old friend walk in.

'You look bushed, mate. You been working too hard or what?'

Bill smiled and shook his head, took another swallow, then replied, 'I wish that was all it was. I could cope with that.'

Then he told Sid how Skates was putting the screws on him to take a commission that was likely to be a right bastard from start to finish.

'I could do it all right enough,' he said, 'and years ago I might have jumped at the chance, but I'm older and wiser now. No, too dodgy by half, Skates and his damned chairs.'

When Bill described how his house had been broken into and a note left on his kitchen table, Sid looked serious. This was more than just an intrusion, it was a downright threat.

'A man's home is his castle, all right, but only until some fucking rat crawls up the drain pipe,' Sid said. 'Want me to weld up a few bars? Firm up that old door of yours?'

Bill said no, he had all that in hand. 'Still,' he added grimly, 'that's Londoners for you. Never had this sort of goings-on in the past.'

Sid had no intention of being fobbed off, however. 'So what can I do to help, you stubborn old bugger?'

'Sid, I really don't want you involved. It's just a bit of a bastard job, that's all. Well, that and this bloody cough that won't shift.'

'You ill?' asked Sid.

'Not as such,' said Bill. 'Just feel like shit some of the time, but working with wood dust all your life, you're bound to get your tubes bunged up a bit. Anyway, I'm having tests.'

Then he remembered he still hadn't phoned the hospital.

To change the subject, he asked Sid, 'And what have you been up to? Any new work for the Frigging Brigadier?'

Brigadier Archie Stanhope-Smythe, Royal Army (retired), known to all and sundry as the Frigging Brigadier, lived a mile or so up the road in what had been a farmhouse of grand proportions. He rode and kept good horses, the right sort of dogs, and the wrong sort of wife. She was much younger than him and pretty in a plumpish kind of way that made some of the older men think of Singapore and its ladies of negotiable affection. She was also kind and generous, and had no airs or graces.

Her husband was the exact opposite. Mean, arrogant, and deeply suspicious of the lower classes, he was a tall, gaunt man with a toothbrush moustache that looked like an angry ginger caterpillar under his long, bony nose. He had a large military pension, and his wife had the fortitude to put up with a man many years her senior who had been institutionalised from boarding school onwards. However, having had enough of being sneered at by the other officer's wives and ignored entirely by the regimental servants, she had prevailed upon her husband to take the offer of retirement and head back to Blighty. He chose the place and she chose the gardener. It was rumoured (well, not so much rumoured as stated as fact by their cleaner, Mabel) that Mrs Brigadier Stanhope-Smythe, Royal Army (retired) was a bit of a lass when it came to strong young men who were good with their hands.

Now, it was not true that time stood still in that part of Somerset, but things did tend to move forward at their own pace. When things needed to be done, they were done, eventually. If you were a local, then by default you were part of a

I don't care. What I do care about is getting what I want. And I want these lovely chairs worked on by you, because you may be a stubborn old fool, but you're the best.'

This statement, which would have been a compliment if made by anyone else, sounded like an accusation coming from Skates.

'Yours not to reason why, Bill. Yours but to do and . . .' there was a deliberate pause before Skates continued, 'get paid.'

But he might just as well have finished the quotation. That much Bill understood and it chilled him to the bone, but it also made him very angry. What right did these two arseholes have to come into his workshop and try to bully him into taking a job he really didn't want? A job that would take a vast amount of time and effort and, truth to tell, a job that was now virtually impossible for him to accomplish.

He leaned towards Skates, who just sat there, implacable, his mind so obviously made up to have what he wanted, and said, 'Now look here, Mr Skates. I don't give a flying fuck how important these chairs are to you. I can't and I won't take this job on. Not now, not ever, get it?'

If Skates noticed Bill's anger, it made no impression on him. He just lounged there and looked at Bill as if he were a toddler having a tantrum.

'Go on,' he said. 'Tell me why.'

Bill thought he saw his way out. 'I'm ill, okay? I'm being tested for all sorts of shit, but whatever the reason, I'm just not as strong as I was. And besides, this job would need some skills I don't have.'

'Such as?'

'The back carving for a start. It's a real specialised job to carve those designs in such a way they will fool an expert. And it's not just the carving, it's the tools to carve with. You can't use modern chisels for the final cuts, it would look all wrong. You have to have a good set of old steels that will leave the same work marks the real chairs have. I don't have those.'

He did, of course, but he was buggered if he was going to admit it.

'Go on,' said Skates.

Bill felt he was digging himself a hole, but he didn't know what sort or how deep, so he carried on.

'The actual body, the carcase of the ruined chair, that alone would take weeks. It's not just the making, it's finding wood to match the original parts.'

Not entirely bullshit, thought Bill, and he went on, conciliatory now as if he really would have liked the job but was baulked by ill health and lack of wherewithal.

'As to making a new chair, that is a real can of worms. Starting from scratch, again you'd need the right wood; not just English oak but the right part of the oak. I suspect the two good chairs you have were made from one tree and that presents a real problem in sourcing the timber because you would have to find a bit of old oak that had all the right characteristics. And, between sourcing the right timber and getting the carving done, it would be nigh on impossible to keep this job secret.'

'Is that all?' asked Skates, as impassive as ever. Bill found his lack of reaction unnerving.

'Staining and polishing would be a tough job. To get all four chairs to look right together you'd have to be lucky to get the right finish on the repaired and the new ones; otherwise you'd have to take the whole lot down to basics and start over from there.'

That was true, though Bill had a talent for finishing that was almost magical, so it wasn't actually all that likely.

'But if all these problems could be dealt with, the job could be done, yes?' asked Skates.

'They could,' said Bill, 'but not by me.'

'I understand about the carving,' said Skates. 'Who do you know who could do it?'

Bill sat back. He needed time to think this one out, and no better implement existed to assist procrastination than the common tobacco pipe. The filling, lighting, and tamping of tobacco can stretch the very fabric of time itself, not even counting the ritual that preceded this; the patting of the pockets in the search for the tobacco pouch, the gentle reaming of the pipe. Bill was a past master at these things and he used the time to rifle through his memory for some poor sod to stand next in line when he had dropped out. But there really was only one person who had the skill to do this job.

'Eric Howler comes to mind. He's a hell of a good carver and once spent time with the National Trust tickling up some bits of Grinling Gibbons and the like. Another thing in his favour is he did a lot of work in Hampton Court a few years ago, so he knows his Tudor.'

What Bill failed to mention was that Eric Howler was known in the trade as 'The Howler Monkey' because he had a tendency to get very drunk and tell everything he knew to anyone who would listen. Oh, and while he had indeed done some work at Hampton Court, he was also well known at the county court for various unsavoury reasons. Yes, Eric would do nicely, and Bill felt only the smallest qualm as he named him.

But Skates's next words showed Bill that even that qualm had been wasted.

'I will pay you £20,000 for this job. Cash. Half now and the rest when it's finished. You can use whoever you like to do the bits you can't, but if even a rumour about this job gets out, then whoever has shot his mouth off will be in a world of pain.'

Bill opened his mouth to object, but Skates spoke over him.

'Bill, I have chosen you because you're the best. I have chosen you because I want this job done in a reasonable amount of time and with great discretion. I have also chosen you because I know –' and here he leaned forward until his face was just inches away from Bill's, '– just what levers to pull. I have met your family. I know what they look like, where they live, and what car they drive.'

Then he leaned back and calmly lit a cigarette.

Bill felt sick and dazed, but managed to ask, 'What if I have to go into hospital or become too ill to work?'

Skates replied, 'If you don't take this on you will indeed go into hospital, and you might just be joined there by that lovely grandson of yours. Understand this: you will do this work for me, it will be done to your usual degree of excellence, and you will get paid handsomely for doing it. When the job is done and I am happy with the results, then you can be as ill as you like.'

Bill got up and walked out into the yard, his mind boiling with a rage the like of which he had never felt before. He looked about him, at his place, his workshop, his home. That this man should threaten him was bad enough, but this arsehole, this fucking animal dared to threaten his family! It was too much.

As Skates followed him out of the workshop, Bill turned

and flew at him, landing a blow that surprised the man more than it injured him. Bill was no fool and he knew Warren was close by, but he didn't care; he just wanted to hurt this bastard as much as he could before he was dropped. He would even welcome a beating if it put paid to any chance of him having to work for Skates.

Bill never landed a second punch, however; he was thrown onto the ground like so much laundry and Skates stood over him, wiping blood from his mouth where Bill's punch had caught him.

'Well, Bill,' he mocked, 'life in the old dog yet, eh?'

Bill lay flat on his back in the yard, the breath knocked out of him. Bess, confused and concerned, ran to his side.

Skates extended a hand to Bill. 'Get up,' he said.

Bill was too winded not to use it, so he did. Immediately Bill had regained his feet, Skates turned the hand hold into an arm lock that forced him to his knees.

'You need to be taught a lesson, Bill.'

Then, without releasing his grip, he turned to Warren and raised his voice. 'What was it I said, Mr Warren? 'Life in the old dog yet?' Well, perhaps there is and perhaps there won't be, eh?'

Warren said nothing, but bent down, took hold of Bess by the back of her leather collar, and pulled her up by it. Her legs thrashed the air as she struggled to get away, gasping and choking like a condemned man on a gibbet.

Bill, held in the vice-like grip of Skates, was unable to do anything to help her. He prayed to God they would let her go, do anything they liked to him, but not his dog, not dear old Bess, none of this was her fault.

As Bess continued to writhe, Warren's other hand went to his pocket and, over the sound of Bess's suffering, Bill heard a metallic click. The blade of a flick knife caught the light from the workshop door.

Warren looked at Skates, who nodded, then with one swift motion, he cut Bess's throat.

Blood, almost black in the gloom of the early evening, gushed over the yard and spread in tendrils along the cracked cement. So much blood. Bess's struggles grew weaker and then ceased. She sagged in Warren's hand and he let her drop to the ground. She made no sound, just shivered once as if she was cold, and then was still.

Skates let Bill go and then he, too, dropped to the ground. Skates bent over, shoved a large envelope into one of Bill's coat pockets, and patted him on the shoulder. Then he stood up and walked to his vehicle, all without saying a word.

Warren looked down at Bill with a sneer, gave Bess's body a kick, then walked over to the car, held the door open for Skates, got in, and drove away.

Bill crawled over to Bess and cradled her in his arms. For what seemed like hours he just held her and said 'I'm sorry, girl' over and over. At last he got to his feet, went into the kitchen, and came back out with Bess's blanket. He spread it over her, then went and found a shovel.

Night gave way to dawn as Bill slowly dug a hole under the cherry tree in his private little garden, his progress impeded by frequent bouts of coughing. Finally, he wrapped Bess in her blanket and placed her with all the love in his heart at the bottom of the grave. He stood there when the job was done, feeling wretched and broken.

'The only time you buy love is when you buy a dog,' the gypsy had said.

And when you bury one, you bury part of yourself.

~~~

Later that morning, Bill packed up all of Bess's things: her beds, her blankets, her bowls. The sight of each newly emptied space cut into his heart as if he were somehow betraying her memory, but he had to keep busy, he couldn't let himself just sit and brood. If he was going to deal with Skates and Warren, he needed to look outward, not fold in on himself like a crumpled wreck.

Bill knew he would have to do Skate's bloody job now one way or another, but inside he seethed with hatred. He remembered Harry Pexton saying, 'It's no use getting old if you don't get artful.' Well, he was old and he was ill, but he was cunning and he would sort these bastards out and to hell with the consequences.

While he was packing up Bess's things, his phone rang, but he didn't answer it. He wanted to speak to no one; words would be too hard to find. The ringing went on and on.

Finally, too emotionally and physically exhausted to do any more, and dreading having to go back outside and clean the place where Bess had been slaughtered, Bill sat down at his kitchen table. He had not eaten all day. The loneliness and desolation that engulfed him seemed at odds with the intense light of the midday sun that streamed in through the open door. The sunlight so conflicted with his feelings that he cursed it as it flowed into the room.

The only thing of Bess's he had not yet boxed up was her

leather lead. This he held in his hands, not wanting to part with it, but not wanting to see it in its old place over the back of his chair, either. The plaited leather was worn and the clasp at the end broken, but holding it brought her back to him.

Suddenly, he heard a vehicle drive into the yard. If it was them again, by gods, he would do for them, he really would! All his tools were in his workshop, but he had a sharp carving knife in the rack by the sink. He took it out, wiped the tears from his eyes, and, carrying the knife close to his jacket so it couldn't be seen, turned to go outside and face whatever was there.

Into the square of light that was the doorway stepped what looked to Bill's tired eyes like a golden shadow. It said, 'Bill, I tried to phone. It's taken me ages to find you.'

As the shadow moved into the room, it resolved into Lucy. Lucy, standing there looking at him with his eyes all red from crying. The knife clattered to the stone floor and he stood like a puppet with all its strings cut, head bowed, shoulders hunched, motionless. Lucy ran to him and put her arms around him.

Bill was so overcome by her totally unexpected arrival and the warmth of her embrace that all he could say was, 'My Bess. My old dog Bess. They killed her. The bastards killed her!'

And then he broke down.

Chapter 13

SUNDAY, 2 SEPTEMBER

L ucy took over. She found what she needed to make a pot
of tea, she found the knife on the floor, she found Bill's
whisky, and she found her heart going out to this man who
was being brutalised by the same bastard who had caused her
so much pain.

When Bill was seated at the kitchen table with a cup of
tea in his hands and a large dose of whisky close by, she pulled
out a chair and sat next to him without saying anything, just
being there. She looked around the room; it told her a lot about
Bill. The house wasn't very tidy, but it was definitely a home.
The person who lived here was solitary and self-contained, but
not lonely. And yet somehow she didn't feel like an intruder.

She put her hand on Bill's arm and in a soft voice brought
him back from the dark, silent place he had withdrawn to.

'Bill? Bill, tell me what happened.'

He looked up at her. She seemed a different woman from
the last time they had met. She was dressed in her usual jeans
and T-shirt, but she appeared to be a lot younger than he
remembered her. She was lovely. He put a hand up to touch
her face, as if to assure himself she was real. She took his hand

and held it while he told her everything Skates and Warren had done, and how afterwards he had buried Bess under the cherry tree.

When he was done, Bill felt completely spent. Lucy suggested he go lay down for a bit, and he simply nodded and got to his feet. She sighed as she heard him slowly climbing the stairs to his bedroom.

Suddenly, she remembered poor Clive, who had been left in the car all this time. She went outside and, keeping him on his lead and carefully avoiding certain areas, she walked him around the yard. Then she tied him up in a shady spot and got busy.

Bill awoke after a few hours' dreamless sleep. When he remembered about Bess, he wished he hadn't. But, hearing the chink of dishes downstairs, he made himself get up and go to the kitchen. It was late afternoon, and Lucy had put on a couple of lights. Everything looked so homely, so normal, but he knew there was no such thing as 'normal' anymore.

He sat down in his chair, and Lucy put a cup of tea in front of him, then asked if it would be all right if she brought Clive in. 'He's been tied up outside for quite a while and he's not used to it.'

'Your dog,' he said, immediately rising from his chair. 'Yes, of course, you must.'

As he walked out to the yard, he was surprised to see it looked the same as it always had (apart from an old green Volvo estate car abandoned at a jaunty angle in front of the house). He had somehow expected the violence and wickedness of the past twenty-four hours to be marked on the buildings, the fields, even the sky. But it was all just the same, except where it wasn't.

There was a large, clean patch of concrete, and signs of water and foam were still visible. It had been scrubbed and cleaned, and on a doorstep next to one of the outbuildings by the yard tap there was a brush he recognized as the one he kept under the sink. It glistened wetly in the fading sunlight, its once-white bristles now showing a hint of pink. He stood a long time looking at this scene, and it moved him almost to tears.

'Thank you,' he said, not daring to look at Lucy.

She said nothing; just placed a hand on his back and gave it a quick, light rub.

Clive was laying down in the shade of the car, his lead attached to a door handle, but when he saw Bill he jumped up and yelped, his tail going round in excited circles. Lucy untied him and he ran frantically this way and that, trying to greet Lucy and Bill and sniff everything all at the same time.

Daft hound, thought Bill affectionately, and called the dog to him, then ruffled its head.

'He must be thirsty. I'll get him a bowl of water.'

Bill walked back into the kitchen and took a large pudding bowl from a cupboard, filled it from the tap, and took it into the yard. It was not Bess's bowl, nor would he give Clive any of her other things. Well, the expensive dog food, maybe, but nothing else.

After Clive had drunk his fill, they walked him a little way along Bill's usual evening route so he could stretch his legs and perform other needful functions. Afterwards, back in the kitchen, Lucy fed Clive his dinner in an antique soup tureen. He seemed to like it, or at least the food it held.

Bill asked Lucy if she was hungry, and it turned out neither of them had consumed so much as a morsel all day. Bill suddenly felt ravenous. He pointed Lucy towards the huge fridge that stood in the kitchen like something out of a sci-fi film, and she rummaged within its chilly depths. Luckily, there were enough bacon and eggs to make a good fry-up, to which was added the baked beans that were also a staple of Bill's diet. Stale bread made good toast, and homemade marmalade turned the meal into a feast.

They piled the plates next to the sink and sat on, talking, with a fresh pot of tea and an ever-diminishing supply of whisky.

~~~

Lucy's experiences since Bill had last seen her were far less dramatic than Bill's had been, but they were not without interest. After Bill's visit, she had become aware that she really was living in a prison of her own making. She was afraid to leave the house, yet all the time she was there she was terrified that Skates would turn up and start making her life a misery again. Now, for some reason, it seemed possible that there were other places she could go. She had £500 and two friends in the whole world: one by her side, the other in Somerset.

She made herself walk Clive a little further from home every day, and the more she did it, the easier it became. Ilford being an East London suburb, it had a touch of the Wild West about it. Cosmopolitan, but full of dodgy characters scratching a living on the margins. Her walks took her past a house that had a forecourt with several cars parked in it and a garage at the back from which poured loud reggae music blended with the sound of metal being hammered. There were cars in the road in front of the house, too, and one had a 'for sale' sign on the window screen, but no price.

Everything was a bit run-down, and a large sign on the small gate leading to the battered front door of the house warned people to 'Beware of the Dog'. One day when she was walking past she saw a tall West Indian man come out of the door holding a large Alsatian on a chain. Clive was on his lead and pulled her forward, eager to engage this black and grey monster in canine conversation. She pulled him back sharply and walked on as fast as she could.

A rich, brown voice with a beautiful Jamaican accent called after her: 'It's all right lady! He as soft as butter; just looks a bad boy!'

She turned, looked from man to dog, and said, 'I bet he says the same thing about you.'

The man's laughter followed her up the street. She liked that; it felt as if she was rejoining the human race at long last.

Eventually, she decided to do as Bill had suggested and buy a car. She had a license, but the only vehicles she had ever driven were her father's and that had been a long time ago. Lucy got a local paper and went through all the adverts for second-hand cars. There were pages and pages of them, and she didn't have a clue what all the abbreviations meant. She thought of that man with all the cars around his house and, summoning her courage, decided to go and talk to him.

Leaving Clive behind this time, Lucy walked to the garage. The music sounded as loud as ever, but instead of banging, this time there was smoke and laughter coming from the building. She went up into the forecourt and looked at the vehicles parked there. All of them had obviously travelled some long roads to reach this final stop before the breaker's yard.

A man with long dreadlocks and greasy overalls poked

his head out of the garage, smiled, and went back in. A few moments later, the big man she had seen with the Alsatian walked out from the gloom of the interior and, seeing her, smiled.

'Pretty lady, where's that lovely dog of yours?'

'I left him at home today. I want to buy a car, but I don't have much money.'

The big man opened his arms wide and, with a grin, said to her, 'Winston's Motors are here to help!'

He beckoned her into a small office attached to the garage. It was full of car parts, both loose and in boxes, and was decorated with innumerable calendars that showed more than just the months of the year. Winston was a good listener and soon found out more about Lucy than she probably realised. He offered her tea, a cigarette, and something more exotic if she wished it. She declined them all, but thanked him for his kindness.

'So, pretty lady Lucy,' he said, 'if I guess right, you're running away, yeah?'

Lucy said nothing to that, but her look told him everything he needed to know.

'Come with me, pretty Lucy,' he said, and led the way outside the garage and along the street a short way. On the road was parked a large Volvo estate car. It was green in colour, was dented in several places, and looked as big as a bus to Lucy.

'This would be the thing for you. It's safe, got good locks, you could sleep in it if you needed to, and is a good price.'

'How much?' asked Lucy. It looked too good for a banger.

'Well, it's got a lot of miles on the clock, though that don't show 'cos we fixed it, but it's a good motor and reliable. A bit thirsty, but safe and comfortable. You can run a long way in this old bus, lady, a long way.'

'How much?' asked Lucy, arms folded, all business.

Winston didn't price the car up before knocking a bit off as he might have done with other buyers. He liked this woman and saw in her eyes something that made him remember his own times of trouble. It was his chance to do someone a good turn, so Lucy bought the car for £350.

As she paid the notes over to Winston, he smiled at her and said, 'This is a lucky car, pretty lady. I can tell these things, you know.'

Lucy laughed and said, 'I hope so, Winston, I'll need it.'

Then she got in and, somewhat jerkily, drove the car to her house.

It was taxed – just – but without insurance. Not having driven for so long, Lucy decided to leave for Somerset in the wee hours to avoid traffic. She packed a sleeping bag, some bottles of water, and food for Clive, then locked up the house, put the keys back through the letterbox, and set off. With every mile she drove, it seemed to her as if she had gained back a little piece of herself. By the time Lucy cleared London, she felt renewed, hopeful, and almost comfortable driving the car.

One of her purchases had been a map book that showed the village in Bill's address, but of course she didn't know how to get to his house. When she got close, she stopped at a phone box to call Bill and get directions, but there had been no answer. Then she had stopped at The George, hoping someone there might know where he lived. They had, and she finally managed to find him. Her journey was over, for now.

~~~

That night Bill showed Lucy to the room that had once been his son's. With a couple of carrier bags that contained her entire wardrobe, and Clive at her heels, she climbed the stairs. And for the first time in years, Lucy slept in a bedroom without locking the door. In fact, she didn't even notice if the door had a lock. She was exhausted, but lay awake for a little while trying to figure out what it was about Bill that had acted as a catalyst for all these changes in her life.

Chapter 14

MONDAY–FRIDAY, 3–7 SEPTEMBER

W hen Bill entered the kitchen next morning, Lucy was at the sink washing up the previous night's dishes. Clive was sitting at her feet, watching her intently in case she needed him to lick any of them. Bill sat down in his chair and found himself looking at a rack of toast and a freshly made pot of tea.

Lucy wiped her hands on a towel, sat down across from him, and asked simply, 'What are we going to do, Bill?'

There was no anxiety in her voice; it was just a request for information.

Bill wasn't hungry, but he took a piece of toast all the same. And he hadn't missed that 'we'.

'Right now,' he said, 'I need to think, and that daft dog of yours needs a long walk. So let's lock up here after breakfast, have a ramble round the fields, and see what comes to mind.'

When he put on his jacket, he found the envelope Skates had thrust into his pocket. Glancing inside, he saw it was full of £50 notes. He hurriedly shoved it into the top drawer of the dresser. Right now he didn't want anything that bastard had touched.

As Bill and Lucy stepped out into the sunshine, there was trouble in both their minds, but there was none in Clive's, and it did them a certain amount of good to watch him run through the fields demented with joy. But there was a dreamlike quality to everything that made discussing long-term plans impossible. So much had happened in the last few days that Bill felt he was only just clinging to the wreckage of his life, and though Lucy had, in fact, crawled out from the wreckage of hers, she didn't yet know into what. The only thing they settled was that they would try to keep Lucy's presence in Bill's house a secret for as long as possible lest word somehow got back to Skates.

Bill spent the next few days grieving for his dead companion and learning to live with his new one. On Tuesday morning he called his family and told them Bess had been killed in a road accident. They offered to drive over, knowing how much the old dog had meant to him, but Bill said there was no need. The next day he had a lovely card from them all and a letter carefully printed in Jack's best handwriting.

On Wednesday, Bill drove over to Sid's, where he found him in the yard welding up a car chassis. Bill told him Bess had died, giving him the same road accident story he had told his family. Sid put down his tools and did something he had never done before: he hugged his old friend. He said nothing, just crushed him for a moment in his huge arms.

Bill told him he would be going to stay with his son for a few days and would get in touch when he returned. He hated lying to Sid, but he didn't want to risk his dropping by the house for a bit. He just wasn't ready to explain Lucy and everything else to anyone yet.

The only other person he told about Bess was Miss Templeton, and he told her the same story he had told the others. She looked at him strangely as she commiserated with his loss, but was too wise to ask him any questions.

Meanwhile, Lucy had decided the best way to get to know Bill's house was to clean it and everything in it. This not only made her feel more at home, but gave her a much-needed outlet for all the nervous energy she was suddenly having to cope with. Too many changes too quickly were taking their toll on a nervous system that was not in the best shape to begin with.

As time went on, however, Lucy made a surprising and somewhat humbling discovery about herself: she actually enjoyed domestic activities. She had always thought of herself as a rebel against traditional women's roles, and here she was revelling in one. She felt a strong sense of accomplishment when she looked at the results of her labours, and keeping Bill fed and full of tea seemed the best possible way of expressing her gratitude to him.

Bill was a little taken aback to find himself the possessor of ironed shirts for the first time in thirty years, but he never felt Lucy's efforts to be an intrusion. She was finding her way in this new world, just as he was.

On Thursday a letter came from the hospital to remind Bill he had an appointment in the oncology department the following day. Christ, he thought, they don't hang about.

Lucy saw the letter and asked, 'Is this about your cough, Bill?'

He answered, 'Might be,' in such a way as to close the conversation, then took Lucy into his workshop to show her for the first time the things that had already caused so much grief in his life, and threatened to cause still more.

The chairs had an imposing, almost regal presence that was not surprising considering their history. The turned balustrade legs and simple frames, the solid ancient backs with Tudor Roses in low relief under which were carved the initials 'E.R.' all proclaimed their heritage. Bill knew that nowhere else in the world was there a set like these. Being in the trade for so long, his knowledge of the lost gems that haunt collectors' dreams was encyclopaedic. And knowledge was not just power in his game; it was money. Real money.

Bill invited Lucy to sit on one of the good chairs, then sat opposite her on the other and told their story. When he finished, Lucy got up and ran her hands gently, almost lovingly, over the carving on the back panel.

'Why 'wainscot'?' she asked.

'That was a term for real high-quality oak boards. They were originally made into panels to cover up cold stone walls, but got used to make furniture later on.'

As though considering such things for the first time, she said, 'Just think of what these chairs have seen since they were made all those years ago.'

Bill smiled at her. Lucy seemed to be experiencing that almost mystic sense of history that really old furniture always gave him. Her grey eyes looked at him in wonder and suddenly he realized that if he had been younger and fitter this lady could really have turned his head. The idea of it both pleased and worried him and consequently he went all bluff and business-like and said he would have to get down to working out just how he would tackle the task of making a new chair and repairing the broken one.

The next day put all thoughts of grey eyes and old chairs out of Bill's head, however, as it was the day of his appointment at the hospital. He went alone. He hated hospitals and the only times he had ever been to one were on those rare occasions when the sharp end of a machine bit him back.

This was different, though. This was . . . illness. Not to mention a full day of his life given over to blood tests, blowing up damned spouts to test his lung function, then getting mopped up after the lengthy coughing fits that followed. Then, of course, there were x-rays – before, during, and after which he had to stand around wearing one of those hospital gowns that left his arse hanging out. That was enough of a trial in itself. Oh, the people were kind and professional, but it was a bugger all the same, and he drove home in a lot of pain and a really foul mood.

When he walked into the kitchen, he was so depressed and distracted he automatically looked to where Bess's basket used to be. Instead of Bess, however, he saw Clive. Clive laying in the exact spot where Bess should have been. The sight hit him like a physical blow.

With a face like thunder, Bill went in and sat down, breathless and seriously pissed off. The sadness of Bess's death seemed all turned to anger now. Lucy saw the look on his face and it brought back memories of other men coming into other rooms and taking out their problems on her. She turned quickly and went upstairs, Clive scrambling up and trotting after her.

Sitting in his usual chair in his usual place, Bill gradually calmed down. He looked around the room. A water jug filled with flowers gleaned from hedgerow and field sat in the middle of the table. The kitchen smelled of cooking, and everything shone. The copper pots were polished, the stone-flagged floor had been scrubbed, and if there was any dust left anywhere, it had been scared out of its life and gone into hiding.

He got up and walked into the sitting room. All the furniture had been dusted and polished, and the few choice pieces he had were looking better than he had seen them in years.

'Oh, bugger,' he thought. 'What a bloody idiot I am. Poor girl, I'm just what she doesn't need right now.'

He walked up the steep stairs to the landing and then knocked on the door of Lucy's bedroom. After a short pause, a red-eyed Lucy opened the door. Bill took her in his arms.

'I'm sorry, lass,' he said quietly. 'I'm an old fool, but I've had a pig of a day. I'm really sorry.'

Lucy hugged him back and said, 'No worries, Bill. I understand. It's just . . . I've spent so much time on my own these past few years, and most of that afraid. It gets to be a habit, I guess.'

He let her go, smiled at her, and said, 'I smell something wonderful. What have you been cooking?'

Lucy called it 'spaghetti bollock-naked' because she had no Italian herbs; only tinned tomatoes and some mince she had found in the freezer. But topped with local cheddar it made a good meal, and one far removed from Bill's normal catering.

She had also found a bottle labelled 'Damson Wine' at the back of a cupboard. Bill remembered it had come from one of the old girls in the village he helped out from time to time. He thought it had been there for at least three years, but it was still clear, tasted of summer, and was lethal. Under its spell, Bill told Lucy about the day he had spent in the hospital. Somehow, telling it all to her, he was even able to joke about some of the things that had been done to him. They both felt as if they had known each other for years rather than just weeks.

Suddenly, Bill got up from his chair and brought out the cardboard box that held the tea set he had been going to send Lucy. She was overwhelmed, not just by his generosity, but by how thoughtful he was. She had never met anyone like Bill. He had a quiet strength that made him so easy to be around. The fact that he was thirty years older than her didn't seem to matter a damn. He was her friend, and already one of the best she had ever had.

That night Bill's coughing was worse than ever, and it woke Lucy. She went down to the kitchen, filled a glass of water, and took it up to Bill's room. When she knocked on the door and went in, he was sitting up, hunched over his knees, a bunch of bloody tissues in his hand. His face was white, and he looked very old and ill. Lucy took the glass and helped him drink from it, all the while gently rubbing his back through the thin pyjamas he was wearing.

'I'm sorry,' Bill gasped.

The spasm was over, but he felt drained and his chest hurt like hell. Lucy got his painkillers, propped him up on his pillows, and stayed with him, holding his hand until he became drowsy and finally fell asleep.

Chapter 15

SATURDAY–SUNDAY,
8–9 SEPTEMBER

Bill slept to nearly 10 on Saturday morning. Lucy waited until she heard him stirring before making his tea and toast. As she was setting his breakfast on the table, she heard a car enter the yard. Peering out of the kitchen window from behind a fold of curtain, she saw it was a big white Range Rover. Skates was driving it, and he was alone.

Bill must have heard the car as well because he came rushing down the stairs, hissing to Lucy to go hide in her room, keep Clive quiet, and stay there till he called her, no matter what she heard. Lucy immediately complied, her heart pounding.

Bill opened the kitchen door and stood there on the threshold. In his hand was the huge carving knife he had held a few short days ago. This time it was not hidden, but kept where it could be seen. Skates drove up to where Bill was standing and the window of the Range Rover purred down.

'Only a courtesy visit,' said Skates with mock amiability, his smile as valueless as a turd farthing. 'Nothing to worry about. Just wondering how you're getting on. I expected to see you in your workshop, beavering away on my chairs.'

Bill replied in a voice full of loathing, 'It's Saturday. I don't work on Saturdays. And tomorrow's Sunday; I go to church on Sundays, okay? Your fucking chairs will be done when they're done.'

Skates said nothing, just looked pissed off, spun the vehicle around in the yard, and drove away in a cloud of dust and gravel.

Lucy came downstairs when she heard the vehicle drive away. She was shaking; this was the first time she had set eyes on Skates since the horror days in London. Bill put an arm around her and gave her a brief hug, then they sat down at the table and made a 'sort of' plan. Bill would start the chairs today; he couldn't put the job off much longer in any case, and he probably felt as good as he was likely to in the immediate future.

But before he started, he needed to pay a visit to the neighbouring farm. Bill made a quick phone call, drove off up the road, and was back within the hour, carrying a long object wrapped in a sack. He took it and Lucy into the field behind the yard, out of sight of the lane.

Bill unwrapped the package. It was an old double-barrelled shotgun with hammers, and in his pocket he had a box of 12-bore cartridges. The gun was not heavy, but he guessed Lucy had never held one before, probably hadn't even seen one outside of the telly or films.

It was a huge surprise, therefore, when Lucy took the gun from him, broke open the breech, looked up the barrel, snapped it shut, pulled back the hammers with an impressive click, and brought the gun up to her shoulder in one practised movement.

'Where in hell did you learn to do that?' he asked in both alarm and admiration.

'My father used to go shooting a lot in the season.'

'Game shooting?' asked Bill, still slightly in awe.

'He did,' said Lucy, 'but I wasn't allowed on those trips. If he was in a good mood, though, he would take me when he went clay shooting. I enjoyed that.'

'Good for you,' said Bill. 'Want to have a go with a couple of rounds just to get your hand back in?'

Lucy did, and soon the quiet countryside was filled with the sound of gunfire. With ears ringing, Lucy broke the weapon and extracted the empty cartridges.

'Gives a good kick,' she said. 'And the hammers are a bit stiff.'

Bill nodded, and they walked back to the house, Lucy carrying the gun. Bill didn't usually fancy leaving a loaded weapon around the place, but being as it was an old-fashioned type and couldn't fire unless the two hammers were fully pulled back, he guessed it was safe enough. They decided to keep it at the back of the kitchen, close by the dresser and near the door to the downstairs hall. All it took to hide it completely was a large towel hung from a hook on the dresser's side. That looked suitably domestic and in keeping with its position.

They had a bit of lunch, then Bill went into the workshop to get started on the chairs. As he started to sort out the bench he would be working at, Lucy came into the workshop with a broom. She might just as well have come into the place with a flaming torch.

'Don't!' yelped Bill in a panicked voice that stopped Lucy in her tracks.

'No, please. Please, don't ever!' he begged in anguish, as if she were going to run someone over or sweep shillings into a drain.

Lucy just stood there with the broom in her hand, at a complete loss as to what Bill was on about. Parts of the workshop were ankle-deep in shavings, and every surface had a deep layer of dust on it, not to mention all the cobwebs, which were thick enough to make Miss Havisham's dining room look like an operating theatre by comparison.

'Some of these chippings have been here for years, decades; some are probably older that you,' he pleaded. 'I know where everything is and I really like it the way it is, please!'

Lucy laughed and started back to the house. Bill let out a sigh of relief.

'It's probably for the best,' Lucy said over her shoulder as she went. 'If someone came in here and saw it all cleaned up, they'd know something was up!'

After a while Lucy came back, this time with Clive. They had been out for a run, and by the look of Clive, it had been a good one. Lucy had brought a bowl from the kitchen and filled it with water. After he had drunk his fill, Clive slumped down, panting, in the doorway. Bill looked over as he was moving the chairs and felt a pang. Bess was still on his mind, but having Clive in the workshop didn't upset him as much as he had feared it would.

He put the two good chairs on the bench and, taking a notebook from a drawer, started to measure each component. Lucy reached over and took the pencil. As if they had been doing this for years, Bill stated the measurements and Lucy wrote them down. As they worked, Lucy asked all sorts of questions, not just about these chairs but about antique furniture in general.

Bill loved it. Lucy was interested in a way his son Philip had never been. Oh, Philip had helped his dad in the workshop whenever he was asked, but it was never really his thing. He did it because he loved his father and liked sharing his company. Lucy was doing it because she was really interested in the subject.

Bill had done all the measuring he needed to do and was now drawing each piece in clear, stark lines. Lucy went into the house and came back with two mugs of tea, setting one down by Bill, and just sat quietly watching what he was doing, trying not to spoil his concentration. His old hands were scarred but confident as they drew.

As they continued to work, it became clear that Lucy had an agile brain; she was not afraid to ask questions and she remembered the answers. Bill watched her as she sat at a nearby bench making her own drawing of a dovetail joint and using callipers to measure the dimensions. In her jeans and T-shirt, with her fair hair tied back in her usual ponytail, she looked delightful. It made him sad to think that if he had known this woman twenty years ago, he might have had a partner by now. Ah, well, other places, other times, he mused as he stood up from his task and lit his pipe.

On Sunday Bill gave Lucy directions to a large supermarket not too far away where she could get all the provisions and ingredients she lacked to show how well she could cook if she really wanted to. And for Bill she found she really wanted to. He was so appreciative of her meagre efforts thus far that she wanted to see his reaction to real meals with all the trimmings.

Lucy hadn't had much occasion to cook for the past couple of decades, but she had memories of quiet, peaceful, safe afternoons when she was a girl, helping her mother's cook in the kitchen. She had also found a cache of cookbooks that Beryl had left behind. Her current favourite was a first-edition *Food in England*, rich with pre-war recipes that somehow felt right in her current surroundings. She couldn't wait to see Bill's reaction to the roast beef, potatoes, gravy, and Yorkshire puddings she had planned for him.

His response turned out to be all she could have wished, and her ears were still ringing with his praises as they moved through to the sitting room at the front of the house after dinner. It was a warm evening, and the scent of honeysuckle that came in through the open window was beguiling. Bill lit some candles that were in brass candlesticks on the mantelpiece, and their soft light was reflected in the glass of a large mirror.

One of Bill's numerous deals had earned him a huge leather Chesterfield. He had re-sprung and reupholstered the sofa, meaning to sell it on, but had never got around to it. Its soft, comfortable embrace acted as a magnet. Bill and Lucy both lounged in cosiness and companionship while Clive spread himself out on the big Turkish rug in front of the fireplace. Bill looked around this room full of old furniture and pictures, all polished and looking loved again after Lucy's efforts.

'I never come in here normally,' he said. 'Silly, really. You live so long in a place and somehow you don't really see it anymore. Well, I do now, thanks to your magic touch.'

'Magic touch!' cried Lucy. 'Elbow grease and a good dose of polish, more like.' But she laughed, and so did Bill.

'The bugger of living alone is that you just tread the same path,' mused Bill. 'You do the same things after work, sit in the same chair, eat the same grub, and then stagger off to bed. Life just becomes a series of habits.'

Lucy understood this; her own life had been one long, dismal, lonely habit until Bill had turned up, clipboard in hand, and opened up doors that had been slammed shut for years.

After a while, Bill said decisively, 'Tomorrow we register and insure that tank of a car of yours. I'll do it in my name and have you as a named driver; that way I can do most of it over the phone. Then we'll have a run into Taunton and you can buy some new clothes.'

'Why?' asked Lucy in surprise.

'We're going to need a couple of old oak panels to repair the back of the damaged chair and create one for the new chair. And that means scouring a few auctions and having a bit of a tickle round some sale rooms.'

'And the new clothes for me?'

'Arrr, sweet wench. *You* are going to be the one who buys the stuff. I'm too well known and if I'm seen sniffing around, word will get out that I'm working on something special. And we are going to keep our heads so far down on this bloody job, we shall have eyes in our arses.'

Lucy laughed and soon afterwards went off to bed.

Before he locked up, Bill took Clive for one last walk and a pipe. He still missed Bess terribly, of course, but he couldn't help liking the daft bugger all the same. The warm summer night air was fragrant; moths flittered and bats streaked silently across the yard as they walked under the old yew and into the small garden. There stood the cherry tree under which Bess was buried, a slight breeze causing the leaves to move as if in greeting. Bill stood there for a while, remembering her and the days before his illness and Skates, both of which had crept into his world like some malevolent trailing vine, determined to stifle and destroy everything.

Turning back towards his house with a sigh, Bill looked up and saw in the grey mass of stone one lit window. A warm light behind faded curtains: Lucy's room. Well, thought Bill, at least I'm not alone anymore.

Chapter 16

MONDAY, 10 SEPTEMBER

On Monday morning Bill decided it was time for Lucy and Miss Templeton to be properly introduced. Bill had told her about the old lady who lived in the cottage up the lane, but Lucy had never actually seen her. Once or twice, as she had moved around the yard or taken Clive for a walk, she had felt she was being watched. No, not watched, but *observed*. There was a difference. So it was with some trepidation, as if she was being summoned to the headmistress's study, that she followed Bill up the leafy lane.

Miss Templeton saw them before they saw her and came out of the gate to meet them. In the back of Lucy's mind had been a vision of some old crone complete with black pointy hat and cauldron. She had never mentioned it, of course, because Bill obviously held the woman in much esteem, but the image was there cackling away whenever Miss Templeton's name had been mentioned.

What she saw now was an elderly lady, thin and straight as a pencil, but obviously full of vitality. True, her grey hair was pinned back in a bun, but she was wearing bright, colourful clothes that looked downright exotic in this English garden.

The most striking thing about her, though, were her eyes. They shone like bright blue sapphires from under a brow lined with age, and Lucy had the impression they could see right inside her head.

Miss Templeton held out her hand; Lucy took it, fighting down the urge to curtsy. Miss Templeton smiled and said, 'I have seen you and your dog about the place, young lady. Are you a relative of Mr Sawyer's?'

Quite why she answered the way she did, Lucy could never explain, but she said simply, 'No, Miss Templeton. I'm in hiding and Bill has given me sanctuary.'

Bill was about to protest or at least try to explain, but Miss Templeton stopped him by saying, 'Ah, that's what I thought, my dear. And you chose the right word; this hill is a place of sanctuary for all of us in one way or another.'

She then made just enough fuss over Clive for him not to feel left out and, for the first time in all the years Bill had known her, invited them in to take tea.

They were shown in through a small, well-swept backyard in which there was a large kennel and run Bill had built for the times when Bess stayed there. Clive went into this without any fuss and was rewarded with a large bone.

Built as a gamekeeper's cottage in Edwardian times when the land it was on was part of a great estate, Miss Templeton's small house had all the charm that resulted from the lavish attention to detail paid by builders in those days. Fretwork gables and decorated brickwork sat under a high slate roof.

Inside the house, they sat in Miss Templeton's kitchen, which was obviously the room she used the most. A scrubbed deal table and four chairs on a rag rug took up the middle of the room. An old Aga stove sat within a fireplace next to which was a neat pile of logs. One wall was all shelves upon which were books, bowls, cups, jugs, and ranks of Kilner jars filled with heaven only knew what. Bunches of herbs hung from hooks in neat rows and scented the room with the fragrance of summer. There was a butler sink with one tap above, and a large cupboard took up a good part of one wall. No fridge, no hot water by the look of it, and no electric cooker. It was like stepping back into the 1950s, or even the 1940s. Bill bet that somewhere there was a meat safe just like his mother had when he was a kid.

The only decorative elements in the room were on the mantelpiece over the fireplace. On this, in between two old Berwick figurines, were several framed photographs, some in silver and others in wood or Bakelite. They were mostly of groups of women, some in uniform, but all, dating by the clothing styles, from around the early 1940s. Miss Templeton saw Bill looking at them and came and stood by his side.

'All dead now except me,' she said matter-of-factly. She then invited them to sit down and began to make the tea. When it was done, she put a brown teapot on the table, got mugs down from the shelves, and poured out. When they were all served, she took one of the photographs down and handed it to Lucy. 'That's me in the roll-neck jumper and coverall,' she said.

The photograph showed a slim woman with her hair pulled back (in a bun, Lucy assumed) looking directly at the camera. Wearing no discernible makeup, Miss Templeton's face was nevertheless flawless, with eyes that were bright and intelligent, and a full mouth with just a hint of a smile playing at the corners.

Lucy looked at Miss Templeton. The eyes were the same, but they were now surrounded by wrinkles. Her lips had lost their voluptuousness, and her mouth was now straight as a knife edge.

As if reading her thoughts, Miss Templeton said, 'Yes, 'in me thou seest the twilight', as Mr Shakespeare puts it. I've never minded losing whatever looks I once had, but I do resent not being as fit and agile as I was in that photo.'

Lucy looked at the picture again and this time noticed that the boiler suit Miss Templeton wore was set off with a very serviceable web belt and pistol holster.

'The gun . . . was that usual, Miss Templeton?'

The old lady's eyes twinkled with mischief and memory. 'It certainly was for some of us, dear.'

'SOE?' asked Bill.

Miss Templeton only nodded, then leaned over and pointed at the photograph in Lucy's hand. 'I was very fond of the big chap on my right, but he had a wife back in Prague. We didn't know it then, but she had been shot by the Gestapo a few weeks before that picture was taken. By the time I found that out, so had he.'

This was said without any pathos, but Lucy was still unable to respond. Miss Templeton then dispelled the awkward silence with a statement that changed the subject utterly.

'You have visitors who are not always welcome,' she said.

Before either of them could reply, she continued, 'When and if you wish to tell me more, I will always be ready to listen, but either way I shall, of course, look out for you as I have always done. I might not be as active as I once was but I still have excellent eyesight and I'm happy to put it to good use.'

She then took them to her attic room, three flights up and originally built as an observation point for the gamekeeper.

It had clear views across the fields on three sides of the house.

'It used to give almost a complete view of the land all around, but trees have grown since it was built so now I can see only some parts through my field glasses,' she told them.

Bill could see over the hedges and into his yard. There was also a clear view of the road and the parts of the lane that were not obscured by trees. No wonder she had been able to tell him he had had unwanted visitors last month! He picked up a pair of binoculars that were lying on a very serviceable stand that could be wheeled around the room.

'I thought you'd like those, Mr Sawyer. German Navy, the best. Spoils of war,' Miss Templeton said, laughing quietly.

As they were leaving, she invited Lucy to call again. Bill said nothing, but in all the years he had lived there he had never seen anyone other than the postman go up the lane to her cottage.

As they walked home Bill said, 'Well, I think you've made a new friend up there on the hill. One more on our side, eh?'

'She's lovely,' said Lucy. 'And I didn't dare ask in front of her, but what's SOE?'

'Special Operations Executive. Top secret during the war. They had very advanced views on women in armed combat. Did a lot of undercover stuff with various resistance networks.'

Bill's voice lowered automatically as he added, 'Extremely high fatality rate.'

Next on the list was insuring Lucy's car, which didn't take long. That done, they loaded Clive and his kit into the big Volvo and drove to Taunton, about an hour away.

Bill had fought down his disgust and taken a wodge of Skates's money out of the dreaded envelope. It helped him to think about what some of this cash would be spent on. It had been years since Lucy had bought herself clothes from anywhere but a charity shop. When she had lived with Skates he had clothed her as he might have done a dummy, primarily to show off his wealth. And some of those garments were for his and Warren's pleasure, certainly not hers.

When he told Lucy that it was actually Skates who was paying for this treat, she went to work with a will. And there was no doubt the lady had taste. She didn't go for the latest fashions, but for classic style and quality. Breeding will out, thought Bill, and Lucy undoubtedly came from the sort of people who knew what to wear in addition to what fork to use. When Bill saw all the bags Lucy accumulated from the various shops he was glad all he had to do was wait outside with Clive.

'What about you?' Lucy asked. 'Aren't you going to get anything?'

'Got everything I need,' he answered.

Lucy said nothing but darted into M&S and eventually came out with a carrier bag, which she handed to Bill. They went to a pub, ordered lunch, and sat in the garden so Clive could be with them. After they ate, Bill peeked inside the bag and nearly choked.

'How did you know I wear that sort? And shirts as well! I normally go to a market stall for them.'

'I washed your only other pair along with your shirts before you were up this morning, and all they're good for is rags.'

'Bloody hell,' thought Bill, 'I'm under new management, all right.'

That afternoon they hit the auction houses. There were five in Taunton: one was top notch, up there with the West End crowd; two were good county houses where the gentleman farmer bought and sold; and two were indifferent to dodgy. Bill was known in them all, so it was Lucy who slipped in and collected the catalogues for the next sales.

On the journey back they stopped at a nice hostelry and turned some of Skates's money into a really grand meal. Clive was watered and left in the car, but he looked at Lucy with such sad eyes that she not only asked for a doggy bag for the steak she had left on her plate, but also inveigled the nice young waiter to see if there were any unwanted bones in the kitchen.

Lucy was on top form. She had had a wonderful day and told Bill so, repeatedly. He drove home, she fell asleep, and Clive put his head out of the back window and enjoyed the night air.

Chapter 17

TUESDAY, 11 SEPTEMBER

B ill spent the next day sorting what old oak he had in his workshop. Lucy explored the depths of the barn and ferreted around in dark corners, emerging regularly with cobweb-covered and dust-encrusted treasures that she would ask him about excitedly. He had never worked with anybody who had such a thirst for knowledge, and although it slowed things down, he was happy to tell her everything she wanted to know.

That afternoon, when he walked behind one of the outbuildings that backed onto the meadow, he saw Lucy sitting on the grass, leaning against the sun-warmed stone wall, reading one of his books on antiques. He thought she looked about eighteen years old. He said nothing, turned, and, smiling to himself, walked back into the cool dark of his workshop. She was getting hooked.

His audit of timber complete, Bill decided he probably had enough of the right lengths of old oak to do all of the straight pieces, but panels for the carved back of the new chair would have to be sourced. He had been through the sale catalogues they got from the auction houses and seen two items that might just do. Both were chests.

One, listed as Jacobean, was being auctioned by Taunton's top-dollar dealers, Messrs Teasel and Oats, Fine Antiques and Auctions Since 1950, or so their catalogue proclaimed. They were known in the trade as 'Weasel and Stoats' but the business was, in fact, run by one Tristram Hoare-Bennet. He was ex-public school with all the right connections and as sharp as knives. He sold mostly to serious collectors.

The other chest was listed as being a 'large coffer or blanket chest, possibly seventeenth century'. It was being auctioned by Fortnum's Fine Arts, a concern run by two brothers, Harry and Dave Snelling. Their handle in the trade was 'the Smellings', not because they had problems with body odour but because some of their deals really stank. Both brothers were as bent as nine bob notes, one of them having done time in years past for selling stolen goods.

As Bill had explained to Lucy, he could not be seen to have any interest in the chests because it would arouse speculation and might be remembered later, so she would be the one doing the bidding. Bill was sure that with only a small amount of coaching she could do the job, but the fact remained that he would have to look at both chests himself to make sure they were indeed what was needed.

Both sale rooms held a preview the day before their auctions, but Bill wanted to play it safe and avoid those as well if he could. Teasel's auction was on Thursday, which meant the preview would be held on Wednesday (the Smellings' auction was not until Saturday). Bill knew one of the porters at Teasel's and, more importantly, knew where this bloke did his drinking. Therefore, it was decided that Bill would drive to Taunton that evening and slip his contact a £20 note for a preview of the preview. Fortunately, this auction also had a set of top-notch Chippendale chairs up for sale; if Bill could get into the store room, ostensibly to weigh these up, he could just 'happen' to spot the chest and give it a quick once over.

But when he got to Taunton there was good news and bad news. The good news was that his pal the porter was indeed at his usual pub enjoying a quiet pint. The bad news was that he no longer worked for Teasel and Oats.

Just on the off chance, Bill walked around to the auction warehouse after leaving the pub. This was down a side street at the back of the sale room and had huge wooden doors the height of the building. In one of them was a small wicket door, and standing by this was a dealer he knew. The man was acting like someone outside a brothel, looking left and right, up and down, as shifty as hell.

Bill sidled up, clapped a hand on his shoulder, and said, 'You naughty man, Morris. You're not waiting here for a sneaky once over, are you?'

Before the man could answer, the wicket door opened a little way and a florid face under a flat cap peeked out. Bill didn't know him, which was a bonus, and he squeezed through the door close behind Morris, who was still recovering from the shock of Bill materializing out of nowhere.

'Who the hell are you?' enquired flat cap.

'I'm with him,' said Bill, pointing at Morris and edging further into the big warehouse. 'We're married, you know, been like it for years.'

'I wasn't told,' said flat cap truculently.

Bill eased a £10 note from his pocket into the man's hand

with the skill of a conjurer. With a grunt and a scowl, flat cap muttered something about them only having half an hour, and went back into his office somewhere in the gloom.

'What the fuck are you doing here?' hissed Morris. 'I thought you had retired.'

'I have, but I know someone who's after a nice set of Chips for their dining room.'

'You sod off, that's why I'm here,' said Morris. Then he added with avarice aforethought, 'How much are they willing to give? Maybe we could split the deal if there's enough meat on the bone.'

'That depends. Who else is dipping their wick on this lot?'

'The usual, I expect, but these are going to make big money so it narrows the field a bit.'

They walked down aisles of furniture and long tables piled high with goods. At last, finding the Chippendale chairs, Morris began lifting aside the sheets that covered them. He took out a small torch and, bending down, started to examine them in detail. Bill looked as closely as he could in the dim light and thought they were indeed good chairs. He didn't recognise them, and he would have done if he had been part of their recent history. So, big bucks then.

Morris turned to him and said, 'These are out of your league, Bill, unless you know something I don't.'

'I thought I might,' said Bill, 'but now I've seen them I'm pretty sure they're not the ones I was thinking of.'

With that, Bill drifted off as though the reason he had gate-crashed was no longer important. Morris stayed with the chairs, looking even harder in case there was something dodgy about them.

Bill mooched around, occasionally picking up bits to examine in a half-hearted way. As he moved to the part of the warehouse where flat cap had his lair, he saw the man's face was glued to a television screen, and he slipped quietly past.

Then he saw it. With no dust sheet on it, the dark polished wooden chest sat solidly on its base as it might have done since the time of James I. Even from a few feet away it looked right to Bill, and when he got closer he knew by the carving and patina that it was the real thing. In the half-light it was impossible to tell for sure, but Bill thought it had been catalogued incorrectly. Its size gave it away; this was at least five feet long by two-and-a-half feet wide and a couple of feet deep. Also, there was no large key hole as there would have been on a regular chest or coffer. No, in his mind this was a blanket chest. The three side panels had some nice linen fold carving on them, but they were large enough for his purposes.

Bill moved on up the aisle. He could see Morris's torch across the room; he was having his own rummage round. Bill decided to make his way down a different aisle and come back to the chest another way. If the base or top were from one piece of wood, then that alone might swing it. The side panels were carved, after all, and might not have enough meat on them for carving anew. No, it was the top or bottom that he would base his decision on.

Morris was now making his way towards the small office; his business done, he wanted to get out before anyone else crashed his party. Bill moved quickly back to the chest, but only had time for a brief look at the top. It was solid, no decoration, some cracks, but it looked original to the rest of the piece.

He caught up with Morris by the door and they exited like

a pair of prisoners escaping from a nick, looking round in case anyone they knew saw them. Bill suggested they go for a pint. Morris looked at Bill in his old tweed jacket and shabby cord trousers and declined the offer, which Bill had been pretty sure he would.

Morris walked off, but Bill stayed behind, ostensibly to see what kind of car Morris was driving these days. It was a big Jag, the poncy bastard. Fair enough, crime pays, thought Bill, and started to bang on the door. Eventually, flat cap poked his ugly head out, scowling like a bulldog with piles. Bill gave an embarrassed smile and ingratiatingly asked if he could step inside just for a second because he had dropped his keys somewhere.

'What do you mean, *somewhere*?' snarled the merry porter. 'This place is huge and I'm not putting the fucking lights on just so you can wander about. They'll be seen by all and fucking sundry and then that's me in the shit again.'

Bill told the man he was pretty sure he knew where he had dropped them. It was only £5 this time as Bill didn't want to look too keen. He asked if he could borrow a torch and you would have thought he had asked for the man's wallet by the fuss he made, but eventually a torch was grudgingly passed across.

In its dim light Bill looked around the floor by the Chippendale chairs. Old flat cap had gone back to his hole and his television by the time Bill got to the blanket chest. Being as quick as he could, he measured the lid with the span of his hands and then lifted it up. One big piece of timber and, yes, some cracks, there were bound to be, but nothing that couldn't be lived with. The bottom of the chest had been repaired in times past. It was made up of planks and they looked like another wood entirely and not polished at all. Good enough.

He made his way to the office, returned the torch, and was virtually thrown out of the building.

'See you again soon, I hope,' said Bill.

'Fuck off,' said flat cap, and slammed the door shut behind him.

It was late when Bill got home, and the house was in darkness. As he unlocked the kitchen door and put the lights on, he saw the kitchen table was laid for two, and there, in his armchair by the stove, was Lucy, blinking up at him. She had obviously been asleep.

Bill said, 'Sorry I'm late, love, got held up.'

As Lucy put a pile of sandwiches on the table and made a fresh pot of tea, the domesticity of it all struck him. It was like that bit in the middle of a tornado, he thought: the place that was calm while everything else swirled around and around in a destructive circle.

Bill took out his notebook and drew a plan of the blanket chest using the rough measurements he had taken. It would do the job, but he really didn't like the idea of destroying such a nice object just for the lid. It seemed criminal somehow.

Lucy was far more pragmatic.

'It's us or it,' she said.

Chapter 18

WEDNESDAY–FRIDAY,
12–14 SEPTEMBER

B ill awoke tired on Wednesday morning, having slept badly the night before due to his anxieties about the auction. Over breakfast, he shared his concerns with Lucy, his primary one being that the Jacobean chest might go for big money.

'A chest doesn't have the same desirability as some other antique furniture,' he said, 'but Weasel and Stoats don't sell cheap antiques, and if someone outside the trade really wants the thing, then it could go for a lot more than it's really worth. And if something goes for a lot more than it's really worth, then it gets talked about and possibly remembered somewhere down the road. For example, when some exceptionally rare chairs turn up and are being authenticated.'

Bill's estimate for the chest was in the region of £800. If he had still been in the trade and there was a dealer's ring at the sale, he could have called in a favour or three and maybe got it for £300–£500. But, with Lucy doing the bidding, a greedy auctioneer might bounce bids off the wall to drive the price up. That was the bugger of having the general public bidding at auctions: if someone got a bee in their bonnet and just *had* to have the piece under the hammer, then no one was at home to Mr Prudence and silly prices were paid. Bill decided they could bid up to a thousand, which was far more than the chest was probably worth, but they had to have a ceiling.

Lucy managed to calm him down a little bit and suggested he give some thought to what the other auction house was selling, just in case. The catalogue only described the item as a 'large coffer or blanket chest, possibly seventeenth century' and gave the measurements, which were about the same as Teasel's Jacobean chest. The Snellings' auction was being held on a Saturday, however, which told Bill it was much more downmarket than Teasel's and would probably have hundreds of lots, most of them junk from house clearances.

They spent the rest of the day preparing for the first auction as much as they could. Lucy went upstairs and tried on the outfit she had bought for the occasion. With her hair worn loose and a pair of fashionably large sunglasses perched on her head, she felt reasonably pleased with the result. She felt even more pleased when, as she came downstairs to show Bill, he exclaimed, 'Bloody hell, girl, you look the business!'

He wasn't simply being polite, either. Lucy didn't just look good, she looked *expensive*. She had seemed almost emaciated to Bill the first time he saw her back in London, but now, in these clothes, her thinness would be taken as an indication of wealth rather than hard living.

Thursday morning they lodged Clive with Miss Templeton and headed off to Taunton. They arrived at Teasel's about an hour before the auction was due to start and Bill parked as far away from the building as he could. Lucy's car was pretty inconspicuous, but he was still mindful of the danger of his being seen and recognized.

Lucy went inside about half an hour before the start of the auction, registered as a buyer, received her bidding card, and was ushered into a big, oblong room that reminded her of a theatre or church. There was a low stage at one end with a viewing platform in the middle and spotlights above it. On one side of this stood the auctioneer's lectern, and on the other a couple of tables with a row of telephones for the auction house staff. Wide aisles either side of the seats led from front to back, and the seats themselves were placed in rows facing the stage. The main entrance was right at the back, around which there was enough space for people to stand and observe the proceedings.

Bill had said this was a big, prestigious auction with many valuable items up for sale; it would therefore be well attended. Thankfully, the lot number for the chest was after the Chippindale chairs, and he thought the place might empty a bit once these had been sold.

Lucy positioned herself at the side of the room closest to the auctioneer and stood near the wall. From here she would be able to catch the auctioneer's eye while also being able to see who else was bidding. That is, if they made it obvious. Bill had told her some silly buggers, mostly rank amateurs, thought they looked like big players if they bid with a raised eyebrow or a slightly lifted finger. The only thing likely to come of that, he said, was a lost bid.

The room was filling up quickly, and soon people were sidling along the wall near Lucy, looking for seats. It was the same on the other side of the room, and there was a clump of people standing at the back as well. The room was buzzing with conversations as people came in and milled about.

She was gently nudged by a rather county lady, who asked her if she had a spare catalogue. As she turned to answer, Lucy heard a voice that made her freeze. Thankfully, her back was to the main door, where the voice was coming from, and there were a lot of people between her and that part of the room. She carefully turned her head just a fraction and, out of the corner of her eye, saw Skates standing in the doorway, talking to an elderly couple.

There was no mistaking him, and although she was not in his direct line of sight at the moment, she knew she had to get out of that place before he made his way further into the room. He appeared to be alone, but Warren might be right behind him, or perhaps waiting outside in the car. Either way, she had to do something, and quickly.

The auctioneer had mounted the podium, and porters were carrying the first lot onto the display plinth. Lucy lowered her sunglasses, then edged towards the wall, slightly behind a portly gentleman who was leaning out to get a better view. Once the auction started and all eyes were on the stage in front, she made her way to the back of the hall. Her passage was slow because people were crowded in the aisle, in some cases right up to the rows of seats, but she wormed her way through, muttering quiet apologies as she did so.

To her incredible relief, at the end of the room she found a closed door that had 'Toilets' written on it. She dared not turn around to see if Skates had spotted her, so just opened the door and went in.

Lucy found herself in a short corridor that had a gents on one side and a ladies on the other, and a door at the end marked 'Private'. She entered the ladies and locked herself in a cubicle, then sat and wondered if she should stay there until the end of the auction. She quickly realized, however, that if Skates had seen her, he would be outside the door she had entered no matter how long she waited.

She went back into the corridor and tried the door marked 'Private', praying it wouldn't simply be full of brooms. It was locked. Desperate now, Lucy gave it a good, hard kick. It sprang open, the blessedly puny catch on the other side giving way.

Quickly closing the door behind her, she found herself in a small office full of filing cabinets. Luckily, there was also another door, this one unlocked, through which was a larger office containing a desk and other executive trimmings but, more important, a door marked 'Fire Escape'. It had a crash bar that opened without a crash, thank goodness, and Lucy was at last outside the building.

She stood in a small car park that looked like it must have been for staff only as it was a mixture of small family saloons, plus one enormous Rolls. Adjusting her hair and with her sunglasses still down, Lucy took a deep breath and, looking like she owned the place, walked out into the street. She followed this round till she came to the entrance to the big public car park in front of the auction house. In the disabled bay near the main entrance was Skates's Range Rover. No one was in it. She walked slowly and carefully, looking round all the while in case Skates or Warren were lying in wait somewhere. They weren't and her car was where she left it. No sign of Bill, though.

As she reached the car, he emerged from the other side of the car park where he had been hiding behind a small van. They got into the Volvo and, without a word or a backwards glance, drove out and away. Nothing was said until they stopped at a small pub outside Taunton. Then, sitting in the garden with a couple of pints and a packet of crisps, they exchanged stories.

Bill had seen Skates pull up and go into the auction. He could not follow as there were too many other people milling about the entrance, some of whom he knew. He was in a blind panic and considered finding a phone box and calling the fire brigade, saying he saw smoke coming from the building. He hid behind the van so he could see all the car park and the main entrance, and was just about to see if he could get in anywhere else when Lucy turned up. They both reckoned that if Skates had spotted Lucy, he would have done something about it then and there, so he must not have. It had been a hell of a close shave, though.

One thing was decided: Bill would have to purchase a mobile phone. He hated the idea and had always resisted getting one no matter how hard his daughter-in-law had pressed him to do so. He had one phone that was at the end of a perfectly serviceable landline, and from this he and Sid had run an extension into the workshop. That was as mobile as he ever wanted to be, and the last thing he needed was some bloody instrument squawking at him when he was out and about, invading his privacy and probably souring his beer. Lucy told him there was no way she was going through that ordeal again, however, so he caved in.

It was late afternoon by the time they got home, and they were both exhausted from the strain. After collecting Clive from Miss Templeton's, they took a bottle of wine and some sandwiches and picnicked on the field's edge. Clive enjoyed a manic half hour in the pasture before coming back to the pair of them to see if he could cadge a snack, which of course he did.

On Friday they made the trip into Yeovil and found a shop that sold mobile phones and other mysterious devices.

They purchased a simple phone for each of them and all the arcane paraphernalia necessary to keep them working. Bill paid cash and asked for a discount, which was politely refused. When they were back home, Lucy showed Bill how to work the thing, and he slipped it into his top jacket pocket.

'Not in the same pocket as your pipe, Bill, dear,' said Lucy.

That afternoon they started sorting through the wood Bill had culled from his collection as being suitable for Skates's chairs. Lucy held a piece of the badly damaged chair in her hands. It was an armrest that Bill would have to rebuild. She felt the smooth, silky surface that had been created by countless hands and arms rubbing against it for hundreds of years.

'Look at that wood,' said Bill. 'See the long, dark grain? That's English oak, and from a good-sized branch, too. The wood in your hand now was a sapling when Henry IV was king about fourteen hundred and something. The tree this came from grew for at least 130 years before it was cut down.'

Lucy watched Bill as he told her about the way such oaks were felled and then cut up for use, and how his own name, Sawyer, came from one who had done such tasks. Talking about his craft, sharing his knowledge, the years didn't exactly drop away from him, but his illness did, and Lucy caught a glimpse of the man Bill had been before sickness and Skates had invaded his life.

He leaned against the stone wall, smoking his pipe and musing.

'Now, whoever made these chairs knew his joints and how to cut them right; the sort of skills only a good craftsman would have. But not top drawer. Local man, local timber. Whoever made these chairs would have used whatever wood of the right sort he could get his hands on. Just like we're going to do.'

Chapter 19

SATURDAY, 15 SEPTEMBER

Saturday morning was bright and full of sunshine. Lucy took Clive up to his 'dacha', as Miss Templeton called it, then she and Bill set off for the Snelling Brothers auction. They arrived early enough to see the wares stacked in the yard of the so-called showroom. It was, in fact, a former garage on the outskirts of Taunton set amidst dodgy double glazers and other businesses that relied on gullible customers seeking cheap deals.

The showroom's wide glass doors were rolled back, and the big forecourt was being used as the sales floor. The auctioneer's podium was set just inside the showroom where it could be seen above the crowd and yet remain dry if it rained. Just like the 'Smellings', thought Bill: they stay dry while their punters get soaked. Well, being punters of the Smellings, they were in for a soaking, anyway, if they weren't careful.

Lucy was well dressed, but not as expensively as for the previous auction, and she had added a large, wide-brimmed straw hat. The plan was for Bill to go in a little while after her and do a wander round in a leisurely, disinterested sort of way. If he saw anyone he knew or was accosted by either of the brothers Snelling, he would say he was just there to get a feel on prices as he was planning to shift some stuff he had accumulated over the years.

All the larger lots, including the chest they had come for, were in rows near the auctioneer's podium. Bill noted some more modern pieces of furniture and a nice set of 19th-century mahogany dining chairs. The smaller stuff was piled here and there on trestle tables. The way Snelling Brothers auctions worked was that numbers were chalked on the lots, and as the numbers were called, a porter would go around and, if he felt like it, hold up the small items so they could be seen by the bidders at the back. Larger lots would be pointed at, sometimes.

The place was filling up quickly, and with so many people milling about it was easy for Bill to stand in the lee of the wall nearest the chest and, lighting his pipe, become just another onlooker. Then, puffing away and trying not to cough his lungs up, he wandered over to the chest.

As he went forward to have a look, so did a grey-haired man in a battered pork pie hat. Next to the chest was a wooden crate containing a pile of ancient hand tools. The man picked up a rusted old G-clamp and showed it to Bill, who now stood opposite him.

'Look at that,' said the man in disgust. 'Makes my heart bleed to see a useful bit of kit allowed to get into this state.'

Bill agreed and, taking the clamp, looked at it and then absent-mindedly placed it on the lid of the chest. The man continued to root around, so Bill asked him if there were any spoke shaves in the box.

'Hang on,' he said, and delved further.

This gave Bill a chance to lift the lid of the chest and peer inside as if he was more interested in what it might contain than the chest itself. He had a very good visual memory and studied his quarry as well as he could in the few seconds he had. There was some carving to the front, but the lid was plain and appeared to be made from a single piece of timber. Whether the chest was true Jacobean or a Victorian copy, however, it was impossible to tell based on such a cursory examination. One good thing was that the bottom of the chest had small feet (and they had been knocked about, which should reduce its value to anyone else), but the floor itself looked reasonable. The size was right, and the two planks that made up the back looked like they were still almost rough-sawn on the inner side, which meant they had been handmade rather than machined.

'Nah,' said the old boy, emerging from the box and rubbing red muck from his hands. 'A couple of claw hammers and a load of drill bits all stuck together. Nothing but scrap iron now,' he added sadly.

Bill threw the old G-clamp back into the box, nodded to the man, and walked away. He went right round the other side of the yard and nestled up close to a drainpipe in a shadowy place on the wall, the most inconspicuous spot he could find. He was almost out of sight of the auctioneer's podium, and there were any number of people in between. All he wanted now was to be able to see Lucy. Based on the information he had been able to glean, they needed that chest.

The auction started, and the big stuff was going through much more quickly than Bill had thought it would. The only long bidding joust was over the nice set of chairs, and he was able to see the bidders from where he stood. One was a probable dealer and the other a punter on a mission. The latter was a big woman with a helmet of tightly permed hair under a headscarf. Bill thought she looked a bit 'horsey'. After each bid she glared around like a bulldog with a bone, daring anyone to bid against her.

There was still no sign of Lucy. Bill kept looking out for the big straw hat among the throng and was therefore surprised to have it suddenly materialize right in front of him. Lucy had meandered up to stand with her back to him as she looked into the sales area. There were a few other people in their vicinity, all with their faces turned like sunflowers to where Harry Snelling was doing his stuff. Lucy turned around with a cigarette in her hand as if to ask him for a light. Bloody hell, he thought, she's really living her part today!

As he proffered her a light, she asked him quietly, 'Yes or no?' He nodded yes.

'How far?' she murmured through the smoke, all calm, cool, and lovely.

'As far as it takes,' he replied softly, relighting his pipe.

Lucy turned away and moved to the middle of the sales floor, where it would be easy to make eye contact with the auctioneer. Bill stayed where he was, nervously watching the show and trying to spot other bidders who might damage their chances of winning the chest.

Gradually, the lots were whittled away. Nothing was making really big money, which pleased Bill. Then the chest was up at last, and because there were no photographs in the catalogue, Snelling described it for those too far away to see the thing for themselves.

'An antique chest, possibly early, possibly not, but a nice chest all the same, and we all like a nice chest, don't we?' he tittered and smirked. 'The size being three feet by two feet six inches and some eighteen inches high. With some very fine rustic carving to the front panel and, ladies and gentlemen, a beautifully polished surface that with just a little TLC will render this piece an heirloom to cherish. Probably oak with only the merest hint of wear and tear as is often found on a piece of furniture of this age.'

The majority of the crowd took no more notice of this item than they had of the other lots, but Bill saw a few stiffen and adjust their stance to get a sight line on the auctioneer. From where he stood he counted five possibles, including Mrs Bulldog.

Standing near her, Bill saw the man in the tweed cap, the one who had looked at the tools with him. He pushed his way to the man's side and nodded a greeting.

Snelling beamed down at the crowd in front of his podium. 'Let's start the bidding with two hundred pounds, then.'

No response.

'One hundred, then. This really is a nice chest and would make a good blanket box.'

Still nothing.

Undeterred, Snelling grinned like a loon and suggested fifty pounds.

At that, several hands went up.

Smelling, seeing a number of bids at fifty, started going up in twenties. Eventually he reached £210, and at this point only two people were still bidding: some punter well down in front and Mrs Bulldog. Bill had told Lucy to hold fire until only one bidder remained.

Bill turned to his neighbour and, in a louder voice than he

would normally use in such a place, said to him, 'Bloody hell, that's a lot of money for a worm-eaten old box, ain't it?'

The man in the pork pie hat was still thinking of the box of tools they had been examining and obviously had not been paying attention to what was being bid on.

'Damn right,' he said. 'Full of worm and falling apart! Anybody'd be daft to give more than a fiver for the thing!'

Bill saw the headscarf turn slightly in their direction.

'Full of worm, you're right,' he said. 'Get that in yer house and you'll be infested in no time.'

'Two hundred and ten pounds I have, ladies and gentleman, two hundred and ten pounds, any advance on two hundred and ten pounds?'

Whoever had been bidding down in front must have dropped out, leaving Mrs Bulldog in the lead and looking very uncomfortable.

Come on Lucy, thought Bill, get in there.

'Two hundred ten pounds once,' said Snelling and raised his gavel. Bill couldn't see Lucy from where he stood now, but Snelling must have done.

'New bid, two hundred and thirty?' Lucy must have agreed because he went on, 'Two hundred and thirty now, any advance on two hundred and thirty pounds for this nice old chest?'

Bill's heart was thumping. He saw Mrs Bulldog stir as if it required a physical effort for her to let someone else win an item she had shown interest in, but then the seed of doubt planted by Bill's remarks took root, and she stood stock still and silent.

'Two hundred and thirty pounds it is, then. Two hundred and thirty going once, going twice, sold!'

And bang went the gavel on the podium top. Bill breathed

out, then slid away through the crowds and outside of the yard, where he lit his pipe and waited for his heart rate to return to normal.

It was another hour before he saw Lucy, followed by a weedy porter and some other minion carrying the chest to her car. She looked triumphant and oh so ladylike. With a gracious smile, she tipped the two men. Bill waited until they had gone, then walked to the car and got into the passenger side.

Lucy, her big straw hat now in the back on top of the chest, put her arms around Bill's neck and gave him a huge, smacking kiss.

'We've done it! We've bloody well done it!' she exclaimed, then started the engine and drove away at such a speed that Bill was pushed back into his seat.

They stopped in a layby outside of Taunton and covered the chest with blankets. Bill didn't dare look too hard at their prize yet just in case it was a dud, so they drove straight home and carried it into the workshop, where he could examine it properly.

Lucy walked up to Miss Templeton's and collected Clive, then returned to the farm and made a pot of tea. She brought two mugs and a plate of biscuits out to the workshop, where Bill was busy with a magnifying glass. Every now and again he would point something out to Lucy, puff on his pipe, cough a little, and get close in again.

Finally, he sat back and said, 'It's old, but probably not Elizabethan. More like Jacobean, which is a good bit later. The bottom is rough and has had some damage a while back. There are stains on the wood that look like it could have had a soaking donkey's years ago.'

'But is it any good? Can we use it?'

'Yes, it's all here. Enough good wood to make two chair backs if we need to, especially with what we've already got in the workshop. Now all we have to do is make the damned things.'

'How long will it take?'

'A month; possibly a bit less, probably a bit more. A lot depends on how quickly we can get the back panels carved.'

'So, October if all goes well.'

'I'd say more early November, just to build in a bit of buggerage, but we'll get it done as soon as we can, that's for sure. I want this job out of the way and those bastards out of our lives just as soon as possible.'

After supper that night, Bill lit his pipe and took Clive for a walk. They made the now-traditional circuit around the field at the back of the barn, then Clive was allowed to sniff round the yard on his own while Bill made a stop at Bess's grave under the old cherry tree.

As he stood there, he contemplated a plan that had been growing in his mind these last few days. A plan that Lucy would probably not like one little bit, but one that, for her sake, might just have to be put into play. Finally, having made his decision, he heaved a sigh, said goodnight to Bess, rounded up Clive, and went inside.

Chapter 20

SUNDAY, 16 SEPTEMBER

The weather was not quite as good the next day, but it was good enough that Lucy was not made suspicious by Bill's suggestion that they take a trip to the seaside to celebrate their triumph at the auction and recruit their strength before starting work on the chairs. He had told Lucy about his visit to Seaton with his family earlier that summer and now, he said, he wanted to show it to her.

They went in Lucy's Volvo, which was much more comfortable than Bill's old van. This he hid up in the dark depths of one of the cow sheds with a tarpaulin over it. He reckoned if he wasn't at home, his van shouldn't be, either.

They reached Seaton before lunch and did an explore. It was the first time Lucy had been to the seaside in years. She seemed to like the place, and the fact that she could let Clive off his lead to make an arse of himself chasing the waves was a real bonus. No big hotel, no big pubs, and no big crowds. Just a few flocks of old biddies hobbling around like penguins in woollen cardigans clutching enormous handbags. It would do, thought Bill. Skates would no more visit this place than he would a church hall jumble sale.

Bill and Lucy mooched around, looked in some of the junk shops, and strolled along the prom. Lucy was back in jeans but wearing a new waxed jacket. Bill wore his usual tweed one. Some people took them for father and daughter, but others assumed they were husband and wife. All Bill and Lucy knew was that they were enjoying this time together in a place where they didn't have to worry about prying eyes.

Lucy found a fossil and Clive found a friend. The latter was a small, delicate, well-manicured poodle that was whisked away by a stern-looking matron as soon as she determined that Clive's intentions were definitely not honourable. Lucy dragged Clive back, apologising as she did so.

Bill asked her if Clive had been 'done'.

Lucy said yes, certainly he had been 'done'.

'Shame no one told him.'

After a pub lunch, Bill suggested a drive to the caravan park that was halfway up the headland on the only bit of level ground before the summit, ostensibly to look at the view. At the entrance to the site was a large wooden building with a sign over its brightly painted door that read 'Harmony Caravans and Camping', under which, in rainbow letters, was written 'Peace and Harmony'. Under that, in much smaller black letters, was printed 'All Dogs On Leads'.

Bill parked as far away from the wooden building as he could, near a wide footpath marked with a sign saying 'Solstice Walk and Headland'. He suggested Lucy take Clive for a jaunt along this path while he saved his breath for his pipe. He would admire the view from here.

As soon as she was out of sight, Bill walked across the car park to the building at the entrance. Behind and slightly to one side of the wooden building was a long brick one with its own concrete footpath that was well signed as being 'showers'. It had a strong, municipal smell and a small copse of Tibetan prayer flags planted to one side. As he watched them flutter in the breeze, Bill hoped some of them represented prayers for the prevention or healing of verrucas and other such blocks to spiritual enlightenment.

There was no one else about, and the warm sea breeze rustled the long, dry grasses that grew up all around. A sort of street lamp stood opposite the brightly painted door and bore a hand-painted sign advertising 'Tarot Readings'. In the big window that looked out onto the car park was another sign, this one letting people know there was 'Crystal Healing' on offer.

When Bill opened the door, a small bell chimed his arrival. He entered a large room and saw a counter in front of him on which were the usual dispensers holding tourist guides, maps, and other holiday bumf. The front was decorated with old posters in a psychedelic riot of yesterday's dreams. There were bookshelves round the walls over which bright lettering declared them to be a 'Free Library' and encouraged people to 'Bring and Borrow'. The shelves were full of books, paperbacks, magazines, and comics.

In the middle of the room was a small coffee table on which more pamphlets were spread, an armchair with a vast, multicoloured blanket over it, and a long and seriously decrepit sofa similarly draped in a riotous variety of coloured throws. The low wooden ceiling was hung with mobiles made of driftwood and feathers, along with threaded shells that put Bill in mind of small bleached skulls.

It was a bit 'alternative' for his taste, and yet something

about it was so pleasing that he smiled as he walked into the big room. From behind the counter where he had been curled up in rattan saucer chair rose one of the tallest men Bill had ever seen. He was wearing faded denims that were mostly patches, and his hair was long, grey, and tied in a ponytail that reached well below his waist. Bill put him at about fifty, but that was only a rough guess as the man's long beard hid most of his features. What it didn't hide, however, were clear, penetrating eyes behind round, metal-framed glasses.

Putting his book down on the counter in front of him, the man gave Bill an engaging smile and a slight bow and, in a warm voice just tinged with an American accent, said, 'Greetings, friend. Are you here for a booking or to fix the damned door on number 53?'

It never surprised Bill that he was so often taken for a tradesman. He might as well have worn dungarees and a flat cap, and carried a spanner or tool bag.

'Looking at renting a caravan for a month or so,' he said.

'The season's moving on,' said the man with a sigh, and for a moment Bill feared he would take out a guitar and start crooning some folk song about the end of summer, but he soon recovered. 'Yep, we got enough. For how many?'

'Big as you've got and with a loo if possible. Oh, and there's also a dog, but he's well-behaved.' Bill actually crossed his fingers when he said that. Clive was well-behaved, of course, on occasion. But then so were the hordes of Genghis Khan, on occasion.

'It's something we can talk about,' said the tall man noncommittally. Moving out from behind the counter, he put his hand out and introduced himself as Dylan, then ushered Bill to the armchair and lowered himself onto the sofa. As he did so, the bell over the door shook musically, and Lucy walked in.

She saw Bill sitting there and said, 'I've put Clive in the car. The window's open, but he could really do with a drink.'

Dylan, who had risen from the sofa upon Lucy's entrance, now put his head slightly to one side like an inquisitive heron and looked at her. Lucy looked back. She spoke a bare millisecond before he did.

'Dylan?'

'Lucy?'

And with that he walked forward and enveloped her in his long arms. Bill felt very surprised and, to his horror, a bit jealous, but also suddenly less worried. In fact, if was reading the scene right, this development could be very helpful to the success of his plan.

Dylan untangled himself from Lucy and, still muttering 'how wonderful', 'how super', and other genuine platitudes, went through a door behind the counter and emerged with a big aluminium bowl brimming with water. He and Lucy went out the door, and soon Bill heard Clive being given nearly as warm a greeting as Lucy had received.

When Dylan and Lucy came back in, they both sat on the sofa, Dylan with his long frame tilted sideways towards Lucy, and Lucy with her back towards the arm of the sofa and her hands round her knees. As Bill had guessed, these two had met in the Peace Convoy when Lucy had first left home. She had been befriended by Dylan's girlfriend, Gabby, who had guided her through the first difficult weeks when there were more than enough randy buggers desperate to introduce her to a bit of 'free love' in all its moist and interesting guises. Dylan and Gabby had looked after Lucy, regarding her as family, almost.

When the convoy was broken up, Dylan and Gabby had looked for Lucy, but with American passports they were vulnerable to deportation, so they had split as soon as they could and headed west, where they bummed about for a bit doing a bit of busking here and there before settling down in Glastonbury and getting married. They opened a shop and used their contacts in America to import crystals and semiprecious stones from Mexico and Arizona which they sold at a huge markup along with Tibetan bells, incense sticks, and other mystic paraphernalia.

'We became born-again capitalists,' said Dylan. 'What happened to you?'

'Lots,' Lucy replied. 'Most of it shit. No, to tell the truth, all of it shit, until I met Bill.'

Dylan turned and looked with renewed interest at Bill, who for the first time in decades was in real danger of blushing.

Lucy then asked about Gabby, and the look of interest on Dylan's face dissolved into one of sadness. 'She died two years ago,' he said. 'Breast cancer.'

Lucy leaned forward and took his hand. Dylan went on to say they had bought this site about three years ago, hoping to turn it into a healing centre for those who wanted a spiritual dimension to their holidays. 'It's on the right ley lines, and the natural energy levels are so good in this part of the country.'

It was late afternoon by now, and Dylan suggested they should stay for dinner. Lucy seemed to like the idea; it was obvious to Bill that she had found not only an old friend, but someone who was part of her life before Skates and therefore not tainted by history. Bill was up for it, too, because he had not yet broached the subject of why he had really brought Lucy here.

They moved to Dylan's mobile home, which was just three rooms long but somehow felt huge. The central room was full of books, pictures, sculptures, and other treasured flotsam, and a table not unlike the one in Bill's kitchen. Everything was lit by gas lamps that cast a gentle glow and reminded Bill of his grandmother's cottage before she had got electricity.

They sat around the table eating fish and chips from a nearby shop, Lucy and Dylan drinking wine while Bill had something ethnic and fruitful because he would be driving later. 'Tastes quite nice,' he thought, 'but I'm bloody glad I'll be near my own toilet tonight!'

Of course Dylan wanted to know what Lucy was doing these days and received a very high-level overview of her and Bill's situations. Lucy wasn't exactly on the run from her ex-husband, but she was endeavouring to lay low, and Bill was having trouble with a dodgy client.

Finally the conversation hit a lull, and Dylan asked, 'So what do you need a caravan for?'

Lucy looked at Bill, at first with surprised laughter in her eyes, sure there had been some misunderstanding, and then, when he only looked at his feet instead of meeting her gaze, with growing suspicion. Dylan looked from one to the other of them and felt extremely uncomfortable.

Finally, Bill looked up at Lucy and said gently, 'The thing is, love, I really think it would be better, safer I mean, if you got away for a while.'

Lucy said nothing. Bill hurried to put more words into the gap that had suddenly opened up between them. 'Think of all the close calls we've already had,' he begged. 'We can't risk it, lass, we just can't.'

'For a while or forever?' asked Lucy in a voice so cold it froze the air around her words.

'Of course not forever!' He got up and went to her, taking both her hands in his. 'When the chairs are finished, we'll settle up with Skates, and I need you beside me for that, I really do.'

'And how will we do that?' asked Lucy, thawing slightly.

But Bill would not be drawn on that subject yet, especially not in front of Dylan. The truth was he had only the roughest idea of any end game, but it was obvious that Skates and Warren would have to be neutralised somehow if he and Lucy were ever to have any peace again.

Dylan halted any further discussion by saying that Lucy was more than welcome to stay if she wanted to, and there was a spare caravan she could use. He also made it quite clear that as far as he was concerned, everything was on a need-to-know basis. He was happy to provide a safe haven but doubted he had any other talents they could call on. That was good enough for Bill, and it mollified Lucy somewhat, but it was not a happy lady who sat next to him in almost complete silence the entire journey home.

As ever, caution ruled, and Bill turned his headlights off before driving slowly up the lane to the yard entrance. There were no other lights nearby, and the house was in darkness. Bill stopped the car and checked a couple of the surreptitious markers he had set up to tell him if someone had driven into the yard since they had left. Someone had.

He switched off the engine and felt for the large spanner he kept in the car door pocket. Holding this makeshift weapon, he got out and motioned for Lucy to lock the doors and stay in the vehicle. Lucy being Lucy, she immediately got out and followed him.

They both knew the place so well that the starlight alone was sufficient for their purposes. They searched the yard and tested the lock on the workshop, then moved on to the house. They found all secure, and there was no sign that any lock or door had been tampered with.

What there was, however, right in front of the kitchen door, was a red metal petrol can with a box of matches placed neatly on top of it.

Chapter 21

MONDAY, 17 SEPTEMBER

On Monday morning Bill walked up to Miss Templeton's to ask if she had seen or heard anything the night before. She told him she hadn't seen anything, but had heard the sound of a motorbike just as she was going to bed at a little after ten o'clock.

Lucy was still not happy about leaving, and oddly enough the nasty little hint from Skates made things harder for her rather than easier. 'I feel like I'm running away and leaving you to face everything alone,' she told Bill.

'You're not running away, lass,' he replied. 'You're not even retreating. We're just clearing the decks for action.'

They discussed how Bill should react to the can of petrol. Lucy recommended he telephone Skates and do his best to sound like a man in fear who had made up his mind to do as he was told. She said Skates wouldn't let up until he was sure Bill had been whipped into submission.

The phone call was almost one-sided. Skates was brusque at first, but when Bill told him the job was under way and progressing as well as could be expected and he needed no reminders of that sort again, thank you very much, Skates became greasily conciliatory. He actually asked if he could stop by on Friday to see how things were going. Bill had no choice but to say yes.

When he put the phone down, Bill's hands were sweating, and his cough and chest pain had come back with a vengeance. He told Lucy it wasn't so much that he was scared; he was just so *angry* it made him feel physically ill.

Lucy considered digging in her heels and refusing to leave, but she understood the reasoning behind the move and, more importantly, she knew how much it would upset Bill if she didn't go. So they established times to telephone and a code for Bill to use in case he was unable to speak freely. Yes, his phone was charged; yes, he would always have it with him; yes, he would be careful. Then, with a hug and a quick kiss, she was gone.

Bill sat in his kitchen and felt more alone than he had in years. His eyes went around the room, conjuring up visions of Lucy at the stove, at the sink, sitting at the table opposite him with a mug of tea in her hand, Clive between them looking up expectantly but patiently, knowing there would eventually be furtive handouts from one or both of them. Suddenly he felt like an old man. A sick old man.

But not a beaten one, he finally decided, and the sooner he got to work the sooner Lucy would be back.

For the rest of the day, Bill did all those things one does to put off whatever it is one should be doing. It was always like this to a greater or lesser degree, depending on the work in hand. Like a cat having a shit, he thought, as he brought out chisels to test their edge and gathered up all the other tools he might need when he finally got down to actually working instead of just preparing.

Finally, he decided he needed a drink and, more importantly, a bit of company. It had been weeks since he had been to the pub. It hadn't occurred to him to go when Lucy was around, and in any case he wouldn't take anyone he really liked to that hole, but right now it suited his mood.

He walked out of his workshop into a half-hearted rain. For some reason, probably due to his sudden loneliness, Bill caught himself looking around for Bess. She had always made this journey with him, walking jauntily and looking forward to her customary biscuit when they reached their destination. But she wasn't there tonight, and never would be again.

When Bill finally got to the bar, he ordered two glasses of gin in addition to his usual cider. He took them to the table in the back room where he knew Sid would be and, without saying a word, poured one into his glass and one into Sid's.

'Blimey,' said Sid. 'We hanging one on tonight?'

'No, just need warming up.'

'It's cold as a witch's tit, all right,' said Sid, but he watched very closely as Bill took out his pipe and filled it from his battered tobacco pouch, and didn't like what he saw.

'Been a while since you've been in,' he said evenly. 'Saw you in a beat-up Volvo with some bird last week. What's that all about?'

'Not what you think,' said Bill firmly.

Sid could tell that subject was closed, so he said no more. But he continued wondering.

Bill took a large swig of his cider and looked at Sid. 'I need to build a pole lathe. You game to help?'

'Bloody hell,' said Sid, 'Never seen you use one of them before.

Making something special, are we?' And then he murmured in a singsong voice, 'Something old, something new, something dodgy, someone screwed.'

'Fuck off,' said Bill, but he smiled. 'It's just a repro job that has to be done right.'

He took another swallow, another puff, and a sideways look at Sid, who sat comfortable in his skin, rolling a cigarette the size and elegance of a piano leg.

'I want to set up a pole lathe in the back of my workshop. The light is better there and I can keep out of the weather.'

He said 'weather' but Sid knew he meant 'sight'.

'I want you to rig me up some sort of spring that will act as the pole but not be as hard to work as the real thing.'

Sid said nothing, just lit his rollup and went to the bar for another round. As Bill waited for him to return, he suddenly realized he was feeling quite a bit better and was somewhat surprised to see that his gin-laced cider had evaporated. No wonder his world was, in a small way at least, a better place than when he first came in.

Sid sat down with all the ease and elegance of a man who didn't give a shit, dropping into his chair like a sack of bricks, and regarded Bill from under his bushy eyebrows.

'I smell a game afoot.'

'No,' said Bill, 'just a paying job.'

Sid gave up for the moment and they discussed various options in regard to the pole lathe. Sid said it might be two or three weeks before he could get over as the Frigging Brigadier had a bigger than usual project going. Bill said that was fine.

After a little while, Bill got up and prepared to leave, then, as if just thinking of it, said, 'Remember that desk you helped me get back from the house clearance in Wooton? Heavy bugger with a secret drawer we only found when we tipped the thing up on its side to get it into the van.'

'Yeah,' replied Sid, 'and apart from the bloody hernia I got lifting the damn thing, that drawer nearly broke me toe.'

He stopped suddenly as he remembered what had fallen out of that drawer.

'Christ, you still got that?'

'Yes,' said Bill. 'Never did get rid of it. Don't know why. Just thought it might come in useful someday.'

'Useful! A bloody great revolver of that age, useful! What for, shooting elephants?'

'No, but I might need to sort out some vermin. You told me once your dad left one like it in his garden shed from when he was in the home guard. You still got it?'

'The thing was all rusted to buggery, so I threw it. Why?'

'No real reason. Did you chuck that box of ammo that went with it?'

'Still there, I expect,' said Sid, then looked at Bill long and hard. 'Shall I bring it with me?'

'Why not? Probably the wrong sort, but it won't hurt to find out.'

Bill patted Sid gently on his balding pate and left the George. It was still drizzling with rain as he walked back home, but he whistled a merry tune as he went.

Chapter 22

TUESDAY–FRIDAY, 18–21 SEPTEMBER

On Tuesday Bill had a letter telling him he had an appointment with the oncologist at the hospital on the 27th. He decided not to think about it right now and pinned it on the wall next to the calendar.

He spent the next couple of days carefully disassembling the damaged chair, taking measurements, and making detailed drawings. It was a slow, painstaking process. He had part of the carved back panel and one good baluster-turned arm support and armrest. The seat itself was split; that really didn't matter in a piece of furniture this old. But all the stretchers that separated and supported the chair legs were broken, and he only had one acceptable baluster-turned leg.

In an effort to get some way inside the mind of the man who had made the chair, Bill measured the parts using the width of his thumb as a guide. When this chair was made, a craftsman measured by eye and hand. The width of a thumb was about one inch; the span of a hand, nine inches. The distance from nose to fingertip or the length of a man's pace was a yard.

With Skates due to visit on Friday, Bill wanted the job to

look as complicated as he could make it. He knew that once he was no longer any use to Skates, he would probably be silenced, one way or another. At the moment Skates regarded him as cowed and beaten and wanting to finish this job, get paid, and go back to being a sick old man eking out what little life he had left. But for now he was needed, and that gave him some time to manoeuvre. These thoughts went round and round in Bill's mind as his hands worked on loosening the chair's joints and dissolving the glues that had held them in place for over 400 years.

He would need to match the baluster turning on the originals, but with Sid on board to make the pole lathe, that should be no real problem. What was a problem, however, was his health. He was not eating properly; on his own he never did. Old habits die hard, and there are not many vitamins in shop-bought pasties and pies, eaten cold as often as not.

Lucy had only been gone for a couple of days, but he had already reverted to 'old man living alone' mode. One plate used for every meal and washed up when needed. Ditto one set of eating irons and one mug. The whisky bottle now sat next to the big, budget-sized bottle of brown sauce and the mustard jar that had an ochre encrustation around its lid like some impasto refugee from an impressionist painting.

He and Lucy talked by telephone each evening, which helped a little. Dylan was keeping her busy repainting some of the caravans, and Clive had the run of the place. Bill told her about the progress he was making with the chairs. What he didn't tell her was that his coughing had gotten worse, so much so that he hardly liked to light his pipe now of an evening.

Bill knew things were really going downhill when he found

himself picking up his battered copy of *Lord of the Rings*. He knew the book backwards and only reached for it when life was seriously getting him down. When he came to 'Tom sodding Bombadil' and found himself singing along, half pissed, he knew things were getting serious.

Somehow he had to get Lucy back sooner rather than later.

After a long night of deep thought, he set to work with a renewed will, and by Friday morning he had the two good chairs and all the components of the damaged chair spread out on the big bench in the middle of the workshop, illuminated by strong lights.

He made a few other arrangements in preparation for Skates's visit, then did a bit of tidying up in the house and grounds. Every time he walked through his yard he avoided the spot where Bess had been killed. There was no mark on the cement, but there was in his heart, and when he saw the big Range Rover drive up that afternoon, he felt the bile rise in his throat.

Both Warren and Skates got out. Warren was wearing a black leather jacket that looked very expensive. If anything, he looked more menacing than when Bill had last seen him. Skates himself was dressed in a way that indicated real money and a good tailor. Smart, smooth, and deceptively casual.

Bill had a small hammer in the pocket of his jacket that he knew would be as much use as a chocolate kettle if it came to mixing it with these two bastards, but it gave him some comfort anyway. The old shotgun was within easy reach in his workshop, hidden away where he could get to it if things took a dangerous turn. He didn't really think it would come to that, however; not with the little show he had arranged for their entertainment.

Bill did not smile; he left that to Skates, who did it for all of them. There were no greetings and no handshakes; they just followed him into his workshop where they could see the chairs under the bright lights. The stars of the show. Bill stood behind the bench on which the chairs and components were placed as if he was going to give a lecture. And in a way, that's just what he did. It was impersonal, factual, and comprehensive.

Warren stood just behind and to one side of Skates, looking at him rather than at Bill or the chairs. He was always simmering with rage, always on the edge. Even the way he stood, poised on the balls of his feet like a boxer or street fighter, showed this. Bill couldn't imagine the man in repose; he probably slept clenched.

Skates asked how long the job would take now that Bill had all the components separated.

'I'd say a month or a bit more, depending on how things go. I'll be erecting a pole lathe so as to make the baluster-turned legs and arm supports look contemporary with the rest of the damaged chair. But then there's the problem of the back panels. The one that's split can be repaired and I have the right wood to make the new panel but, as I told you before, someone else will have to do the carving.'

'Yes,' said Skates, 'and you said you knew a man around here who was up to it. I think using someone in London would be better. I don't want anyone to even *wonder* if this job has anything to do with me.'

'There's only one person I know of who is capable of doing this kind of carving and that's Eric Howler. He drinks too much and he smells bad, but there's no one else good enough, not even in London. Besides, if it's secrecy you're concerned about, the London antiques community is so bloody incestuous you can't even visit a couple of markets without someone gossiping about it.'

Skates smiled at that and took his point.

'Besides, I'll take the work to Eric's shop and he'll have no reason to come here. He lives on the outskirts of Chard and from what I hear he's on another driving ban, so it's unlikely he would in any case.'

It was agreed that Bill would commission the work for the new back panel and oversee the project. Skates wanted Eric's address and Bill had no hesitation in giving it to him. He had no love for Eric and sometimes two birds can indeed be stuffed with one packet of sage and onion.

Bill straightened up. 'One last thing,' he said. 'You will not come here again until I call and ask you to, and that probably won't be until I have the finished chairs to show you.'

Both Skates and Warren stared at him as though he was suddenly speaking a foreign language.

'This is my home and I am not well. If you want me to finish this job before I die, I need to be able to work without worrying about some fucking lunatic prowling around and popping up like a rat in a lavatory bowl. I will do the job, you will stay away. This is not negotiable.'

Warren lost it. He sprang towards Bill, who was still behind the big bench.

'No, you fucking don't,' said Bill, who was suddenly holding a full petrol can in one hand and its top in the other.

He lay the can down on the bench and its contents flowed out, pouring around the chairs and the components and onto the floor around him. Despite the fact that he was now standing in a growing pool of petrol, Bill lit his old Zippo lighter and held it aloft.

The stench of the fuel was overpowering and the pool had widened until it nearly reached Skates's feet. He stepped back, pulling Warren with him.

'Don't be stupid, Bill,' he said quietly.

Bill was now shaking with fury and strain. The fumes were really getting to him. His chest was constricted, his breathing laboured, but still he stood defying them. Anger and shame – shame that he had allowed these swine to kill Bess and threaten his family – drove a rage that lent him the strength to dominate these bastards, if only for a short while. He had been pushed around and menaced for too long. If he didn't make a stand now, he would be forced to do anything they demanded.

Besides, he wanted Lucy back.

Bill came around to the front of the bench. The petrol had flowed across the concrete floor and was almost at the door where Skates and Warren now stood. The air was a little better here.

'He who can destroy a thing, controls a thing,' he said. 'I read that in a book once. Never really got it until you left that can of petrol outside my door. Well, I control these fucking chairs, get that?'

Skates nodded, then turned to Warren and told him to go to the car. Warren glared at Bill, but obeyed.

'Tell me what you want, Bill,' Skates said, his voice low and mollifying. Not pleading, but seemingly aware that he might have pushed Bill a bit too far, for now at any rate.

'I'll do this job my way or not at all. No fucking about, no sending your nasty playmate over, no calling in uninvited.'

Skates nodded in agreement.

'I'm doing this for two reasons and two reasons only. One, after this I retire, and if I'm going to retire I want to put my tools down after doing something really special. These chairs are really special. You might not care about that, but I do.'

Skates nodded again.

'Two, you pay me the twenty thousand you promised me.'

Skates nodded a third time, then turned, walked to the big Range Rover, and climbed into the front passenger seat. Not much of Warren could be seen in the interior of the vehicle except a pair of white knuckles gripping the top of the steering wheel. Bill liked that. Wind the bugger up tight enough and he'd tear his own bollocks off trying to get at you. Something to bear in mind.

Skates lowered the car window and said politely, 'Phone me if you need anything, and I would like to be kept informed as to how things are going.'

Bill nodded, and they drove away. As they disappeared from sight, he nearly collapsed to the ground, but managed to stagger to the kitchen, where he slumped down on a chair, exhausted both physically and emotionally. His trousers smelt of petrol, so he changed them, throwing the old pair outside.

Then he got out the bottle of whiskey. Then he burst out laughing. Then he called Lucy.

~~~

It was nearly seven that evening when Lucy arrived. Bill saw her drive in and went out to meet her. She threw her arms about him in an almighty hug that nearly knocked the breath out of him. Clive ran around them in frenzied circles of happiness.

Then they were in the kitchen, Lucy sitting opposite Bill once more, holding his work-worn hands, her face aglow with joy at seeing him again. As the tea brewed, Bill explained all that had happened that afternoon. On the phone he had only said that he had sent Skates away with a flea in his ear. Now he told her the situation had got a bit 'incendiary', then laughed himself into a coughing fit.

When he was able to continue, he said, 'It was that petrol can that finally gave me the idea. Skates has dabbled in a bit of arson himself, so I figured threatening to set fire to his precious chairs would make him think a bit. I took him through all the work that needed to be done to the chairs, just to whet his appetite, then I sprang on him what I wanted. To be left alone to finish the job.'

'Just like Greta Garbo,' said Lucy with a grin.

'Then Warren lost it and went for me, but I'd worked out the distances and that bench would take some getting over, especially with the chairs on top. The cap was off the petrol can and my lighter was filled and ready in my pocket,' he said, standing up and adopting a Statue of Liberty pose, a big grin all over his ruddy face.

'Did the petrol harm the chairs at all?'

'Ah, the petrol, said Bill, with a twinkle in his eye. 'The thing is, my lovely friend, there was only ever about a cup full. Well, maybe a bit more, but not a whole can, not how that bastard left it when he stuck it outside our door. You see, petrol is lighter than water and just sits on top while the water goes all over the place. Enough water to cover the bench and flow all over the floor, and enough petrol to stink the place out. When liquid comes pouring out of a petrol can, especially a petrol can that you yourself filled to put the frighteners on, you don't stop to wonder if that liquid is actually petrol.'

Lucy lavished praise on him for his cleverness, eventually ending with, 'But it really was an awful risk, Bill.'

'Aye, lass, but I had to find some way to get you . . . to get him to leave me alone.' Bill paused to clear his throat and glanced sideways at Lucy, whose eyes were suddenly, inexplicably filling with tears.

'Besides,' he went on, 'I doubt I'm well enough to do everything on my own now. I'll be needing an assistant to do some of the donkey work.'

Lucy hit him with the tea towel.

'Skilled donkey work,' he added quickly.

Chapter 23

SATURDAY–WEDNESDAY,
22–26 SEPTEMBER

The next day they discussed whether they could trust Skates to keep his side of the bargain. Lucy thought they could up to a point. He might not make an unannounced visit himself, but that didn't mean Warren wouldn't. Besides, Skates undoubtedly had other men in his pay, so they decided to devote a few days to taking what security measures they could.

After putting Lucy's car into the cart shed and draping a dusty plastic sheet over it to get it out of sight, they took a good look at all the other buildings and sheds that skirted the yard to see where someone might hide. They secured all the doors as best they could, even if it was only with wire and bailing twine. Over some doors they nailed sheets of corrugated iron, planks, or scaffold boards, then hung empty tin cans and bottles in places where they would drop and make noise if the doors were forced open.

Then they focussed on cleaning up the large steel gate that was half hidden by weeds and undergrowth against one wall by the entrance to the farmyard. The hinges were corroded, and the metal bars red with rust and age. But with a bit of bodging and a lot of grease they got it closed, and it did the job of keeping vehicles out once again.

On Tuesday they went around the fields that bordered the house and buildings. Both Bill and Lucy knew them well as places to walk the dog and see a bit of the local flora and fauna, but neither of them had ever walked the land with an eye as to what someone who had been sent to spy might be able to see. They were girded by ancient hedges that had marked the boundaries on this landscape for centuries. Amongst the hawthorn, blackthorn, hazel, dogwood, and spindle there were oaks that had stood there when horses were the only form of transport. Amidst the hedges stood ash trees; once pollarded for their upright poles, they now spread leafy fingers to the sky. The hedges were hardly ever trimmed or cut back and were full of wildlife of all sorts. Hugh Dawlish, who owned all the farmland around, was a man who liked his shooting, and these hedges gave good cover to his game. They would also give equally good cover to anyone approaching Bill's home and workplace.

As they walked back to the meadow gate, it was nearing dusk. The air was chilly; soon autumn would colour the trees and vegetation in russets and gold. Bill looked up the hill, and there at the top he could see the roof and the dormer window of Miss Templeton's attic. He waved just in case she was sitting up there watching out for them as she had said she would.

~~~

On Wednesday Lucy went off in the estate car to do a big shop at the large supermarket about half an hour's drive away. Bill was in and out of the barn, getting it ready for Sid to set up the pole lathe. Clive was following him around and generally getting under his feet. What with swearing at the dog, then relenting and throwing an old tennis ball for him, then clearing a space for the pole lathe amidst the benches and trestles, he was hot, out of breath, and not in the best of moods when he heard a car drive in.

The gate into the lane was open to let Lucy back in, but she hadn't been gone long enough and he could only think it must be Skates or Warren turning up to make a point. He'd give them a fucking point all right, he thought, and picked up a rusty pitchfork he had unearthed from behind a pile of lumber. He held it in front of him like a spear and walked out of the dark workshop into bright sunlight.

He stopped a short way into the yard and there, petting Lucy's dog, was his grandson. He threw the pitchfork aside and went towards the boy. By this time Gloria had got out of her car and was walking towards him. Thankfully, she had not noticed what was in his hand when he came out of the building. Her eyes were on her son, who was entwined with a large mutt; the two had obviously decided to be the very best of friends as evidenced by furious petting and hugging by one party and joyful tail wagging and face licking by the other. One small, delighted boy and one foolish but ecstatic dog. It was smashing, if lacking in hygiene, so Bill and Gloria went into the kitchen, where he sat down to get his breath back while she made a pot of tea.

If Gloria was surprised that Bill had got a new dog so soon after Bess's death she didn't say so, but Bill knew she must be wondering.

'Not mine,' he told her. 'Belongs to a friend of mine. Clive, he's called.'

If Bill had not been so knackered, he might have put that differently. As it was, he simply went on to tell Gloria that he had a friend staying with him who was helping out about the place, doing a bit of cooking and housekeeping.

Gloria looked around the big kitchen. It was certainly much cleaner and brighter than she had ever known it. No dirty dishes piled up on the draining board. No saucepans filled with water while they soaked on top of the stove. No underwear or shirts draped over chairs to dry. Yes, there was quite a difference. The flowers in an old enamel water jug in the middle of the table certainly were a difference. Cut flowers, beautifully arranged, and in a ruddy vase, even! This Clive, she thought, must be quite a chap.

'A good sort, this Clive?' she asked.

'Oh, he's all right,' replied Bill. 'A bit daft. Friendly enough, though.' He sat back in his chair, sipping his tea. 'A little too young and boisterous for my taste is all,' he added with a smile.

Gloria was spared further confusion by a car driving in and stopping close to the open kitchen door. Bill got up and walked outside followed closely by Gloria, who saw a large, slightly battered, green Volvo estate car with a blonde woman bending over its open tailgate gathering up a large number of shopping bags.

Bill walked up to the woman with comfortable ease and, turning to Gloria, introduced Lucy.

'She's the friend who's staying with me for a while,' he said, and smiled benignly at them both. He then bent down to hug his grandson, who had run up with Clive.

Lucy had heard about Bill's family, of course, and been

shown photographs of them. Gloria, on the other hand, had had no idea of Lucy's existence. One minute her father-in-law was quietly leading a bachelor's existence, and the next he had a woman living with him who was young enough to be his daughter!

She tried not to stare despite her surprise, but still took in every detail, from Lucy's long, fair hair tied back in a casual ponytail to her close-fitting jeans and oversized, multicoloured jumper. Bill was oblivious throughout this examination, but Lucy was not. She knew she was being weighed up and guessed that Bill had never told his family about her. Well, that was Bill; the art of communication was not his strong suit except when it came to his precious bits of wood.

Leaving the boy and the dog playing, they went inside and sat round the big kitchen table. Bill sat in his usual place. Lucy sat at the far end of the table and watched as Gloria make a fresh pot of tea.

Bill was nonplussed. He had assumed that by some strange osmosis Gloria would know all about Lucy. He had never made a secret of her, had he? But of course he had. Insofar as it was possible, Lucy had been hidden from everyone and it now dawned on him that this included his family. He looked down into his mug of tea and then across the table at the two women silently sitting opposite one another and knew he had mishandled the situation.

Lucy sat forward, her arms on the table, hands playing with an old silver spoon, turning it round and round as it caught the light. She looked slightly anxious while Gloria, her usual elegant self, gazed at her and Bill in turn.

Finally, Lucy followed her instincts and told Gloria pretty

much what she had told Dylan: she wasn't exactly on the run from her ex-husband, but she needed some peace and quiet in her life and the only way for her to get it was to be where he couldn't find her.

When Gloria asked how they knew each other, Bill said they had 'mutual acquaintances in the antiques trade'. This seemed to satisfy Gloria, who looked at Lucy with much less suspicion now. She and Phillip had been worried about him not taking proper care of himself, especially lately. The cleanliness and comfort she now saw all around her spoke volumes for Lucy's ability to 'do' for Bill, and if he could repay her by providing a safe haven, it looked like being an excellent bargain on both sides.

After a little more small talk, Gloria said it was time for her and Jack to head home. Leading the way into the yard, Bill veered off to where dog and boy were still engaged in a game with the old tennis ball and joined in so the two women could have a chance to talk without him around.

They did, for quite a long time, and Bill was pleased to see that any reservations Gloria might have had must have been allayed. In fact, at one point he heard them both roar with laughter at something one of them said. (He asked Lucy later what had been so funny, but she pretended not to remember.) As Gloria and Jack drove away, Lucy stood beside him, smiling and waving.

Over dinner, Bill told Lucy more about his family and, in doing so, made her feel slightly more a part of it. She knew she still had to be hidden away from most eyes, but now that his family knew of her, she felt a lot less isolated. Bill understood this now and was grateful that Gloria had called by. One little problem solved, he thought, as he sipped a small whisky before bed.

But as he undressed that night, a bigger one loomed: the bloody hospital. Tomorrow was the day of his appointment with the oncologist. He knew his health was deteriorating, and he was sure Lucy had noticed it, too. Sometimes he caught her looking at him when the coughing got bad or when he couldn't finish the meal she had placed in front of him. His chest hurt almost all the time now, and he was weaker than he ever remembered being. He felt this illness as a personal affront; his own body was letting him down just when he needed all his faculties more than at any other time in his sixty-seven years.

Chapter 24

THURSDAY, 27 SEPTEMBER

On a rainy Thursday afternoon, Bill drove himself to the hospital. As he wandered through labyrinthine corridors, medicos hurried by, their white coats flapping like wings. Nurses wearing crisp uniforms, sensible shoes, and utilitarian smiles passed silently by. Porters moved blanket-swathed lumps from place to place on beds and trolleys, the wheels of which squeaked and rattled as if warning the unwary of their passage. Visitors who knew where they were going moved purposefully with expressions of faith, hope, and charity. Others, like himself, looked anxious and awkward as they negotiated their journeys to consulting rooms or treatment centres.

In the Oncology Department, the wait for out patients was endless, or so it seemed to Bill as he sat in his hard plastic chair. There were rows of them, their pale blues, greens, and reds scuffed and tired but still the most colourful things in this drab, sad area. Waiting along with him were other patients, some with friends or relatives. Hardly anyone made eye contact; conversations were hushed. The hot, stuffy room had no windows through which one might see a world going about its normal, ordinary, pain-free business.

Eventually Bill's name was called, and a nurse showed him into a tiny, cramped consulting room, the walls of which were covered with posters, charts, and signs warning against smoking and other terminal recreational pursuits. A white-coated young man (Bill thought he looked about fourteen) got up from a small desk that was set against one wall and shook Bill's hand. The desk held a large computer screen, piles of medical notes, and a pencil pot bearing a withered note asking that its pens not be taken. It was empty. Bill thought of putting in one of the big, square carpenter's pencils he always kept in his jacket, but didn't. Instead, he sat down in the chair next to the desk, his back against the shabby wall, and looked up at the doctor.

The doctor looked back at Bill and saw a face that was grey and lined, but with eyes that were still fiercely alive. He also saw a pipe sticking out of the top pocket of Bill's worn tweed jacket like a small, wooden periscope. This appeared to have a negative effect on his composure. He sat down at his cluttered desk, turned towards his computer screen, and fiddled with the mouse. Bill sat upright and silent, looking at the notices on the walls and occasionally at the youth in the white coat.

Finally, the doctor attempted to adopt a grave expression, one he probably copied from a senior colleague and practiced in front of a mirror. Bill thought he needed more practice as it just made him look vaguely petulant. It was clear the poor little sod was embarrassed for both of them, like a new vicar discussing unnatural desires or sex before marriage. The idea made Bill smile, which threw the medic entirely, causing him to finally blurt out that the tests Bill had taken, the X-rays, the biopsies, and all those other indignities he had endured a few weeks ago, all showed he was in the last stages of lung cancer.

He was in the median something, blah blah four, and various other things besides. His jargon meant little to Bill.

'So in other words I'm riddled with rot like an old beam and wouldn't even make good firewood. How long have I got?'

The doctor consulted his notes, fiddled with the computer again and, with many more 'err's and 'hmm's hedged round with 'might's and 'hopefully's, told Bill that, though there was no cure for the cancer that was destroying his lungs, there was treatment that could prolong his life. It would mean giving up work, smoking, drinking, and eating anything worth having, but it would prolong his life. For a while, anyway. Probably.

Bollocks to that, thought Bill, and it showed in his face.

'How long without?'

'It's difficult to say for sure,' replied the doctor, squirming as he looked down at Bill's paperwork yet again. 'Weeks. Maybe months. Certainly not years. And it will get more painful and debilitating. Of course, we can help with that, and there are other symptoms you might develop that we can mitigate to some extent.'

He stopped talking at that point, knowing that, for all practical purposes, neither he nor medical science could do fuck all. It wasn't that he was unsympathetic, he just found this old man intimidating, impenetrable, wooden. Glancing down again at his notes, he read what Bill did for a living. That was it; the man was an antique himself, all hard surfaces and dovetailed joints.

He asked Bill if he had someone who could look after him.

'I'm sorted, thanks.'

'There is help available if you apply for it,' said the young man a little desperately. 'Hospices and the like. We'll be in touch with your GP.'

He gave Bill a leaflet and a limp, apologetic goodbye. Bill folded up the leaflet and put it in his pocket, then threaded his way back through the long corridors to where his van was parked. He got in and looked through the dirty windscreen at the rows of cars and the few people who were scurrying about in the rain. His mind was strangely clear.

'That's it, then,' he said.

He drove home slowly and carefully, his mind on the road and not on what he had just been told. Driving into the yard, he closed the big metal gate behind him and went into the kitchen. Lucy was cooking. She turned to him, but before she could say anything Bill raised his hand and shook his head a little. Lucy took the hint.

He sat down heavily in the his armchair by the stove. 'I'll get this thing lit again. It'll take the chill off.'

Silently, Lucy put a mug of tea by him and went back to her cooking.

After drinking his tea, Bill got up and said he would take Clive for a walk before dinner. He changed his coat, took a walking stick from the rack, fixed Clive's lead on his collar, and went out. It had stopped raining, but everything was still wet and dripping. There was a mist over the fields, and the hedges around them were just showing the beginning of autumn. Dusk was not a long way off. Letting Clive off his lead to run himself out, Bill walked along paths he knew well and used often. Along hedges that had bounded these fields for centuries, with trees still in leaf that dripped second-hand rain on him as he passed underneath. He walked in silence through a soundless landscape that was grey-green in the soft light. Even the rooks in the trees above had ceased their quarrelling.

After a while Bill felt tired and walked to a fallen tree that had left a natural seat amidst the hedgerow: a wooden throne under a tall oak that spread its branches above. This was a place he often used to rest and look over the countryside around him. He would light his pipe and ponder things while Bess wandered off on her own for a while. A short while only, then she would silently return and Bill would feel her warmth leaning against his leg. With that memory, Bill's hand automatically reached down to pat her as he had used to do.

But she wasn't there. He was alone, and the memory of her death came like a whiplash out of the past and opened a wound in his heart that had barely begun to heal. He cracked and broke like a beam on which too much weight has been placed.

The soft machine that is the human mind can at times withstand a tempest, and at others be shattered by a single thought. Bill felt crushed and powerless. He sat, head in hands, and sobbed his heart out. He cried like a child, not caring who might hear or see him, oblivious to anything other than his regret and despair.

He thought of his son and his family. Of the grandson he loved so much and whose teenage years he would never see, nor the man he might grow into. Of the new grandchild he would never meet, never hold, never love. It broke his heart.

He also thought of those cursed chairs. He feared he would never be able to finish them now and – one way or another – remove the threat of Skates and Warren from Lucy and his family.

Finally, spent and exhausted by the emotions that had crashed through him, he became calm again. The world around him was quiet and slowly growing darker. Suddenly he felt movement and, looking down through eyes still stinging with tears, saw Clive's head in his lap. Soft brown eyes looked up at him with unmistakeable concern.

'You been talking to my old Bess? You've been learning from her, haven't you, you soft bloody fool.'

Clive blinked and swallowed in bliss as Bill's old hands caressed his ears.

It was enough. As if taking strength from the landscape around him, from the bones of the land beneath his feet, Bill rose above his cloud of despair and stood up. He had lamented his fate and grieved for his old dog and his own future. Now he had to pull himself together, to plan and scheme.

Anger gripped him like a clenched fist and gave him strength. He would survive long enough. Not clinging to the wreckage and bewailing his loss, but fighting back and giving the bastards the kicking they deserved.

'First things first,' he said, as he made his way back home. 'First things first.'

He stopped at the tree under which Bess rested. He said nothing; he didn't need to. Even Clive took a moment and just sat at his side while he stood there.

After a while, Bill said to Clive, 'Let's go see that lovely Lucy of yours.'

And after that, he would call Philip and Gloria. He knew he could no longer walk alone. If he was to succeed, he would need all the help he could get. But his heart told him it would be there, until the end.

Chapter 25

THURSDAY–SUNDAY, 27–30 SEPTEMBER

B ill walked through the door of the kitchen into warmth and light and the savoury smell of supper. Lucy was curled up in his armchair by the stove. She had been crying; the leaflet he had brought back from the hospital that afternoon was in her hand. He walked over and gently pulled her to her feet. He enfolded her in his arms and she laid her head on his shoulder.

'I hung your jacket up to dry near the stove,' she sobbed. 'The paper fell out.'

'There, girl,' he said calmly, enjoying the fragrance of her hair. 'There, girl, don't fret. What is, just is. We'll weather it, you and I.'

He held her as the tears ran down her cheeks. Finally she gave him one long, strong hug as though revelling in the warmth and reality of him, then stepped back, smiled, and wiped her eyes.

Without any more discussion, they agreed not to talk about Bill's illness or anything else that would cast a shadow on the evening. After they ate, they sat in front of the stove together, just chatting about nothing. Tomorrow was tomorrow was tomorrow. The now was comfort and companionship, with added dog. Clive lay between them basking in the heat of the stove, its warmth filling the room and the fruitwood burning within it scenting the air.

~~~

Over tea and toast the following morning, they planned. Actually, they schemed, which is far more detailed. Taking down the calendar from its nail on the kitchen wall, Bill tried to work out how long it would take him to finish the chairs. He said they would have to treat his illness as just another part of the problem. He would have no sentiment brought into the equation. It was there, and no amount of crying would make it go away.

'We factor it in as best we can, that's all,' he said. 'There's no other way, and we can't afford to get soppy about it.'

Leaning back in his chair, he rubbed his chin and reached for his pipe, which earned him a look from Lucy, but no comment.

'It's all down to time,' he said, 'and there just doesn't seem to be enough of it.'

It was Lucy who finally provided at least a hope of a solution. She told Bill to break down all the work that needed to be done into two sorts: what a novice (i.e., Lucy) could do, and what only he himself could do. As he did this, it became clear that, providing he stood by and talked her through it, there really were quite a lot of things she could do, and she was more than willing to have a go at them. This would make a difference, he said; they might gain some days, even a week this way. And the more Bill thought about it, the more he liked the idea of teaching Lucy his craft and passing on at least some of his skills to her.

The next subject of discussion was Bill's need to tell his family about his diagnosis. As difficult as that would be, they both knew it couldn't and shouldn't be put off much longer. Lucy couldn't help feeling that the best thing she could do was to leave him to get on with it in his own way, so she suggested she go visit Dylan for a day or two. Bill reluctantly yet gratefully accepted this plan, knowing it was right, but also that it cost both of them something to be apart.

The next day dawned bright, sunny, and gently warm. Bill waved Lucy and Clive through the gate, then closed it behind them and went back into the kitchen. He did very little that day; only enough to put off calling his son for as long as possible, with naps in between. But eventually he did call and suggested they get together for Sunday lunch the next day. Philip was mildly surprised, especially by Bill's instant acceptance of his offer to stop by and pick him up, but didn't ask too many questions.

The venue was definitely not the sort of place liable to be patronized by Skates, but even so Bill kept scanning the room during the meal next day. He still didn't have any idea how to tell his family what he had to tell them, and it wasn't until they got back to the farm and Jack went off with a catapult his granddad had given him (some recompense for not having that bloody dog to frolic with) that he was able to say anything about his condition. He finally decided to just tell it like it was, with no fancy wrapping and no false hope. They were intelligent people and grown up enough to take it.

Or so he thought. In the end it was him comforting Gloria while Phillip walked out into the yard. Eventually Philip came back in, red-eyed and very quiet, by which time Gloria had calmed down somewhat, though she wouldn't let go of Bill's hand.

He reassured them as much as he could. It helped that Lucy was staying with him now, and they were pleased that he had bought a mobile phone. Of course he then had to find the bloody thing to get his own and Gloria's numbers, as well as charge the battery. Still, you can't have everything, he said, as he plugged it into its charging dock, hoping it might lighten the atmosphere. It didn't. He promised he would see his doctor just as soon as he could and would keep them informed of whatever he learned. Yes, yes, he promised.

They left in the late afternoon, and Bill felt relieved to see them go. Not because he didn't love being with them, but he found it tiring to put on a brave face for so long. He was more tired now than he liked to admit, plus when a coughing fit took him he felt embarrassed by it. Stupid, he knew, but in the back of his mind lurked memories from his childhood about the way TB sufferers had been ostracised.

And he was hurting. Hurting because of the pain he was causing them, but also because he didn't like to take the painkillers he had been given. They made him feel as though his brain had been put in a sock, or belonged to someone else. Distant from the world around him. When he read on the package that you weren't supposed to operate machinery or drive if you took these pills, he nearly threw the bottle away. He didn't, though. He kept them beside his bed like a book not yet opened but there just in case.

Lucy returned and that made things a little better. Dylan had sent his kind regards, a cake, and one of his wholesome organic loaves. The cake was delicious and they shared it by way of supper. The bread, well, there was only so much goodness a bloke could take, Bill said. He would face that another day. Perhaps.

Chapter 26

MONDAY–TUESDAY,
1–2 OCTOBER

F irst thing Monday morning there was a call from his doctor's
surgery telling him to come in the next day. Wonderful,
thought Bill, with only mild sarcasm. At least Dr Hall could
be counted on to speak plainly.

After that a call, quite polite, from Skates enquiring
how things were going, please. Bill made no mention of his
condition but said he would be getting the panels to the carver
this week, probably on Wednesday. Otherwise all was going
according to plan, and he would contact Skates if he needed to.
Skates muttered something indistinct and hung up. Bill smiled
but was glad it had been he and not Lucy who had picked the
phone up. That underlined the care they still had to take.
No bad lesson, that.

So it was the doctor's on Tuesday, and then he would have
to get his arse over to Chard and see Eric on the Wednesday.
He was not looking forward to either encounter, but Eric's
would probably be the more challenging (and nauseating).

Lucy said she was up for either or both trips if Bill didn't
feel like driving. He said he'd prefer to go to the doctor's alone,

but admitted it would be a great help if she could drive him most of the way to Eric's. They would find a place close by where he could drop her off and continue on his own. As he said, Eric was a notorious gossip, and it just wouldn't be safe to let him see her with Bill, but it was really much more than that.

'The fact is, lass, Eric is not a nice man. Not a nice man at all. It's well known that he's done time, and in the 'fraternity' it's assumed his conviction had something to do with his being a carver of quality forgeries, but I know different. I know the mother of the young girl he interfered with.'

Lucy's face paled, and she put down her mug of tea with a deep, disgusted sigh.

'Aye. But he did pay for that crime. Prison is not easy on his sort. It took months for his groin to heal from the boiling water with which the inmates of Chelmsford jail baptised his crotch.'

'Well done, the inmates of Chelmsford jail,' said Lucy. 'But that doesn't really help the young girl, does it?'

'No, but it might prevent some other young girl from being hurt the same way. Or not. Anyway, as you can imagine, none of that served to curtail Eric's drinking habits, and when he gets drunk he talks. Always at the wrong time and always to the wrong people, going on and on about what jobs he's done and sometimes even for whom. Naturally, this has resulted in fewer and fewer jobs over the years, certainly from the more lucrative and sensitive end of the antiques trade. And the bugger of it all is that he's good. Really good, with a feel for wood better than most and an uncanny eye for what's right.'

This cut no ice with Lucy, but if Bill said he was the only person capable of doing the job they needed, then they'd just have to cope.

After fortifying himself with another mug of tea, Bill was finally able to bring himself to phone Eric. 'I see you're doing well enough to pay your phone bill, at least,' was his opening remark.

This was answered only by a damp sniff.

Bill told him in as few words as possible that he had a carving job for him and he'd be bringing it over on Wednesday morning.

'And if anyone else is due to visit that day, put them off. No fucking about. This is a nice, juicy job but it'll go elsewhere if I get buggered about, right?'

'Right (*sniff*),' said Eric.

When Bill put the phone down he called to Lucy, who was in the pantry doing something domestic.

'Have we got any disinfectant wipes?'

'What for?' she called back.

'I want to clean the phone. Been talking to Eric. Always makes my ears feel soiled when I've done that.'

The final call of the day was to Sid, who said he would be able to come set up the pole lathe late the following week. That was good enough for Bill as he had plenty of cutting out and other work to do before anything would need turning. He also reminded Sid about 'that little box of fireworks' they had discussed last time they met. Sid said no, he had not forgotten and, yes, he would bring them with him.

The rest of the day was spent in slowly dismantling the old chest and getting the top ready to take to Eric for carving. Bill found it very useful to have Lucy working alongside him. She was quick to learn, and when he felt tired or a coughing fit got too bad, he could sit down and she would carry on.

~~~

The next morning Bill had his appointment with Dr Hall. No fireside chats about antiques this time; he was seen in the doctor's surgery with the letter from the oncologist and all of his test results ready to hand. Dr Hall had a very practical approach to telling people the news he had to give. With some patients you had to dress it up, to wrap the inevitable in layers of hope, like coating a nasty-tasting pill with sugar. But with a man like Bill you told him exactly how things stood and what options, if any, were worth considering.

So Dr Hall described all the possible ways Bill's cancer could impact his life and what medical science could do to mitigate some of them. Bill listened and took in as much of it as he could. The one thing he was really concerned about was how long Dr Hall thought he could keep working.

'I can't really answer that, Bill. There are so many factors involved, not the least of which is willpower. And pain control is always a balancing act. You'll have morphine-based painkillers to deaden the pain, but they'll also make you feel sleepy and slow. So that's what you'll have to learn to balance: how much pain you can tolerate before you can't function efficiently, and how much drug you can take before you're too zonked out to care.'

Then Dr Hall said something that shook Bill more than anything else he had been told that morning.

'When things get really bad, Bill, and you know the game is nearly over, I can get you into a hospice. Because you live alone you're warranted a place.'

Picking up a glossy brochure like something from a holiday company, he handed it to Bill and suggested he make a visit to talk things through with their medical admission counsellor. Bill couldn't think of anything to say, so he just folded up the brochure and put it in his pocket. Then he went home.

The sun was out, the day was as crisp as a new apple, and Bill refused to be smothered by the information he now had lodged in his brain.

Driving into the farmyard, he saw his daughter-in-law's parked car. The kitchen door was open, and at the table sat Lucy and Gloria, mugs of tea in front of them, close in conversation. Bloody hell, he thought, those two look as thick as thieves. As he sat down at the table with them, Lucy got up and poured him a large mug.

'Just been made,' she said.

'So what have you two dreadful viragos been discussing?' he asked as he sipped his tea.

'You,' was the instant and unanimous reply.

Of course they wanted to know what the doctor had said, and as he was starting to tell them he remembered the brochure he had been given. Even folded, it was a little large for his pocket and it came out with a jerk, hit the sugar bowl, and landed half open in a drift of white crystals. Gloria picked it up and looked at it briefly, then without a word handed it to Lucy and walked out into the yard.

Bill looked at Lucy, shocked and ashamed of himself. He had had no intention of being so cavalier about it all. Lucy reached over and squeezed his hand quickly, then got up and followed Gloria. Through the window he saw the two women embracing each other, comforting and being comforted in return. The sight, though sad, was nevertheless a consolation to him. If these two were becoming such good friends, it would make his leaving them easier.

Coming back inside with the bravest grin she could manage, Gloria put her arm around his shoulders. She said she and Phillip would find out about the hospice, and when Bill felt able, they would take him to look the place over. He nodded, but said nothing.

As Gloria prepared to go, Bill looked in vain for some visible sign of pregnancy through her oversized jumper. She noticed him looking and said, 'If it's a boy we're going to call him William, you know.'

Bill pretended to grimace, but most of it was a smile. 'And if it's a girl?' he asked.

Gloria appeared to think for a while, then brightly and with some malice aforethought said, 'Wilhelmina.' She laughed as her father-in-law nearly choked on his tea.

When Gloria had driven away and Bill had locked the gate behind her, he felt completely wiped out and in a lot of pain. His chest, his back, and really his whole body was giving him grief. In addition to the tablets next to his bed, he now had a big brown bottle of some gunk that was serious stuff according to the label. He chose not to think about it, however, and fell asleep in his armchair trying to let the warmth from the stove relieve some of his discomfort.

Lucy looked at him. He was more loose-skinned than when she had first known him. His shirts hung on him and the collars were too big for his neck. The incident with the hospice pamphlet had brought home to her how little time they might have left together.

She decided to let him sleep for a while and went to lock up the workshop for the night. Later on she woke him and fed him what little supper he could eat, his appetite being completely eroded by pain. Like a small boy, he allowed her to help him up to bed, where she administered a spoonful of sweet syrup from the big brown bottle, after which he slept a deep, narcotic-fuelled sleep full of dreams that cascaded in coloured confusion through his mind.

Chapter 27

WEDNESDAY, 3 OCTOBER

Awaking much later than his normal six in the morning, Bill made his slightly muzzy way down to breakfast. Lucy was up and about and had already been in the workshop putting the old chest lid in a box and carefully wrapping the piece to be copied.

Bill's contribution to getting underway was to take £500 out of the Skates pile and put it in an envelope. Whatever the final price for the job might be, he figured half a ton would be enough to get Eric started.

While Bill did the best he could with a piece of toast and some really strong coffee, Lucy walked up to Miss Templeton's and asked her to keep a particularly good watch on the place as they would both be out for a large part of the day. Then they set off on the small roads that interlace like green veins all over this part of the county. The land was now turning perceptibly towards autumn. The light was different, clearer somehow, if not as strong. The morning dew took a long time to disappear, and there was a moist edge to everything.

For Bill, it was strange to be out in his van and not driving it. Lucy handled it well, not crunching the ravaged gearbox too often and, more importantly, not trying to overtake anything faster than a cyclist. Clive panted behind Bill's right ear, wishing he could get his head out of the window.

There was a large supermarket with a café on a trading estate just outside Chard; this is where they decided Lucy and Clive would wait for Bill. He assured her he was feeling much better now, much stronger. He was in some pain but not enough to slow him up. As he said to Lucy, 'It gives me an edge.'

He drove along small lanes that got even smaller until he saw a turning he recognised at the top of a hill, then drove onto a track that led to a gate in a tall chain-link fence. The gate had a crude handmade sign that read 'Keep Out' and another on which 'Beware of the Dogs' had been scrawled. Bill knew that both signs meant what they said. Two, sometimes three great savage dogs were allowed to run free at night and were usually tethered on long chains even when Eric was in his workshop. They knew their business and would happily tear your arm off just to see how you tasted.

Bill sounded his horn and waited. Eric knew he was coming, so the dogs would be chained up (he hoped). Eric came out and opened the gate, and as Bill drove through, he looked around. The high chain-link fence was topped with razor wire and formed a large square. On every corner of the high fence was mounted a large halogen light with a motion sensor. Bill thought all this gave the place the look of a gulag; definitely more prison than fortress, anyway. On one side of the square was the dilapidated caravan in which Eric lived, its original colour now lost beneath encrustations of old leaves and filth. On another was his workshop, a large wooden building with a wide door and a window on the front. The rest of the square was paved. It was also littered with dog bowls, dog chains, dog shit, the stench of rotten meat, and, to Bill's surprise, one small yellow rubber duck, much chewed.

What he didn't see were any actual dogs, but he could hear them all right. They were in the caravan, which rocked slightly as they bounded from window to window, barking, snarling, and scratching to get out and maul this stranger who dared to enter their yard.

Bill placed his bundles on the bench that took up the centre of the Eric's shop. The bench itself was a work of art, copied from an 18th-century joiners manual. With vices of all types fixed to it and peg holes for clamps, it was beautiful and could replicate every work mark you might expect to see on a piece of antique carving.

On the bench was a craftsman's cabinet of the sort apprentices used to make as examination pieces, its lid carved in an intricate foliate design. Bill recognised the handiwork and sighed inwardly. Eric might be a complete shit of a human being, but he was a superb carver by anyone's standards.

You can tell a lot about a craftsman from his workshop, Bill explained to Lucy later. Eric's was surprisingly clean for a start. Eric was a smoker, but there were no ashtrays here and no dog ends on the floor, nor was there much in the way of wood shavings. There were a few woodworking machines, the sort anyone would have in his trade. A large bandsaw stood against one wall, and there was a very nice wood-turning lathe, well lit and with as large a selection of turning chisels as Bill had ever seen outside a catalogue. On one wall was a row of G-clamps. Huge bracket clamps hung on pegboard, some of them obviously new, as was a rack of carving chisels of such quality that Bill almost drooled.

Overall, a lot had changed since Bill's last visit. A large amount of money had been spent on enlarging the shop, as well as on new tools and equipment. Bill saw no work in progress, however, nor even any signs of recent work having been done. This meant one of two things: either Eric was out of work and would take any job offered him right now, or what he was doing was so bent he had hidden it before Bill got there. Either way, it was interesting.

Eric himself had not changed. He was still wearing the same greasy flat-cloth cap and he still had the same unhealthy complexion. His face was ferrety, lined, and bore the stubble of someone who habitually shaved in the dark. Thin lips hid a few brown, tombstone-like teeth in a scowling mouth that produced a constant whine. He returned Bill's look through glasses filmed with nicotine. Short and emaciated, he lived on tinned fish and cheap gin. And he stank. Bill kept as far away from him as he could. No one ever got close to Eric Howler by choice.

Bill carefully unwrapped the old chair panel and laid it on the bench. Eric moved closer and picked up the carving, holding it up to the light and moving it slightly as if reading the story the shadows told. Putting it down gently, he drew his fingers across the carved surface with the delicacy of a blind man reading a braille love letter. He turned to Bill and a sly look crossed his face. 'Is this what I think it is?'

'I'm not paying you to think,' said Bill firmly. 'I'm paying you to carve, and carve well. This is to be a museum-quality reproduction and I've brought you the wood I want used. Follow the pattern of the sample, but make it unique, with all the right chisel marks and only a cursory rub down. Finish with fine sand on chamois leather, not wire wool, and no polish, got that?'

Eric nodded without comment. Bill asked to see the tools that would be used. There could be no new steel tools on this job. The gouges and flat-end chisels had to be handmade and tempered so the cut marks, even when aged and polished, would show the authenticity that only came with genuine antiques (or the cleverest copies).

Eric opened the lovely tool chest on the bench. There inside, set in a velvet-lined rack, was a collection of gouges, swan-necked scrapers, and chisels Bill would have killed for at one time. They were beautiful: some old, with cutlers marks on the polished steel that Bill recognised as being 18th century; others newer, but so well made they had the same feel as their antique companions. Bill was impressed. He had heard about Eric's private collection but never been privileged to see it. They made his own assortment of antique tools seem meagre by comparison.

Next, Eric examined the chest lid closely. Eventually he said it might need a bit of smoothing on the back but that was about it. Yes, it could be done. Now as to price . . .

Bill had in mind between £1000 and £1500. Cash, half up front, the rest on delivery; all the usual terms and conditions for this sort of job. But he hadn't liked the look on Eric's his face when he had first examined the carving. It was like seeing a rat smile. Consequently, when he pitched at a thousand and Eric agreed without squirming or even much of a whine, he knew something was lurking at the back of that shifty bastard's mind. However, he put the envelope down on the bench, and within seconds a scrawny hand had it open, counting the cash.

'Five hundred,' said Bill.

'Five hundred,' agreed Eric, then sneered, 'Do you want a receipt?'

Bill said nothing about receipts, but enquired as casually as he could how business had been lately. He admired the workshop improvements and examined the new machinery, all the while congratulating the little man. Eric tittered nervously but explained nothing. For a person who loved to gossip, that was very strange. When the talk turned to mutual acquaintances in the trade, Eric was his usual chattering self, imparting all manner of scurrilous rumours and bitchy innuendo: who had overbid on what and who had been turned over by whom. But of his own doings, nothing. An enigma wrapped in a bad smell, thought Bill, and he left it at that.

Price and time agreed (two weeks or thereabouts), Eric let him out of the big gate. Bill couldn't help shuddering as he looked in his rear-view mirror and watched the horrible little man lock it and then scurry back into his workshop.

Stopping in a layby, he phoned Lucy and suggested they have a bite at the supermarket café before returning home. Lucy said she and Clive would meet him in the seating area outside. She also added that she had bought a big packet of antiseptic wipes. Bill laughed, blessed her, and drove there as fast as he could.

They sat in the weak sunshine drinking mugs of coffee, and Bill told Lucy of his meeting with Eric. In describing the man, he resorted to a sort of visual shorthand using film actors he knew. However, his knowledge of movies was so out of date that it turned into a game along the lines of 'Do you remember so and so? Well, a bit like him but thinner and with a different face.'

When Bill recounted Eric's stranger than usual behaviour and the way he accepted the price offered without whining or protestations of crushing poverty, Lucy asked, 'Do you think he might be going to try a bit of blackmail? Could he have recognised the carving as being from a valuable set of chairs?'

Bill agreed it was possible. 'After all, I knew about them before I set eyes on them, so Eric might, too. The Blakeney Chairs are famous in their way and he might have seen some illustration of them somewhere. Sod's law the little shit is currently looking through old catalogues and antique trade journals for confirmation.'

That gave them both food for thought, of the sort that causes mental indigestion.

Lucy drove them home, Bill's exertions of the morning having made him very weary. Instead of driving straight into their yard, however, Lucy drove up the narrow lane to Miss Templeton's cottage. She had seen them coming and met them at her gate, acknowledging Bill with a kindly smile and telling him he was looking wan. Bill thought 'wan' sounded just about right.

After tea had been offered and politely declined, Miss Templeton told them there had not been any visitors to the farm in their absence, but a motorcycle, a big one, black in colour and with a short, thick-set man in leathers riding it, had stopped at the junction. The man was wearing one of those all-encompassing helmets, so she could not see any features. He had not got off his bike and would only have seen an empty yard. When he left, she had used her powerful binoculars to track him as far as she could up the road towards Brewton. He had not stopped.

It was Warren, they were sure. Whether he had slipped his leash and come on his own account or whether he was under instruction from Skates was impossible to know.

Looking at Lucy, Miss Templeton suggested she might like to pop up for a chat once Bill was home and settled in. Bill was happy to reach his comfortable chair in front of a warm stove, and Lucy was glad to have someone to talk to while he napped, especially someone as interesting as Miss Templeton.

During their visit, Lucy asked her how she had gotten involved in the war. Elenore Templeton had been a schoolgirl when war broke out and had joined the WAAFs just as soon as she could when she was 17½. She spoke perfect French and, with the help of a friend's introduction to the 'right sort' of people, joined the SOE when she was 19.

'Only 19!' Lucy exclaimed. 'You were still a teenager!'

Miss Templeton laughed at that. 'There were no such things as teenagers in those years, my dear. They are a post-war phenomenon and delightful they are too, all gaudy and vibrant, like so many exotic birds all strutting and showing their finery. But I sometimes feel sorry for them, too. They have so much need to prove themselves and no great cause in which to do it. No wonder so many of them end up in trouble.'

Lucy gave this serious consideration. If there had been a war on when she was 19, she probably wouldn't have ended up in Skates and Warren's clutches. She hoped not, anyway, but the truth was she really didn't think she had Miss Templeton's kind of courage.

~~~

Bill woke in the early evening, refreshed but still tired. He knew now he would never really feel well again, not unless it was due to some chemical crutch. But he was grateful for the rest, the warmth, and the savoury smell that now filled the kitchen. Over dinner, Lucy told him about her visit with Miss Templeton.

'She's had an amazing life. She didn't get into too much detail, but hinted at some really scary stuff. Did you know she worked for the Ministry of Agriculture after the war? She said it was awfully dull after the SOE, but they didn't let women have any of the really fun jobs after the men came back.'

'Fun jobs!' laughed Bill.

'I hope you don't mind too much, but I told her the truth about what's going on with us. She had most of it figured out in any case, and there's just something about her that makes you feel daft if you try to hold anything back. Like you're only fooling yourself.'

'It's probably just as well, lass. As she said, she's going to keep looking out for us anyway, so she may as well know exactly what to look out for.'

'Well, one thing came across pretty clearly. She thinks our problem is a walk in the park compared with all the horrors she and her colleagues had to deal with. She said our job was simple: we only have two enemies, we know what they look like, and we know where they live. The rest is down to opportunity and timing.'

'Christ, I wish it were that bloody simple!' exclaimed Bill, mildly peeved.

Lucy laughed, 'Simple is not the same as easy, and I'm sure she doesn't think for a minute it's not going to be dangerous, she just takes it for granted we'll be able to cope with it.'

'Well, I hope she's right,' said Bill.

Lucy cleared away the dishes from the table and put them on the wooden draining board. Going to the huge fridge she called 'Beryl' after Bill's ex-wife, she took out some ice cream concoction and placed a small bowl of it in front of him, then sat down in what was now 'her' armchair. They discussed Warren's visit and agreed it was probably just him being his usual devious self rather than a statement of some kind from Skates. That he had not come into the yard was a good thing, but finding a way to keep him away altogether would be preferable. Bill suggested they sleep on it. The truth was he felt very tired and was hurting, so it was out with the big brown bottle and hello to the morphine.

Chapter 28

THURSDAY–THURSDAY, 4–11 OCTOBER

Over the next few days, Bill and Lucy got on with making the components of the chair that needed to be restored. Bill thought that by doing this job first he would get his eye in for the big job, which would be making the entirely new chair from scratch. All the timber they would need had been sorted and, with the dismantled chair as a guide, the work would be exacting but not too difficult. The real bugger would come later in the finishing.

For Bill, sitting down while Lucy worked took some getting used to. He had to show her what to do, of course, but even that became less frequent as she picked things up. Long years at his craft made the jobs look effortless in Bill's hands, and trying to emulate his actions was hard for Lucy, as it would have been for anyone, but she was bright and had natural hand skills. They worked together in such a way as to conserve Bill's strength. It was not easy, but Lucy made light of it and rarely got upset when Bill was a little short or impatient with her. Once again he mused that she would have made a good apprentice, but there was no time now, even if she had wanted it.

As Bill and Lucy worked, they discussed ideas for keeping Skates at bay. It was not him spying out the work on the chairs that really worried them, it was what might happen if he learned that Lucy was there. There was no way of knowing if Skates had even realised yet that she had broken out of her prison, but one thing was sure: he would try and silence her if he found her with Bill. For that matter, there was no question of her leaving again to hide with Dylan or anywhere else: in his current condition there was no way Bill could complete the work on the chairs without her help.

By Monday morning the bones of the chair that was being restored had begun to take shape. Making a new arm meant looking for a piece of timber that had been split from the main log rather than cut. Sawn timber was sometimes used, but the craftsmen in Elizabethan times liked to use wood when it was green and would split along the grain. This was preferred because of shrinkage, and its natural shape being sympathetic with its end use. Looking closely at the elegant bend in the armrest, Bill could see that the grain followed the bend. This showed it was a branch, split rather than sawn, and shaped with an adze before finishing with chisels and scrapers. One of the complete chairs had arms made of wood like that. Thankfully, the other was from sawn timber that had been carved into shape, the grain running across the wood rather than following the contours. That was solvable; Bill had the right size oak beam, which he had rescued years before from a demolished cow shed. The beam was old and small enough to have knots. It couldn't be split now as it was far too dry, but it could be carefully shaped to match.

The old oak was like iron, however, and Bill was forced to

use modern power tools to do the shaping, which meant dust, and dust meant coughing up his lungs. Somewhere Lucy had got hold of a box of dust masks, but Bill hated them; they were hot, uncomfortable, and actually made him cough more.

It seemed like stalemate as he sat on a chair outside the workshop door, head in hands, emptying his diseased lungs onto the cement beneath his feet. Blood-streaked phlegm pooled in the dirt and sawdust. He could feel his chest crumpling in and out like a greasy paper bag. His arms were weak, his head was hurting, his lungs were wrung dry with relentless heaving, and all he had been doing was using the big, heavy-duty bandsaw. This was a piece of piss in the old days, the work of less than an hour or so. But not now, not ever again, he thought. And they had at least ten more jobs like this to do. They had to use this machine because to try and saw the old oak by hand was stupid. It would take an age, and of all the steps that had to be done, this was the one that could be done on a machine.

Lucy went into the house, brought out a glass of water, and stood by him as he gulped it down. Her hand on his shoulder moved down to lightly and slowly rub his back. His tweed jacket felt very loose on his bony frame. She wanted to cry. Not for the chairs or what might happen if they couldn't be finished, but for this lovely man, whom she loved, and who was dying by inches. Tenderly, she took his arm, helped him up, and walked him into the kitchen where she sat him down in his armchair by the stove.

'Must have been a bit of wood dust went down the wrong hole,' she said soothingly. 'No big deal, soon go away.'

After a slight pause she added, 'You'll have to show me how that machine works. It can't be too difficult as long as I take it slow.'

Bill's voice was weak but his reply was adamant.

'That is the one machine in the entire workshop that you are never, ever, to try, love. That bandsaw is probably the most dangerous and unpredictable machine I own. Not just mine, anyone's. If you're going to lose a hand, that's the thing that will do it, in an instant and without even clogging up with bones and gristle. No, it will have to be me, somehow.'

Lucy told him to rest for a bit and he would undoubtedly think of a solution when he was less tired. Out came the big brown bottle and out stretched the arms of Morphia to welcome Bill into a pain-free dreamtime.

Meanwhile, Lucy set herself to work on the problem. If it wasn't for the coughing, Bill would have the energy to work if he was careful, and she was pretty sure she could see that he was careful. That meant something had to be done about the dust.

Looking through the Yellow Pages for dust-extraction equipment, she remembered something she had seen when staying with Dylan. She made a quick phone call and then drove off, leaving a note on the kitchen table to say she wouldn't be gone long.

A short time later she returned to find Bill wandering round the workshop sorting through various hand saws. Under her arm was what looked to him like a space helmet. In fact, it was a full-face protective respirator. It took clean air in through a filtered compressor worn on a harness at the back that fed fresh, dust-free air into the helmet. This blew down over the face and out under the wide, clear visor, which ended below the chin.

'Where the hell did you get this?' asked Bill. 'It looks like something out of a science fiction film.'

'I saw a guy wearing one when he came to spray for fungus in Dylan's shower block,' said Lucy.

She had made the man a cup of tea and examined his headgear out of curiosity, finding out a bit about how it worked. Bill was impressed, especially when Lucy told him it was only on hire from a local outfit and would not cost a great deal.

It worked, though not without Bill moaning at the noise, the draft, the smell, and the dust that occasionally stuck to the outside of the visor and had to be wiped off. The fact that he was moaning from inside the thing without dissolving every half hour into a coughing fit seemed beside the point to him, but not to Lucy. The only member of the team who couldn't get used to the contraption was Clive. He hid whenever it was switched on.

~~~

That night after supper, Bill showed Lucy a large cupboard under the stairs that he said was one of the oldest parts of the house. It was actually more of a small room than a cupboard, but Lucy had to bend in half to get in through the tiny door. Then she went down four or five worn stone steps and into a small, odd-shaped space with a flagstone floor. Bill stood outside the door, directing operations. Thankfully, he had rigged up a light that revealed wide shelves just above floor level on which sat several huge stoneware flagons. The room smelled of damp stone, great age, and apples. Pointing to the vessel nearest where she stooped under the low, cobwebbed ceiling, he asked Lucy to hand out the jar. It was heavy and covered in dust.

'And don't shake it, for God's sake,' he said.

She handed it to him, then emerged brushing the cobwebs from her hair and the dust from her clothes. Bill placed the old flagon on the table. The small top was sealed with wax. On one side was impressed a maker's mark, and under that '3 gallons'. Bill smiled as he gently wiped it down with a damp tea towel.

Lucy enjoyed the sight of Bill's pleasure in unearthing the jar and asked what was inside that was so special.

'Applejack,' replied Bill, caressing the container and carefully examining its cork.

'What's applejack?'

'It's a kind of liquor made from apples,' he replied. 'Well, mainly apples.'

They sat drinking mugs of tea, the large flagon sitting at one end of the kitchen table like another guest, and Bill told her the story of old Jimmer, the best cider maker for miles around, and his illegal still.

'This stuff's been down there for years. Jimmer had been given the nod he was going to be raided by the police, so I hid his stock for him. He never wanted it back, too dodgy I expect, so there it stayed.'

'And why are you dragging it out now?' asked Lucy.

'Two reasons,' Bill answered, with a big and slightly wicked grin. 'First, we've got some wood stain to make. And second, Sid's coming round.'

Chapter 29

FRIDAY, 12 OCTOBER

Lucy knew *of* Sid but had not yet *experienced* Sid. Bill told her enough about him, however, that she felt prepared when his battered old transit van pulled into the yard early the next morning. Out clambered a large, exuberant man, his huge frame enclosed in dungarees that had more patches than pockets and were stained with oil, paint, and other indicators of his many and varied pursuits. Clive greeted him with an enthusiastic nose to the crotch, which Sid brushed away with a practiced air that indicated this was not an unusual occurrence.

The kitchen smelled invitingly of bacon when he entered it, and Bill sat facing him at the head of the familiar table, brown sauce within easy reach. Lucy turned from the stove, an enormous frying pan in her hand.

'You must be Sid,' she said.

Putting a massive pile of bacon on a plate and setting it in on the table, she returned the pan to the stove, walked over to where Sid was standing, and shook his hand. Her grip was firm, no mere flutter of fingers, but a real grasp, and her smile was easy to return. She then poured him a large mug of tea the colour of teak, just the way Bill had told her he liked it, and pushed the sugar bowl across.

Bill had not often seen Sid lost for words, not even when pulled over by the police or challenged by a short-changed barmaid. But if Sid had any sangfroid he certainly had not used it as aftershave that morning. He said nothing; as far as Lucy was concerned, he didn't need to, for his broad smile and the way he demolished his breakfast said it all.

But as he sat there lathering brown sauce over crispy bacon, Sid was paying attention. He had lived a ramshackle sort of existence, had loved unwisely and too often to keep a wife, and he had no kith nor kin he cared a scrap for, but he was a good judge of character and a wise observer of the human condition. So, as he sat eating the simple meal, drinking his tea, and listening to Bill and this lady natter on, he was fast coming to the conclusion that there was some special connection between them. He noticed how Lucy made sure Bill had everything he wanted, and always had an eye to his comfort. She obviously cared a lot for his old friend. Well, one thing was for sure, this lass knew the way to a man's heart was through a good breakfast, and that was rare wisdom these days.

For Bill's part, he knew Sid was a cunning man, and so were his ways. Bill was no longer under any illusion: he and Lucy needed all the cunning they could get and then some. For that reason, he had decided to tell Sid everything. As he said to Lucy, he hated to involve Sid in something so potentially dangerous, but he just didn't see that they had a choice.

So, as they sat amongst the breakfast debris, Bill told Sid the true state of affairs with Skates, and Lucy told him how she fitted in. Sid had always known there was more to the story than he had been told and that Bill would put him in the picture when the time was right, but when he heard what had been done to Bess, his face darkened and his knuckles whitened on the mug in his hand.

'Look,' he said, 'if there is anything I can do, you got it, right?'

And that was it. Bill went off to make final preparations for the pole saw to be set up in the workshop, and Lucy helped Sid unload the van. Lucy was impressed that Sid had been able to create a device out of elastic bungee rope and a few metal bars that would take half the effort of a traditional lathe but deliver the same sort of results, and it was fascinating to watch him set it up.

During one of Sid's many cigarette breaks that morning, Lucy told him just how ill Bill really was. Sid shook his head at this news, saddened but certainly not surprised. To cheer her up, he recounted a few of the things he and Bill had got up to over the years. These made her laugh and like him all the more. It was obvious to her that he held Bill in high regard, and she looked forward to hearing more of their history of combined naughtiness.

After lunch, Sid wandered off for a smoke while Lucy cleaned up and Bill took his midday pills. A little while later Bill was just walking back towards the workshop when he heard a strangled scream. He thought it came from outside the yard, but somewhere fairly nearby. Running down the passage between the barn and the cart shed, he hurried through the meadow gate, then stopped to try and see what was making the noise and where. He was afraid it might be someone pinned under a tractor or one of the many other rural opportunities for serious injury, but then he saw what it was. It was Sid hammering a man against a tree.

They were at the edge of the field, not far from where Bill was standing, and the man was no longer screaming, but each time he hit the tree, he made a sort of shrill bubbling sound.

When Bill came panting up, he saw that Sid was holding a large, well-muscled man dressed in camouflage jacket and trousers who had a really nasty bruise already coming up on his greasy forehead. Blood was running from his nose down the front of his jacket. He was stubble-headed and had a round, coarse, blubbery sort of face. Glancing down, Bill saw a long, nasty-looking hunting knife shining in the grass at Sid's feet. Nearby was a large and very new-looking pair of binoculars.

'This stupid bastard pulled a fucking knife on me!' said Sid indignantly.

'Didn't,' said the man, trying to squirm free.

'Yes. You. Fucking. Did,' said Sid, each word accompanied by another thump against the oak tree.

'What are you doing here?' asked Bill.

'Bird watching,' said the man. 'I'm a bird watcher. I got permission, you know.'

Suddenly, Sid let the man down. Stepping back and adopting a more conciliatory tone of voice, Sid asked, 'Oh, was you looking for the black-winged woodpecker we're famous for in these parts?'

The man nodded his head vigorously in agreement.

'Yes, that's the one. Very rare in the rest of the country.'

Sid's right arm, moving at tremendous speed and with a remorseless attention to detail, punched the man in the pit of his stomach. He folded over at Sid's feet.

'Prat,' said Sid. 'No such fucking bird. Now, why are you here?'

'Never mind,' said Bill in a tired voice, 'I know.'

Reaching down, he picked up the expensive binoculars and smashed them against the trunk of the tree just inches above the man's head.

'Tell Skates if he sends any more of his little thugs here he won't get them or his fucking chairs back in one piece. Understood?'

The man said nothing, but was obviously glad to be let go. Holding his stomach and dripping blood, he hobbled away as best he could. He didn't even look back.

Lucy had heard the commotion and got the shotgun, but had waited out of sight, holding Clive by his collar. When Bill and Sid walked back into the yard, she ran up to them and, seeing the red mark on Sid's forehead where he had administered a 'Glasgow kiss' to Mr Peeping Git, took him into the kitchen to administer a bit of TLC to her new hero. Sid shrugged it off but quite liked the unaccustomed attention.

Bill got out a whisky bottle from the dresser. Not bothering with glasses, the two men drank a goodly drop from their tea mugs. Sitting there, the excitement ebbing away, Sid examined the shotgun. Breaking it open, he extracted the two cartridges with a theatrical 'tut-tut' and put the gun on the table in front of him.

After another slug of whiskey, Bill went to the phone and called Skates's number. After a short while the telephone was answered by a voice Bill didn't recognise.

'Mr Skates, please,' he asked, trying to keep his tone neutral.

'He's not here,' was the reply.

'When will he be back?'

'Who's calling?'

This is like verbal fucking ping-pong, thought Bill.

'An old friend,' said Bill, and suddenly realized the voice was Warren's, so he continued. 'Was that fucking idiot in the camouflage jacket Skates's idea or something you thought up in your own tiny, pox-infested brain?'

No reply, just a bit of heavy breathing, so Bill went on.

'Well he's not a happy little twitcher now, I can tell you. Ran into a mate of mine who had been doing a bit of welding on my van. Silly bastard tried to frighten him with a fucking great knife. Not a good move, that.'

A grunt and then silence.

'So Skates is away and this is your own bit of arse-licking initiative, is it? You trying to think like a grownup, you dumb, muscle-bound fuckwit?'

'You do what Mr Skates wants or you'll have the same as your fucking dog,' was the reply.

'I'll do what I want,' said Bill. 'And what I want is to get on with these chairs without a lot of stupid interruptions, get my fucking money, and have you piss off back up Skates's fundament. But if I see a shiny black motorbike or any more camouflaged twats around my place I will burn those fucking chairs and take my chances.'

Bill slammed down the phone and turned around to a sudden burst of applause from Lucy and Sid.

'All right,' he said, smiling, 'back to work, you two.'

Finally, the lathe was up and tested, all the arms had been cut with Sid's help, and the two long back timbers for the new chair were ready to shape. Having both Sid and Lucy really made the job a lot quicker and easier for Bill. Sid knew his way around wood a bit, and machinery even more. Lucy was organised and had sorted the timbers out to size so they were ready to be coarse-trimmed, and Bill was there, out of the dust, fussing it all through.

Lucy invited Sid to stay for supper; he was delighted to accept as he lived on his own and his meals were usually from a tin or a microwave packet. That evening, Lucy fed them the mother of all beef stews, full of vegetables and crowned with huge, fluffy dumplings. Bill had not eaten so much in weeks, and Sid not eaten so well in years. This was followed by an apple pie of heroic proportions with a whole jug of custard.

Bill got out some cider for himself and Sid, and Lucy opened a bottle of wine. The men sat back in their chairs, replete and content. Bill had not felt so well in an age. He could see the way forward now, for a bit anyway.

When the table was cleared, Sid rolled a cigarette, Bill lit his pipe, and no sign of reproach crossed Lucy's face. It was too good an evening. Bill said how much he appreciated Sid's help and what a difference it had made, and Lucy agreed, adding that, without Sid, there could really have been a problem with the snooper in the field. Sid shrugged it off, but it was true and he knew it.

Then Bill got out the huge flagon of applejack and carefully removed the wax seal from around the cork bung. Putting an empty whisky bottle next to it, he had Lucy hold a large copper funnel while he carefully decanted some of the liquid into the bottle. It had a pale yellow tint and a peculiar fragrance of apples with just a hint of turpentine.

'Christ, is that old Jimmer's horizontal fluid?' asked Sid, with awe in his voice.

'The same,' said Bill, 'the very same.'

'Horizontal fluid?' asked Lucy, looking down into the copper funnel, the inside of which was now much brighter than it had been. 'I thought you said it was applejack.'

'Oh yes,' chuckled Bill. 'You drink too much of that particular applejack and you'll be horizontal, all right.'

'Possibly even permanently,' added Sid.

Bill got out some tiny glasses from which they all took small sips. Lucy coughed, her eyes watered, and as the liquid burned down her throat, she knew she wanted no more. It was getting late and she was tired. It surprised her that Bill was staying up so long, and then she realized he must have something he wanted to discuss privately with Sid.

Sid had drunk too much to drive home safely, much less legally, so Lucy made up a bed for him in the spare room, reminded Bill to take his medication, and bid them both goodnight. After she had climbed the stairs, Bill asked Sid about the ammunition. Sid went out to his van, came back, and put a small brown cardboard box on the table in front of Bill. The faded green lettering on the top said '24 Cartridges Revolver .455 DCM' and there was also a date stamp: August 1942.

Opening it up, Bill poured the cartridges onto the table. The lead bullets were a dull, dark grey and the brass cartridges stained by time, but despite their age, they still looked usable. He walked over to the dresser, opened one of its bottom drawers, and pulled a locked wooden box from deep within it. Back at the table, he unlocked the box and took from it an ungainly shape wrapped in an oily cloth. It made a dull thump as he placed it in front of him. He pulled away the cloth, and a huge, ancient army revolver gleamed dully in the soft light of the kitchen. It had a proof mark for 1917 stamped on it, but it was oiled, cleaned, and still obviously in working condition.

Bill released a catch on the side, and the revolver split open to reveal the empty chambers in the cylinder. He picked a round up from the table and slid it into a chamber. It fit perfectly. Then another and another, until all six cylinders were loaded, and he closed the gun with a metallic click.

'That's lucky,' he said. 'I was afraid they wouldn't be the right size.'

'I don't know about lucky,' said Sid, then added impatiently, 'Give it here, you're like a cow with a gun.' He laughed at the unintended joke. 'You ever fire one of these?' he asked Bill, standing up. Holding the gun in a practised hand, he pointed it at the floor, testing its balance and weight.

'No,' said Bill.

'I have. Lots. Not as big as this; ours were all modern, only thirty-eights, but the principle's the same.'

He held the revolver up, his arm straight out in front of him, then changed to holding the heavy gun in both hands, the right hand holding the large butt, index finger along the trigger guard, his left hand supporting his right from underneath.

'Unless you get close, really close, you won't hit a barn door with this. I couldn't, and I've been trained.'

He broke the gun, extracted the bullets, closed it again, and put it down on the table. Then he rolled a cigarette.

'How about I show you what I mean another time, when we're were both completely sober?'

Bill nodded. Suddenly he felt completely exhausted. Somehow having this gun out from hiding and with ammunition to hand was more unsettling than reassuring. For a start, what would Lucy make of it? Shotguns for intruders were one thing, but this? This had to do with an end game that seemed barely real even to him.

Chapter 30

SATURDAY–SUNDAY, 13–14 OCTOBER

The next morning Bill repeated how grateful he was to Sid for all his help and asked how much he owed him. Sid finished chewing a mouthful of bacon sandwich from which dark brown sauce dripped, adding another bit of gastronomic history to the front of his dungarees.

'Fuck all!' he said finally, with a wink at Lucy. 'Sweet fuck all!'

But neither Bill nor Lucy were having any of that. Bill took out an envelope he had prepared earlier. Sid was a good mate, but even so it was right to pay him properly for his work. He placed the envelope on the table in front of him and sat back. Sid looked inside.

'Hey, there's real money in here, you daft bugger. Notes with big numbers on!'

'Two hundred and fifty pounds,' said Bill. 'And when we need you again, there's more. That and the rest of the bottle,' he said, indicating the applejack, of which only a small amount had been drunk.

'I'll pass on that, thank you,' said Sid with a brief shudder, grateful for Lucy's offer of paracetamol first thing that morning.

'Anything else I can do?' he asked.

Lucy was at the stove with her back to them, and he made a sign with two fingers like a gun at Bill.

'Not right now,' said Bill, who had hidden the firearm and ammunition away in his bedroom the previous night. 'But I'll let you know when there is.'

'Any time,' said Sid. He got up, went over and gave Lucy a peck on the cheek, then walked out into the yard. Bill followed him out, and as Sid climbed into the driver's seat of his transit van, he looked down at Bill and said, 'You take care, mate. We might have scared your little chum away for now, but in the end . . . well, in the end . . .' He made the sign of a gun again, only this time he mimed the gun firing.

'Thanks,' said Bill. 'I'd have been a bit buggered without your help. I owe you one.'

Sid closed the door and wound down the window. 'Nah, what goes around comes around, and it was just my turn to be around for you. Say, you know what I'd do if I was you? I'd call the Dawlish brothers and tell them you've seen strangers on their land. Maybe even plant a few feathers in the hedgerows for his gamekeeper to find, eh?'

'Sid, you're a bloody genius,' said Bill, and he meant it.

Sid laughed. 'Been telling you that for years!'

And with a cloud of black diesel smoke, the old van pulled away. Bill closed the gate after him, then walked back into the kitchen and told Lucy about Sid's idea.

'The land 'round mine is owned by two brothers who really like their shooting, and they get seriously pissed off if anyone poaches their game. Anyone they catch would be lucky to just be handed over to the police. The lads are a little old-fashioned in their ways,' said Bill, smiling grimly at the thought of the beating Warren or his minion would get if they were found by the brothers or any of their men.

They went to a local butcher who sold game and bought a brace of pheasant, then walked the meadow around Bill's house. They left a wing and some tail feathers tucked in the spot where their last illicit visitor had lurked, and Bill identified a couple of other places that could be usefully spiked. Then he phoned Hugh, one of the brothers who owned the land, to say he had seen what he took to be poachers. Hugh sent his head gamekeeper, Garry, over to investigate, and when Garry saw the planted evidence he took it for what it might have been. This field was away from the main farm and only got shot over at the end of the season, but Garry said he would look by now and again, just to keep an eye out.

Bill knew that was as good as he could hope for. Between Miss Templeton keeping an eye on things with her powerful binoculars and Garry putting these fields on his watch list, he felt they were a bit more secure and could turn their attention back to the chairs.

With all the wood cut, the shaping and such surface carving as there was to do took the best part of two days. The hardest part was cutting the mortise and tenon joints. Only Bill could do this, but they were second nature to him, and he used his antique chisels only on the last finish, which saved time and effort.

He and Lucy had fun with the pole lathe. Sid had done a tremendous job of adapting the medieval construction of the machine to something that gave the same result with a fraction of the physical effort.

'This sort of kit was used for donkey's years,' Bill told Lucy. 'Those Windsor chairs in the kitchen you like so much were turned out by bodgers over a hundred years ago. Same bit of kit, same technique, same cut lines on the wood.'

Bill had boxed a bit clever by rough-shaping all the turned areas in the chairs' arms and legs on his big lathe. This used different turning tools, but it was much more efficient and started with a big green button rather than a wobbly leg with dodgy knees. It was only the final finish he had to do with the pole lathe, but that alone took a whole day.

And then there was the carved chair back to collect from Eric. Bill had a bad feeling about that – not to do with the quality of the carving, but with Eric's strange behaviour.

He phoned him on Saturday morning and Eric said, yes, the back was ready and Bill could collect it any time he liked, just phone first and, of course, bring the money. There was no hint of Eric raising the ante, but Bill didn't think there would be until he was in the man' workshop with the finished piece in front of him.

'What worries me,' he told Lucy, 'is that Eric is no fool. The little shit will have some way of protecting himself. I doubt it will be a minder; that would cost money and besides, minders can become keepers if they feel so inclined.'

'But isn't that what he's got his vicious dogs for?' asked Lucy. 'I remember Skates having dealings with some very unsavoury characters who didn't needs guns because they had these damn great attack dogs frothing at the mouth instead. All they had to do was take off the muzzles and point the horrible things. Even Warren was afraid of them.'

'Was he?' mused Bill. 'Then perhaps he ought to come with me when I collect the panels.'

At first Lucy was appalled at the idea of having any more contact with Warren or Skates than they had to, but Bill eventually brought her around to the idea.

'I don't have the strength to put the fear of God into Eric myself anymore,' he said. 'I may as well use Warren for that.'

'Oh well,' said Lucy, 'with any luck, he'll get his throat torn out while you're there.'

Bill thought that unlikely, but having Warren around would provide some control over Eric, and it might even make Skates feel more in the picture without needing to resort to the use of birdwatchers who didn't know a great tit from an albatross. He went to the phone and called up Skates. Again, Warren answered, but this time when Bill asked for Skates he came on the line.

'How's the work going?' he asked.

'Well enough,' said Bill.

'When can I see what my money's buying?'

'If all continues to go well, I should be able to show you the finished pieces in late October or early November. But right now I've got a small problem you might be able to assist me in solving.'

Bill told Skates his suspicions about Eric. Skates hit the roof, blaming Bill for using someone he knew was flaky. Bill calmly and quietly explained that it was all a bit late for that and reminded Skates that he had used Eric because he was the only one good enough for the job. Not really mollified but a bit calmer, Skates asked Bill what he proposed. When Bill told him, there was a short, muffled conversation between Skates and Warren, and then Skates agreed.

Bill then phoned Eric and said he'd be by on Monday around eleven in the morning to collect the panels. Eric reminded Bill he still owed him a 'monkey', and that was it.

All the cutting was finished on the small components now. The seat for the new chair was being made out of the back panel of the chest they had bought in the auction. It worked in well, and when finished it would be indistinguishable from the original. As Bill cut the board, he thought back to the auctions he and Lucy had attended and all that had happened since then.

After a while Lucy came across the yard, bringing him a mug of tea He was sitting just outside the workshop door in the afternoon sunlight on a small bench that had been dragged out into the fresh autumn air, away from the dust. He was working away while the radio played, measuring and sawing the ancient oak board, his pipe clenched in his jaw but not, she was pleased to note, actually lit. With his stained carpenter's apron on, she thought he looked quite happy and it pleased her to see it. Clive, who followed in her wake as usual, was far more pleased by the fact that Bill always shared the biscuits Lucy brought him with his tea.

Lucy was intrigued by the strange device Bill was now using to saw the wood. It looked more like a huge kitchen knife with a crudely serrated edge than one of the beautiful, wood-handled saws he kept in racks in the workshop. Bill explained that this saw was an exact replica of those used in the 16th century.

'If ever this board is examined by experts,' he said, 'they will be hard pressed to know when it was cut. No tines at an angle like a modern saw. These things chew the wood more than cut it, but that's how it was done until a couple of centuries later when saws like we use now were invented. Details like this matter when you're making history.'

Chapter 31

MONDAY, 15 OCTOBER

I t was history of another sort that Bill made on Monday. As arranged, he met up with Warren in the same supermarket car park that he and Lucy had used when he visited Eric just under two weeks ago. From there, Warren would follow Bill on his motorbike until they got to the lane before the turning into Eric's bosky gulag, then he would park the bike up out of sight, get in the back of Bill's van, and be taken unseen into the compound.

Warren was wearing his usual black leathers and, with his bald head covered in a blanket, was virtually invisible in the dark rear of the van. Bill, with malice aforethought, made sure the blanket was a very old and smelly one. He had considered rubbing it in dog shit or some other noisome substance, but Lucy had vetoed it on the grounds that they didn't want the bastard throwing up and giving the game away.

It worked like a dream. Eric met Bill at the gate as before and didn't even glance into the back of the van. There appeared to be no dogs loose in the compound. Bill parked right by the shop door and followed Eric inside. The place was much the same except that on the bench in the middle of the room were two carved panels and a large book.

As Bill walked up to examine the carvings, he heard a low growl that raised the hair on the back of his neck. On the other side of the bench was an enormous Rottweiler chained to a hook in the wall. Eric moved to stand beside the dog, which was straining at its chain in an attempt to launch itself at Bill. The sneer on Eric's face gave him the appearance of a self-satisfied rodent.

'Adolph was very sorry not to get to meet you the last time you were here,' he said.

Bill made no comment, just bent down to look at the carving on the bench in front of him. It was perfect. The new panel was sculpted with the same amateur vibrancy and enthusiasm as the original, the chisel marks were just right and softened in all the correct places, just as they would have been by centuries of wear.

Eric could see Bill was impressed. 'Look as hard as you like,' he said. 'When I age a carving I do it right.'

He then added, with a contemptuous smirk, 'It's why I'm so expensive. Especially when I know what I'm working on.' He laid his hand on the large book and looked at Bill, his eyes bright with greed.

'Page 56. Nice piece on the Blakeney Elizabethan wainscot chairs. Lots of lovely detail.'

He was obviously enjoying the power he thought he had over Bill.

Bill leaned over to read the cover title. It was not a book he had in his library. He knew it, of course, but it was as rare as an honest auctioneer. *Bane's English Furniture: 1200 to 1700,* Volume 1, printed in 1930, gold lettering on the cloth cover.

He didn't open it, but just looked at Eric, who suddenly had a lot to say.

He wanted money, of course, as much as he could get and then some. 'I'm fed up with doing dodgy jobs for dodgy dealers for a few quid and all the risk. I'm fed up with snide remarks from you and all the other miserable bastards who rip me off every job I do. This one is going to pay for a long holiday in Thailand, where a man can indulge his private interests without fear of incarceration. Those chairs are worth a fortune and you are not going to reap all of the reward for them, not by a long fucking chalk.'

Bill said nothing to all this, just turned to the open doorway behind him. As he moved, the dog growled and renewed its efforts to get at him.

'Don't do anything rash, Bill,' said Eric with a malicious giggle. 'Adolph doesn't seem to like you and, do you know, I think I forgot to feed him this morning. What a silly Billy I am, and you fucking well would be, too, if you tried anything,' he added with some venom.

'Fuck off,' said Bill. 'Just lighting me pipe.' Which he then proceeded to do.

This was a signal to Warren, who had climbed out of the van and was waiting out of sight by the workshop door. Now he burst in, and his hand came up holding a small black object. Three loud bangs rang out, like enormous firecrackers, followed by a high-pitched scream. Bill saw the dog slumped on the floor amid a growing pool of blood.

Eric, still screaming, had his back to the wall, trying to get as much distance from the dead dog and Warren as he could. The crotch and legs of his boiler-suit showed the laxative effect of sudden shock.

Some nervous reaction prompted Bill to say, 'That'll take some washing out.'

He was appalled by the violence – he couldn't help remembering what Warren had done to Bess – but part of him knew it had been necessary.

Warren stepped to where Eric was now quivering and moaning in terror and slapped him, very hard, in the face. 'You have forfeited your deposit,' he said. 'Where is it?'

Eric was completely cowed now and showed Warren a safe hidden on the wall behind a rack of tools.

'Open it,' demanded Warren.

Eric did.

Bill was still standing by the door and peered outside to see if anyone had been drawn by the sound of the gun being fired. All he could hear was the other dogs in the caravan, barking their heads off.

Turning around, he saw that Warren had scooped out the contents of the small safe and thrown it all on the bench. Bill saw the envelope he had given Eric, opened but still looking full, and a few blue-covered invoice books.

Then he noticed the magazines and photographs. He knew such depraved things happened but had never seen actual pictures before.

Warren was transfixed, picking up photographs of children and adults, some in colour, some in black and white, but all very amateur in quality. Eric had slumped into an evil-smelling heap at Warren's feet. Suddenly, Warren started to kick him, punctuating the blows with incoherent shouts. Eric had his arms and hands over his head, protecting what he could from the relentless attack.

Bill made no move, nor any protestations. Somehow he knew that do so would be tantamount to suicide.

Warren's motorcycle boots made very little sound as they connected with the body hunched on the floor, and this may have annoyed him because he stopped kicking, looked around, and took a wood carver's mallet down from a nearby tool rack. The heavy, round, wooden head struck the cowering man, making a sound like a paddle hitting a bag of wet washing. Eric screamed. This, apparently, was better.

Turning to Bill, Warren said simply, 'Get out.'

Bill did. He took the carvings, and for a split second thought of taking the furniture book as well, but just as rapidly decided he wanted nothing else from that place. He even left the money in its envelope on the bench. The alternating sounds of thuds and screams continued behind him.

He got in the van as quickly as he could, stopping only to make sure the carvings were well wrapped up, then drove home carefully, slowly, and with the windows open as if the chill air might blow away the horrible visions that played over and over in his mind. He was still in shock when he reached home, and when he got out to open the yard gate, his hands were shaking. By the time he had driven in, closed the gate, parked, and entered the kitchen, he was in a bad way.

Lucy was immediately at his side, as was Clive, jumping up to be petted. It was putting his hand down to the dog's head and feeling the soft contours under the fur that really got to him. His face ashen, he slumped into his chair.

Lucy waited for Bill tell the story in his own time and at his own pace. She sat opposite and listened, holding his hand across the table. When he'd finished, she got up and fetched the two carvings from the van and placed them on the table between them. Bill sat, silent and drained, his fingers tracing the sculpted designs on the old wood. The new back was not polished and the old oak had a mellow, almost golden glow. It was a superb piece of carving. Picking it up, Lucy turned it to catch the light.

'To think that such a vile man carved something as beautiful as this.'

'Yes, well, it's unlikely he'll ever carve anything again. Warren's attack was . . . manic, frenzied. Beyond anything needed to subdue a little shit like Eric. It must have been the photographs.'

'Oh, I'm sure it was. You haven't forgotten about Warren's childhood on the Isle of Man, have you?'

Bill shook his head and Lucy continued. 'I doubt very much Eric is alive right now. And if he is, he certainly wishes he wasn't.'

Bill groaned and said he could really do with a smoke. There was no complaint from Lucy when he lit up, nor when he reached for the tissues she had so thoughtfully placed on a small stool by his chair. He coughed and coughed, then finally, pipe alight and chest subdued, he went over where he thought they were and where they might be going next.

'I think we can assume that Warren will somehow clear up his own mess. He's got previous for a bit of arson, of course, and it won't surprise me if Eric's workshop mysteriously burns down.'

'True,' said Lucy. 'There's nothing to link you to it, though, is there?

Bill shook his head. 'I only touched the two panels and

we have them here. I left the book on the bench. I might have touched it, but so would a lot of other people in the past. Same with the money I left behind. If it doesn't all end up ashes, there's nothing to say when I paid him or what for. But I can't see Warren leaving it there in any case.'

He paused, took a sip of his tea, and then reached down to pet Clive, who was laying at his feet. 'I understand why that bastard shot the dog. There was no other way. But Warren does like killing things, that's for sure.'

'And hurting them,' said Lucy quietly, more to herself than to him.

Bill looked at her as she sat opposite him. The nearby stove mumbled away, keeping the chill of the night air at bay, wisps of smoke occasionally escaping to scent the huge old kitchen. It all seemed so peaceful and innocent, so far away from the things Lucy had suffered in the past and he had witnessed today.

Lucy made him eat something, then told him to put his feet up and rest in his chair for a bit. He napped uneasily until just past six, when the phone rang. He got up and went to the instrument, lifted the receiver, and said wearily, 'Yes.'

Lucy could only hear Bill's side of the conversation, but it did not last long. When he put the phone down, he came back to his chair and sat down.

'It was Skates, of course, wanting to know what happened. As you heard, I just said I collected the carvings and left. Saw nothing, heard nothing, did nothing.'

'What did Warren tell him?'

'Buggered if I know. Probably some, possibly all, who knows? But I'm a witness and Warren will try and do me, that's for sure, regardless of what Skates does or doesn't want.'

Lucy gave him a worried look.

'Don't you fret,' he told her. 'We can be pretty certain nothing is going to happen until after those chairs are finished and delivered into Skates's hands. That will give me time to figure out how to get that nasty bastard before he gets me.'

That really did little to comfort Lucy, but she put on a brave smile.

Bill went to the dresser and took out a bottle of whisky, poured two large measures, and handed one to her. He sat back down, sipped his whisky, and took up his pipe again. He hardly noticed the coughing spasm that followed, it was so much part of his life now.

'I figure we've got about a week's worth of work putting the chairs together,' he said. 'The actual construction of the repaired chair should take only a day or two. The new chair, to put it all together, glue and peg the joints . . . three, maybe four days if all goes well.'

Lucy knew he really meant was if he was well.

'It's not a hard job now all the pieces are ready,' he continued. 'It's only a matter of fine-tuning the mortise and tenons a bit and hand-drilling the peg holes. You can do that bit while I glue and fix. The real bugger is going to be the aging of the wood, and that can't be done until the chairs are fully constructed. Normally on a job like this I would take three, maybe six months to really make the magic, but of course I haven't got that long.'

The words carried no bitterness; he was just stating a fact.

'But on the bright side,' he added, 'these chairs only have to be good enough for folk music, not a whole bloody symphony.'

'Folk music?'

'What I mean is that it's not as if they'll be examined by a real professional as soon as they're delivered. Skates will want to keep them for a bit while he gloats. Dealers and collectors, especially low-life amateurs like Skates, often equate possessions with power. It gives them a kick knowing they have something other people want. He won't do anything about selling them until he's had them awhile.'

Chapter 32

TUESDAY–SUNDAY,
16–21 OCTOBER

B ill and Lucy worked to a plan now, and the chairs came together better than he had dared to expect or even hope. It was as if, this being his last job – his swan song – all the skills he had acquired over the long years of pursuing his craft were rising to the challenge. The repaired chair accepted its new pieces as if it enjoyed becoming whole again, and time almost seemed to turn in on itself as the new became the old.

Lucy's world was now one of evil-smelling rabbit-skin glue, and she spent most of her time cutting pegs to the required lengths. As she worked, her appreciation of Bill's talents, and those of the craftsman who originally made the chairs all those centuries ago, grew and grew. Her own skills continued to develop as well, her hands learning to find marks and dents in the wood her eyes could not see.

Towards the end of the week, all the main fitting had been done. The new chair was looking good. Even Bill was pleased, and the carved panel fitted beautifully. He lined all the chairs up, side by side, and Lucy could only tell the old from the new by the colour of the wood. As far as the style was concerned, they were unquestionably a set, each with its own subtle characteristics – but definitely a set.

Now the work of aging and polishing could begin. Despite what Bill had said about the chairs not really needing to be museum quality, his pride would allow nothing less. No matter how much he hated their owner, the chairs themselves demanded and deserved as much.

But all this work was taking its toll on him, so Lucy insisted they both take the Sunday off, completely, with no arguing or sulking. Bill knew she was cooking something special because the rich smell of a game stew filled the kitchen, but she just smiled and told him to make himself scarce.

'And do *not*, emphasis on the *not*, go into the workshop.'

She shooed him into the front room, where she had lit the fire. He was a little bemused but did as he was told and sank into a huge leather club chair.

With the radio on and Clive taking up most of the hearth rug, Bill sat in front of the roaring log fire and read. Eventually the book slipped from his hand and he dozed, only to wake to the sound of voices in the house. As he was struggling to get out of the chair, he was surprised and delighted to be set upon by his grandson. He marvelled at how much the lad had grown and allowed him to help him to his feet. Then, with his old arm around Jack's young shoulders, they walked the short distance to the kitchen.

There he saw the table covered with his mother's damask tablecloth and laid out with all the old silver he never used; even the condiment set had been polished. The main overhead light was turned off, and candles were lit all around the room. An ancient candelabra, now polished and less bent than he remembered it, was placed in the middle of the table. It looked to Bill almost medieval with the flickering candlelight, the bright silver, and the antique china on the white cloth.

Gloria and Lucy were at the stove decanting saucepans of vegetables into tureens he had forgotten he owned. Philip was opening bottles and arranging his father's antique wine glasses at the places set around the table. They sat Bill at the head, his family (which now included Lucy, of course) all around him. In the centre, like a flotilla of ceramic ships, bowls steamed and brimmed with delights of all sorts.

Bill was dumbfounded. It was a Christmas dinner! A wonderful Christmas dinner, and it was happening now. His family were giving him his Christmas. They were giving him the one gift they could that would really matter. Showing him just how much they loved him and, in their own way, putting two fingers up to fate. If he couldn't make it to Christmas, then Christmas would make it to him.

Gloria sat opposite Bill with a large casserole to hand. She lifted the lid and a rich, savoury smell filled the room. She served out a wondrous stew onto plates that Lucy then put in front of each person. Deep red wine shone like rubies in the glancing light of the crystal glasses. Even Jack, who sat next to his grandfather, was allowed a 'taster'.

Beside each plate was a linen napkin. as Jack lifted his so he could tuck it into his collar like granddad did, he found that several small, brown, hard biscuits had been hidden underneath. Lucy caught his eye and winked. Jack slowly lowered one of the biscuits under the table. A warm, wet mouth engulfed it, and a large, furry tail semaphored the owner's delight and gratitude.

When the meal was well under way and the first helpings

were making way for the second helpings for those who still had corners to fill, Philip stood up and banged on the table with a spoon. Raising his glass, he said, 'A toast, ladies and gentleman! A toast to my dad, Bill.'

They all stood and raised their glasses, and with a lot of clapping and even more joy, they drank. Bill then rose to his feet and took up his own glass.

'Thank you, all of you. Right now I couldn't be happier.' Then, bowing to Lucy and Gloria: 'You cunning wenches, bless you.'

He sat down, then leaned over to Jack and said very quietly, 'Happy Christmas.'

Jack looked slightly puzzled, but decided being a granddad meant not knowing when it was or wasn't Christmas. Strange, but that's grown-ups for you.

The feast continued, relaxed and slow, and all the dishes that were placed in front of Bill he recognised as being his favourites, right down to the strong local cheddar that followed the apple pie and custard. When it was finally over, and the smell of fresh coffee began to waft from the stove, he and Philip were sent into the front room to put their feet up and get out of the way of the two women. Jack was sent outside with Clive to burn off a bit of energy in their favourite pastime of losing the tennis ball and finding it again.

As father and son sat opposite each other in their comfortable old armchairs in the comfortable old room, Bill was finally able to ask Philip about his work and how things were going. He knew that his son really wanted to start up on his own, and he understood that: he had never wanted to work for anyone, either. Philip told his father just how frustrated he was in the current setup.

'I know more could be done for some of the clients we handle, but the senior partners are all for a quiet life and big Masonic dinners.'

Bill looked at his boy. He was slim, and taller than his father. His fair hair was thinning, but his smile was ready and engaging. He looked more like a teacher than an accountant. When he began telling his father about some of the clients he had who were small businessmen or craftsmen like Bill, he became quite passionate.

'They're paying good money for a service that's just about adequate, but doesn't really answer all of their needs. Not the way it should do, or at least not how I'd like to do it.'

Bill understood that only too well. He had employed a canny bookkeeper for years who knew the ropes and was well in with the local antique fraternity. She was getting on, however, and there would be a gap when she retired. He could certainly see that someone who was familiar with the problems of the self-employed might be able to carve out a good niche for themselves.

He asked Philip what sort of capital he would need to set up on his own, and it turned out to be not as much as he had feared. Philip explained that he would work from home, which would save a lot of expense. That gave Bill an idea. He leaned forward and looked at his son.

'I'm not going to beat about the bush, lad. You know I'm for the chop.'

Philip said nothing, just nodded, knowing that to deny the truth would only upset his father. Bill was grateful that his son made no stupid protestations. A chip off the old block, he thought.

'Now, you'll get all this anyway,' he said, waving a hand in the general direction of everything. 'Lock, stock, and every bloody barrel. So figure out how to make these assets work for you and give you the freedom to do what you want to do.'

He leaned back, searching for his pipe, thought better of it, and continued.

'Look, son, when you work for yourself, it's your life you lead and you can choose how you lead it. Your clients, customers, call 'em what you want, you treat them well and give them your best advice and you'll never want for work because word gets 'round. You'll work harder and longer hours when you work for yourself, but it's your business and you reap the benefits in more ways than one. With the sort of clients you'll be dealing with, for example, you'll never have to worry about getting a bit of building work done or moving a few antiques to a new home.'

Philip laughed at that.

'Anyway, you and the family move in here after I'm gone,' said Bill. 'There's bags of room and, trust me, there are some nice little earners tucked away that will bring in a goodly shilling when they're sold.'

Philip thought there was a lot of sense in all his father said. He and Gloria could sell the place they were currently living in, which was a small, modern house on a new estate just outside Dorchester. Gloria was fed up with the lack of room, especially with the new baby coming, not to mention their arse-clenching neighbours. He also knew Jack would get a better education here than he would at the rather second-rate comprehensive school near their current home. He leaned forward and put a hand on his father's knee.

'I'll talk to Gloria about all this, Dad, but what about Lucy?'

'I'm glad you asked me that, son. I'm making provision for her, of course. Truth to tell, I never could have got this far without her.'

'We know that, Dad. We'll make sure she's looked out for.'

Philip turned to look out of the window. It wasn't raining, but the landscape was suddenly blurry.

Bill, too, was silent now, staring into the flames of the fire in front of him. The huge fireplace, blackened by time, gave out the only light in the room now that dusk was falling.

But life rather than death beckoned when Jack came bursting in with a very muddy Clive panting beside him and sat down on the wide leather arm of his grandfather's chair. Out of breath, muddy, and smelling of the countryside (a certain amount of which he had, in fact, brought in with him on shoes and trousers), he put his arms around Bill's neck and delivered a big hug. When he was finally released, Bill smiled at his muddy grandson.

'How did you get past your mother? She'll skin you alive when she sees the state you're in.'

'I just scooted through. Mum was busy at the sink. Aunty Lucy saw me but she just winked.' Then he added, 'I like her, she's fun.'

'She is, isn't she?' agreed Bill.

Teas and coffees were brought in. The sitting room was suddenly full of family, more logs were put on the fire, and the room became hot and cosy. They all talked and laughed together, especially when Clive farted and Philip blamed it on Jack.

A family together, but not for much longer, Bill thought.

His illness was getting bad. He was in a lot of pain most of the time now, and that made even everyday things like shaving tiring. As soon as his family left, he went to bed. He was absolutely whacked.

'Happy but knackered,' he told Lucy as he went up the stairs. And for the first time, he asked her to lock up for him.

Bill's keyring had a large collection of keys on it. Some were as old as the house, some no longer had locks that fitted them, and a few were bright new ones that shone amongst the old like a sixpence in a sweep's ear-ole. Trust Bill, she thought, as she hefted the keyring, he never throws anything away. Gives away, yes; throws away, never.

With Clive at her heels and a heavy, rubber-handled torch in her hand, she made sure the workshop was locked and put the padlock on the big gate. As she did so, she heard the sound of someone walking on the lane just up from where she was standing. It was dark, with just a sliver of moon low in the autumn sky. She stood absolutely still. Clive growled but didn't attempt to get over the gate. Standing there, she realised she had no weapon except the torch in her hand. Her heart pounding, she swung the beam in the direction the sound had come from.

The dim ray of light showed her a small deer daintily picking its way up the narrow lane towards Miss Templeton's cottage. It turned and looked straight at her. Lucy thought she had never seen anything so ethereal in her life before. The old magic of the landscape seemed to be shining in its dark eyes. Then the deer moved gracefully and silently out of the light and disappeared back into the darkness.

As Lucy walked into the kitchen, locking and bolting the door behind her, she wondered if there had been some sort of message in the encounter. As she got into bed a little later, it came to her. The stew they had all enjoyed so much that day had contained venison. Sweet little deer were apt to become someone's meal if they didn't watch out, weren't they? So the message was: *Don't go out at night without a fucking weapon.* How very mystical!

Chapter 33

MONDAY, 22 OCTOBER

Bill had a bad night, indigestion and pain making horrendous bedfellows. Lucy left him dozing in bed and opened up the workshop. About eleven a car she didn't recognise drove up to the gate. Peering from around the corner of the barn, she saw it contained a man in his forties with a shock of red hair. He wore heavy, horn-rimmed glasses that were slightly askew. He certainly didn't look like anyone who would be employed by Skates, so Lucy decided to risk it and let him in.

As the man got out of the car, he smiled and, in a deep, pleasant voice, said, 'Hello, I'm Chris Hall, Mr Sawyer's doctor. Is he here?'

Lucy took him inside, and there was Bill sitting at the big kitchen table drinking tea, the breakfast she had left out for him largely untouched. He looked ill and tired, his face lined now with more than just age. But he stood up and greeted the doctor warmly, introducing Lucy as his niece who had come to look after him. This turned out to be an inspired choice because when she asked Dr Hall if he'd like her to leave while he spoke with Bill, the doctor said that, as she was his carer, it was all right with him if she stayed.

So Lucy made a fresh pot of tea while the doctor gave Bill a quick examination. Out came the stethoscope, and Bill was asked to take deep breaths and do all the other things that accompany such soundings. As he sat there with his shirt open and his vest up to his armpits, Lucy saw the hollow chest covered with grey hair and the skin hanging loose where muscles used to be. 'I have to do something,' she thought, but had no idea what.

When the examination was over and Bill was pulling on his clothes, the doctor asked him how his symptoms were progressing. Bill shrugged them off, but Lucy didn't, which earned her a scowl from Bill as she told the doctor of the intense coughing that brought up blood, the loss of appetite, and the constant weariness. Dr Hall appreciated this. He needed to know the truth and he was glad to see that this woman was no pushover who would be cowed by her uncle. Bill was in good hands, he thought, and included her in the conversation as he laid out Bill's options.

Morphine was not a problem. Bill could take as much – well, almost as much – as he liked. The big brown bottle could be a comfort, but was not without some side effects. Bill then got a bit embarrassed asking about some of them. Well, one of them in particular. Lucy cottoned on immediately and said Bill had been daft not to mention it before. Bill squirmed and mumbled. Dr Hall said he had a medication he would prescribe, but 'a good, rough farmhouse cider was probably just as good.'

He then asked Bill if he had looked into a hospice yet for 'the final leg'. Bill admitted he hadn't, but Lucy told him she had spoken with Gloria, Bill's daughter-in-law, and she was getting information on one not too far away. They planned to take Bill there some time in the next couple of weeks.

Bill was taken aback by this news. 'Thick as thieves, those two,' he thought. 'Poor bastard like me doesn't stand a chance.'

As Lucy walked the doctor back to his car, he asked her how she was coping.

'Well enough,' she replied.

'If you like, you can register with me and I'll give you what help I can.'

'I'm only staying as long as I'm needed, and then I'll go home,' said Lucy.

And then it suddenly struck her what a lie that was. She had no home and no idea what she would do after Bill died, especially if Skates and Warren were still about.

The doctor nodded and said, 'Well, if you need anything or just want a bit of respite, call in at the surgery. No need for any paperwork,' he added with a smile.

Clever man, that doctor, thought Lucy, as he drove away. A clever man and a kind one. But the fact remained that she really didn't know what she would do or where she would go after Bill died. They had been so focused on the chairs and how much they could get done each day, she had never given it any serious thought.

Instead of going back into the kitchen, Lucy took Clive and went through the passage next to the workshop into the meadow beyond. She looked carefully at the place where Sid had caught the intruder. There was no sign of anyone having been there since, just the few feathers she and Bill had scattered about. As she walked around the field close by the hedgerow, she noticed the changes being made by the season. Autumn was now in full colour, the hedges just bare branches as they closed down for the winter. Even the old oak that had stood for centuries was losing its gold and russet leaves. They crunched under her feet as she walked.

Clive had run off chasing imaginary rabbits and she was alone. She felt very much alone. She had no family of her own, and she doubted Philip and Gloria would want her about them much, reminding them of the father they had lost. And, for the same reason, would she even want to stay around?

She kept walking, trying to let the spell of the place wash over and comfort her. Finally she made up her mind to return home and was calling Clive when she saw a man with a shotgun under his arm walk out from the gate to the next field. He looked about forty, with a ruddy face and short, dark beard flecked with grey. He had on a well-worn wax coat and green wellies, and looked every inch a countryman, the sort Lucy had seen in county magazines.

'This is private land, I'm afraid,' he said kindly as he walked up to her. His voice had the same mellow, West Country burr as Bill's.

'Yes, I know, I'm staying with Bill, I mean Mr Sawyer,' stammered Lucy, not quite sure why she suddenly felt so self-conscious. 'I, I'm his carer. His live-in carer.'

The man broke open the gun, rested it on his left arm, and extended a strong right hand for her to shake.

'My name's Hugh Dawlish,' he said. 'My brother and I farm this land. We're neighbours of Bill's.'

'Yes,' said Lucy, 'I think I've heard him mention you.'

'I heard Bill was sick. How is he getting on?'

'He's quite ill, actually, but still getting about.'

Hugh smiled at that. 'I bet he is. He's always seemed

indestructible to me. But if there's anything I can do for him, please let me know. He's a good man is Bill, one of the best.'

'Yes, thank you, I will,' said Lucy and was turning to go when Hugh asked how they were set for logs.

'Oh, there's a stack in the lean-to, but I haven't really noticed how many are there.'

'Ah, a townie, then,' he said with a laugh. 'I'll bring a trailer-load 'round soon as may be.'

And with that he turned and went back through the gate. He whistled, and a black Labrador got up from where it had been sitting on the other side of the hedge and ran to its master's side. Hugh turned, waved, and was gone.

Lucy looked down at Clive, who was sprawled panting at her feet, his coat matted with mud, leaves, and twigs. 'Why can't you behave like that?' she asked him.

Back in the kitchen she found Bill looking a bit better, his mood a little lighter. When the dishevelled Clive came in and slumped down next to the stove, Bill berated him with mock severity. 'You're a disgrace to the canine race, you are!'

Lucy told him all about her meeting with Hugh in the meadow and his offer to deliver some logs. Bill laughed at that. 'There are enough logs on the woodpile to see me out,' he said.

Lucy felt stunned, as though he'd slapped her. Her face must have shown the pain she felt because he looked puzzled and asked her what was wrong.

'Enough firewood to see you out!' she said angrily. 'Well what about the rest of us? What about me? What the hell do I do? Where the hell do I go, after you're gone?'

And then, to Bill's horror, she burst into tears.

Between sobs she told him she just didn't know just how

she would cope without him. She didn't want to, couldn't even think of, going back to where she came from, but she certainly didn't want to be a burden on his family. So where could she go, what could she do?

Bill sat there and shook his head. He had no idea such thoughts had been going through Lucy's mind. Stupid of him. He felt guilty and ungrateful.

'Come here, love,' he said, putting his arms around her and pulling her close. 'I'm so sorry. I have been so bloody occupied with my own problems that I completely lost sight of yours.'

Lucy sat back and rubbed her eyes. 'I'm sorry, Bill –' she started, but he cut her off.

'You've nothing to be sorry for. It's past time we talked about this. Now, as we know, we have two main problems: the chairs, and Skates and co. Both are solvable. You, my darling, just need to ponder on what you want to do after they are taken care of. If I work it right, we'll have about sixteen thousand quid in cash from the chairs.'

Lucy looked up at that.

'Do you really think Skates will pay you the ten he still owes you? He won't have to if he lets Warren loose on you.'

'He will if I only deliver two chairs and tell him he won't get the others until I'm paid the remaining ten grand. Oh, he'll plan to have Warren get it back when he knocks me off, but he'll give it to me, especially if I deliver the new chairs first and keep the really valuable ones back. I'll tell him they're wired up to be destroyed or something if I don't get back to my workshop by a certain time.'

'It sounds an awful risk to me,' said Lucy. 'You'll be in their hands, not here. Will Skates even let you go?'

'You are my ace in the hole, love. Neither Skates nor Warren knows I have an accomplice. They'll assume they can get to me any time they want. One old man, sick and alone. That'll make them careless.'

Lucy still had her doubts, and if he was honest, Bill knew the plan still needed a bit of work, but that was tomorrow's problem. What Lucy needed right now was a road she could travel, or at least a few options she could consider.

'Okay, let's move on. The job is done and I'm in a hospice. It won't be for long, and the way I've been feeling of late, honest lass, I won't be sorry.'

Lucy's eyes filled with tears again, and Bill leaned over to take her hand.

'If I were a dog they'd have put me down weeks ago and you know it. So let's look to the living: you, my love.'

'Bill, the problem is I really don't know what I want. I love it here, but without you it will be empty and lonely. But I don't want to go back to London,' she added with a shudder.

'What about Dylan?'

'Oh, no, he's sweet and all that, but I really wouldn't want to spend the rest of my life there.' She gave him a weak smile. 'Not with those loos.'

'How about a holiday, then? Anywhere you fancy going?'

This suggestion took Lucy by surprise. She had never given thought to a holiday; had never really had one since childhood, in fact. 'What about Clive?' she asked.

Bill had a rude answer to that but managed to stop himself saying it in time. 'A dog is no problem, depending where you go. You could take a trip somewhere in the UK that you've never been before. Better still, just outside it. How about Ireland?

You could drive there, even with that daft animal.' He could see she was intrigued by this idea. 'A lovely part of the world,' he went on, 'You can do a bit of sightseeing, and it's not as cold there as here. Wet, yes, but not really freezing. Nice, small hotels and pubs you can stay in. Great food and friendly people. I loved going there.'

'What did you go there for?'

'Irish silver and furniture. More silver than furniture, but if you do your homework right there are some great bargains to be had in some of the smaller towns that don't get infested by tourists. You have a good eye, girl; you could buy a few pieces of nice silver and bring 'em back, sell 'em on. And look,' he added. 'Philip is going to need to move a bit of stuff from here in order to make space, and Sid will be flogging off what machinery in the workshop is worth anything, and he'll need a bloody grown-up around, that's for sure.'

Lucy felt slightly better. A holiday, then back here to review the situation, or at least a break away with time to plan her next move. It was a stopgap of an idea, but it was something to be going on with.

Still holding Lucy's hand, Bill looked her in the eye and said, 'It will work out, my darling. We've got some shit to shovel between us, but it will work out. I promise.'

They had done no work on the chairs that day; now it was too late and Bill was too tired. He phoned Sid to see if he was available for a couple or three days this week, and could he bring over a grain dryer if he had one? Sid said he would look into a grain dryer and, yes, he was available. Rat catching was quiet, and no one wanted any welding, not even his dodgy car dealers, so he would be there in the morning, bacon-sandwich time.

After supper, Lucy asked about the man she had met in the fields that afternoon. Bill told her that Hugh and his brother Alan had inherited the farm from their father and had added to it and expanded it beyond recognition. Hugh was the older son and more of a true farmer than Alan, who had the business brains. Nice blokes, was Bill's summing up of them, and good neighbours who loved the land they farmed.

'Most people think Hugh is a confirmed bachelor, but the fact is he's actually a widower. His wife died in a car crash not too long after they were married. Very tragic, that. She was pregnant with their first child. Ever since then he's kept his head down and just focused on his farm.'

Lucy looked shocked but said nothing, and the subject was dropped.

When Bill went to bed that night, however, it struck him that Lucy had mentioned Hugh twice that day. Something might be made of that, he thought. Each of them had wounds the other might be able to help heal. He determined to sleep on it.

Chapter 34

TUESDAY–WEDNESDAY,
23–24 OCTOBER

Sid returned early next morning and set to work demolishing the huge pile of bacon sarnies Lucy had got ready for him. It turned out he didn't have a grain dryer that worked, which for some reason didn't worry Bill at all; quite the opposite, in fact. He looked downright pleased when he said he would phone Hugh instead and ask to borrow his. After doing so, he went out into the yard where Sid and Lucy were slowly and methodically rubbing down the new chair with fine wire wool to soften its edges.

Working outside was a real bonus, and thankfully the weather was kind. Cool but not cold, and blessedly dry. The rich colour of the old oak mirrored the colours of autumn all around them. Bill kept upwind so as not to breath in the dust, and occasionally suggested they do something here or a bit more there. Lucy could see he was a little frustrated, though, because his own hands were not on the job.

She went inside to make yet another pot of tea. Those two seemed to swim in the stuff, but men who could be made happy with constant cups of tea and good, plain food were still a revelation to Lucy and not something she was ever likely to take for granted.

When she was gone, Bill leaned over to Sid and asked him if he could lay his hands on a better shotgun than the one he had borrowed from Hugh. Sid nodded and asked if he wanted a legal or a special. Bill said he wasn't bothered so long as it was deadly. Sid smiled and said he had just the thing and would bring it tomorrow.

They carried on the long, slow job of rubbing down, now with fine sand on a damp chamois leather. This exposed the grain when it was rubbed along the wood following the natural contours. Already age and wear could be seen blending the new wood into the old on the repaired chair; it was only the colour and tone of the woods that differed. Bill said they would leave the staining until both chairs were completed as that would be 'an arsehole of a job' and they would only have once chance at getting it right.

Sid stayed for supper but left off drinking too much cider as he wanted to get home that night. As Bill walked out with him to close the yard gate for the night, he asked Sid about a quick lesson with the revolver tomorrow.

'Not a problem, but what about Lucy? You still haven't told her you have the bloody thing, have you?'

'No, but she's going into town to get groceries in the morning. We can practice then.'

The next day Sid was there by nine. Bill was not yet up, and Lucy was getting ready to go shopping. There was a cashbox without a key in a drawer in the dresser, and she always took whatever cash she needed from that. Once, early on, she had asked Bill if he wanted receipts when she shopped, and he had said a very rude word that made her laugh out loud.

Before he left, she put a handful of pills in a saucer and asked Sid to make sure Bill took them. Sid stared at the heap of capsules and tablets in the dish. Different colours, different sizes, some looking like sweets and others decidedly not.

'Poor bugger. How is he?'

'Not good,' said Lucy sadly. 'But holding in there.'

'I'll do anything I can, you know that, girl.'

'I know that, Sid, bless you.'

After Lucy had gone, Bill came down carrying a large, heavy box. He ate his usual meagre breakfast and took his pills, then he and Sid went out to the workshop.

From the large box, Bill took out his old revolver and the box of ammunition. From a small box, Sid took out two sets of earplugs. There was plenty of room in the workshop for Sid to pace out fifteen feet right at the back. He chose a place away from the main door and near to the gable wall. It would be safe from ricochets and not easily seen by anyone coming into the building.

Bill had a dining table that was in such poor condition it was only good for burning, but it did have a top of solid wood over two inches thick. On this Sid drew the rough outline of a man's torso and head, then he put the table on a couple of tea chests to raise it to man height. The light was not very good this far into the barn, but that suited Sid, who wanted to replicate the worst-case scenario Bill might have to face.

'Show me how you'll get the gun in,' he said. 'Let's make this as real as we can.'

Bill got out a long, narrow, wooden toolbox, the sort carpenters used years ago for carrying tools on a job site. It had no lid, but the ends narrowed at the top and were connected by a stout wooden handle. There was enough of a gap between this and the box itself to get to the tools inside, and yet the box was still deep enough so you had to look right down into it to see anything. Bill said the gun would be covered with a cloth in any case, and Sid approved the scheme.

Out came the revolver, and Sid took Bill through the best way to hold such a big weapon. Next he had Bill dry fire the gun so as to get used to cocking the large hammer. Sid watched carefully and noticed how the gun wavered in his friend's hands. It was a heavy piece; he reckoned it must weigh near to three pounds. That was a lot if you were nervous and your arms were weakened by illness.

Finally, Bill put the gun in the toolbox, covered it with the cloth, and put the box down on the floor. Sid moved behind Bill, looked at his watch, and said, 'Right, go.'

Bill took the huge revolver from the box, holding it as he had been shown: right hand by the butt, finger alongside the trigger guard, left hand supporting the right from underneath. Standing square onto the target, he cocked the hammer, brought his finger around onto the trigger, and fired.

The noise was terrific. It filled the building and brought dust down from the roof high above. Both men were very grateful for the earplugs. The recoil had thrown Bill's arms high, but Sid was pleased to see he still had it in his hands. Some people let go at first, and it could really cramp your style if you had to go looking for your weapon after each shot.

The grey stone wall several feet behind the target now had a bright crater in it, and there was a large hole in the table right where the head had been drawn. Sid thought it was probably just a lucky shot, but Bill was beaming like a schoolboy.

'Fucking hell!' he said, awed at his own performance.

'Yes, not bad, but that was only one shot, and you might have to take three or four depending on how many people are in the room.'

Bill looked shocked. 'People? Three or four?'

Sid pulled a dusty dining chair from a stack nearby and got Bill to sit down on it. He was looking a bit shaky. Then, with the smell of cordite still enveloping them, Sid looked him in the eye and spoke to him slowly and seriously.

'If you go into Skates's house to kill him and it turns out there are people there besides Skates and Warren, you will have to kill them as well.'

Bill said nothing, just looked down at the gun. The wooden grip felt warm in his grasp, and the dark blue metal of the barrel and cylinder had an oily sheen that reflected the light. This was no toy, this was a weapon, a tool with only one use: killing.

'If there are servants,' continued Sid firmly, 'you can tell them to fuck off. They will, I assure you, but they'll still be witnesses, so it's down to you. But there might well be a minder or two in addition to Warren and if there is, they will have to be taken out. Otherwise, they will do you.'

He paused for a moment to let that sink in, then added, 'If you're really going through with this, Bill, then you have got to go through with all of it. There is no other way.'

Bill knew Sid was right, of course. It was just that so far it had only been talk and now it was becoming real. He had imagined he would walk into Skates's place, shoot the bastard and hopefully Warren, too, then just walk out. Silly, really, to have thought it could ever be that simple.

Then, for some reason Bill found himself telling Sid about the day Warren killed Eric. Sid had read something about someone dying in a fire near Chard, but now he heard the full details. He had never had any doubts about the ruthlessness of either Skates or Warren, but after learning what had happened to Eric he was absolutely convinced they had to be put down.

'They'll never let you live after witnessing something like that.'

'Which is really neither here nor there under the circumstances, Sid, but if I don't do this, Lucy will never be free of those bastards. Besides,' he added softly, 'there's what they did to Bess.'

Sid could see Bill was tired, and not just from the firing practice but also from recounting what he had been forced to witness only last week. The poor bugger, he thought, and suggested they get a cup of tea.

Bill nodded, then emptied the cylinder of cartridges, wrapped the old firearm in its oily cloth, and put it back in its box with the rest of the ammunition. Ever mindful of good housekeeping when it came to evidence, Sid extracted the bullet from the stone wall, brushed dirt over the crater it had left, and took an axe to the table.

Back in the warm kitchen, Sid made tea while Bill went upstairs and returned the gun to his room. When he came back down he sat in his armchair, pensive and quiet. Taking the mugs across to the table, Sid watched Bill spoon sugar into his tea. He spilled some on the tabletop and tried to wipe the sticky crystals up with his handkerchief.

'I hope you're going to be a better shot with that gun than you are with a bloody spoon, mate,' he said kindly, and handed him a wet cloth.

He let Bill rest for a bit, then returned to the business at hand. Sitting back in his chair, mug of tea cradled in his hands, he delivered what amounted to a sermon. A very Old Testament kind of sermon, full of the smiting and harrowing of the ungodly.

'A firearm, old son, is the ultimate leveller. With one, any person – even a weak old granny with a prolapse and no teeth – can be as deadly as a muscular marine with skills in unarmed combat and wielding a fucking great sword to boot. Providing,' he stressed, '*providing*, they have the element of surprise. If Skates has minders, shoot them first. Shoot *accurately*; you need not be quick, but you do need to be accurate. Do not hesitate. Once in, make sure you open fire as soon as the targets are within range. You have six rounds; one each should be enough to put them down. These are big shells, but even so, when you have accounted for all of the buggers, if they're not shot in the head or the chest, shoot the fuckers again. You have to,' he added grimly. 'It's you or them.'

Sid drank the remainder of his tea and went out, leaving Bill a bit shell-shocked. He soon returned carrying something wrapped in dark cloth. He opened it up on the table near Bill. It was a shotgun, but not the elegant hunting weapon as typically found in the hands of gentry plugging away at plump game, posturing and chortling whilst showering the beaters with shot. No, this had once been a gun of that kind, but now it was just nasty, brutish, and short. The barrel had been butchered to less than a foot and the stock had been cut into a butt-like handle. A single lever opened the breach and it had two triggers, one for each barrel.

'This can be held and fired with one hand if you're busy,' said Sid. 'But it's better with two.'

He took from his pocket a box of twelve-bore shells. 'These have been doctored a tad. They'll blow a hole six inches wide through an oak door, so just imagine . . .' He left the rest of the sentence unsaid.

'Now,' he added with a wolfish grin, 'would you like me along to ride shotgun? For free, pro bono!'

Bill thought for a bit, then said, 'No, not with me, Sid, but I'd be grateful if you'd be here with Lucy when I . . . um . . . deliver the chairs.'

Further discussion was put on hold as Lucy's Volvo drove in just then and parked outside the kitchen door. Sid went off to help her bring in the shopping while Bill took the shotgun upstairs and secured it in his room.

Lucy seemed to be in a good mood as she unloaded the grocery bags and put the contents away. 'Open wide, Beryl!' she said with a laugh as she stocked the huge refrigerator with eggs, milk, and other provisions.

Bill, coming back into the kitchen then, only smiled, having heard the joke before, but poor Sid nearly choked on his tea.

'You got that right, girl!' he gasped. 'Large and frosty, that was Beryl all right, eh, Bill?'

Bill grunted and said, 'Not far off.'

When all the groceries had been stowed away, he told them it was time to get back to the chairs. 'One more day of rubbing down and we can start staining. Hugh's bringing his grain dryer over tomorrow, so we need to get as much done today as we can manage.'

As they all trooped into the workshop, Lucy said she

thought she could smell fireworks. Neither of the men made any reply, so she put it down to a quirk of the old stove.

They were able to work in the open again as the weather was still dry. Lucy and Sid cleared out a space in the open-sided cart shed. It was near enough to the workshop to run a power line across, which meant they could put up a few lights to help them see better. Once again Bill took an advisory role until there was something that needed his particular hand skills and experience to finish off.

The day drew to a close and the landscape around the farm softened in the twilight. Sid stayed for supper, during which they discussed the day's work and how everything was progressing. Bill was very pleased and said it certainly beat doing it all himself as he used to do.

Lucy got out a jug of cider she had picked up on her way home from the supermarket. It was good stuff and, at eight percent, very powerful. Sid drank sparingly, but Bill did not and, as a result, became jollier and more garrulous than Lucy had ever known him. Sid got him reminiscing about some of the jobs he had done in the past and the various tricks of his trade, ancient and modern.

'In the real old days,' Bill told them, 'fakers would make reproduction furniture out of green wood, just as the originals were made. Then they would tether them on the sea strand to get battered by waves and rolled against sand and rocks, which would add years of wear in only a month or two. There was one harbour near West Bay that was used by two different families of fakers, and if any poor sod tried to do a bit of fishing around there, he would be chased off right quick. And one time someone saw all this furniture being tossed about on the strand, thought there had been a shipwreck, and cycled miles in foul weather to alert the Coast Guard!'

'When was this?' asked Lucy, laughing.

'Oh, back in the thirties when antique furniture was becoming sought after by the middle classes. The upper crust always used the great inheritance merry-go-round method of furnishing their homes. There were some real first-class fakers in those days. Men like George Furnley, who was known as 'Flashy Furnley' because when he died in 1960 he was still wearing the same suit they gave him when he left the army in 1919. Harry Tasker was another one. He was known as 'Nailer' because he would knock you up a bag of 16th-century nails and screws at five pounds a dozen. All hand-forged and, if you wanted them that way, nicely corroded.'

'What would you want with corroded nails and screws?' asked Sid, a bit confused, though that may have been the cider.

'If a thing ain't right, it's wrong, Sid. A modern nail or screw in a supposedly old chair, that bugger would be as out of place as you in a convent.'

They all laughed, and after another drink, Bill went on thoughtfully, 'Speaking of things that ain't right, I've been giving some thought to where Skates might have come by those chairs of his. The last time any of the Blakeneys was ever mentioned was when Simon Morse sold his two in 1953, and I think the buyer was one Lord Deverill. He had two obsessions, this lord: one was collecting anything related to Elizabeth I, and the other was gambling. A friend of mine in the trade told me it was believed Skates had acquired some valuable Elizabethan furniture from Deverill as payment for a gambling debt, and I think the two-and-a-bit Blakeneys were included in that payment. Morse always said he never could find the other two chairs, but I reckon Deverill already had the damaged one and was still searching for the fourth. He probably even told Skates all about them. It's unlikely he'd find out about them any other way.'

'Well, that's as may be,' said Lucy, getting up, 'but now I think it's time we were all in our beds.'

She could see that, despite the cider, Bill was weary and in pain. He refused to take any morphine, though, because he wanted to be up in good time to get things under way for when Hugh arrived.

'And him being a farmer,' he said, 'I'm guessing it will be bloody sparrow fart o'clock.'

Sid said he would walk Clive and check over the place, then drop the dog back in before he left. The night was cold and there was autumn mist in the air. The light that came from the kitchen window barely illuminated the doorstep, and his white transit van was just a ghostly shape. He walked in a silent world, his boots on the concrete making the only sound. Clive wandered off for a crap and a sniff around; Sid stood waiting for him and smoking a roll-up. His mind went back over the day and then, as if summoned by the remembered sound of gunfire and the smell of cordite in Bill's barn that morning, old memories put their boots on and marched behind his eyes. He was back in Belfast doing what he was trained to do and doing it well. He had been a soldier, he had been a killer, and he knew that it had changed him.

There was no regret, though. He had done what he'd had to do, and if he hadn't, well, he wouldn't be standing here having this fag right now. But sometimes he missed the camaraderie of his fellow soldiers, and he would dig out his sand-coloured beret with its cap badge depicting Excalibur wreathed in flames. 'Who fucking dares wins *what*?' he would ask himself. And that's when he would start drinking, not stopping until he was unconscious or all the bottles were empty.

And now his friend Bill would have to take a gun and kill at least one man, probably two, and maybe even more. What a fuck-up, he thought.

Calling Clive to him, he walked back to the house, stopping for a moment to look through the small square of light that was the window. He saw Bill moving around slowly, putting glasses onto the draining board. He looked as old and ill as he undoubtedly was. Sid sighed, went into the warm, homely kitchen, and said goodnight.

As he drove home, his headlights cutting into the blackness and the hedgerows flashing past, he thought again, *What a fuck-up*. What a right fuck-up.

Chapter 35

THURSDAY, 25 OCTOBER

Hugh Dawlish rattled into the yard at seven the next morning driving a tractor and towing a trailer. At one end of the trailer was a drum-like device and a couple of Calor gas bottles; at the other was a pile of logs, well-seasoned and split, all ready for use. Lucy went out to greet him and soon he was seated at the kitchen table with a cup of tea in his hands.

They spoke little at first, carefully knocking the edges off the difference between conversing with a stranger and a neighbour. Hugh seemed to be comfortable in her presence, and Lucy felt surprisingly relaxed sitting opposite him, drinking her tea. For her, men were something to be wary of, but soon she and Hugh were talking easily, glad to find they both had the same sense of humour. Bill came downstairs and was very pleased to see the pair of them chatting away.

Sid arrived, and they all trooped outside to unload the trailer. Lucy had never seen a grain dryer before, and Hugh seemed to take great pleasure in showing it to her. This was not lost on either Sid or Bill. Sid suggested that it might be helpful if Hugh stayed long enough to see the thing working properly as neither he nor Bill had much experience with such complex pieces of machinery. Hugh knew that was a load of bollocks, but he was happy to stay and help.

After unloading the logs, they set up the grain dryer in the old stable block where the roof was sound and there was enough room to place the chairs in line with the dryer. They rigged up some lights and, putting the machine on a couple of pallets, eventually got a steady stream of warm air blowing through the building.

Lucy then suggested Hugh might like to stay for lunch. He thanked her and said he would, and she walked off to the kitchen to make some sandwiches. Sid and Bill nudged each other as Hugh's eyes followed her slender form across the yard.

'Pretty lady,' said Sid.

'Bloody good cook,' said Bill.

'Had a tough time,' added Sid, sitting down on the trailer and rolling a fag.

'Needs to get out,' said Bill. 'Have a bit of younger company now and again.'

Hugh just smiled and headed for the kitchen. Bill and Sid raised their eyebrows at each other and took their time following him.

When lunch was over, Lucy walked Hugh out to his tractor and watched as he reversed the trailer. He stopped just before going out of the gate; Sid, looking out the window, saw the two of them have a brief conversation. When Lucy came back into the kitchen, he noticed she had a bit more spring in her step.

Bill was tired, so they made him sit in his armchair by the stove and doze while they moved the chairs into the stable for staining, which Bill would have to do as it was a very skilled part of the deception. Even though the wood they had used was from about the right period, the colour was brighter and lighter in tone. This showed up against the dark aging of the original chairs' wood, especially where it had been worked.

The lights they had rigged up showed all the dirt and detritus that had accumulated in the stalls, including an old horse collar, its leather white with dust and bird droppings. There were cobwebs everywhere and ancient bits of straw trodden into the cobbled floor. Sid and Lucy cleaned up what they could for fear that when the dryer was working the dust would be fatal to Bill.

When he felt as rested as he was likely to, Bill had Sid set up an old kitchen table in one of the stalls. On this he placed a carboy, several demijohns, and a small, brown stoneware bottle. He poured glutinous grey and brown substances from these into an enamel bowl and carefully mixed them. None of the containers had labels on and all smelled strongly of wood alcohol. The fumes caught at the backs of their throats, and Bill was forced to wear his space helmet. Sid and Lucy stood upwind. Clive hid.

Bill had a number of offcuts from the wood he had used to construct the new chair, and on these he brushed the mixture from the enamel bowl. The colour looked nothing like that of the wood it was supposed to replicate, but that didn't seem to bother him. He adjusted the mixture, adding a trickle from this bottle, a spoonful from that one, and then a careful measure of something that smelled of rotting lemons.

It was like watching some mystical alchemist at work, though instead of robes he was wearing a very stained boiler suit that might once have been white. Over that he had on a red rubber apron and gumboots several sizes too large for his feet.

They gave him an awkward, shuffling gate as he moved around the table, dripping here and brushing there. At last, he walked away and sat down on a chair they had brought outside for him. He was absolutely exhausted.

'One last thing to do,' he wheezed as he stripped off his rubber gloves and threw them in the corner. 'Lucy, please fetch me that bottle of Jimmer's applejack.'

'Christ,' she said, 'you're not going to clear your chest with that stuff, are you?'

Bill gave a wheezy laugh, then coughed hard and long. When at last he had got enough breath back, he told her it was for the stain.

Lucy carefully carried out the flagon. Under Bill's instructions, she and Sid decanted a small amount into an empty bottle. In the bowl, the mixture was now a viscous, dark brown substance that absorbed the light. Bill poured in some of the applejack, stirring as he did so with a wooden stick. Every now and then he carefully lifted the stick out and checked to see how the concoction dripped off it.

'If it's too thin, it won't do much. If it's too thick, it'll stick like shit to a blanket,' he said.

When he was finally satisfied that enough applejack had been added, the resulting stain was very carefully poured from the enamel bowl into a large, wide-necked Kilner jar. It was not nice stuff and Bill made sure no one touched the bottle without rubber gloves.

'Dangerous, is it?' asked Sid.

'Wouldn't do you much good,' replied Bill. 'The nicotine oil alone would kill you.'

As he leaned over and hawked noisily onto a bit of newspaper at his feet, Sid patted him gently on the back and said, 'Come on, mate, you've done enough for today. You're beginning to sound like a fucking bubble pipe.'

He helped Bill back into the kitchen and the welcoming embrace of his armchair. Sid and Lucy sat at the kitchen table drinking cup after cup of tea in an effort to wash the fumes out of their sinuses.

When Bill began to nod, Lucy said she needed to get out into the fresh air and would take Clive up the lane to see Miss Templeton. She called on the old lady regularly now, and no longer had any secrets from her. Miss Templeton enjoyed Lucy's visits and gave her as much advice from her own experiences in love and war as she could. She understood the pressure Lucy was under as well as the danger she was in, and knew they would both get a lot worse before they got better.

While Lucy was gone, Sid decided he would have a look around the fields. No matter what Bill said, he didn't trust this bloke Skates or any of his scraggy crew not to come snooping round. Setting off through the passage that led to the meadow behind the barn, he went round the back of all the farm buildings, checking to see if any of the boarded windows had been disturbed. As he neared the stable block, the powerful reek of Bill's wood stain reached him, and he moved quickly on to the hedgerows that girded the fields beyond. He made very little noise as he went, moving slowly and carefully with the stealth that had kept him alive in the lanes and fields of Northern Ireland.

The late afternoon grudgingly shed its weak sunshine on the surrounding landscape. Trees that had been a furnace of colour yesterday were now muted. Autumn was getting ready to evolve into winter. But Sid found no trace of any incursion, and that pleased him.

When he returned to the house, Lucy had not yet come back from Miss Templeton's. He checked to see that Bill was still comfortably napping, then he headed home. Sid was not a lonely man; a solitary one, yes, but quite comfortable in his own company. Sometimes the pub and local gossip, sometimes a takeaway and a bit of telly, sometimes the whisky bottle and memories of old comrades. Tonight it would be a pasty from the fridge, a bottle or three of cider, and a bit of strategic planning. There was no way he was going to let Bill and Lucy walk into this sort of danger with their eyes wide shut. Just no fucking way.

Chapter 36

FRIDAY, 26 OCTOBER

O n Friday morning the weather turned cold and peevish, and a penetrating drizzle fell from low, grey clouds. Bill was up, but with a wheezy cough from concocting yesterday's wood stain. Clive had crapped just outside the back door in such a spectacular fashion that Lucy could only assume he had eaten a badger's arse. She was feeling tired and dispirited, wondering how they would ever finish these damned chairs and get rid of them, to say nothing of Skates and Warren.

The phone rang. Lucy almost never answered the phone, but she was standing right next to it and Bill had only just got comfortable in his armchair, so this time she did. She picked it up and, before she could say anything, heard a voice that chilled her to the bone. It was Skates, yelling to someone in the background. She let go of the handpiece as if it were red hot. It swung on its cord, banging against the wall as if chiding her for dropping it. Bill got up as quickly as he could and retrieved it.

While Bill dealt with Skates, Lucy sat down as far away from the phone as she could. The sound of that voice had caused a visceral reaction within her, and just for a nanosecond she had felt as if she were back under his power. She didn't hear what Bill was saying on the phone, but just sat there, shaking and pale.

When Bill hung up, he went over and did what he could to comfort her. She wasn't crying, just closed in on herself, dazed and remote.

The kitchen door opened and Sid walked in. Seeing Lucy hunched in her chair and Bill with his arms around her, he immediately went and sat down on the other side of her chair and asked what was going on.

'Skates called,' said Bill. 'Lucy picked it up.'

'Did you say anything?' Sid asked her.

Lucy shook her head. 'His voice . . . it was stupid of me, it just brought things back. Stupid, stupid, stupid,' she repeated quietly to herself.

'No,' said Bill, 'you are not stupid. That bastard put you through hell. He hasn't hurt me nearly as much, yet every time I hear his voice, my flesh crawls.'

Lucy got up and gave herself a shake as if casting off old memories like dirt from a rug. She smiled gratefully at the two men, and in as steady a voice as she could manage asked what Skates had wanted.

'Just an update on the chairs. I told him I was on schedule and expected to be finished in a week or ten days, depending on the weather.'

'What did he say to that?' asked Sid.

'Not much he could say. Bastard must have heard me wheezing 'cos he asked me how I was,' Bill added with disgust.

Lucy made toast for Bill and Sid, then more toast for Sid, who had an appetite second to none. She didn't feel hungry. That voice on the phone had caught her off guard when she was worried about Bill and just generally tired and pissed off. It made her realise how vulnerable she still was, and she didn't like that one little bit.

Bill glanced around the table and was concerned by what he saw. Lucy looked rattled, Sid looked dangerous, and he could only imagine what he looked like. 'What a team we are,' he said. 'The good, the bad, and the terminal.'

His attempt at a laugh turned into a cough, robbing the comment of what little humour it might otherwise have had.

'So what are we going to do to get Skates and his arsehole Warren out of the picture?' asked Sid, getting down to cases. He had given the problem a lot of thought the previous night, and none of the conclusions he had reached were nice ones.

'I have always said that I would be the one to do for Skates and Warren,' said Bill.

'Yes,' said Lucy, 'but we need to be realistic. With that ancient shotgun you borrowed, you don't stand a chance.'

Bill sighed, held up a finger to signal 'hang on a minute', then went upstairs to his room. While he was away, Sid somehow managed to avoid Lucy's eye. Bill soon returned to the kitchen carrying a large box from which he unpacked the old revolver. Wordlessly, he laid it on the table.

'Bloody hell, Bill!' exclaimed Lucy. 'What is this, the Wild West?'

She went to pick up the gun and looked a question at Bill.

'No, it's not loaded.'

He broke the breach open to show her, then clicked it back and put the gun down in front of her.

'It's huge,' she said, lifting it up. 'And really heavy. How on earth are you going to lift the damn thing, let alone fire it?'

'I'll manage,' said Bill, hoping he would.

Lucy looked to Sid for help, but he said nothing, just reached inside a pocket of the decrepit army parka he had hung on the back of his chair. This was a garment he wore most of the winter months, its camouflaged colours long since muted by time, oil, and grime into a muddy mixture of browns and other browns. Its pockets were usually filled with bailing twine, snares, rat traps, and other tools of his many and various trades, but now he brought out an object wrapped in oilcloth. It was about the size and shape of a pipe wrench.

'This,' he said, uncovering it, 'is a Smith & Wesson model 36 revolver. It weighs about 20 ounces, is just over six inches long, and fires a .38 special round. It holds five shots and has an effective range of 25 yards, but between you and me, boys and girls, five yards is about right. Especially,' he added, 'if the bullets are fixed so they go all naughty inside.'

Lucy looked at Sid anew. *He might be round on the outside*, she thought, *but by Christ he has a hard centre.*

Sid opened the breech to show the chambers were empty, then placed the gun on the table. Delving into his parka again, he brought out a box of ammunition. 'Twenty-Five Rounds' it said on the top, and it didn't rattle.

Lucy reached out for the weapon, and Sid passed it to her with a grim smile. Her fist closed around the small butt, which had been wound round with some black tape that made it larger and easier to hold. She brought the weapon up and trained it on the jar of flowers behind her. Squeezing the trigger took almost no effort, and the small hammer went back before striking the firing pin in a fraction of a second.

Sid took the weapon from her and, with a big grin, said in a low, mock American accent, 'That's my girl. Annie Oakley, eat yer heart out!'

Sid then gave the gun to Bill.

'With this little darling, you only have to get close enough to hit them anywhere and . . . job done. The ammunition is smaller, but with a hollow point and a little bit of extra doctoring it will do nicely. And because it's so small you can keep it in a pocket. They'll never expect you to go armed in any case; it's not your style, mate.'

'Is it traceable?' asked Bill.

Sid put his mind at rest about that; the firearm was completely untraceable, likewise the ammunition. Providing neither carried any fingerprints, there would be nothing to make the police associate the weapon with them.

Bill then went upstairs to retrieve the sawn-off shotgun. Returning, he unwrapped it from its sacking shroud and put it on the kitchen table. It made an incongruous sight, like something medieval next to the more refined examples of the arms trade already resting there.

Lucy gazed with wide eyes at this, but without a word went and fetched the venerable shotgun Bill had borrowed from Hugh and added it to the growing armoury on the kitchen table.

She sat down, saying, 'We could start a ruddy war with this lot.'

'No,' said Sid, 'but we should be able to wage a decent campaign.'

They stashed the weapons in various out-of-the-way places, then Bill said they had better get on with the chairs before the day disappeared. Sid said he would lend a hand, but it was more to see that Bill didn't keel over than anything else. Lucy said they would probably be in need of a good supper that night, so she took her car, left Clive with the men, and went off to shop for it.

Bill had Sid move the two chairs that needed to be stained from the workshop to the stables. Sid insisted Bill wear his 'space helmet' and had him stand as near to the open door as he could. Rain occasionally spattered in from the incontinent clouds, and the air was cold, but that suited Bill because he didn't want the stain to evaporate too quickly.

Sid put the repaired chair on a turntable, then he stepped back and watched a master at work. Bill had the bottle of Jimmer's fiery spirit on one side, the Kilner jar of mixed stain in the middle, and a milk bottle containing turps close at hand. He mixed, diluted, and spread the stain along the grain of the wood, sometimes with a soft cloth and sometimes with a piece of sheepskin. Sid marvelled as the 'new' gradually disappeared until it was difficult to distinguish what was today from what was yesterday.

Finally, Bill moved away, then went outside and sat down. The rain had stopped, and there was a watery sun in the pallid sky. He took off his helmet and breathed in the fresh air. Sid felt sorry for the old boy and wished he could be of more help, but he knew he couldn't; not yet, anyway.

When Bill got his breath back, he tried to bring up the subject of money. 'We need to sort out what I owe you, and I'm not talking your day rates here. There's a bit coming in on these chairs, and I want you to share in it.'

'Look,' said Sid, 'we always have this bloody conversation.

It's 25 quid a day plus expenses, extras extra, and mate's rates apply, except when they don't.'

Both men laughed. They had worked together on and off for years. Some jobs had been nice little earners, others less so, but it had all evened out.

'You share the chair money with Lucy,' said Sid. 'That girl's done a lot more for you on this job than I have.'

'So far,' said Bill, looking at Sid meaningfully. 'I'll do Skates; I know I can, and with that little gun of yours it will be a lot easier than it would have been otherwise, but I still might not manage Warren. He might be too quick for me, I don't know.'

Sid thought for a moment and then asked, 'Have you considered that Warren might not even be there when you deliver the chairs?'

'Why not?'

'Because it makes more sense for him to be here waiting for when you get back.'

Sid sat downwind of Bill and lit one of his dreadful rollups. The smoke from it rose in the gusty air and flew away like good intentions.

'Think about it,' he said. 'No one – no one alive, that is – knows you're working on these chairs. What's to stop Warren lifting the money off you and then starting a nice little fire by way of a warm goodbye? That way no chairs, no witnesses, just another unfortunate accident.'

'That's true,' said Bill. 'It certainly seems to have worked in Eric's case. Have there been any rumours about that? Anything more in the papers?'

'Not that I've heard or seen. Which means Skates believes you are the only one in the know and that, old darling, makes you an endangered species.'

'In more ways than one,' said Bill. He went back in to look at the chair he had been working on.

While there was some light and he had a little energy left, Bill wanted to get started on the new chair, so Sid set it up on another turntable. Again, a drop here and a small spoonful there, the smell of the applejack mixing with the pungent odour of the stain.

The late afternoon was host to yet another drizzle from the darkening sky. The yard looked as if it were underwater, the buildings just shapes in the gloom, as they walked back into the bright, comforting warmth of the kitchen. Lucy had returned some time earlier, and now there was the smell of something savoury and delicious. Bill sat down and Lucy handed him a mug of hot, sweet tea.

'What's for supper?' he asked her.

'Bacon roly-poly with mash, cabbage, and gravy.'

Bill and Sid exchanged looks of such pure bliss that Lucy's heart swelled.

Bill sat back in his chair with an odd feeling of contentment. Despite all that was going on in his body and his life, he had never before known the companionship he was enjoying now. After a little while he got up went into that small, almost underground room he called his cellar and emerged a few moments later carefully carrying a dusty bottle. He placed this on the table, then went to the dresser, took down a crystal decanter, and reverently transferred the contents of the bottle to it. Finally, he held the decanter up to the light. The contents glowed a deep ruby red while the facets cunningly cut into the crystal reflected light into the dark corners of the room.

'What is it?' asked Lucy.

'Port,' said Bill. 'A very special one.'

He passed the bottle to Lucy, who wiped dust from the simple white label and then read aloud, 'Taylor Fladgate 1928. Is that good?'

'One of the best,' said Bill. 'There are other vintages that tick all the boxes, too, of course, but this little darling was a gift from a grateful client ten or more years ago.'

'Some gift,' said Sid.

'Some client,' said Bill, remembering her with pleasure. 'And after our grub, we'll have a council of war over the port and cheese.'

He gave Lucy a worried look. 'We have got cheese?'

'Of course we have cheese!' she laughed.

Bill napped in his chair as Lucy moved quietly about the room putting the finishing touches on dinner. Sid took Clive and did a quick patrol of the meadow and around the backs of the buildings, just to be on the safe side. There was still enough light to see if anyone had disturbed the small indicators he had left in all the likely and even a few unlikely places from which a watcher could watch. A pine cone here and a small group of twigs there; all things that would not be noticed, but would be disturbed should any prying biped encounter them.

After the delicious meal they had their port, which was as good as Bill had said it would be, and then they got down to business. Sid got up and walked over the stove. He was dying for a smoke but didn't want to set off Bill's coughing.

'Okay, try this for size,' he said. 'Skates would be unlikely to have you killed at his place even if you brought all the chairs with you because it's easier and safer having a body move around under its own steam than it is to carry it about.'

'Especially if they plan to give me the Eric treatment,' said Bill.

'Right,' said Sid. 'So we can be pretty sure Warren will be here waiting for you when you return. He'll have orders to get Skates's money off you and set fire to the workshop.'

'So what happens when Bill turns up with only two of the chairs?' asked Lucy.

'Well, that will throw a bit of a spanner into the works, but Skates is no fool and he'll be flexible. He'll probably phone Warren and tell him to hold off until he can collect the other two chairs, or let the killing go ahead but tell him not to set fire to anything until the other chairs are retrieved. On the whole, I think that's the most likely scenario.'

'Should I try to shoot him before he can call Warren?' asked Bill.

'No, you'll have enough to think about, and it really doesn't make any difference. Either way, Lucy and I will be here waiting for Warren, and we can sort him out, even if he brings helpers.'

'We can? Oh, good,' said Lucy, trying not to look as anxious as she felt.

'Surprise is on our side, love,' Sid told her. 'The last thing Warren or anybody else will expect is to meet up with us and our shotguns. And we will not be at home to Mr Merciful, oh dear no!'

As Lucy was drifting off to sleep that night, she thought about what a strange evening it had been. If anyone had looked in at the window they would have seen three moderately normal-looking people conversing around a table laden with food and drink. They might even have smiled at such a picture of domestic harmony. Yet the three of them had been planning multiple murder.

No, not murder, she decided. Self-defence. Survival. It really was the only chance they had.

Chapter 37

SATURDAY, 27 OCTOBER

There's something about a cold, rainy Saturday morning with a mist hanging about like a tax collector in a doorway that makes people want to stay in bed. Bill was drugged up to the eyeballs and Sid was hungover. He came downstairs into a stone-cold kitchen, no one having banked up the stove the night before. He was using a sleeping bag for a cloak, holding it together with one hand while he used the other to put the kettle on and clear the ashes from the grimy firebox.

Lucy, hearing movement from below, came downstairs and into the kitchen. Her long, fair hair was a little dishevelled, and she wore a huge, ex-navy duffel coat as a dressing gown with a pair of very worn fleece-lined flying boots as slippers. When she moved, her bare legs were occasionally visible between the coat and the massive boots. Sid thought she looked like a child wearing a grown-up's clothes: charming and vulnerable at the same time.

He got the stove lit, and the fragrant smell of wood smoke was soon drifting about the room. Lucy let Clive out and shivered as the cold air blew in. Then, having made a pot of tea, she sat at the kitchen table holding her mug in both hands and sipping the hot brew, hunched into her clothes against the chill. Sid took his mug upstairs to get dressed.

As Lucy sat alone in the kitchen, she was warmed by both the tea and her surroundings, which bore witness to how much she had become a part of them. There were flowers in various jugs and vases Bill had collected over the years, there were herbs in bunches hanging from the beams in the ceiling, and there was Clive's basket by the stove. No photographs, though, and memories that only reached as far back as the summer, but she was content with that. The past, her past, was one of the reasons for last night's planning session. She sighed, went upstairs and got dressed, then returned to the kitchen and started making breakfast.

Sid came back down, put on his coat, and went outside to enjoy that first sublime rollup of the day. This was interrupted by Clive's frantic barking at an old Land Rover that had pulled up at the gate. At the wheel of the mud-spattered vehicle was Hugh Dawlish. Sid opened the gate and Hugh drove in, parked, and asked if Bill was about.

'He's not down yet,' Sid told him, 'but I'm sure he will be soon. Come in and have a cup of tea while you wait.'

Hugh followed Sid into the kitchen and was immediately enveloped in the heady aroma of the bacon Lucy was frying in a large cast-iron pan. On the table was a small tower block of bread ready cut for the rashers. There was also an enormous bottle of brown sauce, a large slab of butter in a dish, and a pot of marmalade. Hugh looked at all this and thought of his own meagre breakfast of some gritty by-product of the miller's art and thought, *wholesome grains be damned.*

With a welcoming smile and a warm 'Good morning,' Lucy

asked him if he had eaten yet. Hugh decided that even if he had eaten a full English with all the extras, twice, that morning, he would still have said no.

Bill finally emerged, looking better than he felt, and greeted Hugh warmly. As they ate, Hugh told him the reason for his visit.

'Ian, one of my chaps, was out on the far field next-but-one to your home meadow this morning and saw a man walking this way, keeping close to the hedgerow. Ian was in a tractor and by the time he had driven up to get through the field gate, the man had turned back. He shouted something about looking for a place to pee and went out through a gap in the hedge and onto the road. Ian was going to go over and find out more, but he heard a motorbike roar off so didn't bother. I just thought you should know.'

Bill looked at Sid, 'Warren, by the sound if it.'

'What time was this?' Lucy asked Hugh.

'About eight this morning. My chap was checking some covers we're planning to shoot over, and we always keep a lookout for poachers and pikeys this time of year.'

'There's a small gap in the hedge by the road,' said Sid, 'but no lay-by as such. I'll go see if I can tell where the little shit parked up.'

'So, you know who it might be,' said Hugh, concerned but not wanting to pry.

Lucy looked at him and her face was troubled.

'I'm sorry,' she said. 'We, I, probably should have told you before now. It's someone from my past, a really horrible man.' She looked down at her hands for a moment and then back up at him, smiling wanly. 'We're dealing with it. It's nothing for you to worry about, but thanks for letting us know.'

Bill and Sid murmured their agreement. Hugh didn't want to press the matter and risk embarrassing Lucy, so he just said, 'Well, if I can help in any way, you only have to ask.'

'We will,' said Lucy, 'Thank you, Hugh.'

There were more murmurs of agreement from Bill and Sid. Hugh got up, put on his tweed cap, and thanked Lucy for the lovely breakfast. She had been clearing up, passing plates to Sid, who was at the sink, but now she turned to look at Hugh as he went out. Putting down the dish she was holding, she followed him through the kitchen door and into the yard. The rain had stopped but the morning was still misty, dank, and cold, and she shivered slightly. Hugh noticed this and, without really thinking about it, put his hands on her shoulders. Her face was drawn and anxious.

Looking into her grey eyes, he said, 'I don't want to know your business, Lucy. Your past is your own country, but please believe me when I say I will help you in any way I can. Bill is a good man,' he continued, 'but he's not well. Sid is as good a bloke in a fight as you could hope to have, but if you ever need a third Musketeer, promise you'll ask me.'

Lucy smiled up at him and said simply, 'I promise.'

Feeling as if the sun had suddenly come out, Hugh started his vehicle and slowly drove away. Lucy stood and watched him go, then waved as he turned into the lane.

Back in the kitchen Bill and Sid were in close conversation, muttering away like two rooks on a branch. When Lucy walked in, however, they both stopped and looked up.

'Good chap, that Hugh,' said Bill.

'Excellent farmer,' said Sid. 'Solid character.'

'Not had a happy life,' said Bill.

'Needs to get away from the farm more,' said Sid. 'Learn to enjoy himself now and then.'

Lucy flashed them both a 'that'll do' look and the conversation immediately turned back to the motive behind Warren's intrusion.

'I don't doubt the little shit was doing a recce to see how he could sneak into the yard here,' said Sid.

'If he came into the yard through the meadow gate and that passage, he'd have the run of the place,' said Lucy.

'Aye,' said Bill with a scowl, 'and lots of nooks and crannies to hide up in.'

'Well,' Sid mused, 'with a little imagination we can make that gate very interesting for the bugger.'

'But for now, let's get on with those bloody chairs,' said Bill.

The two newly stained chairs were brought from the stable, where they had been enjoying the attentions of the grain dryer, back into the workshop. The big stove was going full blast, but with such a large space to heat, they had to stand close to it to feel any real benefit. All four chairs now stood in a row. The new chair and bits of the restored one were different in colour, but as a set they looked perfect.

'They do look good,' said Sid, as he stood admiring their work. 'Even without the polish.'

Bill went to one of the many cupboards that hung on the walls above the benches that ran around the workshop and took down an old-fashioned screw-top coffee bean jar. He had Sid place the restored chair on a turntable under a strong light, then he opened the jar. Inside was a dark powder. He spooned a little of this into a small container he could hold easily, then used a soft, long-haired brush to delicately apply the powder around the joints and pegs of the chair. Using a sprayer, he then caused a gentle mist to fall over the places where he had been working. When this was done, he sat down, making sure the small container of dust was well out of the way and safe for the next application.

Lucy had watched, entranced, throughout this process and, when she was sure Bill had his breath back, asked him to explain what he'd been doing. She and Sid were then let into another secret of the dark arts of the antique furniture resurrectionist.

'One of the prime areas of suspicion in the eyes of an expert, and a right bugger to replicate, is dirt. Dirt and dust hidden in corners and around pegs. If it's found on top of the wax or finishes, then it has to be new. In hidden corners, in crevices, in up-and-under hideaways, the gummy residue of years of waxing and polishing and just plain dust and dirt accumulate. Now, some amateurs will try and replicate that with stains or even paint, but that never works if someone who really knows what they're about investigates the piece. It has to be real. This dust,' Bill said, pointing to the dark powder now being carried into the crevices by the water he had so carefully applied, 'is as real as it gets.

'Many years ago I did some jobs for a seriously good faker. He had made a reputation, though not much money, creating oak furniture that had allegedly come from when old King Henry carved up the monasteries. Big money was being spent by Americans just then, driven by several Hollywood blockbusters that had a medieval theme, and Olde English was all the rage. Don't ever think Yanks are daft. There are some very sharp cookies and some seriously clever scholars who can cause any amount of problems if they're employed to really suss out a piece. Anyway, this chap, George his name was, had a maintenance contract with Salisbury Cathedral for an absolute peppercorn payment. Once a month, or whenever called for, he dutifully turned up and frequently he would take me with him. It was all woodwork, nothing stone. And sometimes the choir or some heavy parishioner would bust a bit of furniture and that would need to come back with us for repair. All signed for, of course, counted in and counted out, nice and proper. Well, that gave us a few choice scrapings now and again, but mostly it was Victorian tat. The real benefit came when we were allowed up into the roof space to do a bit of work. This area had not been cleaned or even brushed down for decades. There was dust from really ancient timbers everywhere, and it was dust that had all the right ingredients: candle smoke, incense, bat shit, monks' farts, and bishops' belches. The Dust of Ages, we called it.'

'And that's what you've got in that coffee jar? The Dust of Ages?' asked Lucy.

'The very same. Poor George passed away suddenly, and his wife locked up his workshop and sold everything to a house clearance merchant before I got to hear of it. I had some of the dust, though, and I knew how to get more by offering my services to local churches. The ones that have rood screens and timbered roofs, I mean, none of yer concrete Pentecostal stuff. Anyway, if some cunning professional has a scratch under our joints and sends the result off for a microscopic examination, it'll come back nice and old, just like it should.'

Bill gave the new chair the same treatment, after which he was too tired to do any more, so they called it a day. Lucy suggested they take the next day off so Bill could recruit his strength, and then start again on Monday. Sid said he had a bit of work on that day so couldn't come back until Tuesday.

'God help the poor rats,' said Bill.

'God help *me*,' replied Sid. 'It's a Frigging Brigadier job.'

When nightfall came, Lucy put on a dark woollen cap, slipped into a thick, blue serge workman's jacket, and tucked a loaded shotgun under her arm. As she walked the home meadow and the perimeter of the farm, she was reminded of a village policeman she had known as a child. He was a large man with a huge moustache who smelled of pipe tobacco and beer. He had been cycling by one day, saw Lucy playing in the garden, and stopped for a chat. She had asked him if there were any robbers about. He hadn't laughed at her or talked down to her, just looked serious and told her she was never to worry about robbers, not in his village. She couldn't remember the entire conversation, but he had said his job was to guard everyone, and at night he walked all over the village 'shaking hands with doorknobs' to make sure everything was locked up tight. Now here she was doing the same thing. She felt good about that, and about the gun under her arm, too.

Chapter 38

SUNDAY–TUESDAY,
28–30 OCTOBER

Sunday passed slowly but inexorably, as Sundays do. Bill stayed in bed for most of it, and Lucy called Gloria to keep her up to date on Bill's health. There was still no indication that he was ready to pursue the hospice option, and although Lucy knew why, it was not something she could discuss with Gloria.

On Monday, Lucy and Bill worked together quietly and happily, applying various polishes to the chairs. These were nothing like as pungent as the stains; in fact, the workshop became fragrant with the smells of natural oils and beeswax. The wood began to glow as polish was rubbed on with soft rags and off with pieces of sheepskin. The activity was pleasant and restful somehow. Lucy thought it the best part of the whole process.

Few words were exchanged as they worked. They would apply a layer of polish to one part of a chair, then let it air dry while they went on to another part. They did this again and again until the whole chair had a patina and colour that looked as if time itself had polished the wood. In the light of the lamps that allowed no shadow to fall on the work being done, Bill worked slowly and methodically, his hands caressing the wood. He smiled as he worked, hardly coughed at all, and looked as happy as Lucy had seen him for a long while.

It was a slow process, but after every sequence the colour deepened, and where the Dust of Ages had been applied, the under-stain showed dark against the prominent highlights. Every so often the chair being worked on would be wheeled out into the daylight and placed next to one of the original chairs. There were differences, but they were getting harder to see as the process went on.

The end of October brought storms throughout the West Country, and on Tuesday the few leaves that had remained on the trees and in the hedgerows were all scattered in soggy abandon. In spite of the damp and cold, Bill insisted on carrying on with the final polishing. Sitting wrapped in an ancient tweed overcoat, his cap wedged low on his head and his hands in fingerless gloves, he looked like something out of Dickens. The big stone barn that housed the workshop was a blessing in hot weather, but as winter took hold there were parts of the building that never warmed up. Good for storing wood, but not so good for a dying man.

It was late afternoon before Sid finally rocked up. The yard gate was open and through it drove a small, rather beaten-up truck with the words 'Alvin Tucker, Chimney Sweep' emblazoned on each side. Out got Sid, dressed in soot-stained overalls and with an equally grimy baseball cap on his head. His face had so much soot on it, he looked like someone out of an old-fashioned music hall. Lucy looked inside the truck and saw a number of brushes, poles, and sacks, all equally filthy and well-used.

Bill came out through the kitchen door, laughing.

'Christ, you're not up to that old lark again, are you, Sid?'
He turned to Lucy. 'When the rat catching and dodgy welding
jobs dry up, out comes this gear and he's off cleaning chimneys
with Alvin bloody Tucker. A right pair of crooks, they are.
Like Laurel and Hardy on ladders.'

He laughed so much at his own joke that he started
coughing, and Lucy drove him back into the warmth of the
kitchen. Sid followed them in to wash the soot off his face and
hands. While he was busy at the sink, Lucy poured him tea,
cut him a slice of cake, and waited to hear what he had to say
for himself.

'No, I was not with Alvin bloody Tucker, who, by the way,
is doing a bit of time for having some lead away from a church
roof. I have the pickup because I know where Alvin always
hides it before he goes away on holiday as it were, but I was
not out touting for business as a sweep. Filthy job; dusty, nasty,
and dirty.'

'So what's with the outfit?' asked Bill.

Here Sid became very smug and self-satisfied. 'Been up to
Skates's place, haven't I? Saw the nasty Warren, didn't I?'

'Oh, Sid, no!' exclaimed Lucy. 'What would have happened
if he had recognised you?'

'Couldn't,' said Sid. 'He's never clapped eyes on me before.
The only one of them who has is the prat we found in the hedge,
and for all he knows I really am a sweep. Anyway, there was no
one there but Warren. The Range Rover was gone.'

'What on earth did you go there for?' asked Bill.

'To get a handle on how you're going to get in and out,

mate. To see if there are gatehouses, security cameras, anyone or anything that might finger you or get in the way of the action.'

'Were there?' asked Lucy.

'Not that I could see. The gates themselves have electric locks with a speaker panel on the gatepost, so whoever is visiting has to call first. Luckily for me that gate was open, so I just drove straight in. A bloke was in the garage working on a big, black motorbike, so I figured it must be Warren. When I drove up he came over and asked me what I was doing there.'

Bill and Lucy exchanged worried looks, but Sid continued, 'He wasn't put out, just a bit wary. I told him I was touting for business, saw the gate open, and thought I'd chance my arm. Left him a card. Didn't even get out of the van.'

'Then what?' asked Lucy.

'Then I drove away nice and slow so as not to disturb his gravel and he watched me depart in peace.'

Sid quietly sipped his tea for a bit. Then Bill asked, 'So what do you think?'

Sid took a sheet of paper from his pocket, spread it out, and dusted the soot from it. 'This is a little sketch I stopped and made on the way here while it was all fresh in my mind.'

The sketch included a map of the road from a nearby junction right up past Skates's house to a small hamlet about three miles further on. There were no houses in Skates's immediate vicinity, and there were open fields all around the big house. The drive became a large turning area in front of the house with a garage on one side. There were a few ornamental trees around the other side, but the drive ended there. There was a gravel path round the house, but no other means of vehicle access.

'Big poncy place with three low steps up to a fancy front

door. A cross between a Dulux advert and a neoclassical bus shelter. Big windows to the front, probably lots of bedrooms above, but no sign of any dormer windows in the roof. A typical spec-built mansion that would appeal to politicians or estate agents. But it is certainly alarmed. I could see the boxes winking away to show they were all working. The house faces the road and there's a tall chain-link fence surrounding it. No sign of any dogs, but with such an open aspect and with gravel all 'round, very secure. Place like that would be a nightmare to go in heavy and mob-handed; no places to hide up and the gates are good ones, not easy to bust open. All in all, it's a target that can only be approached openly, by invitation rather than stealth.'

Sid drained his mug and added, 'Lots to think about, but right now I have to put Alvin's truck back where I found it. I can come back tomorrow if I'm wanted.'

'We can certainly use your help, but only if you can spare the time,' said Bill.

'I'll be back. I had to run the digger yesterday, but there's a couple days' work for the others to do before they'll need me again.'

'Well, plan on staying for supper, then,' Lucy told him.

He winked at her and said, 'That would be smashing.' Then he was off, leaving the smell of coal fires and a filthy hand towel behind him.

Chapter 39

WEDNESDAY–THURSDAY, 31 OCTOBER–1 NOVEMBER

On Wednesday, however, Bill woke up feeling worse than usual. He looked worn – diminished somehow, as if his body was giving up even if his mind and willpower weren't. And he was in a lot of pain.

Lucy called Dr Hall, then she called Sid and told him there would be no work on the chairs that day. The doctor arrived within the hour and examined Bill in his bedroom, giving him an injection and talking with him for a long while. When the doctor came downstairs at last, he saw Lucy looking worried and worn out, but bravely offering him a cup of tea. As he drank it, she asked him questions, which he tried to answer with both honesty and kindness. Yes, there was something he could prescribe for Bill's exhaustion, but there were side effects and he would need to use it sparingly. And, he told her, Bill's pain was also getting worse. Pretty soon the only place he would be able to get the drugs he needed would be in a hospice.

Lucy understood that, but she also knew Bill would not go quietly into palliative care while Skates and Warren were above ground. Nevertheless, she phoned Gloria and told her what the doctor had said.

Philip and Gloria arrived the next day just after lunch. Dr Hall's injection of the previous day had helped a lot, and Bill was up and in his chair, listening to the radio. After tea, they took him to see the hospice outside Salisbury.

It was a modern building within beautiful grounds and blessed with a staff who were kind, considerate, and not a bit solemn. Bill was greeted by the matron and made to feel welcome and respected. In her office, which was full of potted plants, she explained the whats, the wherefores, and the way forward for Bill and his family. She would get his latest records, she had already received a letter from his GP, there was a room ready when he needed it, and all he had to do was 'sweep up what you wish to, tidy what you must, and tell us when you will be arriving'.

Bill and his family were invited to look around. They chose not to, but sat in the garden for a while instead. No one said much, then or on the journey home, but somehow it was settled that Bill would pack his bags and go into hospice on the 6th or 7th of November. A week away. One last week in which to do what had to be done.

Chapter 40

FRIDAY–SATURDAY,
2–3 NOVEMBER

Thanks to Dr Hall's 'rocket fuel', Bill felt even stronger on Friday. He had rested well and breakfasted better than usual. Going out into the workshop, he studied the four chairs, now set in a row and looking superb. He and Lucy looked hard at the repaired chair and the brand new one to see if they could spot any obvious differences from the original two. They couldn't.

Late that afternoon Lucy called on Miss Templeton and invited her to come examine the chairs. She might have been elderly but her eyes were as sharp as knives. She walked around the chairs, peering closely, and even took a small but powerful magnifying glass from her pocket to really give them the once-over.

At last she said, 'While I am not, of course, qualified to recognize every detail that might be right or wrong, my overall impression is that these are definitely a family of chairs. My only concern is that they do smell quite strongly of polish. Beeswax, actually, though there is a hint of apples as well.'

Bill assured her that it couldn't be helped and the smell

would fade in time. She stayed for tea, during which she asked them straight out what their timetable was, Lucy having kept her up to date on their basic plan.

'My goal is to deliver two of the chairs on the fifth of November,' said Bill.

'How apt!' cried Miss Templeton, then added 'I shall be here, of course.'

They stared at her, horrified, but she just laughed.

'Do you think I would miss this? Besides you are going to need someone to cover the main gate. Not that that's where Mr Warren will come in if he does turn up, but it's as well to have it watched.'

Lucy looked at Bill, who nodded, then invited Miss Templeton to dine with them the following evening. They could then finalize their plans before lighting the blue touch paper.

'My dear, I am very happy to accept your kind invitation to dinner, but as to lighting any sort of fuse, it was ignited the moment those men killed Bess and threatened Bill's family, not to mention so cruelly abusing you.'

As she was leaving to go back to her cottage, Miss Templeton said to Lucy, 'Pop up tomorrow morning and I'll show you how to wring a chicken's neck. It's something every girl should know.'

~~~

As Lucy lay in bed that night, she thought of the coming days and wondered if she really had it in her to kill Warren or anybody else. She thought of Bill: sick and in pain, but with such a spark of determination in his eyes. Yes, she thought, Bill would be able to do what he had made up his mind to do. But would she? Then she remembered a conversation she had had with Miss Templeton on a previous visit to her cottage.

They had been sitting in the garden enjoying the sight of the late summer sun making the last of the flowers glow from within, and Miss Templeton had looked more than ever like a meek, gentle old lady. 'No sane person sets out to kill or maim unless they are driven to it by circumstances,' she said. 'Oh, you get those like your Mr Warren who are psychopaths or deranged in some other way. They kill without a thought and, in some cases, with a great deal of enjoyment. The rest of us need some kind of key to unlock the mayhem and murder that lies within.'

A bee buzzed by, and there was birdsong and the gentle clucking of hens at their feet as Miss Templeton continued. 'Soldiers are trained to obey without question and to kill on command. Some do, most don't, not even in the heat of battle. Those of us who had to kill not in the heat of battle but when circumstances required it, were given special training. Training, mind you, not conditioning. We had to be in control of our actions at all times; otherwise one is as much a danger to oneself as to the enemy. We were trained to react to a threat, and educated as to what that reaction should be. All very well in theory, actually, but when some huge thug is coming at one with a bayonet, one does have a tendency to act first and think about it later. But even in that situation, there must be something that motivates you, that drives your actions.'

She looked closely at Lucy. 'These men who hurt you; do you hate them?'

'Yes,' said Lucy. 'But if I'm honest, I think I fear them more than I hate them. I mean, I always hated them, but still I stayed. I was too scared to leave.'

'Ah, well, it is sometimes difficult to feel sufficient hatred for things done to oneself. Things done to someone else for whom we care ... now, that is an entirely different matter. One can use that sort of motivation to accomplish some very surprising things.'

Miss Templeton sank into her own thoughts for a while, but whether summoning memories or banishing demons, Lucy couldn't tell. Eventually, she heaved a great sigh.

'Alas, the world views such behaviour very differently in a woman than it does in a man. If a man saves someone's life under perilous circumstances, he gets a medal for bravery. If a woman does the same thing, they put it down to maternal instinct. And, you see, if it's an instinct then you can't really help yourself, so you don't get any credit for it.'

~~~

On Saturday Bill was up and about earlier than usual. Lucy found him in the front room sitting at an elegant side table on which he had piled a box of papers, a John Bull printing set, and several ink bottles. It was cold in the room, so she lit the fire and brought in one of the fan heaters from the workshop. Bill seemed cheerful enough but preoccupied, so she left him to it. She did a bit of housework and listened to the radio. Clive lay beside the stove and dozed.

'I suppose this is how normal people live,' she thought to herself.

About midday she heard a vehicle drive up. Going to the door she saw a now-familiar old Land Rover much splattered with mud. Hugh got out and, when he saw her at the door, grinned broadly. He was carrying a plastic shopping bag. Taking his cap off and wiping his boots on the mat, he came into the kitchen and put the bag on the worktop next to the sink. Inside were three very plump, well-dressed pheasants.

'I thought you might be able to find a use for these,' he said. 'I've done all the necessary and they're oven-ready.'

Lucy thanked him warmly and offered him tea. He sat down and, while drinking his brew, told her the goings-on of his farm as if she knew the name of every field and crop he was talking about. When Bill came into the room, Hugh stood up to greet him as he always did. Lucy liked that; it was delightfully old-fashioned and respectful. When they were all seated, Hugh gave Bill the farming news. Because Bill actually did know the name of every field and crop Hugh was talking about, it was slightly more detailed this time.

Lucy showed Bill the pheasants, and he made appreciative noises over them, then leaned back in his chair and watched Lucy and Hugh talk about the weather. He could see the interest these two had in each another, and he could also see that unless someone took charge of the situation they would probably continue to dither like a pair of butterflies over the same daisy forever. So he had a gentle coughing fit to get their attention and then said what a kindness it would be if some generous neighbour would take Lucy for dinner somewhere pleasant tomorrow night.

Lucy turned red and glared at him, but Hugh only laughed and said he would be more than happy if she would allow him to be that lucky neighbour. Lucy felt both flattered and ambushed by Hugh's obvious delight in the idea, and it was agreed that he would pick her up at seven the next evening. She tried a rearguard action as he was leaving, though, by saying she would have to get Bill's supper, but that was easily defeated by Bill's saying he was not a bloody invalid and she could leave something in the oven for him.

All the same, Lucy followed Hugh out to his Land Rover and asked him if it was really all right; if he had something else on, she would certainly understand. Hugh was adamant there was nothing he would rather do than take her out to dinner. He had heard good things about a new restaurant and they would try it out.

When she came back into the kitchen, Lucy didn't know whether she was cross with Bill or not. The day after tomorrow was the 5th, and she thought it was the height of stupidity that she should be out the night before. On the other hand, she really did like the idea of going out with Hugh, and it would be a real treat to have someone cook for her for a change. She decided she would take soundings from tonight's dinner companions. As Bill had returned to his papers, she started preparing the meal.

Sid turned up early with muddy boots and a wind-burned face, but Lucy was happy to fill him with tea and watch him demolish half a tin of biscuits. She suddenly realized how fond of him she had grown; his company was almost as enjoyable and comforting to her now as Bill's. She was making a stew, and he volunteered to peel the spuds, working beside her at the sink and telling her tales that made her laugh and forget just what this meal was really all about. At some point Bill came in and sat in his armchair to listen to Sid's nonsense and doze.

Miss Templeton arrived at seven carrying a shopping bag that chinked. She was wearing a voluminous skirt, myriad layers of carefully mended fine wool jumpers, and, in honour of the special occasion, a string of pearls and just a hint of lipstick. As she was shown in, Sid rose to his feet and was formally introduced. Then Bill led her to the head of the table and pulled the chair out for her. From her shopping bag, Miss Templeton brought out three bottles of wine. They all bore simple homemade labels with 'Sloe Gin' written on them.

'I thought these might jolly the evening along,' she said.

During the meal, Miss Templeton and Sid got to know each other. They knew about each other, of course, as they had both lived in the neighbourhood for ages, but somehow their paths had never crossed. Now it appeared they had quite a few things in common despite their age difference.

The stew and dumplings were delicious, and Lucy received many sincere compliments on them. She was surprised by how much food Miss Templeton managed to tuck away, but even more at how relaxed she was and how fully she seemed to enjoy the company around her. She was still the grand if slightly eccentric old lady, but now and then a devilish streak would peep out like a red silk petticoat from under a nun's habit. Lucy thought this might be due to Sid's influence, or perhaps it was the sloe gin. Probably both.

When everyone had eaten their fill, the plates were cleared away and stacked on the worktop. Sid got up and fetched a large box of very expensive chocolates he had brought and put those in the middle of the table, then got out the sketch he had made of Skates's house and the surrounding area. Miss Templeton sipped her sloe gin and studied the sketch, then complimented Sid on his reconnaissance.

'Now,' said Sid, 'just to go over our basic plan once more, it is simply for Bill to deliver the restored chair and the new one, then demand the rest of his money before letting Skates have the original two. Simple and not out of character. Skates's reaction will most likely be to send Warren to pick up the two chairs from Bill, take the money back, kill him, and set fire to his workshop.'

'And the key to our defensive strategy,' chimed in Miss Templeton, 'is to create scenarios in which the options open to Skates and Warren are limited both as to time and place.'

They decided to start with Warren. Miss Templeton knew the layout of Bill's farm in general terms but had not been round it with a strategic eye, so she, Sid, and Lucy walked out into the yard. With the only lights above the kitchen door and the workshop, most of the surroundings were just shapes in the shadows. They agreed that if Warren came, he'd probably park his motorbike by the field entrance and walk through the meadow. From there he could get over the meadow gate and into the passage between the barn and the cart shed. This passage was some eighteen feet wide and about thirty feet long. Stone walls rose up either side, and it was not possible to see from one end of it to the other.

It was getting cold, so the three of them made their way back into the house and the warmth of the kitchen. Bill was right where they had left him and looked half asleep, but he perked up when the others sat down and poured more sloe gin into their glasses.

'So, if and when Warren does show up, where and how are we going to deal with him?' Lucy asked.

'Ambushes are a right bugger,' said Sid. 'It's sod's law that wherever you set one up will be the wrong place at the right time or vice versa. We have to make it as easy for the bastard as we can without making it look too easy. For example, if we string a light up in that passage to discourage him from using it, he'll just try his luck through one of the buildings and get into the yard that way.'

'If we trap him in that passage, though,' said Bill thoughtfully, 'he could be dealt with there and then.' And he told them about the man trap he had found in one of his sheds a few months before.

'That could work,' said Sid. 'The passage is concrete, same as the yard, but we might be able to hide the thing with a bit of dirty straw and muck.'

Miss Templeton suggested wrapping a bit of barbed wire round the top bar of the gate but leaving enough of a gap for a hand hold in just the right place where a person making use of it would be bound to step on the trap as they climbed over the gate.

Sid said he would look into it in the morning, but all agreed it was a good idea. The focus then changed to Bill's visit to Skates.

'On the basis that no plan survives contact with the enemy,' said Sid, 'I don't think there is a lot of finessing to be done there. Just get into the house, mate, and then blast away to the best of your ability. After that, your goal is to cover your tracks and destroy as much of the evidence as possible. And for that, you can't beat a good fire.'

'Absolutely,' said Lucy wholeheartedly. 'Arson has been a real signature dish of those two, and it will be quite fitting for them to experience it themselves, even if they are dead at the time. After all,' she added with a smile, 'it's the thought that counts.'

Sid recommended a simple mixture of petrol and Calor gas cylinders. 'A technique much favoured by the gentlemen of the IRA, and very effective it is. Almost untraceable, too, as far as the cylinders are concerned.'

'And how am I going to carry huge, heavy gas cylinders from the van to the house, let alone cans of petrol?' asked Bill.

'The small cylinders like we used for the grain dryer will do fine,' said Sid, 'but you'll need at least two of them.'

'And one Jerry can of petrol goes a long way,' added Miss Templeton. 'The important thing is to spread it around as much as you can. And you will be full of adrenalin after the shootings. Two gas cylinders and even two cans of petrol will present no problem to you as long as you move quickly.'

Bill sat and listened, occasionally adding something, but mostly just taking it all in as if it were someone else who would be doing all these things. But he actually had little doubt in his own mind that he would be able to do them when the time came. Yes, he was ill, very ill, but he believed in the old adage that 'a candle burns brighter just before the flame dies'. His own body was telling him this and, helped by the stimulants he had got from Dr Hall, he believed he would have the strength. He had a score to settle, and in his soul he felt this to be a legitimate blood debt. He simply had to succeed.

So it was decided that Bill would phone Skates the next day and tell him he would have the chairs finished by late Monday and would deliver them that evening.

Miss Templeton then asked to see their arsenal. The guns were fetched from their various hiding places and put on the table for her inspection. She examined the weapons as another elderly lady might have scrutinized handbags in Harrods. The sawn-off shotgun elicited a genteel 'tut-tut', but mostly in sorrow for the butchering of a once-beautiful weapon.

'Nasty things,' she said, 'but very effective. We used these a lot.'

Next she picked up the huge revolver, weighed it in her hands, then brought it smoothly up to the firing position. 'Not bad after all these years,' she said, with some little pride. 'But I couldn't hold it for long and the recoil would definitely be too much for me.'

Then she picked up the pistol that Sid had supplied.

'Now this is better. A model 36. Good balance. Yes, that's lovely.'

This was almost too much for Lucy. The incongruity of an elderly lady with a cut-glass accent politely remarking on the merits of various firearms suddenly struck her, and she was in grave danger of laughing out loud. Must be nerves, she thought.

Miss Templeton went home that night feeling more alive than she had in decades. Bill said his goodnights briefly and went gratefully to his bed, while Lucy and Sid took Clive for his evening walk. As they patrolled the yard, Lucy suddenly remembered she hadn't mentioned going out with Hugh the next evening and asked Sid what he thought about it.

Without hesitation, he answered, 'I think it's a grand idea, lass. None of us knows what the next couple of days may bring. A few hours of normality with a good bloke like Hugh Dawlish will take your mind off things. Besides, if you try to back out now, Bill and I will carry you there!'

This made Lucy laugh and put her mind at rest, at least as far as the next night was concerned. As to the one after that, well, that was another matter entirely.

Chapter 41

SUNDAY, 4 NOVEMBER

Sunday the 4th November was a miserable sort of day: rainy, cold, and depressing. Winter was giving a preview of what it would be up to in a month or so, and the landscape had become drab and waterlogged.

Under Bill's direction, Sid got out the man trap and oiled it up. Lucy came out to watch and make sure Clive got nowhere near the horrible thing. The two crescent arms were nearly three feet wide, and it took a lot of effort to open the jaws and set the spring trap that sat in the middle.

'It looks like a giant metal clam,' she remarked.

'It's a very simple mechanism,' said Sid, then activated the spring by placing a long piece of timber about four inches square on the base plate. The vicious iron teeth came together with a loud clang and the wood was bit in two just about where a man's ankle would be. All three of them stood silently looking down at the evil machine.

'Were these things actually used?' asked Lucy.

'Oh, yes,' said Bill. 'These and lots of other nasty devices like them. Not that long ago, either.'

'Well, it will certainly slow up Wonder Boy,' said Sid. 'Now we just have to work out where to put it and the best way to camouflage it.'

The entrance into the passage from the meadow was through a traditional five-bar gate about six feet wide and just over four feet high. It was ancient and rickety and normally left open. Some of the timbers were rotten and some were missing. When closed it would be easy enough to climb over, but would someone who was unfamiliar with it choose to do that at night?

'How about we pull the gate almost closed and leave the chain and padlock in the ring on the post? asked Bill. 'It'll look like we closed it but forgot to lock it afterwards; the sort of thing that happens when you're in a hurry.'

They agreed it would be simpler to do that than to try and work out exactly where Warren might climb over it and land. Also, it would be easier to camouflage the trap if it was further away, in shadow near the wall. Normally such traps were buried in long grass or undergrowth on a track known to be used by poachers, but on a cement-floored passageway the only option was to try to cover it with straw, leaves, and other rubbish that tends to accumulate in such places. Darkness would help, but the trap was about eight inches high when opened, which made it difficult to hide. Sid tried all manner of ways, but was satisfied with none of them. Finally he decided the only answer was to create a depression for it.

The concrete floor of the passage was badly cracked. Sid levered up a few of the slabs and thankfully there were no cobbles below, so he was able to create a fairly large area of muddy ground all around the gate. He scraped away the rubble and dug enough of an indentation to take the trap, then hauled away the displaced concrete. Then he put the trap into the hole and camouflaged it as best he could with dirt, leaves, and other detritus. They all agreed that this did the trick: the trap was well hidden and in a likely place for someone slipping into the passage to step.

As they left, Sid blocked the entrance to the passage with a hurdle just in case Clive got curious and decided to go for a sniff around the newly excavated area.

Back in the kitchen with a well-earned cup of tea, Sid gave his mind to all the places in which Warren could hide if he did get into the yard. The cart shed where Lucy kept her car was open all down one side. Then there were all the other buildings, including the stables, milking parlour, and cattle shed. All could provide cover and a place from which to launch an ambush. The bugger of it was that the lighting was so poor. However, there was an electric supply run from the workshop into the cart shed and stables, and that cable had been fixed high across the passage, so electricity was near enough at hand to fix up some better lights. He would go into town first thing in the morning and buy a couple of big halogen lamps and put them up. *Bloody hell*, he thought to himself, *this is all getting a bit close to the wire. We should have done this weeks ago!*

Sid had been planning to go home that night, but with Lucy dining out with Hugh, he thought it might be better if he stayed, so he suggested to Bill that he pop out and get some Chinese, 'just like old times'. Bill readily agreed.

Lucy came downstairs about seven. She had released her hair from its normal ponytail and brushed it until it gleamed like spun gold. And she was wearing a dress. It was one of the ones she had bought months ago to attend the auctions, and it was a stunner. Bill and Sid were speechless at first, but Lucy seemed unaware of the effect she made. If anything, she felt a bit embarrassed, as though she were a teenager dressing up instead of a woman in her late thirties going out for supper with an acquaintance.

Hugh turned up right on time and had dressed for the occasion himself, but even so he looked like exactly what he was: a successful but slightly old-fashioned farmer. Lucy was pleased with that, however, and appreciated the fact that there was no side to the man. What you saw was what you got.

As they left, Bill and Sid wished them a good evening but refrained (not without effort) from 'if you can't be good, be careful' and all the other corny sayings they would have trotted out if things had been different.

Hugh took Lucy to a nice but not over-the-top restaurant, and was a good host even if his conversation did tend to centre on his farm. The food was excellent and the atmosphere not overtly romantic, which suited them both. Somehow it was understood that they were building a foundation of friendship rather than simply exercising their hormones. Each hoped they would eventually come to know the other better but, without discussing it, they both seemed to know that this was not the time. When Hugh drove her home, Lucy was glad she'd gone, but also glad to get back.

Bill and Sid were still up, and the kitchen smelled of Chinese takeaway and cider. Lucy started to clear up, but was stopped by Sid, who asked her what she would have to drink. She choose tea and allowed herself to be thoroughly questioned and chaffed about her evening. But there wasn't just one elephant in the room, there was a whole herd of the buggers. All that had been planned, put in place, and worried over for months would be put to the test next day.

Of the three of them, the one who seemed least anxious was Bill. In between coughing bouts, there was a brightness in his eyes that both Lucy and Sid recognised.

But they did not discuss tomorrow.

Chapter 42

MONDAY, 5 NOVEMBER

'Remember, remember the fifth of November; gunpowder, treason, and plot!' carolled Sid as Lucy came down next morning and found him already drinking tea at the kitchen table. She poured herself a cup and looked at him as he sat writing on the back of an envelope.

'Making your will?' asked Lucy.

'Nope, just a list of components I need to set up some floodlights.'

'A bit late isn't it?'

'Just in time, my love, just in bloody time! It won't take long to fix up. We have some of the wiring already in place.' He stood up and flourished the envelope.

'I'm off to B&Q,' he said, and suited the action to the words.

Bill came into the kitchen and Lucy scrutinized him. She decided she had seen him looking worse, but she was still worried about what would happen if he didn't have the strength to accomplish tonight's tasks. That turned her mind to Skates, and she suddenly thought how awful it would be if the bastard wasn't home when they needed him to be.

'What time are you planning to call Skates?' she asked.

'I was thinking about noon. Why?'

'Phone now,' she said with some urgency, 'before his day starts and he has a chance to make other plans.'

Bill set down his teacup. 'Good thinking,' he said, then went to the phone and dialled Skates's number. He told Skates the chairs were ready, he would deliver them that evening, and he expected his money to be waiting for him, all £10,000 of it and not a penny less.

Skates wanted to know why tonight; he had planned on going out. Bill said he was putting the final polish on that day, and once it was done he wanted shot of the bloody things. The next day he was going into hospital, so it had to be tonight. After a little more fussing, Skates agreed to seven o'clock. Bill sat down, face flushed and excited.

Sid was back just before midday. Lucy helped him rig up a powerful spotlight to cover the front of the workshop, and another to illuminate the passage to the meadow gate. The new light over the workshop door illuminated much of the yard even in the soft grey daylight of November. The light down the passage was fixed high up, the switch for it put at shoulder height inside the cart shed next to the passage. Just the place where either Sid or Lucy would be waiting.

The floor of the passage and surrounding yard had benefited from the light breeze and a gentle soaking of rain that had fallen since Sid had buried the trap. If you knew where to look, you could see some disturbance to the area around the gate, but at night it would be unnoticeable.

Lunch was a quiet affair. Sid did what he could to add a bit of cheer, but when he got up to clean and check the weapons, it couldn't help but focus their minds on the coming festivities.

'Well, it'll be a fireworks night to remember,' he said as he stripped the guns, oiled them carefully, checked the mechanisms, and did all the things his days in the army had taught him to do.

The day wore on. Sid took Clive out for a walk; Bill sat in his armchair by the stove pretending to read. The clock on the wall ticked the seconds, minutes, and hours away as it had done for a century or more.

About four, as it was reaching dusk, Miss Templeton arrived. She had replaced her usual flowing garments with flannel trousers, a dark jumper, and an ex-army garment with lots of pockets, some of which bulged. She was wearing sensible shoes rather than her normal plimsolls, and instead of her voluminous patchwork cloth bag she carried a small rucksack, again of army issue and nearly as old as she was.

Returning from his walk with a muddy and worn-out Clive, Sid took one look at Miss Templeton and said, 'Bloody hell, a commando tunic! I haven't seen one of them in donkey's years.'

Lucy made tea. She didn't feel hungry, nor did Bill, but both of the professionals insisted they eat something, so she made a pile of sandwiches. She decided it was probably the strangest meal she had ever eaten. Around a table piled with a variety of firearms and boxes of ammunition, they discussed the best way to pickle onions and whether a hollow-point bullet was as destructive as a cross-cut dum-dum round.

Sid went over the plan one more time. Bill could have done without it, but he listened with good grace. In reality he just wanted it over, one way or the other.

'You'll go in with the chairs first, one at a time, and in no obvious hurry,' Sid told Bill. 'If there's anyone else in the house, they'll probably come out to look at the chairs. Curiosity doesn't only kill cats! Skates has waited so long to see these he'll be all over them, and so will anyone else who's there. Then out comes your little helper and bang, bang, bang.'

'Do get as close as you can,' reminded Miss Templeton.

'If Warren's there, take him down first,' continued Sid. 'He's the one most likely to be armed. If the other goon is about, the one we caught in the field, him next, and–'

Suddenly Bill interrupted him. 'And if there's a fucking dance going on, I'll shoot the bloody bandleader!'

He appreciated Sid's concern, but the truth was he was wound up now and ready to go. Lucy made sure he had his mobile phone charged up and fixed, so all he had to do was press a button to call home. Sid had told him about a field entrance just down the road from Skates's place where he could park and phone them right before he drove in.

The final preparations were made, and Sid loaded up Bill's van. The two gas cylinders went in first, along with two Jerry cans of petrol; these were concealed with the dark grey army blankets Bill used to cover furniture. Then the chairs, swathed in more blankets and wedged in with old foam cushions.

The unaccustomed weight of the revolver in his right jacket pocket made it feel conspicuous, but Lucy said it didn't show. The safety was off but the hammer wasn't cocked so it would be safe enough, yet easy to fire.

Before he left, Bill went back inside alone and put a folded note on the mantelpiece over the stove, saying nothing of it to anyone. Then he phoned Skates and told him he was leaving. It was 6:35.

It was a cold night. There had been rain earlier, and the road shone under the headlights of his van. There was little traffic once he left the main road and entered one of the narrow sunken lanes that criss-crossed this part of Somerset. Bill drove slowly, more slowly that he normally did, not because of his cargo but because for some mad reason he saw himself skidding off the road into a ditch and not being able to keep all the promises he had made.

Eventually he recognised the description Sid had given him of the lane that ran past Skates's house. Up ahead a short distance was the gate leading to Skate's drive. He almost missed the field entrance and had to reverse back. Slowly and carefully he backed into the space as if there were a deep chasm each side rather than straggly hedges. He had just turned off his lights and was reaching for his mobile to call home when he saw a flash of headlights and heard a loud roar as a motorcycle sped by. He couldn't tell for sure if it was Warren, but whoever it was, they were going very fast.

He pushed the button on his mobile as he'd been taught and the phone was answered immediately by Lucy. He told her where he was and what he had seen, then rang off and drove on.

The large, brick pillars of the gates came into view, and he turned into the drive. The gates were open, and the whole front of the house was illuminated. He turned his van around and parked it with the back doors facing the porticoed front steps. There was a wide, shiny door with small bay trees on either side, and the windows on the entire ground floor were lit. Next to the house was a garage, its door open and a white Range Rover parked inside.

Bill got stiffly out of his van. As he did so, the front door opened and through it walked the man he had last seen being thumped by Sid. He was dressed in some form of track suit, and Bill thought he looked bloody enormous.

'Mr Skates is expecting you,' said the man curtly.

Bill nodded and opened the back doors of his van, unwrapped a chair, and put it down on the gravel. The big man just stood there, looking neither surprised nor interested. Bill took out the other chair, stacked it seat down on the first, then closed the doors.

'Take them in, will you?' he asked, then walked behind the man as he did so, making an enormous effort to refrain from putting his hand into the pocket that held Sid's revolver.

He followed the man through a large hall that boasted a massive chandelier and a staircase wide enough to take a horse, and eventually ended up in a dining room. It held a vast mahogany table so highly polished that it reflected the lights from a number of antique sconces that adorned the walls. Between these were large oil paintings and, against one wall, a serving dresser that to Bill's experienced eye looked very good indeed. He could not say the same for the dining chairs, however. They were Hepplewhite in the same way that Skates's manservant was human: they might pass from a distance but would not have borne close examination.

Skates emerged from a doorway somewhere in the back of the big room and came forward to meet them. The man set the chairs down in front of him and stepped back. Skates nodded to Bill but otherwise made no acknowledgment. One by one he examined the chairs, turning them around, lifting them up, rocking them on their legs from side to side and backward and forward.

Finally, he sat in one of the chairs, looked at Bill, and said, 'They reek of fucking polish, Sawyer.'

'Of course they do, and they will for about a week, depending on where you keep them. But it's beeswax, not polish, and you'd smell that in a church on pew-cleaning day, so it's nothing out of the ordinary.'

Then, in a more conciliatory voice he asked, 'So what do you think of them?'

Skates moved to the other chair and sat on it, running his hands on the wood under the seat.

'Not bad. Which one's the repair?'

'I can't tell from here,' said Bill and moved closer. In fact, he really couldn't tell without getting close to the back carvings.

'Yeah, all right,' grinned Skates. 'You've made your point. They're good, I grant you that, but then I knew they would be. That's why I insisted on you doing them.'

He turned to his bodyguard. 'Bring in the other two.'

Bill said, 'They're not here.' As casually as he could, he sat down on one of the dining chairs on the opposite side of the table from Skates, who suddenly looked fit to blow a gasket.

'What the fuck do you mean, they're not here!' he shouted, his normally sallow face becoming scarlet with rage.

Bill sat back, wishing he could pull out the gun and shoot the pair of them now, but he hadn't got his money yet. Instead he raised both hands in a conciliatory gesture.

'Hang on, they're perfectly fine,' he said. 'But if you think I'm daft enough to come here on my own, hand over those chairs, and expect to get paid, or even walk out alive if your Mr Warren has his way, you'll need to think again.'

He sat back and took his pipe out of his top pocket. He needed to do something with his hands to stop them shaking. 'The other two chairs are in my workshop, all nice and safe, providing I get back in one piece and with my cash.'

'And if not?' sneered Skates.

'Then they burn. Easy enough to arrange when you've got all the right kit, and I've got all the right kit. By the way,' he asked, still fiddling with his pipe as if thinking about lighting it, 'where is good old Warren tonight? Out torturing kittens somewhere?'

'He's out with some friends. I sent him away because I know you two don't get on.' Skates shrugged, almost back to normal now. 'Wait here.'

He walked to the door at the far end of the room but, before disappearing through it, asked Bill if he wanted a drink. Bill was as dry as a bone and decided he really could do with one, so he said yes. Skates nodded to his man, who wordlessly went to the sideboard, poured a large measure of amber liquid into a crystal glass, and brought it across. Bill drank some without even sniffing to find out what it was. Not that it would have mattered: he was suddenly so parched he'd have drunk bath water. It was whisky, however, and a good one at that.

Skates had not pulled the door to all the way, and in the reflection of the huge mirror over the sideboard, Bill could see him pick up a phone and make a call. He couldn't hear what was said, but the conversation was short. The minder, seeing Bill's interest, moved to block his view, but Bill was already sure Warren had been told there were still two chairs to come.

Skates came back with an envelope and placed it next to Bill's glass. 'And when do I get my other chairs?' he asked.

'You can send Sonny Boy here for them tomorrow morning if you like. Not Warren, though. I don't want that bastard anywhere near me, understand?'

Skates just nodded.

'And don't get any clever ideas, either. There'll be someone with me in the morning until I go to the hospital, and they'll be at my place all day until I get back.'

'Fine, fine,' said Skates, adding 'Not that you have anything to worry about, providing I get my other chairs.' He walked over to get a drink from the sideboard and, like a guard dog, his minder swivelled his head to watch him.

Bill's mouth was still bone dry despite the whisky. The two men were close together and no more than six feet away, possibly less. Close enough.

Time seemed to slow down as he rose to his feet. He put his hand into his pocket and felt for the grip of the revolver. Pulling out the gun in what felt like slow motion, he pointed it at the big man in the track suit and pulled the trigger. The sound was deafening, terrifying, and Bill saw a large red stain grow on the man's belly before he folded up and lay face down on the carpeted floor.

Bill's arms had been driven upward by the recoil of the gun. With ears still ringing, he brought them gun back down into the firing position. Skates had already started to run towards to the door at the end of the room but Bill stepped forward and squeezed the trigger.

The gun fired, and at first Bill thought he must have missed because Skates kept moving. It turned out he had only been falling forward, though, twisting as he did so, like a worm impaled on a garden fork.

Bill was about to take another step in Skates's direction to follow Sid's injunction to shoot everyone thoroughly whether they were dead or not when his right ankle was wrenched out from under him. He fell backward, his head missing the dresser by inches, and landed painfully on his backside. Winded and in shock, he realized he had dropped the revolver. He now sat looking into the face of Skates's minder, who had dragged himself over from where he had fallen. Holding Bill's ankle in an iron grip, his face contorted in pain and hate, the man was using his powerful arms to crawl nearer.

Bill tried to edge himself away, but his back was against the dresser. The carpet, rough under his hands, provided no grip, but as he put his right hand out to stop himself from slipping sideways, his fingers brushed the barrel of the pistol. His assailant also saw the gun and made a herculean lunge for it that took him across Bill's legs.

Bill, pinned beneath the thug, could smell the man's stale breath and hear the snarl that rattled in his throat. But he got to the gun before his attacker did and, closing his eyes and turning his face away, placed it against the man's head and pulled the trigger. Luckily, most of the resultant gore ended up on the underside of the dining table rather than on Bill. Trying desperately not to look at the ruined head only inches away from him, Bill disentangled himself from the corpse and lurched to his feet.

He immediately collapsed, panting, onto a dining chair. He set the revolver on the table next to the glass of whisky he had drunk from . . . how long ago? A minute, an hour, a lifetime? It was so quiet now, and there was only the faintest hint of gun smoke in the air. He drank the remainder of the whisky and got to his feet. He picked up the revolver and walked over to Skates. Then, thinking he heard a moan, he emptied the gun into Skates's body.

He took the chairs one by one back out to his van, then looked around, listening for any sound that might indicate his vermin-control activities had attracted attention. But the night remained silent and peaceful. He brought the gas cylinders into the house first, then unloaded both petrol cans and stowed the chairs in their place. His system was awash in adrenalin; he thought of Miss Templeton's prediction and smiled wryly. Yes, he might pay for it later, but right now he certainly had the strength to do what was necessary.

Sloshing the petrol around brought on his cough with a vengeance, however. So much so that, after opening the valves on the gas cylinders, he was in such a hurry to leave the house that he almost forgot to pick up the envelope full of money that still lay on the dining table. Quickly stuffing it into the inside pocket of his jacket, he gave one last look around the room. Nothing moved.

Leaving the front door open, he poured a trail of petrol from the dining room, through the hall and doorway, and onto the shallow steps. Some of it ran down and formed a pool on the gravel below. He stepped back, lit a match, and dropped it.

Chapter 43

MONDAY, 5 NOVEMBER

B ack at the farm, Bill's telephone call had put them on the alert. If it was indeed Warren who had flashed by Bill's van, and assuming he was making for the farm, Sid calculated they had something like half an hour before he arrived.

In fact, it was only twenty minutes later that Warren reached Bill's place. He drove up the lane a short way, then turned off his headlights and slowly coasted back. There were no lights on at the farm as far as he could see, so he parked his motorbike well into the field entrance he had used before.

He was waiting quietly in the dark for Bill to return when his phone vibrated. It was Skates. That bastard Sawyer had only brought two chairs and claimed to have the other two booby-trapped. Warren was to get into the old fool's yard and wait till he returned, then do whatever was necessary to get the two remaining chairs before having any 'fun'. Skates had even said he could keep half the money Sawyer would be carrying. It was a treat for him: a reward for all the aggravation he had had to endure over these fucking chairs.

Lucy was stationed in the cart shed within easy reach of the switch for the floodlight that would shine down the passage towards the meadow gate. Wearing a warm jumper and an old tweed cap of Bill's, she cradled the sawn-off shotgun. Staring into the darkness with ears straining for any sound is a soul-destroying activity. Nerves taut, eyes wide, and brain fizzing, she waited for something to happen.

Sid was posted in the workshop, which gave him a good view of the yard along with easy access to the switch for the workshop floodlight. He was experienced at this game, but even he was cold and stiff. 'I'm getting too old for this sodding lark,' he thought as he sucked on a boiled sweet he had found in one of the pockets of his huge parka. He had Bill's ancient revolver within easy reach, and its presence was some comfort.

Only Miss Templeton was not alone. Clive was asleep by the stove, but it was not him with whom she shared her watch. Armed with the old shotgun, she kept an eye on the yard and the big main gate, but her mind was filled with memories of other times, other places, and long-dead comrades with whom she had sat, holding a gun in her hand, waiting for foes to emerge from the gloom.

Warren made his way to the farm. Dressed in his black motorcycle leathers, he was almost invisible. Coming up to the gate in the meadow, he saw in front of him the dark, narrow passage that led into the yard. Having been here before, he remembered the general layout and knew this was the only entrance apart from the big gate to the yard. Unfortunately, it was too dark for him to notice this one had been left unlocked, so he carefully climbed over it. Somehow he also managed to avoid the man trap Sid had so carefully set for him.

Though he knew Bill was currently at Skates's house, Warren held a small automatic pistol at the ready as he entered the dark passageway. You couldn't be too careful; besides, there might be rats or cats to shoot. He moved soundlessly until he had nearly reached the end of the passage, when he disturbed a small piece of broken concrete that made a tiny clattering noise. It was such a trivial sound that it didn't even register with Lucy, but Sid edged around slowly and carefully to see what had made it. He didn't switch on the big floodlight because he wasn't sure it was a human noise, but he moved and that was enough.

Warren fired. His reflexes were superb, but it also helped that he didn't give a damn who he shot. Sid felt a blow on his left arm just below the shoulder and, throwing himself across the entrance to get his gun into play, he fell on his back. Pointing the big revolver where he had seen the flash of the gun, he fired.

Warren's little automatic had made a nasty sharp crack, like a firework. Sid's bloody great war relic made a great smash of sound that reverberated in the narrow passage like the crack of doom. Sid's shot did not hit Warren, but it surprised him enough to prevent him from instantly firing another round into the man who now lay at his feet.

Lucy had leapt up at the sound of the gunfire, hit the switch for the floodlight, which now lit up the entire area, and stepped into the passage. She saw Sid lying on his back, one arm bleeding and useless, struggling to get another shot at Warren. She also saw Warren bring his pistol up to shoot Sid again.

'Ricky!' she shouted. 'Ricky Warren!'

He turned and saw her. It took a few seconds for him to recognize her, though, because instead of the cowering girl he had raped and tortured for years, he saw a tall, confident woman holding a sawn-off shotgun.

Lucy's fear aimed the gun, her love for Sid squeezed the

trigger, and her grey eyes saw the man she hated so much flung back against the wall, a red smear appearing on its ancient stones to mark his passage.

There was no need for the second barrel. There seldom is with such a weapon. Lucy broke open the gun to render it safe and then bent over Sid, who was trying to get to his feet.

Miss Templeton now ran into the floodlit passage, her old shotgun at the ready. Quickly assessing the situation, she yelled at Lucy to 'switch that damned light off in case there are any more of them'. Lucy did as she was told, then they got Sid into the kitchen. On went all the lights and off came Sid's coat, which caused him a deal of pain, but he refused to have it cut off. Then the sleeve of his jumper and shirt were cut away.

Miss Templeton rummaged in her rucksack and produced clean dressings that she pressed onto Sid's wounds until the bleeding had all but stopped. Examining these, she declared the damage to be 'just a nasty scratch. In and out, dear boy, like a squaddie in a knocking shop,' she said, and winked at him.

Sid just sat there staring at her. It hurt like hell, but he knew he was lucky. No bones smashed and, if properly treated, no hospital visit and no awkward questions.

Miss Templeton produced a bottle of iodine and proceeded to paint it over the wounds. This hurt so much that he hardly noticed when she put a stich or three over the exit hole, which was bigger than the small entrance wound.

'Rest the arm a bit,' she said as she made a sling out of a hand towel while Lucy cleaned everything up.

Then Lucy made a pot of tea and brought out the whisky bottle. They sat sipping their drinks in that twilight world that comes after mortal danger has passed. Hot tea laced with rum for Lucy and Miss Templeton, and whisky for Sid. It was 9:30 by the wall clock.

'He should be back soon,' said Lucy, hoping he really would be.

Sid said nothing, but he was worried, too. If Bill wasn't back in half an hour, he decided, he would go and start looking for him. In the meantime, partly to keep Lucy from fretting, he suggested they go out into the yard and consider how best to dispose of the late, unlamented Warren. They all trooped outside, and Sid put on the yard spotlight so they could see what was left of their visitor. It turned out there was quite a lot at either end, but the part in the middle was a bit sketchy.

'We'll have to move it before rigor mortis sets in,' said Miss Templeton.

Lucy was detailed to find the biggest plastic sheet she could while Sid connected the big hose to an outside tap near the workshop. Lucy returned with the sheet, some rubber gloves, and Bill's neoprene staining apron. They rolled what was left of Warren onto the sheet, Miss Templeton going through all his pockets as they came into view. Then they stood and looked at the shiny, plastic-sheeted lump at their feet.

'We'd best put it in the back of my van for now,' said Sid. 'Whatever we decide to do with it, we can't leave it laying around in plain sight.'

It was an ungainly parcel for a one-armed man and a slight woman to get into the back of a van, but Lucy tied bailing twine around it to form handles, and somehow they managed it between them.

There was quite a lot of blood where Warren had lain and this had soaked down through the broken concrete. Lucy took the hose from Sid and washed away as much as she could, including the smear Warren had made on the wall when the shotgun blast had hit him. The water glistened in the harsh light, showering jewels onto the walls of the passage.

Sid got a stick and defused the man trap, then Lucy put it in the back of the cart shed.

Miss Templeton consulted her watch. It was nearly 10; Bill was running late. Sid was just on deciding it was time to go look for him when headlights appeared at the main gate. Lucy ran to open it, and in drove Bill's van.

They helped him out of it and into the kitchen. He sat for a minute or two, saying nothing, clearly exhausted, his face pale, his eyes red-rimmed, and his breathing laboured. They asked no questions, merely plied him with tea and made sounds of general encouragement while they waited for him to get his breath back.

Finally, with a visible effort, he gathered himself and told them what had happened. When he was done, he slowly pulled from his inside pocket the envelope he had got from Skates.

'Lucy, put this on the mantelpiece, will you?'

As she did so, he looked around and seemed to notice for the first time that Sid's arm was in a sling. The little bit of colour that had returned to his cheeks drained away.

'How bad is it?' he asked.

'Gnat bite, mate, a mere gnat bite, and this lovely lady,' said Sid, indicating Miss Templeton, 'has already sorted it out nicely.'

They told him what had gone on in his absence, and the look he gave Lucy when he learned Warren's fate was worth a million pounds to her. After a while he got up and asked to be shown where the action had taken place. The spotlight was still on in the yard, illuminating the area like a crime scene, though most of the blood had been washed away. Sid took Bill through the sequence of events just as they happened, without any embellishment. Lucy said nothing, but stood close to Bill throughout.

They turned off the light and went back into the kitchen. On the table was Warren's motorcycle helmet and a pile containing his possessions, including his phone and bike keys.

'Where is the bike now?' asked Bill.

'Parked up where it was last time he visited, I expect,' answered Sid. 'But we'd better get it moved.' He rose wearily to his feet.

'No, Sid,' said Lucy, getting up. 'You rest here for a bit. I can drive it.'

Taking the helmet, the keys, and a small torch, she went out into the night. *No need for a shotgun now*, she thought as she walked down the road. It was only when she put the helmet on before riding the bike back to the farm that she got the shakes, and that was only because the bastard still used the same aftershave. The helmet reeked of it, and the smell made her gag. But the bike started easily, and she made short work of riding it into the yard and parking it in the cart shed.

Back in the kitchen, she went over to where Bill was sitting, leaned down, and kissed him.

'What's that for?' he asked, looking up at her with a tired smile.

'Because I did it, and I couldn't have without you.'

'And Sid and Miss Templeton,' said Bill. 'Couldn't have done bugger all without them.'

'Yes, I know that,' said Lucy, resting her cheek on the top of his head. 'But you're the one who rescued me.'

'It's not all over yet,' said Miss Templeton. 'We still have a body to dispose of.'

'I've been thinking on that,' said Sid, gingerly rubbing his wound. Lucy had given him one of Bill's painkillers, but the arm was getting very stiff and sore.

'You know I've been doing a job for the Friggin' Brigadier? Well it's a new septic system and all there is left for me to do is to fill in the old one. Lucy can drive me over there at first light, we can pitch Warren into the hole, fill it up, and no one will ever be the wiser.'

'Won't anyone else be about?' asked Lucy. 'What about the general?'

'He never gets up before nine and he's deaf as a post. No one else will be by; I have the keys to the field gate and the digger. I should have filled the hole in days ago, but we were still working on the chairs. My mate who owns the digger just wants a phone call when the job's done and I'm to leave the keys to the machine under one of the tracks so it can be picked up when convenient, same as usual.'

'I like it,' said Bill. 'If Warren disappears, the police, bless 'em, may think it was him who did the dirty deeds because he has done similar ones before.'

After a little more discussion, it was decided that Lucy would ride Warren's motorbike to a mainline-connected railway station. Salisbury was the closest, but likely to have security cameras; Yeovil Junction was half an hour further away, but the car park was well outside the station, which was not manned but had a ticket machine.

'Wear gloves so only Warren's fingerprints will be on it,' advised

Sid, 'and buy a ticket for London on the machine. If the police ever get around to checking railway stations then it won't hurt to have a ticket sale in the right timeframe. But we'll have to get a move on for it to look as if Warren killed Skates and did a runner straight away.'

Lucy stood up. 'We're not waiting on me,' she said.

Miss Templeton said she and Bill would wait up for them, and settled herself in an armchair near the stove. Lucy fetched them both blankets and neither protested as she tucked them in.

Sid drove his van and Lucy preceded him on the bike. The roads were wet and the motorcycle far more powerful than any she had ever ridden before, so she took it slowly at first, but after a while she began to enjoy the exhilaration of riding such a lovely machine. There wasn't much traffic, but bonfires burned on the hills all around, flickering lights through the trees like signal fires warning of danger.

By the time they reached Yeovil Junction, the place was deserted. Lucy parked the bike in a corner, under some trees, away from the few cars that were still there. She took off the black helmet and strapped it onto the bike, then walked to the machine and purchased a ticket for London.

Sid was waiting just outside the carpark, and when she walked up to his van she could see he was in a lot of pain. She motioned him across to the passenger seat, got in, and drove home.

By the time they reached Bill's, both of them were exhausted. When they dragged themselves into the kitchen, the occupants of the armchairs remained asleep. Sid laid his hand on Lucy's shoulder for a brief moment, then went straight up to the spare room and his sleeping bag. He washed down another painkiller with a swig of whisky and crashed out. Lucy did much the same, with the difference that Sid's sleep was full of disturbing dreams, while hers was deep and untroubled.

Chapter 44

TUESDAY, 6 NOVEMBER

Lucy was the first up on Tuesday morning, and though she crept around the kitchen making tea as quietly as possible, she woke Miss Templeton, who stretched in her armchair and smiled up at her.

'You did well last night, young lady,' she said.

Lucy smiled gratefully in return, but before she could say anything, Bill awoke and started coughing. He tried to get to his feet but couldn't; he slumped back into his chair, chest heaving, blood speckling his lips. Lucy got behind him and helped him to his feet while Miss Templeton got a kitchen towel and wiped his pale lips. Lucy called Sid, and between them they helped Bill up to his bed and undressed him. Lucy gave him his medications, then they closed his bedroom door and returned to the kitchen.

Sid's arm was very stiff; the bruising was extensive and colourful. Miss Templeton checked his wounds and, finding no cause for concern, said she would get herself back to her cottage and into a proper bed. Lucy attempted to tell her how much they all owed her, but this was brushed aside.

'I'm sorry, my dear,' she said kindly, 'but I'm just too exhausted to listen to such nonsense.'

Sid smiled at that. As Miss Templeton walked out of the kitchen door, he called 'Ma'am!' and threw her a salute. She chuckled and left, still very upright, still very much the lady.

It was now 6:30 and still dark, but dawn was in the offing. Lucy and Sid decided they would wait to have breakfast until after they had planted Warren. Before they left, Lucy parked her Volvo in the passage right over the spot where the shooting had taken place. They would have to do a more thorough clean-up job when they got back.

It was only a short drive to the Frigging Brigadier's, and the digger was as Sid had left it, near a huge hole at the bottom of which were the remains of an old cesspit, the roof and the drain leading to it just rubble, raw earth, and slime. Sid started the machine, and it roared to life in a cloud of black diesel smoke which helped mask the foul odour lingering in the area. A pile of earth from where the new septic system had been installed was nearby, ready to be used to fill in the pit.

But first they needed to get Warren's body from the back of the van into the hole. Sid drove the digger right up to the rear doors and Lucy was able to use the bailing twine handles to drag the plastic-wrapped parcel onto the bucket. After that it was the work of a moment for Sid to tip the parcel into the bottom of the old shit-pit. Then, with skill and finesse, he used the digger bucket to tear open the plastic shroud.

This disturbed the muck at the bottom of the hole, not to mention Lucy. She backed away from the stench and asked him what the hell he thought he was doing.

'If you watched more television, lass, you'd know that plastic sheeting preserves bodies. This way there will be fuck all left of the little bugger after nature takes its course!'

Sid started tipping clean earth into the pit and soon the stench lessened, for which they were both grateful. The place still smelled of drains but nothing like as bad as when the digger had disturbed the turds of ages past.

By the time Sid finished, the morning had grown soft and bright. Lucy looked around carefully. All that was left of the old cesspit was raw earth piled slightly higher than the meadow around it. The trees bordering the field had shed their leaves and were skeletal now, just as the body buried in that biologically rich environment would be before long. Sid came back from parking the digger and stood by her side.

'Do you want to say anything?' he asked.

Lucy thought for a bit, then said, 'Earth to earth, ashes to ashes, and shit to shit.'

Then she turned, walked to the van, and got into the driver's seat. Sid opened the field gate and closed it again after she had driven through. They rode back to Bill's through weak sunshine, parked the van, and scraped the mud off their boots. Lucy was suddenly very hungry and promised Sid she would make a vast mountain of bacon sandwiches as soon as she had looked in on Bill.

He was still fast asleep. His breathing was shallow and there was blood on the pillow. Lucy went back downstairs feeling slightly less hungry, but kept her promise to Sid.

After breakfast they tackled cleaning up the yard in and around the passage. When Lucy moved her car, she could see specks of gore in amongst the broken concrete, but not as much as she thought there would be. She hosed down the stone wall again and this time dislodged a load of moss and dirt, which ran down onto the floor. Then Sid had her use the hose to drive rubbish from the rest of the farmyard into the passage, which was soon awash with old leaves, twigs, and a few previously hidden deposits from Clive. It wouldn't stand a forensic examination, but it would do to be going on with.

At noon Bill was about the same. When Lucy put more wood in the stove, she realized she was using the new stuff Hugh had brought them. So Bill had been right about that, she thought. There had been just about enough logs on the woodpile to see him out.

Straightening up, she made an effort to shrug off her sadness. Her eyes caught sight of the envelope Bill had given her to put on the mantelpiece the previous night, and for the first time she noticed the note Bill had left before he set out for Skates's. She took them both over to the table where Sid was sitting drinking yet another mug of tea and sat down next to him. Then she opened the note and together they read the following words:

My friends,

If you are reading this, I am probably dead. If I am, well, I was dying anyway and my only regret would be if I didn't finish Skates first, but I hope I did.

There is something like £6,000 left from the advance I was given and that is in the old cash box. Lucy, you know the one.

Split it 50/50. My plan has always been to share the cash with you both. You have earned it, you deserve it.

Lucy, I love you.

Sid, you old reprobate, well, you know.

Bill

Dovetail

Lucy picked up the envelope Bill had brought home. It was thick and heavy. Opening it revealed a wad of cash that totalled £10,000.

Without saying a word, Lucy went upstairs to check on Bill again. She came down looking more worried than ever.

'He's really bad now, Sid,' she said. 'I'm going to phone the doctor.'

'If you do that, Lucy, they'll take him into hospital and he'll die there. He'd hate that, you know it.'

Lucy had to agree, but she insisted on phoning Gloria to let her and Philip know how sick Bill had become. Before she could say much, however, she heard faltering steps on the stairs, the door from the hall opened, and there stood Bill. He made his way past her to the kitchen table and sat down in his chair.

'If that's Gloria,' he said hoarsely, 'tell her I'd be grateful for a ride to the hospice tomorrow. Oh, and I'll want some photos of the family. Tomorrow afternoon, after Jack's got home from school.'

Lucy passed all that on, then, after hanging up, asked Bill if he would like a drink or anything to eat, reminding him as tactfully as she could that he hadn't had anything in nearly 24 hours. He scowled and said maybe a few biscuits, and tea, please. Then he looked at Sid and the pile of money on the table in front of him, with the note he had written lying open on top of it.

Sid saw him looking and smiled at him. 'Silly bugger. What do you suppose I would do with that sort of money? You know me, mate. Most of it would go on wild women and booze!'

'Right,' said Bill, smiling, 'and you'd just waste the rest.'

Lucy came back to the table with some slices of buttered

bread and a mug of tomato soup, a piece of cheese, and Bill's tea. The smell of this simple meal must have whetted Bill's appetite because he tucked in and asked them what they had been doing. As he slowly ate, they told him all about the hole, the burying, and the clean-up afterwards.

Then he told them in more detail what he had done the night before. They had heard the basic facts, but after his long rest and the nourishing food, Bill was now able to fill in the gaps.

'So you're sure that other bugger was the bloke we found in the field?' asked Sid.

Bill said he was sure, which had made it easier to pull the trigger. What he didn't say was that the man's hate-filled eyes were burned into his memory more than anything else from that night. Well, the fire perhaps, he thought, but those unblinking eyes were the stuff of nightmares.

Then he picked up the note he had written. 'Same thing goes,' he said, 'No matter how much it comes to, you share it.'

Lucy moved towards Bill and put her arms around him. 'Three ways, Bill. That's what it ought to be, three ways.'

Sid nodded in agreement.

'Look,' said Bill, 'I've got no use for money where I'm going, and my son will get everything else. There's enough money in the bank for sorting me out. And,' he added, 'there's those bloody chairs. God knows how much they'll fetch if ever they're sold.'

'Shit,' cried Sid, 'I haven't got them out of your van yet!' And he got up, took Bill's keys off the hook, and rushed out into the yard.

Bill laughed, coughed a bit, then reached for Lucy's hand.

'You're going to need the cash for that holiday we spoke of.'

'For running away, you mean,' said Lucy.

'You can't be here for while, lass, you know that.'

He saw her eyes fill with tears and squeezed her hand. 'The police might just think of me having done work for Skates. They wouldn't be able to find a motive, but if you're here you'll be questioned, and if I could connect you with Skates, they surely can.'

Lucy looked at him, tears running down her cheeks now. 'I wanted to be here with you until the end,' she said.

'And I want to be man enough to watch you drive away,' said Bill softly. 'To drive away so you can return again if you wish. No farewells from a damned hospital bed, but from my home, which was your home, our home.'

He stopped, caught her glance and held it. His eyes were tired but as determined in this as they had been in everything else.

'We say our goodbyes from here, Lucy.'

By the time Sid came back in, she had dried her eyes, but he could tell she had been crying and also noted the anguish on his old friend's face.

'The chairs are fine,' he said with as much jollity as he could manage. 'I put them in the back of the workshop along with the original two and covered the lot with some of those army blankets. Then I locked up and here I am!'

Silent nods were all he got from Bill and Lucy.

'Say, how would you like some fish and chips for dinner tonight? I can go get them from the F&C van in the Bell Inn car park. Just a thought,' he added brightly.

Gratefully, they said they would like that very much.

After Sid left, Lucy took Clive for a walk. She used the passage as she had done hundreds of times before, but stopped at the entrance to marvel at how little she actually felt about having killed Warren. He was a rapist, a murderer, and a dangerous psychopath; the world was better off without him, plain and simple.

But she had thought she would feel changed in some way when he and Skates were gone. As though the part of her life they had belonged to would lift from her soul like mist evaporating in the sunshine. But the memories were still there, and so were the scars. She knew now they always would be, but the feelings they conjured up had changed. There was still shame, but it didn't completely overwhelm her anymore. She wished she had been strong enough to leave Skates, but she hadn't been. And there were reasons for that, and, oh well, what the hell, worse things happen at sea, she thought.

As she mused, Clive hoovered the ground with his nose, intrigued by strange scents, tail going nineteen to the dozen. Suddenly he stopped near the place where Warren had been killed, cocked his leg, and pissed on the wall. Lucy laughed out loud. Clive had provided the perfect epitaph for that vile, deranged man.

In the meadow all was quiet and damp in the late autumn air. The sky was dirty white like an old handkerchief, and the washed-out afternoon sun was low on the horizon. Trees and hedges were her only companions. She would miss all this and the people she had grown to love here. One special person would be no more, but this landscape would still be here, and in her heart nothing could ever separate the one from the other.

Back in the kitchen, Bill was doing a lot of thinking, too.

After so many months of worry and planning, it was hard for him to believe everything was over. Yes, there were still some ends to tie up, but he had a day, and a day was all it would take. Then he could let go. He had lived long enough and, right at the end of his life, had killed to protect his own. Not for money, not for power, but to protect his family and repay blood for blood. He was not a religious man, but he thought that if there did turn out to be a God, then he could answer for those actions. Others, well, he'd have to see about those when the time came. Right now, this afternoon, he was in his own kitchen in his own house and would soon be having one of his favourite meals with some of his best friends. And that was enough.

Lucy returned from her walk and turned the radio to the local news to hear if anything was being broadcast about the fire at Skates's house. They'd missed the morning news and the midday, but at six o'clock there was a brief mention that the police were still investigating the fire at a mansion in Long Sutton in which the bodies of two people had been found. No more than that. Bill didn't get a daily paper, and the local rag only came out on Wednesdays. He supposed he should stop and buy one on the way to the hospice tomorrow.

Lucy felt restless and, since she had no dinner to prepare, went to see Miss Templeton. She had a lot to thank her for and wanted to make sure her long night in the chair had caused no lasting harm. The old lady was glad to see her, and they sat in the kitchen drinking tea from fine china cups as always. After assuring Lucy that she was experiencing no ill effects from the previous night's adventure, Miss Templeton asked, 'And how are you feeling today, my dear?'

She knew from personal experience that traumatic events

could leave deep mental scars. But not with Lucy, it seemed.

'I feel fine,' she said, and Miss Templeton believed her, up to a point. She may indeed be feeling fine about killing Warren, but there was nevertheless a shadow of trouble upon her and it was not hard to imagine what was casting it.

Miss Templeton took a shoebox from the sideboard and placed in front of Lucy. 'Open it,' she said, and watched Lucy as she did so.

Inside were several jewellery cases, two small square boxes, a bundle of papers, and a large manila envelope.

'Go on, open them up,' encouraged Miss Templeton.

Lucy did do. In one of the jewellery cases was a string of pearls, and in the others were beautiful jewelled necklaces. Lucy thought they must be worth a king's ransom. In the small square boxes were medals. One was the Croix de Guerre, its simple bronze contrasting with the rich red satin of the box's lining, and the other was the Military Cross. The silver cross and its ribbon of white and purple had Miss Templeton's full name engraved on the back. There was a citation as well, which Lucy took out to read, but Miss Templeton tut-tutted and told her to save it for later.

The big manila envelope contained the deed to Keepers Cottage and a document written on thick, stiff paper bearing the name of a solicitor in Salisbury. The latter stated that, acting under the instruction of Miss Elenore Templeton of Keepers Cottage, Top Lane, Flyton, Somerset . . .

Lucy looked up. 'It's your will,' she said.

'Yes,' replied the old lady calmly, 'and I would like you to read it now.'

Lucy did so, feeling as if she must be dreaming, because

there in black and white was the fact that all Miss Templeton owned was being left to one Lucy Marshall.

She was stunned and shaken, far more than she had been by any of last night's or this morning's activities. But before she could say anything, Miss Templeton took both her hands in her own dry, withered ones.

'Now let me explain,' she said. 'I am old, tired, and have no family or friends left living. If I don't leave what I have to someone, the government will get it, and that, my dear, would be a terrible waste.'

'But why me?'

'Because I like you,' said Miss Templeton, releasing Lucy's hands and reaching for her tea. 'Because you have integrity, honesty, and courage. And because I think you will make good use of this gift. It will give you freedom and, should you wish it, a home of your own.'

'But I'm going away,' said Lucy, near to tears both at the generosity and kindness of this lovely old woman and the fact that she would be leaving here, for how long she didn't know.

'Of course you are. You have to, for a time, but not forever. You belong here now. You are part of this land and its people, my dear. You killed to protect them.'

Lucy was dumbstruck. She had a vision of Sid lying wounded at Warren's feet and remembered the way she had felt. Yes, she had killed to protect him, and to prevent Warren from killing Bill. And she really did regard this tiny spot in the Somerset landscape as home.

'Thank you,' she said, leaning over and kissing the old woman on the cheek.

Miss Templeton patted her hand. 'Once you have a base, let

me know where you are. And take the address of my solicitors and keep in touch with them. As far as they are concerned, you are my adopted heir, and indeed, my girl, that's exactly what you are. I'm a lucky woman to have found one who suits me so well.' Then she smiled and added, 'Now take that dreadful dog of yours and go. You have goodbyes to arrange.'

She took the manila envelope out of the shoebox and handed the box to Lucy. 'You may as well take these with you, and if we don't meet again, think of me when you wear the pearls. They were a gift from a very special man.'

There were tears in Lucy's eyes as she walked down the lane to Bill's house. What she had done to deserve such generosity and kindness from everyone she had met in this place she didn't know, but she had never before in all her life felt so cherished.

When Sid had driven off to get the fish and chips, he had taken the opportunity, as Bill had known he would, to have a pint in the pub and a natter with some of his drinking acquaintances. Apparently, the word on the street was that the fire in the big house was deliberate and one of the bodies found in it belonged to that bloke Skates what came from London and had all those funny friends going in and out all the time. Nobody knew who the other poor sod was, but there were some right dodgy bastards working for Skates. Sid had let his informants rattle on and stood by and listened as others joined in. That nasty bloke who had the motorbike was missing and the Old Bill were looking for him something rotten. There was no mention of antiques, nor Bill Sawyer, nor anything at all to connect him with Skates.

'And long may it be so,' thought Sid as he drove back to the farm with a well-wrapped-up parcel of fish and chips.

It started out as a solemn meal because they all knew it was the last one they would share together, but solemnity didn't stand a chance once Sid got to telling tales about Bill, and Bill retorted with stories of his own about Sid. Anything to put tomorrow where it should be: in the future, not round this table, not right now. As Bill said, 'It's our last supper, my dears. Get out the port and sod the indigestion!'

Once the debris of the meal was cleared away, Bill put the money from the chairs on the table in an untidy pile next to the decanter. He counted it out and insisted that Lucy and Sid have £5000 each for all their work on the chairs. Then he divided the remaining £6000 into two piles.

He turned to Sid and said, 'Philip and Gloria won't be able to move in here for weeks and I don't want this place getting done over, so I'm employing you as a house-sitter.' And with that he put £3000 on the top of Sid's pile. Sid squirmed a bit, but didn't argue.

Then he turned to Lucy and said, 'That car of yours is registered in my name, so take this' – placing the remaining £3000 on her pile – 'and buy a better one. I suggest you get Dylan to register and insure it, with you as a named driver. If the police are taking Skates's life apart, they'll find out he's been married and they might try to find you just out of curiosity. Best if you don't give them any help, and car registrations are easy to check.'

Lucy had made arrangements to stay with Dylan for a day or two after she left Bill's. She handed a bit of paper with the address on it to Sid, who put it into his wallet. 'I'll be in touch,' he said. 'Make sure you phone me to tell me you're all right now and again.'

Lucy smiled at him. 'Don't worry, I will.'

'Well,' said Sid, 'I'd best go home tonight and pack up some things to bring with me tomorrow, always assuming Philip's okay with me staying here for a while.'

'He'll breathe a sigh of relief,' said Bill. 'And you can sort out the workshop for him while you're here.'

'What about the chairs?' asked Lucy.

'Ah, the chairs,' said Bill with a crafty smile that was immediately ruined by a spectacular coughing session. When he got his breath back, he took a sip of port and continued.

'They can't be sold anytime soon without attracting attention. They're far too valuable and well known. If anything was going to provide a link between me and Skates, it would be those bloody chairs. But, like all antiques, time is on their side. We'll tuck 'em away here where they won't be noticed and when enough tempus has fugited, they can be slipped out into the big wide world again.'

'Hide them here for your boy to find in a few years, you mean?' asked Sid. 'That makes sense.'

'Yes, and as the best place to hide anything is in plain sight, we'll move them into the kitchen where they'll get normal wear and tear, and I'll let Philip and Gloria know they're worth a bob or two. I'll say they're for young Jack and to put them on the market when he's 21.' Bill smiled at the thought of that.

Lucy was thrilled with the idea. The fact that it would be Jack Sawyer who inherited their work seemed right and proper in her mind. Sid was happy with whatever Bill wanted.

Then Bill's crafty look returned, and he asked Lucy to get him the big envelope he had left on the side table in the front room. From this he took out a yellowed piece of paper with faded writing and one corner torn off. He placed this rather dramatically on the table in front of Lucy and asked her to read it.

She picked it up and examined it. 'It's a sales receipt from Simon Morse dated 24th June 1953. It says he sold two Elizabethan chairs to the value of three hundred guineas to Mr Abraham Tollis of Tollis Antiques, London Road, Bath.'

'I really did know old Abraham, and did some work for him back in the day,' said Bill. 'He moved a lot of antique oak in his time and he was slapdash in the paperwork department, which is what made me think of him. Caused headaches for collectors ever since. Anyway, he died and his son Lionel took over, but he was useless and the business went bust in 1961. Lionel Tollis sold the property to a developer and quickly drank himself to death with the proceeds, so the shop doesn't even exist anymore.'

Bill's face was grey with strain, but his eyes gleamed and there was a smile on his lips as he prepared to anoint the chairs with a history that would stand the future's scrutiny.

'So the story for posterity is this: After the father died, the son got me in to look at a couple of old chairs. He thought they were Jacobean with Victorian over-carving, nothing too special, but he wanted me to give them the once-over and see if they were worth anything and, if they were, a repair and re-polish where necessary. When I went to see them, there was a third chair in bits next to them. I asked if he had any paperwork on them to give me a clue. He was pissed and just waved me over to a filing cabinet and said 'sort out what you can'. I did and came across the Morse receipt. So I took the two-and-a-bit chairs and the receipt.'

Bill delved into the big brown envelope and put another

piece of paper down on top of the Morse receipt.

'Here's a note in my handwriting torn from a receipt book that has a date in 1960. It's the real thing, apart from what's written on it.' This was '£250 quote for restoration', the word 'Blakeney?', and under that 'Offered £500 for the lot', followed by several exclamation marks and doodles. All made with a strong and vigorous hand in the soft, wedge-shaped graphite of a carpenter's pencil.

The next thing Bill took out of the envelope was a battered, red, common or garden-variety duplicate book bearing dates from 1959 to 1961. It was grubby, carbon-soiled, and dog-eared. A few pages had been torn out, while odd pieces of paper had been added and were held in with rusty staples or pins. He opened it to a page marked with an ancient cigarette packet. This page was numbered and in sequence with the ones on either side. It was the carbon imprint of an invoice, dated 11th June 1960. It showed '£250 owed by Lionel Tollis, Tollis Antiques, London Road, Bath' and the words 'Pay on Collect'.

'But the chairs were never collected, see? So they got moved into the house here and have been sitting around this table ever since. Why did I never sell them? Look around you! People like me hoard all sorts of things or just plain forget about them when they move onto other projects. A small enough mystery amongst the others of life.' Then he put all the bits of paper back in the big brown envelope, sat back, and smiled at them both.

Lucy's eyes shone as she watched this remarkable man play his last trick.

'So that's what you were doing with all the inks and stuff that day,' she said. 'Laying a paper trail!'

'I just dovetailed a little diversion into the story of the chairs,' said Bill. 'First Blakeney, and then Morse. The paper trail there is good enough, and now we have a paper trail from Morse to Tollis to me. We know they really went from Morse to Deverill and then to Skates, but there is nothing to show that and no one left to talk about it. No, I fancy these little scraps will do the trick. Not too many details, impossible to disprove, and looking absolutely kosher. And by the time my boy flogs the chairs, they'll have aged a bit more, the inks will have faded even further, and the dust will be real. Then some clever expert will declare, 'Well, gracious me, I think these are the long-lost Blakeney Elizabethans! Gosh, what a find!'

'You devious old bugger!' said Sid with a huge grin. 'It couldn't be better, mate.'

'What about the new chair?' Lucy asked. 'The one you made from scratch.'

'The one we made, you mean. The three of us. Well, that must never go on the market. The real three can be pored over by experts, no problem at all, and if the restored chair is labelled as such from the start, that's even better. But the one we made, well, I think that should be given a new home.'

He looked meaningfully at Lucy and added 'When you have one to put it in.'

'How do you know I ever will?' asked Lucy.

But Bill only smiled and said nothing. He was exhausted and feeling really ill again now that the big reveal was over. He struggled to his feet, grasped Sid's hand as firmly as he could for a few moments, then, with Lucy's help, went up to bed.

When she came back down, Sid was preparing to drive home. Seeing him standing there, wearing his dreadful anorak and his sad smile, she felt again how much he meant to her. He was made of strength and dependability. She adored his wonderfully rude sense of humour, and she guessed few people, if any, had witnessed the man's courage, compassion, and kindness the way she had. What she really wanted to do, right now, in this kitchen, was to reach out in some way and let him know how much she loved him, and to thank him for all he had done for Bill.

So she took his big, work-worn, oil-stained hands in hers and looked up into his eyes. 'I've never had an uncle,' she told him. 'But if I could have one, you'd be the uncle I'd wish for.'

The moment she said that she wished she hadn't. Was it too soppy? Would he be offended by the uncle bit?

But Sid just laughed and said, 'That's it, girl, I'm yer wicked uncle!' And even though his arm was still very sore, he hugged her tightly to him. He knew he would see her again, but for all his bluff he still found her leaving a wrench. He had said a lot of goodbyes in his life, and so many of them had been forever that he never took tomorrow for granted. But after a while he kissed her, told her to take care of herself, and walked outside to his van.

Sid carried the guns away with him in an old cricket case they had found in Bill's workshop. He would use his skills in the black arts along with his extensive local knowledge to ensure the weapons were never seen again. Lucy watched as her wicked uncle turned his transit van into the lane and drove away.

Clive was wandering about on his final business of the night, so she just stood there in the gloom of the evening for a bit. So much had happened here – happiness and sorrow, life lived and death dealt out. She looked to see if there was a light on in Miss Templeton's cottage, but it was just a dark shape amongst the trees. Suddenly she felt she really did need to be away, to take stock and see new horizons. Well, tomorrow would be the start of all that.

She called Clive and they went back inside. Then she locked the door, took a last long look around the kitchen, and went to bed.

Chapter 45

WEDNESDAY, 7 NOVEMBER

The next morning, Lucy packed her clothes. There were more of them than she had arrived with, plus all those precious gifts from Miss Templeton. She looked around the small bedroom and marvelled at how short a time it had been hers, yet how much had changed during that time! Then she carried her bags down the stairs, leaving nothing behind but the faint scent of the perfume she sometimes wore.

In the kitchen she wound up the old clock on the wall, removed the ashes from the grate of the stove, and made tea and toast. Things she had done for months now and would never do again. Other chores in other places, but not these ones and not here.

She put a letter she had written to Gloria and Philip on the mantelpiece. It wasn't long. Basically it said how privileged she felt to have been part of their family, even for such a short time. She would be in touch in the future, and please give her love to Jack. There wasn't much more she could say without writing a novel, so she didn't try. She thought of leaving a note for Hugh as well, but decided now was not the time. One day soon, perhaps, but not now.

Bill came downstairs and pretended to eat his breakfast but spent most of his time 'secretly' feeding it to Clive.

At last she couldn't stand it anymore, so she simply stood up and carried her bags out to the car. Clive and Bill both followed her, Bill so slowly that Clive had plenty of time to water all his usual spots before Lucy put him in the back of the car.

Bill wordlessly opened the door for her. Determined not to cry, she kissed him quickly; said, 'I love you, Bill'; then got into the car and drove away.

Looking in the rear-view mirror as she passed through the gate, she saw a small, bent old man standing in the yard waving to her.

Then she started to cry.

~~~

After Lucy's car pulled onto the main road, Bill looked around at all the old buildings of his farm. There was no goodbye in their blank stone eyes, but he was glad he had lived among them. He started for his workshop for one last visit there, but was overtaken by a coughing spasm so bad it bent him double. Dark blood dripped onto the ground at his feet.

Gasping and clutching his chest, he made his way into the kitchen and sat down in his chair next to the stove. When he finally had sufficient breath back, he struggled to his feet and went over the dresser. From his pocket he took out an envelope containing his will and a letter to Philip he had written the night before. It read:

I love you.
There are a set of three chairs, the ones you saw me working

on. They are very special and worth a lot of money. I give them to Jack. Sell them when he is 21. Use Christies, if they're still the best. Let them date and value them first. They have a bit of provenance, it's in an envelope in my cash box.

I've asked Sid to babysit the house till you're ready to move in. I would hate to leave the place empty and have it get burgled. I've paid him so you don't have to worry about that. He'll get rid of the woodworking machinery and the workshop equipment. Keep a few hand tools for the boy, just in case. I've packed my old apprentice box with the best. There's a bit of money in the bank and you know where I keep my flute money, so you should be all right for ready cash.

No flowers, no funeral, just the crem and a meal afterwards for those who might like to come. Sid will know who they are. Lucy, bless her, won't be here, so wait for her to contact you. Sid will explain.

Kiss that wife of yours for me and your lovely son. I hope when he grows up you will be as proud of him as I am of you.

Dad

He placed his envelope beside the one Lucy had left, then walked back outside and into his little garden, to the cherry tree under which Bess was buried. He stood there in the cold and wished he could see her, feel her, just one more time. Leaving her behind would be the hardest part of going into that hospice.

The cold got to him very quickly, though, and he returned

the kitchen, chilled to the bone, and collapsed into his chair. By hell, he felt tired. So bloody tired . . . but as he closed his eyes, the pain in his chest seemed to ease.

A little while later he heard a joyful bark, the sort that meant 'It's time for a walk! It's time for the pub! It's time to go, Bill!'

He got up out of his chair. Surprisingly, it took no effort and he felt no pain.

Patting Bess, he took up the lead she had dropped at his feet and together they walked towards the light.

Chapter 46

EPILOGUE

Western Daily Times, August 2008

Marriages: Mr Hugh Dawlish and Ms Lucy Marshall at Wintern Registry office. The Bride was given away by Mr S. J. Mellow. The reception was held at Blackwoods Farm, Flyton, Somerset.

....

2019 Autumn Sale, Christies Fine Art and Antique Furniture

Property of a Gentleman
A set of three Elizabethan carved oak and inlaid panel back armchairs bearing the arms of Elizabeth the first. These are believed to have been made for the visit of Queen Elizabeth to Darrington Hall on her royal progress through Somerset in 1574. Guide price £250,000–£300,000

Bernard Pearson was born on a Friday the 13th in 1946. His father said he was the result of a forty-eight hour leave, his mother made no comment. In his past he has been at times a soldier, village policeman, door to door salesman, potter, sculptor and painter. If there is any theme through these career changes it is the quest to find a job that is indoors and no heavy lifting. Taking the advice from his good friend Terry Pratchett, that writing is the most fun anyone can have with their clothes on, that's what he does now. 'Dovetail' is his first novel and it is believed others are being writ. It's difficult to tell however for the man is a prodigious pipe smoker and the shed he works from so filled with smoke it's like a kipper shed. He lives in Wincanton, Somerset, which doesn't seem to mind.